BARROOMS

Stephen Slattery

ISBN: 0615937934

ISBN-13: 978-:0615937939

For Kylie, Shaun and Dylan. So Someday you can say you saw your name in a book. And of course for Nancy . . .

The most important things to do in the world are to get something to eat, something to drink and somebody to love you.

— Brendan Behan

Cover art by Fiona Slattery. Back cover inspiration by Zack Slattery.

I'd like to thank the Good Lord, but he assures me all the credit coming his way is growing tiresome. Thanks to Jimmy, Jonah and Zack for all the help in editing. Thanks to Amy and Siobhan for the love and support. Thanks to Rory for getting into college and all the wonderful hours spent watching you play baseball and football. I hope you find time to read a book one of these days. Of course thanks to Malachy for getting the pellets and everything else he does, which is a great deal. Thanks to Skeeter Wilson for all the unexpected clouts to the head and hours of SpongeBob. Thanks to the sweetest granddaughter a man could ever have for reminding me the future isn't written and nothing to fear. Thanks to Studley. Another Yankee fan is hard to find in Massachusetts. Thanks to KR, KP, Mr. Marsh and Mr. DiCicco. Without you it never would have been written. And finally, thanks to Nancy for your faith in defiance of convincing evidence to the contrary; for knowing when I need a swift kick in the ass — and most of all, for giving me the time to finish this little tale. I owe you more than I can ever repay, which you have been quick to point out on more than one occasion. Cheers.

1

"Father Bob called me neurotic! Can you believe it, Michael? He said I needed to get a life!"

Mike MacDonnell's dark eyes swept the kitchen ceiling. Several of the tiles had tea-colored water stains from the leaky toilet in the bathroom above. He uncrossed his legs and cleared his throat. "Well, Michelle, you have been spending a lot of time up at the church. Maybe the priest just thinks that — "

"After all I've done for him *and* Sacred Heart? Who organized the Seder Supper this year, huh? And who cleans the rectory every week? And who keeps the cobwebs off the Stations of the Cross, replaces the votive candles when they burn out — and *who* makes sure the announcements get printed for Saturday and Sunday mass? I keep that creaky old copier working! Father Bob can't! He messes it up every time he touches it! I have to fix the bloody thing and get the announcements printed at the last minute! Michael, you don't know what I . . ."

Mike MacDonnell ran a big hand through unruly black hair and stopped listening to his wife. He'd heard this rant, or a variation of it, too many times before. Of course, the priest telling her to stay away was a new wrinkle. It was about time somebody put the brakes on her wildfire religious enthusiasm. Mike certainly hadn't been able to and, truth be told, he didn't try anymore. Mike's Uncle Frank, late of this world, once told him there was nothing worse than a convert. He was dead right.

Michelle twirled around the kitchen floor, red-faced, angry, grabbing dishes, some of them clean, to dump them with a clatter into the sink.

"I told Father Bob he had to clean up the garage. There was stuff in there from Father Mullen's day, for pity's sake. There was an old sink that had become nothing more than a giant rat's nest. I told him if he . . ."

Mike watched his wife for a moment. Sometimes she could be so pretty, when she had a little rest and put on a little makeup; and sometimes, like now, she had a face like a coelacanth. Lately, the Cretaceous Period had been calling loudly.

"I want you to talk to him, Michael. He can't throw me out of the Church."

"I don't think he's throwing you out of the church, Michelle," Mike said. "He probably wants you to give him a little breathing room. Christ, honey, you're up there every fucking day, doing something. There are other members of the Altar Rosary Society who can help out. Why don't you let them?"

"I want you to talk to him." She stamped her foot. "And please don't take our Lord's name in vain."

Converts.

"I haven't spoken to a priest since my last confession when I was fourteen." There was a cup of Earl Grey, made from the last tin in the cupboard, on the table in front of him. He picked it up and took a sip. "And I don't intend to start again — not until I'm really old and pissing-my-pants scared of dying. You organized a Seder Supper? Isn't that Jewish?"

"That's another thing! You not going to church looks bad for me. Sheesh! Just last night, Jackie Thompson asked me why you never attend mass."

"Tell her I'm a fucking druid — or better yet, tell her I've joined Atheists for Jesus. We don't pray, we don't go to church, but we all scream 'Dear God' when we cum."

"Stop it! Why do you have to be so sacrilegious?" Anger narrowed pale eyes and almost made them cross.

Mike MacDonnell knew he'd gone too far, but it was getting difficult not to bait Michelle, not to stick a pin in her pious self-inflations.

"I'm going to the post office to get the mail," he said and stood up. At six feet tall and 275 pounds, he filled the small kitchen with bulk and shoulders and dwarfed his petite wife.

"You get back here soon!" she warned. Michelle timed him when he left the house for any reason. If he was — by her standards — gone too long, she accused him of a variety of nefarious activities, including spending money they didn't have and seeing other women. Recently, she had extended this time-keeping to his bathroom trips: twenty minutes to half an hour, whether showering or shitting, meant he was *really* masturbating, which she considered a form of infidelity.

"Father Bob better watch out or I'll fix his wagon," Michelle resumed her screed. "I do too much for this parish to be pushed around like . . ."

"I'll be quick," Mike promised. He grabbed a black leather jacket folded over the back of a chair, kissed her on the forehead and walked out the kitchen door.

"Father Bob needs to apologize. I can't believe . . . "

Outside, in the driveway, Mike MacDonnell found his salvation: a 1971 Pontiac GTO. It was the only possession in the world he prized. The Pontiac was not stock. The British Racing Green paint was less than two years old and the Judge wing on the rear deck had been added at the same time. Under the hood, poised like Billy Goat Gruff to surprise foreign and domestic ogres alike, resided a 428 cubic inch power plant, bored, balanced and blueprinted. The engine had been pulled out of a wrecked Tempest where it started life rated at 390 horsepower; it was a bit heavier now. The monster gulped gas and oil at an alarming rate and shredded tires almost as quickly; but the car was fast. It was all that mattered.

He slid behind the wheel and cranked the motor over. A deep, threatening rumble filled his ears like music. The car backed onto Main Street, paused and then leaped forward to the shriek of Dunlop tires. MacDonnell watched his house, the house he grew up in, that his mother left him in her will, disappear in the rearview mirror. It bothered him a bit to think this had become his favorite view of the only home he'd ever really known.

The Cornwall, New York Post Office — like the village — was small. The parking lot could not contain a dozen cars at one time, not that it ever had to. Life was slow in the little hill towns scattered along either side of the Upstate New York and New England border. There weren't many jobs to be had. Most people commuted to the bigger towns and cities for work. Cornwall had the advantage, if one could call it that, of hosting a ramshackle factory that produced little green floral picks. It didn't pay much, but if you didn't have a job or a car, it was the only alternative — an alternative Mike MacDonnell hoped to avoid with a successful job interview in Wessex, Massachusetts tomorrow. He'd been out of work for three months. The savings account was wrung out. Michelle, since her conversion, spent long hours at Sacred Heart, but none at a paying job.

Mike left the Pontiac running when he went into the post office. Cars didn't get stolen in Cornwall. He was back a moment later with a handful of bills he couldn't pay. He tossed them on the passenger seat and grabbed a pack of Newports from the dashboard. Things were getting tight. Tomorrow had to go well, or . . .

Mike was nervous about the interview. He had never heard of Blythewood. The ad said it was a school for special needs adolescents in Wessex and it was looking for childcare workers, all shifts available. But what, exactly, were *special needs adolescents* and *childcare workers*? And what did they do? This gave him some pause, but in the end he'd called the number in the ad and scheduled an interview. Now all he could do was hope for the best.

Three months without a job. Three months home alone with Michelle. There was the real cause of his anxiety.

Mike MacDonnell took a deep drag on the menthol. A slight tremor made his hand shake. Two years married and he couldn't abide a few weeks with his bride. How in hell had it come to this? Once he couldn't get enough of her; now he couldn't get away from her fast enough. It didn't stand to reason things could so thoroughly shit the bed so goddamned quickly. Maybe they'd gotten married too soon, just three months after they met and discovered a mutual interest in humping. It seemed like the right thing — the only thing — to do at the time.

He put the Pontiac back on the road and headed home.

Parts of the problem were easy to identify: Michelle's precipitous plunge into religious mania, the corresponding and equally precipitous plunge in their sex life. Twenty-four months ago, he couldn't have held Michelle off with an Uzi. She wanted to screw until he or she collapsed from exhaustion, wanted to screw until they made a baby. When it hadn't happened, and the doctor couldn't give her a definitive reason, she became obsessed with controlling every detail of Mike's life as if he were a gigantic, barely sensate toddler in dire need of constant surveillance. The whole masturbation thing started out as a complaint about the dirty, dirty little man wasting peppy spermatozoa (*"You shouldn't touch yourself, Mikey"*). Then came all the ancient mystery and majestic pageantry of the One Holy Catholic and Apostolic Roman Church. Michelle transubstantiated into a tedious avatar of zealotry; all her boundless generative energies directed towards the church (Mike half-suspected she had a thing for ole' Father Bob) and away from her husband's penis.

Converts.

Mike pulled in behind his wife's old Toyota Corolla, a vehicle used mostly by him in the winter. Michelle would putter around town in it occasionally, but she was a fearful driver and never went more than twenty miles from home. He got out of his car, but didn't go inside, opting instead to steal a few moments for himself and finish the cigarette. His eyes drifted idly up and down the street, a street as familiar to him as the face of his own mother. More so. The street was still here.

Cornwall was an old settlement. Most of the homes on Main Street dated back to the 1700s or early 1800s. The buildings were well kept and the lawns mowed, supplying the kind of quaint charm most little villages strive for. Here there was no evidence of the poverty lurking on the other side of town and thriving in the outlying hollows where some families lived for two and three generations on welfare, and where some families spent ten generations taking nothing from anyone and living off what they grew and what they hunted. Mike had gone to school with children, from deep in the hills, whose accents were so odd, so antique, he had trouble understanding their speech.

"Michael! What are you doing out there?"

Sometimes — too often, lately — her voice held an abrasive, jittery quality which reminded him of the lead guitar line from the Stone's *Sympathy for the Devil.*

"Just finishing a cigarette, Michelle." He took a last puff. The spent butt launched from his fingers into the street.

"Well, thank you for not bringing it inside the house, but I wish you wouldn't litter. Are you done now?"

"Yes, I am."

Jesus, I hope the interview goes well . . .

2

"Hi, I'm Mike MacDonnell. I'm here for a job interview?"

The short, thickset figure with the cigarette jammed in his teeth rose from behind the desk and shook hands. "Rick Pasinetti. Job interview? Yeah, okay. Just, uh, just give me a minute here. I'm not the supervisor. He's in a meeting and I'm watching the office."

"Should I come back later?"

"Naw, naw. Did you fill out an application yet? No? Well, let me look around in the desk. Grab the chair over there and have a seat." Rick Pasinetti opened drawers and pawed through them for a few moments. "Yeah, here we go." He handed Mike MacDonnell a printed form. "Hard to believe it's fucking May, huh? Jesus Gawd, I froze my balls off getting out of bed this morning. You need a pen?"

MacDonnell shook his head; he already had pen in hand. He frowned at the application for a moment, then got quickly to work. Anxiety dampened the hair around his ears with a drizzle of sweat and increased the congenital tremor in his hand as he wrote. He gave the paper back to Pasinetti when he was finished.

"This looks good," Pasinetti said, pretending to examine the form. MacDonnell's seismic handwriting was barely legible. "So, where'd you hear about our little diddlers' paradise?"

"Uh . . . I saw an ad in the newspaper."

"Yeah, they're constantly running ads. Like a lousy motel, we always have vacancies. So, what did you do before, and why do you want to work here?"

"I did some construction and landscaping, but the work dried up and I've got a wife."

"Married? Me too. Never thought I would, but you know, it's the best thing I ever did."

Mike MacDonnell allowed himself a smile. This guy was all right. "Have you been here long?"

"Gawd, no. Nobody's here long." Pasinetti ran a beefy hand over a balding pate. "I still got some hair left." A quirky smiled brightened the round face. "No, I used to circumcise baby elephants at the Catskill Game Farm — until they let me go. The Superintendent of Pachyderms said I was starting to enjoy the job too much. Smoke?" He offered Mike an open pack of Camels.

MacDonnell took one, but pointed and said, "The sign behind you says no smoking."

"Don't pay attention to that shit. Go ahead and light up."

"Think I'll save it for the ride home."

"Suit yourself."

MacDonnell tucked the Camel in his shirt pocket. "What's this place like?"

"The orcs are fucking wild, the staff worse, and the administrators matriculated at the Billy Bligh Academy of Rum, Sodomy and the Lash. But don't worry, they'll give you a job. You're big enough. Just watch your back and keeps your mouth shut about anything you see me do. Well, you sit tight. The supervisor will be out in a minute, then you'll have to meet with the assistant program director, and then — Gawd help you."

3

A few hours later an exuberant Mike MacDonnell was back in Cornwall. He stopped at the Cornwall Cash Market to pick up the gallon of milk Michelle demanded before he left that morning. He wrote a check for twenty dollars more than the total and headed for the Colonial Inn. After all, Michelle wouldn't know how long the interview had taken, and Mike had a reason to celebrate.

The Inn was at the bottom of the Old Plank Road, a treacherous bit of asphalt twisting down from Cornwall Mountain to leap-frog Main Street, tumble a few hundred feet and break at the foot of the state highway which split the village in two. Since the tavern was only a few houses down from his own, Mike put the Pontiac around back where Michelle wouldn't chance to see it should she goose step by on her way to scalp poor Father Bob.

MacDonnell was climbing the Inn's front porch steps when a familiar voice hailed him.

"Hey, Mike! Wait up!"

Sara Stevens banged a door shut and hurried across the street. She lived in an old building which once housed an Arrow Shirt factory, but had since been converted to a few, low-rent and drafty apartments. Sara was Michelle's best friend — or had been. They hadn't seen much of each other lately.

"Come on, I'll buy you a drink," she said, sweeping past him. "I got my alimony check from Danny."

Mike MacDonnell shrugged and followed her. Sara always made him uneasy, on several different counts, but if she was willing to buy, he wasn't going to say no.

Inside the Colonial Inn was dark and chilly and deserted. There was an old cracked mirror behind the bar, and a big, bright, glass and metal upright cooler filled with six-packs and cases for those who preferred their poison in a bottle or needed a couple for the ride home. Mike sat down on a stool. Sara stood next to him, lightly resting her hand on his broad back. She had a round, red mouth, heavy breasts and was several years younger than Mike, which made her just old enough to be drinking in a bar. A few pounds had been added since her recent divorce; but she was still attractive and always smelled nice. Mike wasn't sure if it was from some kind of perfume or an expensive bath soap, but he liked it and he liked the way she was dressed today in black, skintight hip-huggers and a tight pink sweater.

"Hey, Wally," she said to the bartender. "Can you cash my alimony check?"

"How much it's for?"

"A hundred and five dollars and twenty-six cents. Just what the court ordered."

"Yep, suppose so." The bartender nodded. Wally was known for a mild and accommodating disposition — until someone gave him a reason to jerk the baseball bat he kept behind the bar. Mike had been here the night a naked Slippery Jones rode his Harley through the taproom. Wally chased him out of the Inn and down the street, waving the ancient Adirondack and cursing a blue streak. Slippery escaped, but was banned from the bar for a year.

"What do you want, Mike?" Sara asked.

"A draft will be fine." He looked at Sara in the mirror and noticed the pencil eraser bulges of taut nipples beneath her sweater. Must be the cold, he thought.

"And a shot of peppermint schnapps for both of us," Sara said to Wally.

Mike MacDonnell tried not to make a face. He hated peppermint schnapps, or any booze disguising itself as candy.

After their drinks arrived, Sara asked Mike, "What are you doing here today? It's been a while since I've seen you out and about."

"Well, I've been broke," he answered honestly. "But I got a job today, over in Massachusetts."

"Hey, hey," Sara exclaimed, raising her shot glass. "Congrats. What's the job?"

"I'm going to be a childcare worker at a school called Blythewood in Wessex."

"What's a childcare worker?"

"It's kind of a babysitter for retarded and emotionally disturbed kids."

"Little kids?"

"Hell, no. They're all in their late teens and early twenties. They just call them kids." Mike took a sip of beer. "It's a big place. There's an office building, a schoolhouse, three dorms and a lot of land. Seems pretty nice. It's run by a family called the Rumgays or something funny like that. The pay isn't much, but it's better than the nothing I've got right now."

"Michelle must be thrilled."

"I haven't been home yet."

Sara giggled and nodded. "Or you wouldn't be here now."

"True."

"Wow, you know Michelle has really changed since she got religion. Man, she'll barely talk to me anymore. Most I get is a 'hey' on the street."

"Yeah, I know."

"And we used to be so close," Sara lamented.

"I wish I had an explanation." Mike raised the beer glass to his mouth.

"I think she feels guilty 'cause I let her doink me a few times."

"What?"

"Yeah, you knew, didn't you? I was a big mess after Danny split. Remember? Michelle would come over and try to make me feel better. It wasn't no big deal, but she started doinkin' me. She really got into it and I didn't mind. It kinda helped."

"You have got to be fucking kidding?"

"No." Sara laughed and cast a quick glance at Wally. He had his back turned, washing some glasses. In a low voice, "Michelle couldn't get enough of this — " Sara unceremoniously grabbed her crotch.

"Jesus."

"You're not mad at me, are you, Mike?"

"No, Sara. I'm . . . Jesus, I don't know what I am."

"Please don't be mad. Two women doin' it ain't like really cheating. I don't think she's ever been with another guy. She would of told me, back when we still talked."

Mike gulped his beer, ordered another one. Between them, they had $125.26 — less the drinks already paid for. Mike wondered if it would be enough.

Feeling a little guilty, though she wasn't quite sure why she should, Sara leaned in and whispered in his ear, "Mike, I just got a tattoo of a rose on my butt. Do you want to see it later? It's pretty."

4

That night, MacDonnell bungled through the kitchen door, swinging a gallon of warm milk.

Michelle was waiting for him in the dark. She rose like a vapor from the kitchen table, arms crisscrossing her chest. "Where have you been?"

"Got a job, honey. Got a job."

"You've been drinking."

There was no point in lying. "Yes."

"With what money?"

"Did you hear me? I got a job," he said, stripping off his leather jacket.

"And who were you with?"

Had to lie here. "Nobody. What's for dinner?"

"You left this house before noon. It's now . . ." Michelle glared at the clock over the sink, but couldn't make out the position of the hands in the dark.

In a foolish gesture of accommodation, MacDonnell flipped a switch mounted on the wall next to the door. A fluorescent ceiling light flickered on.

"It's now — *ten-thirty!* And you expect dinner?"

MacDonnell put the milk on the kitchen table and tossed his jacket over a chair. He went to the refrigerator and removed a package of boiled ham, sliced cheese and a jar of mustard, piling them on the table next to the milk.

"You expect dinner?" Michelle repeated in a hiss. "And please hang your coat up where it belongs."

"I'm hungry. By the way, I start at Blythewood next Sunday." He plucked a knife out of the silverware drawer, and the butter dish and a loaf of rye from the countertop. "Three twelve hour shifts in a row, and then half a day, more or less, on Wednesday." He began to clumsily assemble two sandwiches. His head was swimming, but in a pleasant sort of way.

In spite of the overhead illumination so generously provided by her husband, Michelle's eyes had disappeared into deep wells of shadow. Her thin mouth clamped shut — only to snap open again when he took a glass down from the cupboard.

"What are you doing?"

"I'm going to have some milk," he replied.

"That's all the milk we have!"

"Yeah? So? I'm only taking one glass."

"That's all we have!"

MacDonnell peeled away the plastic cap seal and filled the glass.

"Listen. I got the job. We won't have to scrimp anymore."

"That's all we have!" Her voice was teetering on hysteria.

Had Mike MacDonnell been sober, he would have recognized the mounting frenzy and employed one of the many strategies he'd developed over the past two years to mollify her. But he was in the red afterglow and only wanted to eat and go to bed.

"Listen, Michelle. I'll get another gallon in the morning. Okay?"

He sat down at the table and took a bite of sandwich.

"No you won't. You won't even get up. You'll be hungover!"

"I'll get up. I always get up." He raised the glass of milk to his mouth.

Michelle screeched and snatched the glass out of his hand, spilling milk down the front of his shirt.

"Michelle! What the fuck are you doing? Give it back."

His wife retreated to the other side of the kitchen and put her back against the sink. "No!"

"Michelle, this is fucking absurd. Give me back the glass of milk." His voice was quiet, but alcohol had loosened the fetters on his closely guarded temper. "Now, please."

"No!"

Mike wearily shook his head. It had been such a fine day, such a successful day. He'd found a job, a free smoke, a free drink and a rose. Now, of course, his darling bride had to pour a little vinegar in the cream.

"Give it back, Michelle." No *please* this time.

She poured the milk in the sink.

"That made a lot of sense," Mike said, rising to his feet. He picked up the open gallon, walked over to his wife and calmly emptied the jug on top of her head.

Michelle froze in horrified shock, mouth open and hands half lifted to her face. Milk streamed from her hair and eyebrows and nose; ran over her lips, in her mouth and down her chin; soaked her back and shoulders and front, all the way to the small swell of her belly; made her nipples spring erect, primed by the flow.

"Well," Mike said. "It was warm, anyway. I'll get another gallon in the morning."

Then he went to bed.

5

Blythewood.

The First Day.

The dowdy, near middle-aged female supervisor makes an introduction.

"This is Justin. He's going to orientate you, help you get to know the clients. That's why we had you come in on a Saturday. Didn't want to drop you in the frying pan right off the bat. Justin's the best CCW on this shift. Follow him around today and see how he handles things."

Out of the supervisors office and over to one of the dorms. Wake up time.

"Paul here don't like to get up," says Justin. "So I help him." No word just a fistful of hair and a violent yank. A wordless screech as a plump body hits the floor. "Now watch. He'll try to bite me — see." Two quick punches to a round angry face. Tears and sobbing. "He'll be fine now."

To the next bed. Top bunk. "This is Harry. Be careful of him. He's a mean autistic fuckster. Last winter we were down at the pond and he went off on me, big time. Fuck, I broke my hand on his head. It's hard as a rock. Told administration I slipped on ice. Got two weeks of workmen's comp. Get up, bitch, or no breakfast." A grin. "Food works with him, mostly."

On to the next. A skinny jumping jack in cartoon-adorned pajamas, babbling, laughing, and grabbing at Justin's hand. "This is Joey. He's a real pain-in-the-ass. Hitting him don't do much good." A perfunctory slap across the silly putty face to no effect. "But he don't like these." A big ring of keys out of a pocket and lashed across the top of a shaggy head. "Want some more?" A high-pitched wail of pain. "It cuts him sometimes, but I tell the nurse he's been scratching at his head too much."

Another CCW standing in the doorway. "Hey, Jus. You wanna go out after work?"

"Fuck-yeah."

Later that day, in the gym.

"This is a little game I play with the boys," says Justin, idly tossing a kickball up and down in his right hand. Some shoving with the free hand, forcing the clients to run in a circle. Then careful aim and a hard accurate throw slams off a small head, dropping the student to his knees. Ball retrieved, fired again. Another one down. Those still on their feet begin to run a little faster.

Justin, laughing, "I could do this all day. Wanna take a shot?"

End of shift. At the door of the supervisors office to get a time card signed for the first time. Opening the door. Justin leaning on the desk, the dowdy, near middle-aged female supervisor sitting in her chair, rubbing Justin's crotch through his jeans and sucking on his fingers.

A loud laugh. "She'll be with you in a minute, Mike."

On the ride home that night:

What the fuck am I doing at that place?

Blythewood.

6

A big wolf spider crept across the dirty floor. It paused, shuffled forward again, broke into a sprint — became a tiny smear.

Mike MacDonnell stood up and stamped his right foot twice to restore circulation. When the tingling subsided, he sat down again on the bench against the wall in the Team One classroom. He noticed the little ruined mess of legs between his feet, took a breath and repeated the same silent vow he made at the beginning of each workday: *At the end of shift, I will go home and never come back.*

In eight short weeks anxiety became a garment he put on in the morning like a pair of frayed socks. Every day he worked shoulder to shoulder with a mélange of personalities, some of whom were decent and skilled at their profession, some of whom were at best indifferent, a few of whom were out-and-out sadistic sons-of-bitches — and breathtakingly, a number of whom combined all these traits into one big, over-sexed, schizoid package of fun and high jinks. And every day — every single shitty day — he was witness, or victim, to innumerable assaults by the Blythewood student body, most of whom were only marginally more demented than the staff.

To a newbie like MacDonnell, terming them 'students' was the worst kind of euphemistic nonsense. It conjured images of carefully presented youth in monogrammed prep school blazers. The reality stooped over battered desks in the Team One classroom, clad in worn blue jeans and

threadbare flannel shirts smeared with drool and snot and bits of breakfast. Their school day was spent sorting nuts and bolts and doodling on
construction paper with broken stubs of greasy crayons. They were an
explosive blend of the hopelessly autistic and the organically impaired; all
of whom shared a fondness for the occasional homicidal rage-out. This
special team had been quite correctly dubbed 'The Bomb Squad.'

There were only two reasons MacDonnell remained at Blythewood
so far. One was the simple necessity of bringing home a paycheck; the
other, less apparent to his conscious mind, strutted around the classroom
like a tiny, preening hen.

Terry Johnson snapped, bickered and bullied this ragged troop into a
semblance of functional humanity. It seemed to MacDonnell, despite
Terry's violent protests to the contrary, the teacher aide actually cared for
these unfortunate souls. She made sure they were always clean, fed and
generally looked after. In their own way, the boys in Team One (including
one oversized childcare worker) adored her for it. Watching Terry Johnson nearly made a hideous job bearable to MacDonnell. Shapely, animated, exciting and excitable, she had the most intemperate black eyes he'd
ever seen. He'd been drawn to her from the first. At best, she treated him
with an ambivalent reserve.

An argument, completely lacking in reserve, unexpectedly broke out
between Terry and the Team One teacher, Charlie Collings.

"Oh, well." Terry folded her arms defiantly across her chest and
stamped her small foot. "This girl is not doing mandatory overtime. You
can kiss my black ass." To emphasis the point, she slapped that admirable
portion of her anatomy.

"Terry," Charlie Collings pleaded. "It's not my fault. Rumgay and
administration made the decision." Collings was a fragile older man with a
perpetually pained expression on a limp gray face.

"Well, you can tell them . . . fuck you." Thunder rode Terry Johnson's brow.

MacDonnell stepped out the back door of the classroom to have a
cigarette. Terry's tirade was amusing, but nerve-wracking. There was
enough ambient clamor at Blythewood to begin with. He lit a Newport,

squinted his eyes against the bright afternoon sun, and willed the hours to fly.

Mike had not taken half a dozen puffs before a commotion erupted inside the building. For a split second he thought Terry and the teacher had come to blows; but the wild din of guttural vocalizations convinced him a student was the source. MacDonnell rushed back into the classroom, dreading participation in yet another restraint.

Davie Kemp, a hapless lad who led a primitive existence of eating, masturbating and physical aggression, had quickly dispatched Charlie Collings with a single, crushing head butt; now he was shredding Terry Johnson with fingers and teeth. The woman battled him tenaciously, trying to bring the berserk student down to the floor by any means at her disposal. The other students sat at their desks, some fiddling with the scholastic junk piles arrayed before them, some staring off into space. One boy violently flapped a sheet of paper in front of his face and made a grunting sound like a woodchuck rooting around in the neighbor's garden.

The fearful uncertainty which hobbled MacDonnell in his first few weeks at Blythewood broke like string. It was time to sink or swim.

He moved with a surprising turn of speed and lifted Davie Kemp straight up in the air.

Terry, still clinging to the boy like a pit bull, cried out, **"SHIT!"**

MacDonnell brought them all crashing down on the carpet. Davie Kemp's nose sprayed blood upon impact. MacDonnell wedged an arm between Terry and the student in a single-minded effort to secure his grip, then levied his entire weight on Davie Kemp's back.

Davie lay immobilized, breathlessly babbling one of the three words he knew, "Daddy, daddy, daddy."

MacDonnell's adrenaline subsided. He became acutely aware of Terry's breasts pressing against his arm, the lower half of her body pinned beneath his. He turned his head to look at her. Their faces were inches apart. The fragrance of her hair and sweat filled his nostrils. He had never experienced such complete physical contact with a woman outside of lovemaking.

"Are you all right?" he asked her.

"I'm okay," she panted.

He could feel the warmth of her breath on his cheek, in his ear. "Are you sure?"

"I said I was okay. Are you deaf?"

"What?"

"I said, are you deaf?"

"What?"

"Are you . . ." Terry paused. Her big eyes grew wider as she realized MacDonnell, in the middle of steam pressing a student, was teasing her.

"Fuck you!" She burst out laughing. "You blockheaded, Puerto Rican bitch."

"Uh, I'm Irish and you suffer from some sort of gender dyslexia."

"Yeah? Well you look like a Rican, or a Mexican — or something like that."

"Funny, I was just about to ask what part of Scandinavia you hail from."

"Norway, Jose."

"By the way, how's Charlie?"

"I don't know. Dead?"

"You better go check."

Terry slid her body from beneath him — a delightful sensation — and hurried over to the fallen teacher. "Mike? Charlie's . . . he's out. Should I call a nurse?"

"Maybe we should let him nap. He looked tired today."

Rick Pasinetti chose that moment to saunter into the classroom.

"What's going on, anything? I heard some noise."

"Davie knocked out Charlie," Terry said.

Pasinetti glanced at the motionless figure on the floor. "Yep, yep, he did. Anybody got a smoke? I'm out."

"I think ours are crushed," MacDonnell answered.

A Blythewood staff had once compared Rick to Father Christmas. The resemblance was there, from the bushy almost-white beard to a wry gleam in lively brown eyes that would have done any polar elf credit. But today, Santa was taking and not giving. Pasinetti strolled over to the unconscious teacher, squatted down and removed a pack of Kools from the man's shirt pocket. The burly childcare worker hesitated, looked over at MacDonnell. "You don't think he'll mind, do you?"

"Noooo," MacDonnell replied in an exaggerated foghorn voice. "Grab me one while you're at it."

"Me too," said Terry.

Pasinetti grinned a wicked grin. "Vultures."

7

A swarm of cars encircled the Stanton Club on Bartlett Avenue. It was 7 pm — the official starting time for the annual Blythewood Christmas Party. Already the old building was packed to the rafters. MacDonnell and his wife had been forced to park nearly a quarter of a mile away on a side street. His wife complained bitterly about this inconvenience. He tried to explain there was simply no other choice. This was not accepted.

"Come on, Michelle. Don't start this," MacDonnell pleaded as they neared the front door of the Stanton Club.

"Start what, Michael?" Michelle's voice had that dire singsong, little-girl-axe-murderer sound he'd learned to dread. "If we had gotten here earlier, we could have found a decent parking spot."

"Michelle, if you could have decided what you wanted to wear, instead of changing outfits half a dozen times, we could have been here a whole lot sooner." This was a bad tactical error. MacDonnell knew better than to blame his wife for anything. Accountability held neither a prominent color nor thread in the plaid weave of her personality.

"I had to find the right clothes, so I wouldn't embarrass you." Michelle was loud. A few people, about to enter the Stanton Club ahead of them, turned to stare. "If you wanted me to look like a dirty old hag, you might have said so, before I came to this stupid party."

MacDonnell put his hand on her arm, trying to appease her. "You look great, honey."

Abject surrender was always his best recourse. It had the desired effect. A plaintive smile, disturbing in its ease, stole across her red lips. Tonight, Michelle was — by anyone's standards — looking fine. Her makeup and hair were done just right. The outfit she'd taken so long in deciding upon was flashy, trashy and undoubtedly sexy: a black leather motorcycle jacket, black lace see-thru top, and a black leather miniskirt that barely concealed anything and did not conceal the tops of her black thigh-high stockings. Gaudy gold rings dangled from each ear, flashed on every finger and thumb. Michelle looked like she was playing at high-priced call girl — odd for someone who spent so much time proclaiming religious devotion, and the consequent self-righteous, self-denial of the flesh. MacDonnell had to admit he liked the look, even if it did make him feel uneasy in a way he couldn't quite put his finger on.

They entered the Stanton Club arm in arm, a slightly skewed picture of wedded unity.

MacDonnell made a beeline for the bar, but before he got there a familiar face erupted from the crowd in front of him. Rick Pasinetti was sweaty, red-faced and desperate. He paused to glare furiously at Mike MacDonnell.

"This place." Pasinetti half raised his hands as if to ward off an oncoming assailant. "This place is fucking nuts. Get me the fuck away from these termites."

MacDonnell started to say something, but Pasinetti shook a single bead of perspiration off the blunt tip of his nose and continued his rush towards the nearest exit, shoving bodies aside as he went. MacDonnell shrugged and proceeded on. He'd seek an explanation from Rick later on; if there were an explanation to be had. Sometimes, Pasinetti would go off for no particular reason. Mike considered it part of the man's unique charm.

It was standing room only in the taproom that night. Blythewood employees were a thirsty lot. Nonetheless, MacDonnell managed to carve out a spot at the bar for Michelle and himself. He ordered a whiskey sour for her and a beer and a tequila double for himself. The tequila disappeared as soon as it arrived. For her part, Michelle sipped diffidently at her drink, keeping her eyes tacked on her husband.

Several people, drifting by in the tidal surge of bodies, said hello to MacDonnell. Seven months in Team One had firmly established his reputation as a 'hammer,' one of a select few who were called upon to physically contain the students when things got out of control. This designation made him friends among the line staff, who were beaten up on a day-to-day basis, and a few enemies among the professional class of clinicians and nurses and administrators who had little direct or lengthy contact with the students.

One of those individuals, who fell somewhere between the opposing camps, approached MacDonnell now. Her name was Janice Chambers–Thomas. She was a consultant at Blythewood, commuting twice a week from a private practice in Connecticut to advise the clinical department at Blythewood. A small birdlike psychologist in her late thirties, Janice was wealthy and well-spoken with a hint of carefully contained insecurity.

Tonight she'd had a bit too much to drink.

"Michael MacDonnell!" The woman advanced on him in a giddy rush, a lopsided grin sliding off a flushed face. She was trailed by a dry stick of a man who MacDonnell absently designated as a husband.

"Hello, Janice," MacDonnell greeted her politely. "This is my wife, Michelle."

Dr. Chambers–Thomas didn't glance at Michelle. The psychologist stood swaying unsteadily before MacDonnell. A swath of perfect teeth grew large as she tried to bring her eyes into focus on his chest. Mike was wearing a new chamois shirt beneath the plain, black leather jacket which he habitually wore (it was the only coat he owned). The shirt proved to be a well-made garment — only two buttons popped off when she reached up with both hands and tore it open.

"Jesus!" MacDonnell rarely expressed genuine surprise.

Dr. Chambers–Thomas, braying laughter, rubbed his bare chest.

Michelle gasped.

MacDonnell instinctively retreated from the woman's touch. He quickly buttoned his shirt — what he could of it. By the time he finished, the inebriated psychologist was already merging back into the crowd, dismal husband figure mutely and obediently in tow.

"What the hell was that?" MacDonnell laughed uneasily. His attempt at a lighthearted attitude only succeeded in forcing a thin smile from his bride. "I need another drink. It isn't every day you get attacked by a shrink." He turned back to the bar and ordered another tequila boiler-maker. The corner of his eye was reserved for monitoring Michelle.

For the next half an hour she was terse in her conversation but seemed in control. Mike MacDonnell was beginning to relax when an arm fell across his shoulder. Sharon Murphy, gassed to the point of vertigo, leaned heavily against him. Her face was nearly the color of her brilliant red hair.

"How the fuck are you, MacDonnell?" Murphy ran the words together like a herd of unruly horses. She was rough and hard as any man and almost as solidly built in a female way. Murphy and MacDonnell worked the same shift and become quick friends. MacDonnell would never admit he found her attractive, which he did, and it wouldn't have done him much good anyway. She was wearing a man's tuxedo. It suited her.

"How are you doing, Shar?" MacDonnell asked. At any other time he would have been delighted to see her, but now there was Michelle to consider.

"I'm fucking fine," Murphy bawled merrily.

MacDonnell introduced his wife. Murphy proffered her a nod of the head and then, in a stage whisper Michelle could not have failed to hear, asked, "She the one who called the cops 'cause you were an hour late getting home from work?"

A pained expression was the only reply MacDonnell could muster.

"You and I stopped for a quick one that night, didn't we?" Murphy continued digging his grave.

A quick one? Why, in the name of God, did she have to say a quick one? MacDonnell wanted to hide.

Murphy mercifully changed the subject. "Did you hear about Justin? Somebody, who shouldn't have, finally caught the evil bastard playing his little games. He's gone. They may press charges. Took 'um long enough. You know something, MacDonnell? Blythewood is fucked. It's the most fucked-up, dysfunctional place I ever worked." She drove a finger into his shoulder. "You're the only decent staff there — you and me. Hey, what happened to your shirt? It's missing buttons?" Her face went slack as she lost the train of thought.

MacDonnell cleared his throat. "Do you want a drink, Shar?" He was relieved when Murphy roused and removed her arm from around his neck.

"Yeah, let's have a drink," She agreed. "You haven't seen Reggie have you? She was supposed to meet me here." Reggie Sparks was Murphy's girlfriend.

"No, but she'll turn up."

They made small talk until the young woman arrived a few minutes later, also wearing a tuxedo. Reggie was a new staff and not unattractive. MacDonnell liked her too (he'd developed a fascination for lesbians, cute ones anyway), but prudently kept his greeting brief and politely distant; once again for fear of Michelle.

Murphy and Reggie Sparks soon drifted away, arms locked together, and MacDonnell braced for Typhoon Michelle — but his wife was unusually placid. Perhaps it was the noise and the crowd restraining her. This was his hope. He himself was not comfortable in such large gatherings. To compensate, he usually drank too much and became loud and often aggressive. Sometimes he would offset these tendencies by being genuinely funny. Sometimes he was just genuinely obnoxious.

Tonight, with Michelle at this side, he only wished to survive. He would not have even attended this event except for his wife's frenzied insistence they needed a night out together.

Michelle tugged at his sleeve. "Michael, I have to use the bathroom."

MacDonnell groaned inwardly. Now commenced the 'Ritual of the Potty.' His wife expected him to escort her to the ladies room and post sentry while she was within. If she happened to take an unbearably long time — which was not unusual — he was expected to remain steadfast. There could be no drifting back to the bar, or even a quick visit to the men's room for his own relief — that was all strictly forbidden. He must stand, immovable as Gibraltar, until she finished her dainty toilet compulsions.

MacDonnell sighed and took her hand. They threaded their way through the crowd until he spotted a single occupancy bathroom without a waiting line in front of it. A cute blond in a clingy red dress was just emerging.

Michelle watched the girl walk away. "I bet you wish I looked like that, eh?"

MacDonnell cringed like a dog before a rolled up newspaper.

"Honey, you're prettier than she is."

"Don't lie to me. I know I'm old and soiled looking."

MacDonnell raised his hands in a gesture of surrender. Michelle spun on her high heels and stalked into the bathroom.

MacDonnell's relief was short lived. She reappeared and yanked him in after her.

She locked the door.

"Michelle? What the fuck?"

His wife pushed him back against the nearest wall with surprising strength. "You wanted that girl?" Her breath sizzled in his ear. "And those two lady-lickers?"

MacDonnell lost the power of speech. He was a big Irish deer caught in the headlights of oncoming traffic.

Unexpectedly, Michelle stamped a violent kiss on his mouth that left his lower lip bloody. She started fumbling with this belt buckle and zipper.

"Would that little yellow-haired slut do this for you?" Michelle sank to her knees.

For the second time that night MacDonnell was genuinely surprised. Fellatio in the ladies' room of the Stanton Club was entirely serendipitous.

Michelle applied enough suction to drag an aircraft carrier through a koi pond — but just shy of event horizon, she bit down hard on the head of his penis.

Tears rolled from Mike MacDonnell's eyes, but he did not, could not, make a sound.

"Sorry. I caught a tooth," Michelle chirped, wiping her mouth on the sleeve of her motorcycle jacket.

MacDonnell bent into a half crouch, clutching his injured member, afraid to view the damage done. Finally he summoned the courage and looked down. There were purple tooth marks and either smeared lipstick or blood. His head began to swim.

"Come on," Michelle said. "It was an accident. You might at least say thank you."

MacDonnell fought the dizziness and gingerly returned his wounded manhood to shelter. Michelle waited long enough for him to zip before she unlocked the door and walked out. There was a spring in her step. MacDonnell followed much more slowly. His spring was sprung.

By this time dinner was being served in the main dining room. MacDonnell limped to a table and sat down with his wife. The food presented was appalling: rubbery strips of roast beef tough enough to repel bullets, and bowls of underdone frozen vegetables hard enough to shatter the teeth of hyenas. Baskets of stale Parker House rolls, and tiny pats of tooth-tarter-yellow butter substitute on ice, did not rescue this repast. MacDonnell was amazed. He assumed Oleo had ceased to be manufactured some years back and by the way it tasted — an explosion of freezer burn on the tongue — it had.

Michelle devoured her supper with rare gusto. "This is good," she declared between mouthfuls.

MacDonnell put his fork down and turned away. He could not bear to watch her chew anything.

Dessert proved to be crystallized nuggets of chocolate and vanilla ice cream. Michelle ate both servings. After finishing, she was in such a fine mood, she actually offered to get him a beer from the bar. MacDonnell instinctively placed a hand over his crotch when she walked past.

Once the dinner was completed, a dance floor was opened in the middle of the hall. A Top 40 cover band was summoned to a small stage and began cranking out reasonable facsimiles of popular hits. The music was not to MacDonnell's taste, but once again Michelle approved. Soon she was humming along with the lead singer. MacDonnell did not ask her to dance. Instead, he spent the time searching the crowd for familiar faces. He recognized several, but the one he was seeking, Terry Johnson, proved to be absent. MacDonnell still chose not to look closely at the carnal urges he felt for her. After all, he was happily married and he had recently discovered Terry lived with a man (someone she rarely mentioned and rarely brought to Blythewood parties) named Ben.

Mike MacDonnell glanced at Michelle and sighed.

He took a few minutes to study the great table at the head of the assemblage. Here sat the Rumgays, father and son, the founders of the feast. As befit royalty, they were screened by their men-at-arms, Blythewood's board of directors — a well-dressed assortment of well-heeled cronies, including a few relatives, a judge and a couple of prominent area businessmen. Their chief function was to provide Blythewood School with an aura of respectability and, more importantly, protection.

The Rumgays and their housecarls were seated at a dignified distance from the squirming mass of employees, to the left and behind the little stage erected for the band. Cyril Rumgay, a shock of brilliant white hair and pink scalp, was the patriarch. He'd migrated from Boston thirty years ago, founded Blythewood with something like good intentions, piloted the school through waters both calm and stormy, and finally arrived at the port of profitability.

MacDonnell idly wondered how many of the affluent citizens of Wessex were aware of Blythewood and its unique clientele. The school, smuggled into a densely wooded, sparsely populated area on the outskirts of the trendy community, was carefully shielded from the scrutiny of the town's residents — a neon cathouse would have offered a better fit to the Wessex image and caused considerably less consternation.

Cyril created the school for clients with organic brain impairments, but when the prison systems grew overburdened, the warehousing of dangerous adolescent males proved to be a lucrative growth industry. Blythewood mutated from a barely solvent way station for the handicapped into a tollhouse accepting any and all, so long as the coin had the proper jingle. It managed this profitable evolution without any corresponding and expensive adaptation in the physical environment. Blythewood boasted a roster which now included an eclectic mix of adjudicated sex offenders, urban gang members, murderers, thieves and the older core of violent, mentally disabled students — all contained without benefit of walls, gates, locked cells, or guards.

The Rumgays did their best to calm the disquiet of staff by explaining these cold-eyed 'youngsters' were the heart wrenching products of dysfunctional, often abusive family settings, and each and every one deserved a second chance. At Blythewood, they got that second chance and assaults and runaways quadrupled in number. Thankfully, most of the escapees did not tarry in the vicinity of Wessex, but headed back to their points of origin either by bus, hitchhiking or auto-theft. This last method of transportation caused administration some anxious moments, but ultimately nothing the board of directors and the lawyers couldn't handle.

Cyril had recently retired (rumors whispered he had been forced out), turning over the reins to his son, Bill. At the moment, father and son were sitting side-by-side, the perfect picture of familial cordiality, awash in the affectionate attention of wives and friends and grateful retainers. MacDonnell had never gotten close enough to say "hello" to either man.

Mike's eyes twitched as Annie Wilson, one of the supervisors on his shift, glided across his line of vision. She didn't see him and he made no attempt to gain her attention. Annie was the reigning sex symbol at Blythewood. Most of the male (and quite a few female) employees at Blythewood thought she was drop-dead gorgeous. Mike didn't understand the attraction; to him, she was not, as his father used to say, "The kind of woman who could make Jesus abandon the Apostles." There was something aloof about her, something refined and aristocratic which put him off. Perhaps it was a deep down recognition that girls like her didn't waste spit on guys like him.

MacDonnell spread his feet apart, leaned back in the chair and forced himself to listen to the band.

Unforeseen disaster, in the form of a brunette overnight staff named Cindy Martinez, stopped at their table. MacDonnell barely knew her. Only God could tell what compelled Cindy to be the catalyst of his final excoriation.

"Hi, Mike. I heard you got nominated for employee of the month on Annie Wilson's shift."

"Hey, Cindy. Yeah, surprisingly I was."

"Well, good luck."

"Thanks."

The conversation was innocent enough, but MacDonnell noticed Michelle had stopped humming.

"Are you, uh, about ready to call it a night?" he asked his wife. She stared straight ahead, wordlessly. MacDonnell shrugged and went back to picking faces out of the crowd.

Five minutes passed before he became aware of an unusual noise, like steam escaping from a rupture in the Number 2 boiler on the Lusitania. His ears quested the air, revealed the sound to be a steady stream of expletives escaping from a rupture in Michelle's psyche.

" . . . filthy, fucking cunt!"

Unfortunately MacDonnell was leaning towards his wife when she finished her verbal barrage and opened up a physical one. Her fist, bony and hard, smashed into his nose. The next punch, less accurate, bounced off the side of his face. Five more strikes followed in rapid succession, with varying degrees of success.

The people at the surrounding tables reacted in a variety of ways: some stared in open-mouthed horror, some laughed cruelly and some merely yawned. This *was* the Blythewood Christmas party. Anything was to be expected.

Much later, at home in bed, Michelle apologized. "I'm sorry, so, so, sorry." She nestled close to him, gently patting his swollen face.

MacDonnell had no choice but to accept her apology. It was sincere. He searched his wife's wide green eyes, found there a misery of the soul with no distinct origin and no visible end.

"We could make love?" she suggested. This was a demand sweetly disguised as an offer, a test of his enduring loyalty, a symptom of her congenital insecurity.

Despite residual soreness, he climbed on top of her.

Afterwards they lay side-by-side in the dark.

"You'll leave me someday," Michelle whispered.

"No, never."

"Nobody can love me."

"I love you."

Much to his surprise, he still meant those words.

8

Sundays, once dreaded by MacDonnell because he was left alone in Team One without benefit of teacher or TA, became welcomed islands of calm. There wasn't the hustle and bustle of school to contend with, nor the prying eyes of administrators and clinicians, all waiting to note staff imperfections in word or deed. The Bomb Squad was allowed to sleep late, enjoy a leisurely brunch and spend most of the day doing whatever MacDonnell decided they should do.

The boys rarely 'went off' on him anymore. Despite their limited intellectual capacities, they instinctively grasped he was too big, too fast and too strong. This led them to accept his absolute authority. And because he was never harsh when he didn't have to be, because he never abused or belittled them (unlike a few of the more senior childcare workers), they also came to implicitly trust him.

Only Davie Kemp was guaranteed to do something unpleasant on these tranquil Sundays. It usually started without a definable cause, could last for an hour — or all day. Today's episode began while Team One was in the Rec Center after lunch. Davie, screeching like a howler monkey, launched himself across the room at MacDonnell. The big childcare worker was smoking a cigarette near an open window. He calmly waited till Davie was almost upon him, then nimbly stepped out of the way. Davie banged headfirst into the wall, bounced backwards, and landed on his rump, stunned. MacDonnell continued smoking his cigarette.

Rick Pasinetti stuck his head in the Rec Center door. "Everything all right in here, Mackerel? I was walking by and heard the Call of the Wild."

"Just Davie, as usual." Mike answered.

Pasinetti rambled in, a cup of coffee in each hand. He was wearing what he always seemed to be wearing: an old army field jacket, a khaki safari shirt beneath, worn jeans with a tiny hole in the crotch or somewhere else, and a pair of scuffed-up sneakers. "Mind if I take my break in here?"

"No, I'd welcome the company."

"So what's going on, anything?"

"Same old shit. I hear you had some trouble with Kenny Disanti over Christmas."

"What a sick bastard he is," Rick Pasinetti said, eyes lighting up. "On Christmas Eve, me and Ron Montgomery had to drive all the way to Framingham to pick up the sorry son-of-a-bitch. He'd gone home for the two week vacation and didn't make it two days. Right in the middle of Christmas Eve dinner, with the entire Disanti family gathered around, he strips off his clothes and chases his ten-year-old sister around the house with a carving knife and a twelve inch erection. What a fucking mess. The parents put out the SOS to Blythewood, so two hours later me and Ron strolls in and finds three uncles holding Kenny spread-eagle and bare-assed on the dining room table. Most of the Christmas *feast* is hanging from the ceiling, the mother is crying hysterically, and the father is kicking a turkey around on the floor like a soccer ball. Jesus Gawd. There's this one old ginzo — must have been the grandfather — still sitting calmly at the table, drinking a water glass full of grappa." Pasinetti massaged the top of his balding head. "Kenny starts bawling his eyes out when he sees me. I actually felt bad for the dirty slob. I gets him dressed and hauls his sorry ass out of the house — with the mother hanging off his neck at every step. She's telling him how sorry she is he has to go and how much she loves him. Gawd, it was awful. Merry-Fucking-Christmas and to all a good night. Me and Ron got off shift later and hit every bar in town."

"Happy Holidays."

"Yeah, how 'bout it." Pasinetti glanced at the phone hanging on the wall. "Hey, can you get an outside line on this thing?"

"Dial nine first."

"I needs to call Wifey Dearest. Let her know I'm gonna be doing some overtime."

"You're working the overnight?'

"Gawd no. I'm going out drinking. I'm just a lying beast."

While Pasinetti was on the phone, Davie Kemp began to yowl again, creating such an obstreperous racket Pasinetti's wife heard it over the telephone and asked what was going on.

"The music of childcare, Light of My Life," Pasinetti answered, and then, "Hit him again, Mac! Hit him again!" as MacDonnell planted Davie in the floor.

After Pasinetti hung up, Mike apologized for the ruckus.

"Don't worry about it, dogboy," Pasinetti said. "She was giving me the red-ass. I needed an excuse to get off the line. Jesus Gawd, why in hell did I ever get married?"

Mike MacDonnell might have asked himself the same question.

"So, Cousin Mongo?" Rick grinned. "Wanna be my date tonight?"

Mike's head tilted from side to side a few times as he considered.

"Why not. Hand me the phone?"

9

Newbury, population 55,000 and falling, was an old, comfortable, once thriving manufacturing town passed over when General Electric handed out futures. It was, give or take, 10 miles from the city center south to the center of Wessex — a light year away in terms of attitude. No pretense of snobbery to be found in Newbury. There were nice neighborhoods, there were bad neighborhoods, there were neighborhoods caught in-between. North Street, the main drag, still offered some good restaurants, a few nice shops, but there were blank windows too, businesses that failed when the mall arrived outside of town. The side streets maintained car dealerships, auto body shops, the occasional small fabrication plant, but if you continued along, the pavement buckled and cracked, the streetlights grew farther apart, and only night hid the decaying bodies of fallen giants: huge factories and warehouses, empty, silent, waiting to collapse.

This was Pasinetti's hometown. He had lived here, off and on, for most of his life. After work he took MacDonnell to a quintessential Newbury saloon, Shea's Lounge. The place, like its address, had seen kinder times, back when it was a carbonated hub for working men and women with cash to burn. It still clung to vestiges of those better days. The booths and barstools were made from real wood and padded in leather; the smoked back mirror was six feet wide, frosted and etched at each corner. Smaller, no less fancy branded mirrors were scattered throughout: Old Bushmills, Calvert Extra Vintage, Crown Royal, White Horse, Smirnoff, Crown Russe, Jack Daniels, more. Each of them captured the low ambient light, gently returned it to create a cozy twilight. The bar rails, top and bottom, were brass and polished by hand. An enticing blue halo danced above ranks of liquor bottles and clean glass ware.

"This place is nice," MacDonnell said as the two men claimed their barstools.

"Yeah, it don't smell of piss," Pasinetti replied. "I like it anyway."

Angela, the bartender—owner, glided over to take their order. She was in her late forties with big, starch-sculpted hair straight out of the '40s, pretty dark eyes crowned by too much blue eye shadow, and smooth, creamy skin that had never seen acne or a wrinkle.

"The usual for me, Angie," Rick said. "Something frilly and queer for my buddy here."

"A shot and a beer," MacDonnell clarified.

A few minutes later, when she was down at the other end of the bar with a customer, Pasinetti nudged MacDonnell, and asked, "Would you fuck her?"

"Honestly?"

"I would, but I think she's my cousin,"

"Well . . . just make sure you don't get Eleanor pregnant."

"Hey, Angie! Dogboy here thinks I'm FDR. He's either a raging lunatic or blasted off his ass. Either way, don't give him anymore to drink." Pasinetti's voice boomed like a depth charge. It was still early; no one else in the bar was speaking above a quiet murmur.

Angela dismissed him with the flutter of a slender hand.

"So, Rick," MacDonnell paused to unwind a pack of Newports. "How come you didn't take the assistant soups position? I heard they offered it to you."

"Didn't want a thing to do with it. 'Assistant Supervisor' means jack-shit. You're still just a childcare worker with a fifty cent raise — until they can't find anybody else to finger if something goes bad. Bullshit! I'll stays where I am."

"Christ, Rick. You could have changed things for the better. Been an innovator, a reformer." MacDonnell punched the air to emphasize his mock enthusiasm.

"*Blightwood* will never change. I don't know why we stay in the fucking place. Jesus Gawd. And it ain't the orcs that drive you nuts. It's the fucking administration. No matter what happens, no matter how bad it gets, the Rumgays are never — ever — to blame."

"They're cut from a finer cloth than you and me, Rick, and it's stain-resistant. Maybe if you moved to Wessex, bought yourself a posh little condo, it might elevate you high enough to at least kiss their asses, and enjoy it."

Pasinetti sneered. "I fucking hates Wessex. It's nothing but a resort for rich Nazi-snob-bastard-vaginal-flows."

"Don't talk about your betters. What if somebody heard?"

"Blow me, Boy Scout."

"You're too damn ugly."

"By closing time, I'll be an irresistible vision."

"Nope."

"That's what they all say, just before I kisses 'um," Rick Pasinetti waved his hands in the air like he was trying to surrender. "Angie, could I have another one of these?" He tapped the empty glass in front of him.

"You're putting them away quick," Mike said.

"I needs my tonic," Pasinetti replied. He paused. "You know, I have been thinking about taking a little vacation from the booze. Wifey Dearest ain't happy, though she drinks like a fish herself. I may go on down to the VA in Springfield. They hand out antabuse like candy."

"Are you sure you want to take that crap?"

"It works. Unfortunately, it can send your blood pressure through the roof. Jesus Gawd, I took it back in eighty-four and almost had a stroke."

"Well, look at it this way," MacDonnell said, "if you're slumped in a wheel chair, drooling all day, you won't have to worry about falling off the wagon."

"Fucking inspirational. Thanks."

The two men continued drinking heavily. Shea's Lounge slowly filled with the mixed assortment of Newbury patrons it attracted: a fallen yuppie crack-dealer, a tastefully dressed drag queen (Rick called him Manly the Translucent, said he was a mail carrier in Worcester and a meth addict), and a few working stiffs looking for a quick buzz.

At quarter to ten, two pretty Puerto Rican girls wandered in and sat down on the stools next to Pasinetti. He paused to eavesdrop on their conversation, all in Spanish, and then asked "Do you ladies speak English?"

The girls smiled shyly. One said, "Not so good."

Rick smiled back. "Then let me give you the only English lesson you'll ever need. Repeat after me," His smile became a leer and he held up a thick index finger like the baton of a Tanglewood conductor. "I . . ."

The girls glanced at each other, shrugged and chorused in charming accents, "**I** . . ."

"Love . . ."

"**Love** . . ."

"Ricky . . ."

"**Ricky.**"

Pasinetti continued, "Ricky is . . .'

"**Ricky is** . . ."

"Muy macho . . ."

"**Muy macho!**' The girls flashed beautiful teeth.

Pasinetti turned to MacDonnell. "They're mine."

The girls did allow him to buy them each a drink.

As the night wore on, the noise level steadily increased. Before long someone was slamming coins in the old, jewel-bright jukebox. A bombed-out landscaper, three toes missing because he drank on the job and ran the mowers, had become increasingly fascinated by Manly the Translucent and began shouting out along with the music:

"STROKE ME, STROKE ME!"

The raucous clamor incited Pasinetti. He heaved his bulk on top of the bar, knocking over MacDonnell's beer in the process, and began grinding out an impromptu hula dance, hands behind his head, hips wiggling furiously. A chorus of catcalls, hoots and curses served only to encourage him. Rick was — in the foggy jargon of Blythewood — *over-stimmed.*

"Want the Full Monty, you sick bastards?" Pasinetti roared to the patrons.

More obscenities shouted back; Manly the Translucent clapping perfectly manicured hands.

Rick unbuttoned his safari shirt, shook his hairy belly in a grotesque mockery of seduction — and promptly lost his footing in a puddle of beer. He cartwheeled into an adjacent booth full of startled drunks, striking his head sharply against the edge of a tabletop.

The audience responded with wild applause.

MacDonnell helped his friend to his feet. Thanks to the subdued lighting inside Shea's, he did not see the blood beginning to surge from a gash on top of Rick's head.

"I'll give the dive a ten for innovation," MacDonnell quipped, "but the form was a little sloppy."

Pasinetti did not reply. He stood swaying on his feet, slowly blinking his little eyes.

Mike MacDonnell's heavy brow furrowed. "Are you all right, Rick? Jesus!" For the first time he saw the blood running down the side of his friend's head.

Rick came to his senses. He took an unsteady step backwards and propped himself against the bar. "I'm fine," he said. He touched the top of his head and looked at his fingers. "Is this blood or steak sauce?"

"Blood."

"Fuck me. I need a bar towel."

"You might need a doctor. It looks pretty bad."

"I'd rather be gelded with a chainsaw."

"I thought you had been?"

Angela hurried over with a clean cloth. She'd been an anxious observer of the entire incident.

"Thank you," Pasinetti acknowledged her assistance with aplomb. Then, noticing the worried expression on the woman's face, said, "Don't worry, Angie. It's not your fault I act like a complete asshole. I've never sued anybody in my life. Lawyers give me a crotch rash. I wouldn't mind another vodka, though."

Pasinetti began dabbing at his wound with the cloth, pausing long enough to gulp the drink Angie brought him.

MacDonnell asked, "Are you sure you don't want to go to the emergency room? I'll drive."

"Get me a broad and I'll be fine."

"Wait here," MacDonnell said. "I have to take a piss. Maybe I'll find something suitable lurking outside the men's room." His huge head swung back and forth, he added, "God knows, there are enough *lurkers* here tonight."

"I ain't particular,"

By the time MacDonnell returned from the bathroom, Pasinetti had polished off another vodka, wrapped a fresh towel around his head like a turban, and was actively engaged in conversation with a young prostitute of his acquaintance.

MacDonnell sat down on his stool. "You're looking better."

"Mackerel, let me introduce you to Kelly LaBounty." Pasinetti salaciously exaggerated the pronunciation of the girl's last name.

Mike MacDonnell nodded to the girl. She was dark-haired and not bad looking.

Rick said, "I'm hoping to convince Ms. LaBounty to give up her life of fornication-for-profit, and become my personal concubine."

"Christ, who could resist?" MacDonnell asked.

"I gotta go, Ricky," the prostitute said. "I'm glad you're okay." She smiled at Mike and left.

Rick Pasinetti watched the girl walk away. He turned to Mike and said, "I grew up with her old man. Good family. Now that poor soul sells her ass to any drip-prick that'll buy her a bump of crack. Newbury ain't what it used to be."

"There are worse places."

"Yeah? Too bad for them." Pasinetti adjusted the towel on his head. "Newbury was a goddamned good place to grow up in, the best — before Neutron Jack come along, anyway. Look at all the creepy fucks in this place tonight. Jesus Gawd, at any minute I expects Lee Marvin to come through the door and lead 'em on a suicide mission behind enemy lines, me and you included. Ain't the Berkshires beauty-full?"

"Rick, you're a sentimentalist. I never would have guessed."

"Go rape a snake, cum-eater."

10

The winter passed slowly. Michelle's renewed interest in sex didn't survive the holidays. Consequently, Mike worked as many hours as he could get at Blythewood. For some reason Michelle didn't protest this; possibly because of the good paychecks he was bringing home, possibly because Father Bob relented and allowed her to swarm on Sacred Heart everyday — or possibly because some quirky manifestation of her quirky thought process convinced her Mike wouldn't dare masturbate at work. In the end, it might have been nothing more complex than out of sight, out of mind.

MacDonnell took advantage of her liberality by exaggerating the number of hours he was working and spending the time at bars with new friends.

One of his favorite hangouts became the Four Tables, just down the road from Blythewood. The bar was built on a hillside overlooking the main highway into Wessex. It's bi-level parking area rose steeply behind the building, creating, from time to time, some interesting mishaps for tipsy patrons on their way in and out. Inside, the place was divided into two sections: the smaller taproom, containing a few more than the original four tables and the bar itself, and a larger room filled with over a dozen tables, flocks of chairs, and an array of windows on three sides that allowed customers to view Wessex prosperity in all its glory. The Four Tables was clean, well kept and made great sandwiches, or so Mike MacDonnell had heard. He never ate until he was done drinking. It killed the buzz.

He could be found there every Wednesday, payday at Blythewood. The supporting cast varied from week to week, but it usually included Terry Johnson, Sharon Murphy and a new childcare worker with whom Mike quickly established a friendship, Kevin Marshall. Rick Pasinetti generally avoided these gatherings. He and Mike often drank together, but usually it was just the two of them, and usually it was only at the seediest gin joints in Newbury.

A February afternoon found Mike, Terry, Sharon, her girlfriend Reggie Sparks, and Kevin Marshall sitting together in the Table's big room. It was a small crowd by Wednesday standards. Terry was sipping a frozen strawberry daiquiri and chatting about everything and nothing and making it all entertaining to MacDonnell.

"When Mike walked into the classroom that first day I thought he was Hercules Hernandez. Swear to God. I say to myself 'Uh-oh, this ain't gonna work out.' I figured administration must be punishing me." Terry darted a glance at Mike. "And then I think, this Rican's gonna throw me down and rape me before he gets fired." Terry sprang to her feet, bent over the table and pantomimed a vigorous rear assault. Fortunately, the big room was vacant except for the Blythewood group.

"The thought never crossed my mind," MacDonnell said dryly. "Humping munchkins really isn't my style." He'd given up trying to convince her that he was Irish.

Terry thrust a hip in his direction.

"You couldn't handle it, baby."

The other staff — with the exception of Reggie Sparks — were amused by Terry's performance. Reggie seemed mildly disgusted so much attention was being showered on MacDonnell.

"I knew Mac would make it," Sharon Murphy declared.

Kevin Marshall said, "Yeah, I thought he was nothing more than a dumb, beer-swilling redneck when I first met him." Marshall paused to let a wry smile arrive beneath his long nose. "Then I got to know him, and realized he was a *smart*, beer-swilling redneck."

"Is that curly blond hair of yours natural, Kevin?" MacDonnell asked. "Or do you dye and perm?"

"Mike, you're a bitch," Marshall returned. This phrase was Kevin's patented response to all things MacDonnell; it encompassed everything from 'Hello, how are you?' to 'Goodbye, and let's get drunk later,' to 'Go to hell, you ignorant bastard.' It was Kevin Marshall's personal, New English equivalent of *aloha*.

Reggie Sparks put a thumb under her front teeth and gave the handsome young childcare worker a look that was speculative, enigmatic, and devoid of the faint distaste she reserved for MacDonnell. Sharon Murphy noticed it and frowned slightly.

"Well, the kids don't fuck with Mike anymore," Terry Johnson said. "Even the gang kids shit their pants when he walks in the room."

"Don't we all," Reggie Sparks said, pulling her thumb out of her mouth.

The conversation, mostly about work, ebbed and flowed, until Terry turned to Mike and asked, "Do you go down on your wife?" There was a peculiar kind of sexual provocation in her question.

"None of your friggin' business," MacDonnell replied.

"You do," Terry blared triumphantly. "Mike's a carpetbagger! Mike's a carpetbagger!"

MacDonnell's right hand dragged the length of his face. "Terry, the term you're looking for is carpetmuncher."

"You wish," Terry shot back. It made no sense really, yet it brought a blush to Mike's face.

Reggie Sparks pretended to gag herself with a middle finger.

11

"Where's Michelle today?" Sara asked.

"Church. Where else?"

"She won't be back soon?"

"Fuck no."

"Good, good." Then, panting, "I've got great news, Mike."

"What?"

"Danny and I are getting back together. I'm . . . moving out . . . out to Troy with him, Oh, fuck," Sara groaned. "Ohhh, fuck, that's good."

"Oh . . . yeah?"

"I really miss Danny," she said, reaching down to wipe sweat off Mike's face. "I'll be a good wife this time."

12

"Father Bob wants to have an egg hunt on the Saturday before Easter. I told him, he shouldn't put too much candy in the plastic eggs. You know, kids get enough candy on Easter as it is. Easter isn't about candy, after all. It's about Our Lord's . . ."

Guilt.

More than he could handle.

He would never — ever — do it again.

It was a mistake. I'm not that kind of man. I'm not.

"And I told that Father Bob not to place the flower vases so close to the heating vents this year. What a mess I had on my hands. I had to replace . . ."

Sara was gone to Troy. Temptation removed.

Terry.
Terry . . .
No, I'm not that kind of man.

13

It was a warm spring and an early spring that year. The snow was gone for good by the second week of March. The first buds appeared on the trees before April was finished. Mike MacDonnell made some effort to limit the amount of time he was spending in bars, but quickly lost his resolve. Michelle became increasingly controlling, and odd, when he was at home. When three days of rain ruined her plans to play groundskeeper at Sacred Heart, she levied the blame on her husband.

"Michelle for Christ's sake, I'm not in charge of the weather."

"You might have looked into it. And please, please, **stop** taking Our Lord's name in vain."

Blythewood became something of a haven, almost a second home for him; a home that was often unpredictable and fraught with perils both concrete and ambiguous. Oddly enough this was its greatest appeal to Mike MacDonnell. Working under conditions of physical and emotional risk has a predicable psychological effect on most people: quickly or slowly, it wears them down — wears them out — by eroding their internal state of balance and well-being. But MacDonnell was different. In some peculiar fashion the violence had a calming effect on him, allowed him to sleep easier at night, curbed the crazy chatter in his head which would eat at him when he had nothing to do — and of all things, made his hands shake less. Blythewood became a steam vent for all his innate frustrations. To be sure, it caused him to drink a lot and made him want to fuck all the time, but then, when he stopped to think about it, boredom enhanced his thirst and sexual appetite more than anything else. At least now these urges had direction and a singular clarity.

Mike certainly understood Blythewood was not a place to spend your working career. Staff came and went with the rapidity of pimples and country music stars. But for good or ill, that place and those people (to whom applying the word dysfunctional was a laughable understatement) emerged as the central focus of his life. Little by little, step by step, it all became a lasting part of him — and he of it.

The gateway to this assimilation — the ferry keeper on the River Acheron — was of course Terry Johnson. She was the magnet drawing him during those times when his attention should have naturally wandered onto more wholesome objects than Blythewood. He ignored one or two alternative employment opportunities when they came along, suppressed a periodic, if lackadaisical, yearning to further his education, and unconsciously allowed his relationship with Michelle to free fall; though he would have stoutly insisted he was doing his level best to keep the marriage together had anyone asked.

He never missed a day of work and he was never late — all because of Terry. Mike finally met her boyfriend, Ben, at some bar and found he was a decent enough guy. MacDonald watched them together and instinctively knew Terry, although she rarely spoke of him, loved Ben like the devil; and, sooner or later, she was going to destroy the relationship. She couldn't help herself. Mike wondered if Blythewood caused this self-destructive impulse, or if the facility attracted people intent on blowing their lives all to hell with their own powder. Maybe a little of both, he decided. He made every effort to convince himself that he could not, in all good conscience, participate in the destruction of Terry's relationship, however inevitable it might be. Of course this resolve didn't help much on those nights he awoke so out-of-his-mind horny he would have gladly cut Ben's throat while he slept, just to have Terry in the same bloody bed.

MacDonnell was caught like an oversized minnow in these conflicting tides of powerful emotions. He wanted to help Terry, protect her, care for her — and at the same time, possess, control and use.

Use it till it was all used up, as a dumb, whiskey-swilling redneck in a bar had once advised him to treat women.

The biggest Blythewood party that spring season was at one of the teachers' homes. It was the first such affair Mike MacDonnell attended. The teacher was a dim-witted, but pompous sort who constantly sought to score with the teacher aides, without much success. Convincing proof, in and of itself, as to how innately unappealing this man truly was. Tufts of wiry hair stuck out on his neck, chest and arms, making him look like a ripped mattress. In an effort to change his fortune, and to get laid by other than his usual fare of creaky prostitutes and homeless teenagers, the teacher hosted the staff at his lair on a Friday night. Food and booze were provided. Nobody had to bring their own. It was a massive turnout. Unhappily, the man also memorized two Shakespearian soliloquies, to be inflicted upon the prettiest teacher aides whenever the opportunity presented itself.

MacDonnell happened to be sitting next to Terry when the teacher arrived at their spot. Without preamble or explanation, the man launched into a bit of Hamlet. The lines were delivered without respect for meter, rhyme or, in several instances, proper pronunciation. About halfway through the performance, Terry turned away and began talking to Mike again. Undeterred, the teacher droned on to the end with ugly earnestness. He then executed a pretentious little bow and drifted off to the next group. Usually MacDonnell would have laughed at such a ridiculous performance; but it had been imbued was such deep conceit, such an obvious sense of intellectual superiority, it made him want to pop a few more beers and then pop the dumb bastard.

Terry Johnson, sitting on the floor next to Mike, tossed a cheese puff in her mouth and said, "What was that all about?"

MacDonnell shook his head and grunted. He was left to wonder why the fool thought the Immortal Bard was going to get him any pussy. The girls of Blythewood were not exactly summer refugees from an English Lit program. This left only one conclusion: the teacher was convinced it made him sound smart and would thus irresistibly lure, or intimidate, some stupid piece of ass into bed. The fact most people, however dicey their educational attainments might be, can usually tell a fraud when he reaches well beyond his own capacities, never occurred to the man. He kept going from room to room, girl to girl, bleating the same words, until one young lady, who *was* an English major working a part-time job at Blythewood, pointedly corrected him on several counts. In ice cold exasperation, she asked if he actually knew who Shakespeare was, in what century he lived and from what country he came. This closed the show without an encore. The teacher retreated to his kitchen and drank until he threw up in the sink. MacDonnell found him there a while later, in a crumpled heap on the floor. It smelled like the man had shit his pants.

Denied violent entertainment, Mike wandered aimlessly around the teacher's house, unconsciously trailing in Terry's migratory path of socialization. When he, for whatever reason, failed to arrive promptly at her location, Terry would keep one eye hovering over her shoulder until he managed to catch up. It was a mating dance of a kind, though neither one of them understood how it should, or could, be brought to its natural conclusion. Not surprisingly, it ended in frustration for both of them.

Terry, a little drunk by now, was sitting on a couch with another teacher aide discussing the relative merits of their respective boyfriends, including length, width and hardness; frequency, intensity and variety of positions, and how loud things got. MacDonnell, leaning against a wall behind Terry, overheard the entire conversation. He was both embarrassed and lasciviously intrigued. Women's crude sex-talk, always unexpected, never failed to excite him. And when it was Terry doing the talking, it could become an intense form of auditory stimulation, the words a hot, wet tongue filling his ear with whispered promises and obscenities. Unfortunately, this evening, Mike's erotic musings were abruptly curtailed when Terry veered headlong into a frank admission of past and current infidelities.

"I can't help myself. I keep screwing around on Ben. I don't want to, but I see a cute guy and I just do it . . ."

Some men would have been delighted by this revelation. It would seem to mark an easy path to carefree sexual conquest. After all, it was giving the girl what she wanted. But somehow it made MacDonnell uneasy, and the next words Terry uttered hit him like a steel toe in the gut.

"Maybe, maybe it's because I was molested when I was ten. Maybe it messed me up, somehow . . ."

Something shriveled inside of MacDonnell. He felt ashamed; not for her, but for himself. Terry was so vulnerable, in so many ways, to take advantage of her would be the worst kind of repugnant self-gratification. Yet there it was, a tool presented him, a psychological pry bar to open her thighs. MacDonnell's powers of metacognition were sufficient to warn him that he was more than intelligent enough, more than manipulative enough, to effectively use this to his advantage. It would be easy to offer her a little comfort, a little understanding, and then, well, surrender would surely follow. And to be fair, why should childhood sexual abuse exile Terry from the world of mature, consenting intimacy? It was like punishing the victim for the crime.

MacDonnell took a mouthful of beer from the plastic cup in his hand, found it hard to swallow. So many possible rationalizations to employ. So many plausible excuses to justify whatever action he took.

Mike pushed away from the wall. "Terry, I've gotta get going."

"What?" Surprise in her deep eyes — disappointment?

With those eyes upon him — those lovely eyes — MacDonnell felt truly ugly.

"I'll see you at work on Monday," he said softly, and then he was gone.

Terry was quiet for the next hour or so. She drank a lot and smoked a few joints and finally started talking to a boy, not from Blythewood, barely out of his teens. Later she followed him upstairs to a bedroom.

In the next few weeks, MacDonnell struggled to strike a balance between conscience and lust. It was difficult. He found himself searching for Terry Johnson's face behind the wheel of every car he passed that resembled her little knockabout Renault. And Michelle would have been horrified to discover who he was thinking about during the few times they made love.

14

At the tipping point. . .

"Did you hear Sharon Murphy quit?"

MacDonnell looked up from the newspaper he was reading. "Yes. I'm sorry about that."

Terry and Mike were sharing a break in the Blythewood staff lounge, a musty cement room in the basement of the main building. It contained a Coke machine, a microwave, a couple of chairs and couches and a few thin streamers of green mold on the walls.

Terry continued, "Sharon got in a big fight with Faith about sick time." Faith Minor was the assistant program director, Bill Rumgay's second in command and his second cousin. She had a fearsome reputation among the staff.

"I heard it was messy. I'm beginning to think administration can't tell the difference between good staff and bad staff. The stupid prick they made employee of the month for May is the biggest fuck-up I've ever seen — and he's scared of his own shadow."

"Yeah, but he knows how to kiss the right ass," Terry said. "Reggie Sparks told me she's thinking about quitting too, because of Sharon."

"Well, that's not unexpected. You know how it is around here. One staff gets the axe and a line forms at the chopping block." Mike liked to call it the Blythewood Lemming Effect.

"I like Reggie. I hope she doesn't quit. She's a good staff."

"Wouldn't be any skin off my ass. She hates my guts."

"No she doesn't, not really."

"Yes, really. Somebody told me Sharon's moving to Delaware. That'll be the end for her and Sparkles, anyway."

"I didn't hear that." Terry said letting her voice drift away. She was quiet for a moment before getting up from her chair to stand in front of MacDonnell. "Mike?"

"Yeah?"

"Can I ask you a question?"

He really wanted to finish the article about the Packer's off-season acquisitions, but he nodded and said yes.

"How do you have an orgasm?"

"Excuse me?"

"How do you have an orgasm?" Terry lowered her voice though there was no one else in the lounge.

"How do I have an orgasm?" Mike MacDonnell began squirming in his chair. He wished the newspaper was a Kevlar shield.

"Not you. How do I have an orgasm?"

"You . . . well . . . uh . . . Jesus. You've never had an orgasm?"

"I get excited, then nothing happens."

"Well, there are lots of ways to . . ."

"Maybe I need someone to show me," she said. The words were grenades — pins pulled — tossed in the air.

Goddamn it, I'll show you, he thought. But nothing more than a dry rattle escaped his mouth.

Mike MacDonnell shrugged helplessly and buried his nose in the sports section.

And again . . .

Sitting at midnight, outside the Four Tables, in Terry's car. They were sharing a joint and laughing about something stupid. Both of them were drunk and high, but young enough to avoid getting sloppy.

Mike always contended he wasn't a big-breast man, but Terry's breasts were so captivating — in their almost Frazetta-perfect size and shape, in their wanton sway and bounce when she walked, in their scalding firmness when she would accidentally (or not) brush against him — he'd become unblinkingly fascinated by them. During a lull in their rambling conversation, Terry noticed him staring at her chest. Without a word, she finished the joint and dropped the roach in the Renault's ashtray. As her hand came back it lightly brushed his inner thigh and came to rest there.

Two pairs of dark eyes sought each other, found liquid reflections both indistinct and mysterious, held for a long moment . . .

Mike MacDonnell coughed. "Do you want to go back inside for another drink before the bar closes?"

"Okay, Mike."

15

Summer brought heat and little rain. During the hot months, the Blythe-wood academic program observed a modified schedule: regular classes in the morning, field trips and outdoor activities in the afternoon. Terry Johnson liked taking the team to Taconic Lake Park where it was cool and open. Mike MacDonnell didn't object. For several hours he could sit back, smoke cigarettes, occasionally yell at the kids, and watch Terry, which was his favorite pastime. The teacher, Charlie Collings, rarely joined them. He always seemed to have lesson plans which needed fixing. Mike and Terry were just as glad.

That afternoon, they parked the van next to a picnic table shaded from the bright sun by a stand of maple trees. Because there were no lifeguards, the students were not allowed to go down to the lake itself, but they were permitted to play in the thick grass a few yards away from the stony beach. MacDonnell took his accustomed position, back to bark, and began burning menthols. Terry settled down next him, gathering in her knees with both arms.

"Go out tonight?" she asked.

MacDonnell nodded. Terry was wearing tight red shorts and a stretchy ribbed top which detailed the surface of her flat stomach and the full, round swell of her breasts.

Terry reached over, casually took the cigarette out of his mouth and put it between her lips. She took two slow drags and gave it back to him.

"I left my smokes at work," she explained.

Mike nodded. There was no need for them to share a cigarette. He had plenty in his pack, but the intimacy of the act prevented him from offering her one — nor did she ask.

"Mike?" She pulled her legs tighter against her chest. "What do you want to do with your life?"

"Whaddya mean?"

"What do you want to be?"

"I don't know — a childcare worker."

"No, you dumb cracker–fuck. I mean, what do you want to do after you leave Blythewood?"

"Haven't thought about it."

"I have."

"And?"

"I want to be something — somebody." She cast a sidelong glance with those moist, black eyes. It made him feel all the things a married man shouldn't. "And I want to have babies. I think I'll be a really good mother."

MacDonnell smiled. "I'm sure you will be."

"Do you want to have babies?"

"I've tried and I've tried, but I can't seem to get pregnant. I was thinking of looking into fertility drugs."

"You're an asshole."

"Most likely."

Terry grew quiet for a moment and then said, sadly, "I'm too dumb to be anything."

"Oh, bullshit."

She lowered her head. "Then why don't I know what it is?"

"Nobody does."

"No, that's not true. What about doctors and lawyers?"

"Okay, rich people know they want to stay rich, so they send their larvae to universities. But for people like us it's different. Nothing's that easy or clear. Sometimes we just have to let things sneak up on us and hope for the best."

"That ain't good enough, baby." Terry stood up and dusted off the back of her shorts.

"I never said it was."

Unnoticed by the two staff, a golden retriever wandered into the vicinity. It padded over to the little group and evacuated its bowel a few feet from Joey Rondeau, a herky-jerky little sprite with a wild shock of hair and a face like a fresh turnip. Rondeau didn't hesitate; he grabbed the dog crap and began dancing gleefully around his fellow students, waving it in their faces.

The golden retriever ran off to piss on the tire of a Ford Mustang.

Davie Kemp lunged for Rondeau.

"Joey!" MacDonnell yelled.

Rondeau, screaming with laughter, flung the shit in Kemp's face and ran behind Terry. Davie's rage rendered choice of target unimportant. He grabbed the front of Terry's shirt, dragged her towards the parking area.

"MIKE!"

MacDonnell rushed up behind Terry and seized both of Kemp's wrists. He searched for pressure points.

"Get him off me!" Terry cried.

The front snap of Terry's bra had given way at the first grab. Between Davie Kemp's tugging and Terry's resistance to being towed, the neckline of her shirt stretched out more than a foot from her body. Leaning over her shoulder, Mike MacDonnell was confronted by the fleshy reality of bare, perfect breasts and erect, coffee-colored nipples.

"Let go, Davie." There was something surprisingly feeble in Mike's command. The pressure points were proving elusive.

Terry instantly diagnosed the problem. "Stop looking at my boobs and get him off me!"

"I'm trying."

"No, you're fucking not!"

While all this was going on, Chucky Hoover grew more and more agitated. He was a severely retarded young man whose left arm ended in a withered stump at the elbow. Unable to contain his anxiety any longer, he dashed out into the middle of the parking area. He began jumping straight up and down like a kangaroo on an invisible leash. The height he achieved in these vertical leaps was astounding; it would have shamed many a professional athlete. At the apex of each vault, Chucky would slap himself in the head with his existing hand and shout something which sounded like:

"Bugadga-bugada-ratshitinthetubaba."

This unique display was elevated to an even higher realm when, owing to his extreme thinness, Chucky's loose fitting pants and underwear slid completely off his body. This proved, beyond the shadow of a doubt, the only stubby thing on Hoover was his left arm.

Two elderly ladies, carrying a large wicker picnic basket between them, happened to walk by. One squeaked in horror, dropped her end of the basket and scuttled for the safety of her automobile. The other woman stood stock-still and stared at Chucky. A full minute passed with her chin lifting up and down, up and down, in time to Chucky's salmon leaps. At length, and with great conviction, she said, "If he doesn't stop jumping, that thing is going to hit him right between the eyes."

Several hours later, at the Four Tables, Terry said to Mike, "You were too staring at my boobs."

"No, I wasn't."

"Were too."

"Was not."

"How come you're blushing, then?"

"I'm not. You are."

"You can't tell if I'm blushing."

"Oh, yes I can."

Terry rolled her eyes and took a sip from a tequila sunrise. She put the glass down on the table. "I'm going to the little girls room."

"Where else could you go?"

Terry took three steps away from the table, stopped and turned around. "Next time, don't send one of the kids to do your dirty work, you big-headed, bubble-eyed Rican Bitch. If you wanna look at my titties. . ." she presented her back with an impudent wiggle. "Ask."

Terry did not see him gag on his beer.

16

The Alley was aptly named. It was a dark, narrow little Newbury dive on the edge of town, frequented mostly by professional alcoholics and skid row royalty. The only illumination was provided by beer and liquor signs, a Rolling Rock clock, and the glow emanating from the lighted sinks and taps behind the bar. It was the kind of place where the patrons kept to themselves and most *citizens* kept away from.

It was also one of Rick Pasinetti's favorite haunts.

Mike MacDonnell smacked him on the shoulder and sat down on the next stool.

"Mac!" Pasinetti said. "I'd about given up hope."

"A couple of the gang kids in Team Four got into it at shift change. I had to go over and help out. Christ. It's freezing in here."

"Thank Gawd for air-conditioning. It's hot as a billy goat's pecker outside." Pasinetti emptied the mixed drink in front of him and held up the glass for the bartender to notice. "Less ice this time, Donatello, and more gin."

The bartender nodded and took the glass.

MacDonnell waited a moment, then quietly asked, "The guy's name is Donatello?"

"Naw, I just calls him that 'cause he looks like one of them Mutant Ninja Turtles. Ain't he an ugly fuck?" The bartender returned with a fresh drink. Pasinetti said to him, "My friend here thinks you're an ugly fuck, Donatello."

The man shrugged. "I get laid."

Pasinetti raised the glass. "It's all that counts."

MacDonnell ordered a bottle of Genny and a shot of Jack Daniels, then stuck a Newport in his mouth. He asked Pasinetti for his lighter. Rick handed him an old Zippo. It was scratched and dulled by long use and years swimming with key and coin. Mike flipped it open and thumbed the tiny wheel, kindling a small torch against The Alley's chilly gloom.

"How many orcs did you kill today?" Rick asked pleasantly.

"Seven restraints. None from my team."

"They're starting to use you like a bouncer, boyo."

"Starting?"

"Terry must be pissed you're out of the team so much?"

"She doesn't say anything."

"No?" Pasinetti smiled wickedly. "Do you and her got something going, dogboy?"

"What?"

"Have you fucked her?"

"Rick, come on. I'm married."

"I'd fuck her."

"You're married, too."

"That ain't exactly true. Me and Wifey Dearest have come to a parting of the waters."

"I'm sorry."

"Don't be. I'm not. Two years together was two years too many." Pasinetti gulped down his drink and ordered another. "You know, when we were first together, I stayed by the dirty bitch day and night for a week, helping her kick a pill habit. I wiped her nose and I wiped her ass. Jesus Gawd, there were times when she'd howl like a dog. And what did I get for my foolish devotion? *Married*. Wedded-fucking-bliss. A couple years down the road and she's out at a different bar every night, running up my credit cards, and fucking everything that would hold still, including a Vietnamese midget and a meter maid with a plastic leg. But I guess we all gets what we deserve, including me." Pasinetti ran his tongue along the inside of his lip. "She has nice tits, though. Perfect tits really."

"That's too bad, Rick."

"How long you been married, Mac?"

"Not that long," Mike MacDonnell boasted, but without any great conviction.

"And you're sure nothin's going on with — "

"No."

"I wouldn't blame you. Terry's salt of the earth, and she's got a body to make Liberace reconsider the sequins, the capes — and the fucking candelabra."

Or Jesus abandon the Apostles.

A large figure, reeking of Old Spice, shambled out of the gloom and dropped onto the barstool next to Mike. Greg O'Brien was a CCW at Blythewood, forty something and a confirmed boozer.

"Hey, boys, what's goin' on?" he asked in a slow deep voice.

"I didn't know you were here," said Rick.

Greg's broad, fleshy face composed itself into a sloppy grin.

"Yeah, all day. Parents were killed in a plane crash on the way back from California this morning. Been drinkin' since I got the news."

Tears began leaking from his droopy eyes.

MacDonnell was stunned. "Jesus, Greg, that's terrible — "

"Don't listen to his shit," Rick snarled. "How many times does this make for your parents going down in flames, Greg? Four? Five? What the fuck is wrong with you cunt? Out of cash and need some kind-hearted slob to buy you drinks? Take your act and get the fuck out of here. I ain't in the mood."

Still crying and grinning, O'Brien used the bar to lever himself into an upright position and stumbled away.

"What in hell was going on?" Mike asked.

Pasinetti shook his head. "Greg's all right most of the time. I've known him for thirty years. Sometimes though he gets weird. Probably because he's never been laid. I use to think he was gay, but he's not. He's what they call painfully shy around women. Always has been. About ten years ago he was hot for this broad named Sherry. She was a CCW, too. We were all working at this shitty group home. He'd stare at her all day at work, make stupid little jokes, and go out of his way to do cute little things for her. Made my stomach churn. I think she liked him too, but he never asked her out. He did, however, start parking his car out in front of her apartment every night — until she noticed and called the cops. That was the end of that."

"I never would have guessed. He seems fine at work."

"Oh, it's not like he's a bad guy or nothin'. He's a good childcare worker and good in a restraint. And if he likes you, he'll give you the shirt off his back. He's just a little nuts. Gawd, the poor fuck lives in a tow-along camper parked on his parent's front lawn on Hungerford Street. Has since he got out of the Navy. One night I stops in there for a drink, he always has cases of booze, and find the camper packed with the goofiest collection of circle-jerks I ever saw. His poker buddies as he calls them. Most of them looked like they should be swimming in bottles of formaldehyde at a carnival sideshow. I don't know what they were doing, other than gettin' plastered, but it weren't cards."

"I don't suppose you stayed long."

"Long enough to polish off a bottle of Johnny Walker Black. Hey, I ain't a snob. Never went back, though. I have the sneaking suspicion O'Brien and the lads are a nest of vampires."

"That sounds reasonable."

"Yeah, about as reasonable as you saying nothin's going on with Terry."

A wild sob echoed from somewhere back in the black recesses of the bar.

"Sounds like Gregory Pessary found a mark," said Rick.

17

"Where are you going?"

"Out."

"Out where?"

"They called me into work."

"I never heard the phone ring."

Mike MacDonnell wondered if Michelle knew it was a lie.

"Can't you stay home?" his wife pleaded.

"I have to go." He moved past her and put his hand on the door knob.

"When will you be home?"

"When I'm done."

Then he was outside in cool rain and open space. He hurried to the GTO and spun out of the driveway.

A brief glance in the rearview mirror.

Was Michelle standing in the front yard, waving at him?

Mike did not escape a full measure of guilt, but it was tempered by the paramount desire to escape his wife.

He needed a drink and lately Michelle had been unrelenting in her attack on his boozing. She no longer allowed him so much as a sip of beer in his own kitchen without treating him to an essay on the villainy of alcohol.

And then there was Terry . . .

She'd asked him to go out tonight, to meet her at a bar called Seagram's Brook, about five miles north of Newbury. It was a place where you could dance and find a ready supply of coke and weed. MacDonnell told her no. Thursday was not a good day for him to go out. Michelle threw a fit when he didn't stay home on his off-shift.

But resolution weakened as the day wore on. He tried to call Terry, but didn't get an answer at her apartment. MacDonnell had no way of knowing if she was still going to Seagram's Brook or if her plans had changed. It didn't matter. He would find her, if he could.

Mike stepped on the gas. The ancient poison in his blood stream had made him increasingly restless and prone to violent mood swings. To compensate for this, to subvert it, he'd become excessively affectionate to Michelle. He brought her a flower every day, kissed her every time she turned around, said "I love you" so often his gums began to bleed.

It did no good. He didn't want Michelle anymore.

But why? If a man tried hard enough, he should be able to convince himself that his wife meant well, that she loved him, that she was in the same area code as sane. For Christ's sake, they hadn't been married that long. It couldn't — shouldn't — fall apart this fast.

It had for Rick Pasinetti.

MacDonnell knew he must maintain the center, keep the relationship from disintegrating. If you break the bloody glass, how can you hold up the weather?

He kept repeating this to himself, in time to the clacking windshield wipers, all the way to Seagram's Brook.

When he arrived, he jumped out of the car and hurried inside, but Terry was not there. Disappointed, he pushed his way through a dense, noisy crowd and shouldered up to the bar. One drink here and then push on to the next place she might be. The air inside the building vibrated to music so loud it wobbled his legs. He had to yell his order to a baby–faced bartender. Bodies, rank with perspiration and cheap unisex colognes, jostled him on either side. He was not standing at the bar so much as he was shimmed into it.

A glass of whisky came. MacDonnell stared at if for a long time. He closed his eyes and opened them again. The whisky was still there, perfect, untouched.

What did he want?

To fuck Terry till his heart burst.

And then what?

This answer came as easily as the first.

Pain radiating in all directions and everything lost, for everyone.

The music faltered for a few moments. The DJ was getting a hand–job under his pulpit.

Mike MacDonnell raised the whisky glass to his lips. His right arm was accidentally bumped by the big man with the shaved head and pirate earrings standing next to him. The whisky spilled on the bar and on MacDonnell's shirt.

He put the glass down and tapped the big man on the shoulder.

"Sir, you dropped something."

"Huh?" The man turned. "What did I drop?"

"Your teeth," MacDonnell answered pleasantly.

"What happened to your hand? It's a mess," the woman with copper-colored hair and black lipstick almost shouted. She had to. Mick's Pub, a Wessex faux-Irish bar, was loud and swarming with electrified young professionals busily establishing a fluid social and sexual pecking order. MacDonnell hated the place.

He looked down at his bruised and bloody knuckles as if in surprise.

"Fancy that."

"What do you do?" the woman asked.

"As little as possible."

The woman shrugged. She leaned back on her stool, resting both elbows on the bar and casually spread her legs apart. The black snakeskin leggings she wore revealed a cameltoe. She caught MacDonnell looking and opened her legs a little more.

"Do you know what I do?"

"No," Mike answered honestly.

The woman said she was an editor for a successful skin magazine and danced naked, in a gilded cage, over a tank of piranha, at a Boston leather bar on the weekends.

"Must be interesting work."

"It can be," she said. "Do you want another Guinness?"

"No thanks. I'm good."

"You don't look like you're good." She reached inside her gray, snakeskin tunic and wrangled out a bra that was at least a 38 D. She proceeded to bind Mike's wrists with this warm, impressive undergarment. "Let's go in the bathroom."

He wriggled free from the restraint. "I truly appreciate the offer. But I'm afraid you're a wee bit too . . . evolved for me. Besides, I can't drink with my hands tied."

A tall blond, model pretty, stopped and looked at MacDonnell and the bra he was holding.

"You're disgusting."

"So, I've been told," he replied. "Thanks for confirming it."

Where the fuck was Terry . . .

18

On a flutter of wings, a robin settled to the ground and promptly began picking at something, maybe a worm or an insect or a piece of paper. Its beak snapped like a sewing machine needle for a several seconds, then stopped to allow a small, soulless eye to regard the big, black–haired human sprawled comfortably atop a smaller, glassy-eyed member of the species. A cigarette (the second of the restraint) dangled from the lower lip of the large primate.

Terry Johnson ran by, screaming and laughing all in one breath. Rick Pasinetti followed in hot pursuit, chewing maniacally on one hand, waving the other wildly in the air and belling like an organically–impaired stag in rut.

The robin took a dance step backwards, but did not flee.

MacDonnell smiled. His friends were playing Autistic Tag again. He flipped his spent cigarette butt at the robin. The bird chirped an avian curse and took wing.

Terry ran to a group of staff watching students play kickball on the athletic field. One young staff, Sacha Pitell, pushed Terry behind him and stepped in front of Pasinetti. Words were exchanged.

Though MacDonnell was too far away to hear anything, it was obvious Pitell failed to recognize the chase for what it was: a game. The young man took a sudden step backwards when Pasinetti's barrel-like body surged forward. The burly childcare worker began barking like an angry bulldog. After a few seconds of this, Pasinetti threw his hands in the air and walked back in MacDonnell's direction. By the time he arrived, Pasinetti's good humor had been partially restored.

"That's what I like to see — therapy," Pasinetti declared, nodding at the human rug beneath Mike MacDonnell.

"What just happened over at the ball field?" MacDonnell asked curiously.

"The Wog bastard threatened to report me for an inappropriate staff interaction."

"And the Wop said?"

"I told him he wouldn't be reporting anybody with his mouth knocked back down and sideways out his asshole."

"Have you ever considered a position in the Diplomatic Corps?"

Pasinetti made a hissing sound between his teeth. He waved a hairy paw in the direction of the main building. "I'm fed up with this place, Mac."

These words carried the weight of prophecy. A week later Pasinetti failed to show up for work. Faith Minor would receive a collect telephone call and the simple message, "This is Valenteen Savage. I quit. Fuck you." Minor thought she recognized the voice and put two and two together. Rick would board a flight for Miami and a month long bender in the Keys. He would eventually return to New England, tanned, unemployed and not quite sure where he had been or what he had done for thirty days.

Rick Pasinetti stared at MacDonnell and then looked back at the athletic field. "Terry's got great tits. I'd bet my last brass button Gandhi thinks so too."

Mike MacDonnell was able to shrug only one shoulder; the other was planted in the student's back.

19

Terry arrived for work in an agitated state. MacDonnell, in a foul mood after a pitched battle with Michelle the night before, watched with some irritation as Terry buzzed around the classroom. Even by her standards she was acting irrationally. It bothered MacDonnell. He could not decipher the cause of this behavior. Terry's emotional state was usually an open book to him.

Except for the students, they were alone in the classroom today and would remain so until a new teacher could be hired. Charlie Collings had suffered a nervous breakdown and fled Blythewood forever, proving once again the facility was not everyone's poisoned cup of tea.

"Will you stop flitting around?" MacDonnell grumbled at Terry.

Her responding laughter was excessively giddy. She danced over to the teacher's desk where MacDonnell was sitting with his feet up. She dropped one round buttock on the edge and batted her nightshade eyes at him.

"What do you think of Sacha Pitell?" she asked.

Terry was in lust. Mike MacDonnell knew it immediately. It filled him with a peculiar kind of jealously, not precisely anger or hurt, but rather a feeling of regret. "He don't make my nipples hard."

"He's fucking gorgeous. Fucking gorgeous! He asked me to go out with him tonight." She was biting her lower lip, trying to contain intense excitement.

MacDonnell looked out the window.

20

It was chilly the morning Mike MacDonnell received his first promotion and his first formal introduction to Bill Rumgay. Autumn had barely replaced summer, yet the nights already flowed with dark rivers of cool Canadian air, lingering till the sun was well up in the clear skies. Mike was summoned to the supervisors office without explanation. His pace was measured as he crossed the field from the school building, but the short locomotive puffs of breath trailing after him in the crisp air hinted at a mounting anxiety. He was more than half afraid some sort of official invective was coming his way. For what he wasn't sure, but he didn't dare consider the possibility this had anything to do with his application for the supervisor position. Such was the relentless uncertainty plaguing all Blythewood staff. The guiding lights of the facility cultivated a haphazard and thoroughly arbitrary form of discipline. It made nervous insecurity about one's continued employment not only unavoidable, but necessary.

There were two supervisors per shift at Blythewood. Tinker McCann, a middle-aged veteran of the middle-management wars, had left to pursue a career writing redneck anthems in Nashville. MacDonnell put in for his position. Blythewood was entering a particularly violent period. There were innumerable assaults on staff, several serious injuries and a generally stormy climate. Mike's stock was at a premium. This would be typical throughout his career. If the conditions were hazardous, he was hailed as a savior. When things settled into a placid routine, he was reviled as an abusive slacker. There was some truth in both viewpoints.

MacDonnell walked into the office on proverbial pins and needles. Bill Rumgay and the remaining shift supervisor, Annie Wilson, awaited him. Their expressions were speculative, but not unfriendly.

"Have a seat, Mike." Rumgay motioned towards a chair.

Blythewood's program director was small, slight and furtive, with a hint of malevolent slyness. A friend of MacDonnell's had given Rumgay the nickname "Red Squirrel." It fit.

MacDonnell took a seat and nodded politely to Annie Wilson. He still did not like her much. She was too well-educated and too well-mannered. MacDonnell considered her an elitist snob who elected to soil her dainty fingers among the common folk. That she was smart and possessed daunting good looks had not entirely escaped him; but he preferred to ignore the blue, blue eyes and the long, lovely hair which was not quite blond and not quite brown, and instead note that her nose was a bit pointed and her chin a trifle sharp. To his knowledge, she had never initiated or even assisted in a restraint. This marked her, to Mike Mac-Donnell, as nothing more than a fragile dilettante with no business supervising anyone.

"I think congratulations are in order," Bill Rumgay said, flashing a brief uncomfortable smile. He went on to explain that Mike had been awarded the title of Crisis Manager, a rank never before and never after used. This promotion was on a probationary basis, denying him the full authority of a supervisor until such time as he proved himself worthy in the eyes of administration. This was disappointing and spoke loudly for the lingering doubts Rumgay and the rest held about his character and intelligence. MacDonnell was pleased by the dollar–an–hour raise — and the fact he was not being fired.

Over the next several weeks Mike would wryly refer to himself as 'The Commodore,' feeling the naval term accurately represented a unique position which allowed him to loiter in the office, drinking endless cups of tea and smoking endless lines of Newports, till a hysterical call for help roused him to commit some ruthless act of suppression against the bipolar buccaneers swarming over the gunwales. All in all, the position would suit him quite well.

At the end of the makeshift coronation everyone shook hands, brief pleasantries were exchanged and Rumgay hurried off to more important matters.

Mike MacDonnell took a breath and looked around at his new digs. There were two doors, one issuing into the body of the main building, the other out and onto the campus grounds (he instantly decided this represented the schizoid nature of his new job: go left to kiss some administrative ass, go right to kick some sorry ass); a blackboard, displaying all the students' names and current levels of treatment; a plain metal desk, a file cabinet, a couple of chairs, a clock, a telephone and not much else. Just an office, nothing remarkable — except, of course, for the big, bright, laminated Rumgay Company sign mounted like Cosimo de' Medici's gonfalon on a blank wall. There was an ensign like it in every office and lounge in the building, supersized to near billboard proportions at the bottom of the driveway. Beneath the copyrighted Blythewood logo — a stylized sunburst over a placid water — were several glossy photos of smiling children, all much younger and cuter and rational than anything at the school, and the bold legend:

WE CARE

I don't.

Mike MacDonnell took another breath, sensed dead air, an awkward silence. He was alone with Annie Wilson for the first time. He had never bothered to guess what her opinion of him might be; his assessment of her character rendered speculation irrelevant. Now they would be working together and not exactly as equals. She would remain, for the time being at least, his nominal boss.

"So . . ." he began tentatively. "Do you mind if I smoke?"

"I would prefer you didn't," Annie Wilson replied, a hint of stone in her voice.

MacDonnell's gloomiest forecast was confirmed. Silence fell again like fimbulwinter. He mentally cursed his own stupidity in applying for a position which placed him at the disposal of a spoiled rich girl who was likely a health fanatic, probably a vegetarian and undoubtedly a jogger or avid hiker — or worse yet, a skier. How in hell was he ever going to get around this excruciating incompatibility of taste, breeding, personal behavior and hygiene?

MacDonnell stared at a scuff mark on the toe of his right boot for a long moment. What he said next was one part desperation, one part intuitive inspiration, and one part quirky, unconscious sexual aggression.

"I'll have you know there's a portrait of Rin Tin Tin tattooed on my ass, and if you don't let me smoke, I'll show it to you."

Annie Wilson's eyes rolled wide. Her mouth opened slightly to express any number of unpleasant reactions, from patrician contempt to sickened dismay at the crude remark. Instead — taking both people quite by surprise — she started to laugh.

"I like German Shepherds."

Her laughter had a peculiar bubbling sound to it, like a small leak in a circus calliope. Mike MacDonnell found he liked the sound, but wasn't sure why. He was not yet fully conscious of an old verity: to amuse a woman is the first step in seducing her.

"Good Lord," she burped out more words. "That is the . . . *you* are a *strange* man."

Cracks in the facades having been established, a pleasant, and more conventional, conversation blossomed and lasted till lunch time — when Terry Johnson burst into the office, a defiant set to her jaw, spoiling for a fight.

"Are you all right, Mike?" Terry asked, glaring at Annie Wilson as if she had been subjecting him to a prolonged torture session.

"I'm fine, Terry." MacDonnell instinctively positioned himself between the two women. "I got promoted."

Terry lapsed into an immediate state of shock. She knew of his application, but never gave it the slimmest possibility of success. He was a goon. Her goon.

"You're a supervisor?" she asked slowly.

MacDonnell nodded, deciding not to attempt a clarification of his new position at the moment.

"You won't be in our team anymore?"

"I'll be there when you need me."

Terry Johnson's eyes floated down to her cheeks on a tide of tears. She turned and ran out of the office.

"What's her problem?" The contempt in Annie Wilson's voice angered MacDonnell. He almost told her to take the promotion and shove it up her lovely ass. Instead, he clamped his mouth shut and tried to oblige an empty feeling in his heart.

A buck an hour was a poor excuse for letting Terry down.

But he would learn to live with it.

21

Traffic on First Street in Newbury had come to a halt. Motorists climbed out of their cars to join a few pedestrians gawking at a naked young man dangling from a streetlight.

A yellow van, with **Blythewood School** painted on the side, pulled up. Mike MacDonnell got out and ambled over to the scene.

"What are you doing, Adam?"

Adam McCartan stuck out his tongue and climbed higher. He was Blythewood's resident, full-blown schizophrenic and bore a striking resemblance to a young and deranged Peter O'Toole.

"Why did you runaway this morning?" Mike MacDonnell asked calmly.

McCartan wrapped his legs around the post and hung upside down.

"Can I have a cigarette if I come down?"

"You ought to watch out for splinters," MacDonnell advised. "We'll see about the cigarette later. You need to get down from there now, before the police come. I'm dead sure they're on their way. You don't want to go to jail again, do you, Adam?"

"No. I would prefer not to go to jail again." McCartan's tongue began a circular sweep of his cracked lips.

"Then come down."

"Last night the chair in my room grew a penis and chased me around the bed all night. I had to get out."

MacDonnell nodded slowly. "So, you want a cigarette?"

A wrinkled upside-down grin, bad teeth and a conspiratorial stage whisper. "I think there are some sick people at Blythewood, Mike. And I may be one of them."

"I don't want you goin' through my shit," the student protested. He was sitting on the edge of his bed, looking unhappy. "You gonna steal somethin'."

"Thems the rules," MacDonnell replied as he dropped the suitcase on the bed next to the boy. "When you come back from a home visit, I have to check for contraband."

"What's that?" the boy asked nervously. He stood up and hovered at MacDonnell's elbow.

"Crap you're not supposed to bring back here. Cigarettes, weed, porno..." MacDonnell unsnapped the suitcase and began sorting through layers of underwear, shirts, pants, the usual.

Near the bottom, he lifted a carefully folded hooded sweatshirt to reveal a big bag of candy — bite-size Snickers, Kit Kats, peanut butter cups — and an excuse-me .32 Tomcat automatic. This wasn't usual. MacDonnell straightened up in mild surprise, unsure if it was real or a toy.

In one lighting quick motion, the boy grabbed the pistol and pointed it at the supervisor's face. In a fractionally swifter movement, Mike's left hand swept the weapon away and the flattened palm of his right hand drove into the boy's chest, catapulting him headlong into an open closet. The loud crash brought staff running down the hall.

The boy crawled out of the closet on his hands and knees. Two plastic coat hangers, hooks stuck in his thick hair, dangled like gigantic earrings on either side of his face.

MacDonnell examined the automatic. It was loaded and the safety was off.

He cleared his throat and said dryly, "I'd call this contraband."

The boy gasped, "My moms gave it to me to keep the faggots away."

"Yeah? Tell your moms to get you a chastity belt next time. You can keep the candy."

22

"*You* are a fucking supervisor?" Rick Pasinetti hooted.

"Crisis Manager," Mike MacDonnell corrected.

"Donatello. Your finest champagne for my friend here. He's joined the ranks on Olympus."

"We don't got champagne," the bartender said.

"Then a shot and a beer, you crass bastard,"and then to Mike, "Any new broads working at *Blightwood?*"

MacDonnell grinned. "None that would interest you."

"You'd be surprised by what interests me. I met this broad up in Chester last week. She tried to insert her nipple in the head of my cock."

"Why would she do a thing like that?"

"Don't know, but I had to let her try."

"How have things been going, Rick?"

"Not bad, not bad. I'm doing some hours over at a group home on Second Street."

"Is it better than Blythewood?"

"Fuck no. But I haven't worked there before, so they ain't sick of me and I ain't sick of them — yet. I'll probably go back to selling roses for my father in the spring. I've done it off and on for years."

"Is there money in it?"

"Yeah, there can be. The only problem is working for the stingy old Italian prick I call dad. Jesus Gawd, I love him, but he drives me fucking crazy after about an hour."

Donatello brought Mike's drinks. MacDonnell downed the shot of whisky before daring to ask Rick, "How's your ex-wife?"

"You mean Ilsa, She-Wolf of the SS? Last time I saw her, she looked like Death sucking a Life Saver. Which is pretty good for her. I did hear Maybelline hired her to test their new product line. She squirts cosmetics in bunnies' eyes and waits to see if they go blind. They say she's a natural."

MacDonnell rubbed goose bumps on his forearms and peered into The Alley's murk. There were less than ten people in the place and, with the exception of Rick and Mike, none of them were seated together.

"Christ, it's still cold in here, and it isn't warm outside, anymore."

"They keep the air–conditioning on year-round. That way Donatello don't have to remember to turn it on and off," Pasinetti said. "Hey, Donatello? Why are you such a fucking idiot?"

"Because I listen to the bullshit of assholes like you all day."

"They say there are two kinds of people in the world, Donatello. Those who say 'ouch' and cover their face when they gets hit, and those who hit back out of pure hostile instinct. What do you think of that?"

The bartender dangled another gin and tonic in front of Pasinetti, muttered, "Like I said."

Rick laughed, tossed the man a five dollar bill, and turned to MacDonnell. "You made yourself a bigger target by taking a promotion, Cousin Mongo. Remember what I taught you? Lay low, keep your mouth shut, and nobody will remember your name. That way you won't get picked when it comes time for them to fire somebody."

"I know."

Pasinetti lit a Camel with his old Zippo and blew a cloud of smoke above the bar. It hovered there for a moment, indistinct and ghostly.

"Nobody — and I mean nobody — leaves Blightwood happy."

23

The passage of several weeks proved Mike's reliability to Blythewood's administration and he was thus transmuted into a full-fledged supervisor. He and Annie Wilson continued to discover an easy ability to communicate on any subject. It made a harsh winter fly by unnoticed, and created a bond of trust — the most valuable of all commodities in a place like Blythewood. Terry Johnson's fling with Sacha Pitell ended her relationship with Ben. In turn her new liaison fizzled when Pitell's parents ordered him to find another job and another girlfriend who wasn't black. A certain distance grew between Terry and MacDonnell in the meantime, amplified when Annie Wilson stepped into the gap, becoming his most constant companion in after-hours socializing. Terry jumped into another brief, if turbulent, encounter with a childcare worker, and another after that. Because of this, Mike MacDonnell foolishly convinced himself he would (not without regret) be spared any further temptation. He loved to turn a dim eye on himself, and the situations developing around him, when it assuaged his deeply held, but often assailable, sense of right and wrong.

Annie liked to laugh and drink good beer and listen to his amusing nonsense. She even came to fitfully accommodate his smoking, though she developed an annoying habit of unexpectedly swatting cigarettes out of his mouth if he exceeded what she considered tolerable limits of frequency. MacDonnell began flinching spontaneously whenever she raised her hand.

The supervisors' smooth working partnership helped him settle into his expanded role at Blythewood. Only one of his new duties, attending the dreaded weekly management meeting, proved unbearable to him. This gathering of supervisors and department heads, including lead clinician, head nurse, academic director, assistant program director, and the mighty program director himself, occurred every Wednesday morning at 9 am in Rumgay's office. The session was supposed to run for no more than two hours; an ideal observed entirely in the breach.

The meeting originated as a way for management personnel to exchange information and find solutions to programmatic difficulties. This wise and necessary function was immediately abandoned in favor of self-congratulatory panegyric and endless debate between witless, preening egotists.

This hellish trial of endurance was, of course, presided over by Bill Rumgay. It gave MacDonnell an opportunity to observe the program director at close range. What he saw did not fill him with overwhelming confidence in the man's ability.

The first thing anyone noticed about Rumgay were his eyes: narrow, heavy-lidded and perpetually scanning the floor as if he feared stumbling over something in his path. He rarely made eye-to-eye contact when he spoke, and then only in short, painful bursts of twitching pupil and rolling whites. The program director was fond of referring to his days in the 'Trades.' What this meant exactly was never made clear. Certainly his soft hands, slender build, and relentless appetite for the kind of conservative, carefully maintained garments only a doting mother might choose for a pampered son, precluded the possibility Rumgay had ever done any kind of manual labor. MacDonnell decided Rumgay must have delivered coffee and doughnuts to a construction site during some long ago summer break from prep school. The supervisor instinctively knew his 'leader' had a pathological fear of large dogs, dark bedroom closets and anything messy or untidy. He could easily picture a young Master Rumgay trying to iron out those unsightly wrinkles in his scrotum. To be fair, Rumgay did exhibit a satisfactory level of efficiency in the performance of his administrative duties, so long as imagination and rectitude were not required. The school (and by extension the Rumgay family) continued to make money. By this standard alone, Bill Rumgay was a howling success. On the less savory side, Rumgay enjoyed the company of sycophants and could, on occasion, be motivated to harshly suppress manifestations of independence and character in his employees.

MacDonnell avoided Rumgay's censure by keeping his shift under control and letting Rumgay take full credit for it.

At the management meeting, Rumgay set the tone of aimless mental wandering, which most of the others present had long since mastered. These supervisors and department heads would hem and haw, mumble, whine and generally perseverate on insignificant detail and superficial personality clashes. Invariably the meeting dragged on without any clear purpose and at such length that MacDonnell would begin fidgeting restlessly in his chair. His skin would itch and he would start clawing at himself like an animal left too long in a cage.

One such gathering of the 'Liar's Club' (as one Blythewood wag christened it) took place on a March morning in the first few weeks of

MacDonnell's reign as an all-grown-up, middle-tier-flunky. It began with a discussion about moving a student from one team to another. Rumgay inaugurated the discourse:

"We have a new student arriving on Monday. His name is . . . Jeremy Keefner, I believe. It's been decided he should go into Team One. Of course, it means a student from One has to be moved to another team to make room for Jeremy. I'm leaning toward Stevie Corbett as the student I'd like to see transfer out to Team Three, which has a vacancy. I'd like to have the management team's feedback on this?"

"Well . . ." Courtney Merrick, the academic director, began on a congenital note of uncertainty. "I don't know if Stevie fits in with Team Three very well — on an academic level, that is."

"Why not?" Rumgay asked reasonably.

"Well . . ." Courtney Merrick fingered the big hairy mole everyone pretended not to notice on her cheek. "I think the board of education in his home district will object to Stevie being placed in a classroom with students who are so much younger than he is."

MacDonnell stared at Merrick. He wondered how difficult it would be to remove the furry thing on her face with a blow torch.

"How old is Corbett?" Keith Rodgers spoke up. A flabby, balding, fish-belly-white supervisor, Rodgers loved to be noticed as the guy who asked the most incisive questions.

Mike MacDonnell noticed Rodgers' stupid grin; thought, What a goofy looking fuck.

Stevie is . . . uh . . ." Courtney Merrick's unusually thick eyebrows squirmed together like combative caterpillars.

"He's sixteen," Debbie Wittenburg jumped in briskly. The head nurse had just finished her third slab of cinnamon coffee cake. Her mouth was atypically free to offer information rather than safe harbor to vicious gossip and all comestibles.

"What's the median age in Team Three?" Rumgay asked. He could not help noticing Annie Wilson's breasts struggling against a taught, black-and-white-striped knit jersey. It reminded him of something a sultry operative for the French Underground might have worn in an old World

War II movie. The only things missing were a beret and a haze of cigarette smoke. The shirt looked rather warm and he wondered if it was making her sweat. The program director found himself slipping into an explicit daydream in which he played the role of a relentless Nazi interrogator.

"Well . . . the median age is sixteen," Courtney Merrick admitted sulkily. "I thought Stevie was older."

Debbie Wittenburg beamed triumphantly. She had one up on the academic director. There was a long standing squabble between the nursing department and the teachers — though no one could recall what it was about.

"Okay. Three is an appropriate placement for Corbett?" Rumgay asked, squeezing his legs together to hide the Iron Cross his daydream awarded him. He forced himself to look at the head nurse. She was 250 pounds of self-propelled saltpeter.

"What Stevie's functional IQ range?" Faith Minor interjected. "Does it fit well with Team Three?" Minor, typically, looked severe, processed and ultra professional. MacDonnell wondered if she spent her off-hours working as a vinyl-clad dominatrix.

"Umm, I'm not sure," Courtney pouted. "I'll have to review his records."

"Yes, you should," Minor agreed coldly. The assistant program director despised incompetence. It was all around her at the moment.

MacDonnell looked up at the ceiling and hoped it would collapse.

"For now, let's assume Stevie fits within the range," Bill Rumgay said. "Are there any other objections to moving him into Three?" An image of Annie Wilson, naked and writhing and begging for more interrogation, was a worm stuck in the apple of his brain.

"Yes . . . kind of . . . yes, maybe . . ." Andy Fister half raised his hand, appearing more like a frightened schoolboy on the brink of a new fall semester than Blythewood's lead clinician. Fister was the latest in a long pale line of head, head-shrinkers determined to fulfill a tired cliché and find ease for their own prosaically tortured souls by *curing* the clients. His salient personality trait was an inability to forge a coherent sentence on any subject. Moments before, he too had been staring at Annie Wilson's chest; however, his vision of sexual paradise was much, much duller than Bill Rumgay's. Mike MacDonnell had renamed the lead clinician, dubbing him, 'Anal Fistula'.

"Andy?" Rumgay tried to coax the clinician into lucid speech.

"I just wanted to . . . you know, it might not be the best . . ." Fister rubbed his thumbs vigorously against his index fingers. He'd almost completed a sentence.

"I think it's a wonderful idea," Debbie Wittenburg proclaimed. She was sure Bill Rumgay had been looking at her earlier. The head nurse was the one female at Blythewood who found the program director manly.

MacDonnell slowly mined wax in his left ear. He made a decision. Next Wednesday, at precisely 8:59 am, he was going to call in a bomb threat.

"Let's not be hasty," Faith Minor said. Minor would disagree, out of pure distilled bile, with anything anyone else championed. Multitasking, Minor made a mental note to address the issue of Mike MacDonnell's continued sloppy appearance in a formal supervision later in the day.

"Hasty?" Rumgay frowned. "I don't want to be hasty about this. We do have till Monday before . . . now what did I say the new student's name is?" He giggled self-consciously — a startling, high-pitched girlish clatter that made Annie Wilson openly wince and Mike MacDonnell roll his eyes in horror.

"Jimmy O'Keefe," Wittenburg piped in, hoping to shore up her fuehrer's floundering memory.

"Jeremy Keefner," Annie Wilson dryly corrected. Mike kicked her in the ankle. He did not want her to prolong this agony by contributing to it. Wilson looked at him. It was the first time she could remember him purposely touching her. It gave her an odd feeling that was not altogether comfortable.

"Yes. Right. Jeremy Keefner." Rumgay smiled at Annie Wilson. She didn't notice.

Debbie Wittenburg possessed an uncanny ability to sniff out pastry aisles in unfamiliar supermarkets and to detect men's interest in other women. Her colorless eyes beamed pure hatred at Annie Wilson. The head nurse often wondered if Mike MacDonnell suffered from a pathetic interest in his fellow supervisor. But could Bill Rumgay also be falling victim to Wilson's slutty wiles? Wittenburg felt her ponderous chest flattened out like a pair of leaky football-liners. She was reasonably sure even a skinny skank with pointy titties in a push-up bra, like Annie Wilson, would not fall for an ugly slob like Mike MacDonnell. But how would the desperate little jizz-funnel view a *prize* like Willie Rumgay? Oh, that might be an entirely different matter, fraught with dangerous implications.

Wittenburg plucked a lump of cinnamon sugar from her blouse; yet instead of sneaking it into her maw, as a boundless craving demanded, she crushed it into a fine powder between fat angry fingers.

Courtney Merrick briefly wondered if the head nurse was rolling a booger, then said, "Maybe we should consider another student from Team One, or place Keefner in Three, instead of Stevie." Days of relentless anxiety would plague the academic director should she fail to gain the upper hand in this decision. Her naked ambition to succeed was severely hampered by a lazy indifference to almost every detail of her post.

"Another student?" Rumgay widened his eyes reflectively. "O'Keefe in Three? Hmmm . . . interesting."

For the next hour and a half, these ideas were deliberated and debated, rejected and approved, and then debated again. MacDonnell wriggled in his chair. He found it increasingly difficult to breathe the stale air in the office; all the oxygen seemed to have been sucked out of it. He dreamt longingly of a swift and massive cerebral hemorrhage — for everyone in the room.

Arlene O'Connor, the residential coordinator, and the only administrator MacDonnell had instantly taken a liking to because she was direct and never mealymouthed, sat listening to the drifting conversations in silence — until she could take no more and snapped in a crackling Bronx accent, "Is this going anywhere? I've got things to do."

This forced Bill Rumgay to make a bold decision. "I think, uh, I think Stevie Corbett is our man for Team Three." He rapped a fist on his desk top to emphasize the definitive nature of his verdict.

"I agree," Debbie Wittenburg sang gleefully. She batted her eyes at the program director and assured herself all was not lost. Willie must have noticed the eight pounds she had lost over the last twelve weeks. Deal-A-Meal was such a godsend.

Andy Fister almost raised his hand again. "I don't know . . . I still think . . . you know, it might not be the best . . . Team Three is not very stable right . . . what about Team Five?"

Bill Rumgay gave free reign to a native streak of perversity and turned towards the clinician. The program director valued Fister's opinion on any matter. After all, the lead clinician was working on his PhD and titles and degrees, even those bought, stolen or faked, were the hallmarks of royalty at Blythewood. "You don't think it's the right move, Andy?"

Fister managed to shake his head and nod at the same time.

"I . . . now, I . . . didn't say that . . . exactly."

"Well . . ." Rumgay glanced up at the clock and sniffed loudly. It was half past the midday hour, lunch time at Blythewood. "Perhaps we should table this discussion until tomorrow. We have till Monday before . . . before the new student arrives."

It was a non-decision everyone could enthusiastically support. Mike MacDonnell drew the conclusion Rumgay was not hungry, but addicted to prescription nasal spray and in desperate need of a fix. Yet, as the supervisor was about to violently uncoil from his chair, Rumgay slowly raised a wan hand and motioned for everyone to remain seated.

"Before we adjourn," the program director said, "I understand there are two issues causing some friction within this management team. As a team, we need to discuss these concerns openly and find solutions *before* they evolve into systemic aberrations that adversely affect the treatment culture at this facility."

MacDonnell choked back wild sobs of despair.

Rumgay continued, "The first issue involves Parrish Cole." Cole was a sixteen-year-old, emotionally fractured wing nut whose chosen medium of artistic expression was shit. Cole shit himself when he was angry; he shit himself when he was nervous; he shit himself just for the sake of shitting himself. While all this was certainly bad, and malodorous, Cole did not stop at merely soiling his person. He also enjoyed using his excrement as a tool and a weapon. There was always some on his hands and more on and in his clothes. Without hesitation Cole painted any available surface, including walls, text books, television screens, remote controls and furniture fabric. Moreover, he delighted in coaxing the unwary into shaking his hand or letting him drape an arm around a shoulder soon to be defiled.

Bill Rumgay leaned forward in his chair, clasped his hands together.

"I understand there are some who disagree with my decision to allow Parrish to work as a waiter in the kitchen program?"

No shit, Mike MacDonnell thought.

"If there is anyone here," Rumgay said quietly, "who would not accept a plate of food from Parrish Cole, I would like to know about it — right now." Of course this was not an honest inquiry into staff's apprehension at ingesting fecal matter; it was a thinly disguised trap for anyone foolish enough to disagree with Rumgay's widely known view on the matter. "We are here to help these students, not ostracize them. Our mission is to prepare them for the outside world. A job in the food service industry is a distinct possibility for Parrish Cole ... at sometime in the future."

Annie Wilson summoned the pluck for a mild dissent.

"Bill, I think people are concerned Parrish is not wearing gloves when he serves food, which is required by health department regulations. I suppose the problem may really lie with the kitchen staff not enforcing the rules of safe food preparation and handling."

Debbie Wittenburg almost rose out of her chair. "That's not true *at all.* Latex gloves actually promote the retention of contaminates. Touch a dirty surface with a gloved hand and the germs will stay on the glove for as long as you wear it. Bare hands can be washed after each item is touched. It's much more sanitary." Wittenburg's smug, pig-eyes glowed. She had annihilated the anorexic pump handle's objections in one fell swoop. That no one, including the head nurse, had ever seen Parrish Cole wash his hands was irrelevant to Wittenburg.

Annie Wilson shook her head, but Mike MacDonnell was finally moved to speech.

"So, Debbie?" He affected an exaggerated sense of puzzlement. "Are you suggesting we ignore Health Department regulations?"

"No, I mean that —"

"Because it could get us into some serious hot water, should a health inspector turn up. Which they do from time to time."

"What I meant was —"

"And let me ask you something? Would you want a surgeon, who didn't wear gloves, operating on you?"

The head nurse became dizzy with inarticulate rage.

"Let's move on," Bill Rumgay suggested quickly, realizing he was in danger of losing control of the meeting. "The second issue we need to look at, is the matter of Anthony Reese's treatment plan. I understand some of you are concerned about setting a bad example for the rest of the students by allowing Anthony to cook, that is to bake cakes and cookies, when he is in emotional dysregulation."

Reese, an obnoxious, ultraviolent, compulsively manipulative pyromaniac, regularly injured staff, pulled his own hair out in clumps and demanded constant one-on-one attention. Rumgay had been personally responsible for Reese's admittance to Blythewood over the strenuous objections of every department head; all of whom were scandalously ignorant of the roundabout, semi-legal kickbacks Blythewood's upright administrators received from certain funding agencies for accepting the hardcore hard-to-place. The program director further compounded the problem by instituting a treatment plan which rewarded Anthony Reese's deplorable conduct. Whenever he threatened to act like an idiot and hurt someone, or burn something up, he was whisked away to the kitchen and allowed to bake sweets. Reese's behavior did not improve, but he had gained twenty pounds.

"I think the other students realize Anthony presents some unique treatment issues," Rumgay assured them all. "I don't think they are getting the wrong message from it. Not every client's needs can or should be addressed in the same way. We must, all of us, guard against the creeping institutional inflexibility which can quickly ruin a program. And that is the end of this discussion. The matter in not open to further debate — unless you have something to say, Andy?"

The lead clinician flapped his lips like a suffocating cod, but was unable to form any sound.

MacDonnell rushed out of the office and out of the building.

24

Spring.

New beginnings, new hope born on a pregnant and fragrant breeze. The instinctive lure of seasonal optimism was impossible to resist, even for Michael Francis MacDonnell. Coming in from an uneventful security check of the dorms, he had the hint of a smile on his face as he drank the sweet air and admired the little buds reviving every winter-weary branch and twig. He thought about asking Annie Wilson to take a walk with him after supper. Dusk was his favorite time of the day. The sky had a magic to it then, especially in the springtime.

At first he did not notice Salvatore Torre sitting, hands hanging between his knees, on the heavy wooden bench next to the front entrance of the main building.

Torre suffered from both retardation and an extreme obsessive-compulsive disorder. It sometimes took the young man ten minutes to complete the repetitive, jitterbug rituals necessary for him to do something as ordinary as passing over the threshold of a doorway. First he would extend his right foot, then his left, then he would shuffle from side to side while blinking his eyes four times and clicking his tongue on the roof of his mouth three times. This tedious routine would continue until his organic anxiety was relieved and he could proceed on his way. Through the years it had proven dangerous to interfere with any of his many chronic ceremonies. Salvatore Torre weighed a bit more than a bull moose and had a volcanic temper — especially where his personal rituals were concerned. Try to hurry him along, interrupt his meticulous count of twitches, head jerks and nonsense sound effects, and you would produce a large and angry young man bent on destroying everything and everyone around him. The catastrophic devastations he'd wrought in the past were the stuff of Blythewood legend.

Mike MacDonnell was one of the few who did not shy away from interacting with Torre.

"Hey, Sal. What's up?"

Sitting there by himself, 'taking space' as it was called at Blythewood, indicated Torre was having a problem of some sort.

He replied to the supervisor's greeting in a ponderous, dinosaurian monotone, "I'm not doing *reeel* good, right here, right now, Mister Mike MacDonnell."

"Why is that, Sal?"

"I don't know, Mister Mike MacDonnell. I'm not doing *reeel* good, right here, right now."

MacDonnell frowned. "I understand that, Sal. But you need to deal with it, get yourself together, and get back into program. Is that clear?"

"Yes, Mister Mike MacDonnell, that is very, very clear to me, right here, right now."

"Good. You can sit here for a little while longer, then I want you back with your team. Is that clear?"

Torre's head had begun bobbing up and down like a yo-yo. "Yes, Mister Mike MacDonnell, that is very, very clear, right here . . . **right now**!"

The supervisor looked sharply at the boy. Any kind of expression in Torre's voice was unusual and ominous. "Do I need to stay out here with you, Sal?"

"No, Mister Mike MacDonnell. I'll be *goood*, right here, right now."

Satisfied, MacDonnell started into the building.

Only excellent peripheral vision saved the supervisor this day. He hadn't taken three steps before Salvatore sprang to his feet, picked up the bench and swung it like a gigantic baseball bat. MacDonnell was able to duck under and away from the blow. The bench shattered against the plaster facade of the building. Flying shards of old dry wood filled the air.

A tiny arrow pierced Mike MacDonnell's right eye.

The supervisor roared as his vision was instantly obscured by a flood of moisture in both eyes. Salvatore Torre dropped the remnants of his weapon and, shrieking like a damned soul, rushed into the building.

MacDonnell plucked the sliver out of his eye and blindly pursued. Inside, he could see little more than vague, watery silhouettes; but there was no mistaking Torre's bulk, nor the fact the the huge shape was charging headlong across the lounge towards a small, probably female form.

Rage and pain lent wings to MacDonnell's feet. He caught Torre from behind, not a yard from his target, and plowed him into the floor. Mike's tackle knocked all the wind and fight out of Salvatore Torre. The student lay face down, whimpering impotently.

MacDonnell heard the unidentified female gasping, "Oh, my God! Oh, my God!" and recognized the voice. It was Joanie Padalecki, the Blythewood receptionist.

"Hey, Joanie?" MacDonnell asked calmly. "Could you do me a favor and call the nurse?"

"What's wrong? Is Sal hurt?" Her voice shook like an earthquake.

MacDonnell raised his head so she could see his eye.

"Oh, Jesus piss-pot!" she cried. "What happened to you?"

"I was picking my nose and my finger slipped."

"What?"

"Could you please call the nurse?"

25

"This is taking forever."

Mike looked at Annie with his one good eye. "Sorry. . ."

The emergency room was empty, had been for the last hour. Still no one had called him into an examination room.

"Are you sure this is necessary?" Annie asked.

"Well it kinda of hurts and it's kinda hard to see straight."

"As if that's unusual for you."

"Annie, my eye is messed up. I'm not playing this. I don't do that. I would have driven myself, but my depth perception is a little dicey at the moment."

Annie looked at him for a moment with a mixture of contempt and boredom, then sighed. She picked up a magazine from the table in front of her.

He said, "You know I am human, not a load of bricks. If you prick me do I not bleed?"

Annie turned a page. "Quiet down, Sally. I'm trying to read."

Due to the injury Mike MacDonnell would enjoy a week off with pay. The first time Michelle changed the hospital dressing for him, she could barely refrain from gagging. Later she would tell him the eye had been protruding and gray like a raw shrimp. While it would quickly return to normal size and appearance, it would never completely recover normal vision. Forever after, if MacDonnell covered his left eye, the image in the right one would be slightly blurry and unfocused.

Like everything else, he learned to live with it.

26

Rick Pasinetti changed his residence on a regular basis for reasons best known to him. MacDonnell suspected he did this to avoid bad debts and old flames. It often took a considerable amount of detective work on Mike's part to sift through piles of phone numbers and street addresses before he could find Pasinetti's most recent information. Luckily, he'd visited him a few weeks earlier and knew right where he was today — holed up in a garage behind his sister's house in Wessex.

It was half past eleven in the morning when MacDonnell stepped over a coiled garden hose and knocked on the side entrance of the garage.

"Mac," Rick Pasinetti rumbled a cheerful greeting and handed him a beer. "What's goin' on, anything? Where'd you get the eye patch? I prefer a monocle myself. Drives the broads crazy."

MacDonnell just shook his head and opened the beer. He noticed Rick was wearing a hunting jacket and a red, white and blue bandana around his head. "Lovely, uh, uniform."

"I'm stalking big game this morning."

MacDonnell raised an eyebrow.

Pasinetti produced a pellet pistol from a pocket on the hunting jacket.

"I borrowed this from my nephew."

"Uh ... what exactly are you hunting?"

"A man eating squirrel-o-saurus."

"Come again?"

"There's this damn rodent keeps getting into the garage every morning, right around dawn. It's getting into my food and tearing up my shit, and waking me up when I'm hungover. I've had just about fucking enough. I knows the tree it likes to hangout in, so today it pays the ultimate price for Crimes Against Pasinetti."

"I came to get tight."

"Right after I mounts the trophy on the wall."

"Aren't you forgetting the hounds and horns?"

"Life in the colonies," Pasinetti mourned. "I'll be back in a minute. Go ahead in. There's a handle of vodka next to my bed if you want a snort." Then he was off.

Mike MacDonnell wandered inside the garage and waited in damp mustiness on a folding chair. Pasinetti had squared off a rude living space by suspending heavy carpets and blankets from the ceiling. This wolf's den was equipped with a small apartment-sized refrigerator, a two-burner hot plate, a twenty-seven-inch television and video combo; something resembling a cot or a bed or a pile of old laundry, and a gallon of extra virgin olive oil — Pasinetti liked to cook and he was good at it. Rick's final amenity was a big Coleman cooler he kept perpetually stocked with ice and Genesee beer.

MacDonnell had finished a third beer and a third shot of vodka when Rick Pasinetti dashed in, out of breath. He was sweating profusely.

"Jesus Gawd!"

"What the fuck is wrong?"

Pasinetti grabbed a beer and threw himself down on his bed. It creaked ominously. "Jesus Gawd, I think I'm gonna have a heart attack."

"I take it the safari went astray?"

"I chased the dirty beast from tree to tree, up and down the fucking street, firing away at him. Finally I corners the little s.o.b. in the neighbor's driveway. It perches on a tree branch hanging over the guy's new truck. I'm down to my last pellets, so I takes aim and pulls the trigger. . ." Pasinetti shook his head and tossed the pistol under the bed. "Jesus Gawd, I don't know what happened, but the pellet went right into the goddamned windshield of the truck."

Mike MacDonnell whistled. "Did your neighbor see any of this?"

"I fuckin' hope not. The guy's an asshole. He'll have the cops on me in a heartbeat."

"And after all that, the squirrel escaped?"

"I didn't knock a flea out of place."

MacDonnell rubbed his jaw thoughtfully. "Maybe next time you should consider flaming arrows. Why stop at wrecking some poor slob's truck when you could devastate the entire neighborhood?"

"Fuck you, Mac."

"Need a pull?" MacDonnell held up the bottle of vodka and wiggled it.

"And keep 'um fucking coming."

The booze calmed Pasinetti, though for the next several hours he would periodically get up to peer through a dirty little window. No police arrived.

Along about supper time, pissed past the point of caring much about supper time, Rick asked MacDonnell if he'd ever heard of Tempest Storm.

"Who or what is that?"

"She was this big time stripper, years ago," Pasinetti said. "I went to one of her shows. The place was mobbed. They asked if anybody in the audience would like to come up and drink champagne from her tit. Of course, young, dumb, and full of cum, I runs right up on stage and does it."

Mike MacDonnell laughed and lit a cigarette.

"Kinda disappointing, though," Rick continued.

"Why?"

"It wasn't really champagne. It was ginger ale."

"Her boobs were probably fake too. You should have asked for your money back."

"Nah, the tits looked real to me, and boy did she have a set of 'um." Pasinetti tried to get up to take another peek out of the window, failed and collapsed back on the bed. He waved a hand in the general direction of the neighbor's house. "Fuck him. Get me another Genny, will ya?"

MacDonnell dutifully complied.

"I had a thing for strippers for a while, you know," Rick said. "I nailed this one while I was stationed up at Drum. I called her Hungry Helen. I forget what her real name was. She'd only go out if you were Regular Army. No National Guard or TDY. They were only up there for a couple weeks. We fucked good and steady for about three months."

"What happened?"

"Same thing that always happens."

The telephone rang. It was on a rickety old stand within reach of the bed. Rick picked up the receiver and said, "Snuffy Terdlich here. How may I direct your call?"

It was a bill collector.

Pasinetti listened for a moment, and then, "What's your name? Tremon Jones? What kind of a name is that? Is this some kind of a prank? Some kind of a sick joke? Is . . . is it you Bobbie? Bobbie is it you? But Bobbie, you died in Viet Nam . . ."

27

Arlene O'Connor stood outside the supervisors office door. She'd come to welcome Mike back to work, and then scold him and Annie for missing Four's team meeting. Instead, the residential coordinator silently observed the two people inside the office. They had their backs turned, watching something interesting through the office window. Their heads were close together and they were laughing. MacDonnell turned to look at Annie's face. Their eyes met, connected, communicated more than words.

Arlene O'Connor took a quiet step backwards. She smiled a little wistfully and a little sadly and wondered if her two supervisors realized what was happening to them. It was an old story at Blythewood, one she had seen repeated many, many times — sometimes for good, sometimes for bad.

28

One Wednesday afternoon, Annie Wilson invited MacDonnell, Terry Johnson, and Kevin Marshall to a pool party at the house she rented on Northumberland Street in Wessex. It was a big place in an expensive (naturally enough) part of town. Annie shared the home and its high cost with two male college students. Her Blythewood partner was less than pleased by this deviation in his drinking routine. Mike hadn't been invited to a 'pool party' since he was ten, and, more to the point, he preferred the cozy confines of a bar to fresh air and splashing water. However, the opportunity to see a scantily clad Annie Wilson did have its secret appeal.

MacDonnell would not be disappointed in this. Annie's tiny black swimsuit revealed a sleek body of astonishing form and elegant symmetry.

Kevin Marshall caught him staring at Annie as she dived into the pool.

"Having a stroke, Hefner?" Kevin asked.

MacDonnell had always been able to lift the left side of his upper lip in a dog-like snarl. He did so now — but his eyes never left Annie Wilson.

Terry Johnson, standing nearby, glanced at the woman in the pool, then back at Mike. An odd expression weighted her face like lead.

Except for Annie Wilson, no one had a formal bathing suit. Terry's shorts and tank top would do in a pinch as would Kevin's denim cutoffs and T-shirt; only MacDonnell, in black jeans, infantry boots and a torn black sweatshirt, looked out of place next to the pool. He could not have cared less. There was a fifth of single malt scotch in his hand and no intention of taking a dip in anything but the bottle. Only Annie showed bona fide interest in the water. There was a faint chill in the late June air. It had been a warm spring, but so far a cold and rainy summer.

Mike sipped continuously from the whisky bottle as he prowled along the edge of the pool. His gaze was drawn time and again to Annie Wilson. He felt a strange giddiness as if pure oxygen were being pumped directly into his brain by some reactivated, vestigial biomechanism.

"So, Mike?" Kevin intercepted MacDonnell's orbit around the pool. "Looks like the Red Sox will be good enough to make the playoffs this year."

"If there's a God, they won't." MacDonnell was a Yankee fan.

"Red Sox Nation, Mike. Love it or leave it," Marshall replied with nauseating sincerity.

"You know, Kevin, I would have thought you were into more . . . unconventional sports, like men's free style gymnastics or figure skating."

"Mike, you're a bitch."

"And where is Shelley today?" MacDonnell asked. Shelley was Kevin's longtime girlfriend. Mike was convinced she didn't like Kevin hanging around with him, based on the observation she rarely, if ever, attended any of their get-togethers.

"Wouldn't you like to know?"

"No, not really."

MacDonnell handed Kevin the bottle of whisky. He took a small sip, made an ugly face. "This shit tastes like whiskey. Do you drink this swill to keep warm at night while tending your flocks in Cornwall?"

MacDonnell ignored him and turned to Terry Johnson. "Want some, Terry?"

She shook her head wordlessly.

"Why are you so quiet?" MacDonnell asked.

A soundless shrug.

MacDonnell turned his back and whispered, "What's wrong with her?"

Kevin raised an eyebrow. "Nothing that wouldn't be cured if you stumbled into a blast furnace."

"What?"

Kevin's voice went low. "I gave her a ride here, and all the way over she kept saying, 'Mike doesn't love me anymore. He loves Annie now.' It was fucked-up."

"What?"

"What? What?" Kevin mocked. "You sound like an owl with a speech impediment."

"I'm not in love with Annie."

"It's not what Terry thinks."

MacDonnell shook his head. Annie Wilson poised for another plunge off the end of the diving board. Water streamed down her neck and shoulders and tensed thighs. "I'm not in love with Annie."

"If you say so, Captain Kirk."

MacDonnell smiled. "There's nothing but a black aggie in my chest, Kevin."

"Can't say the same for Annie," Kevin grinned lewdly. He panto-mimed squeezing large breasts.

" Ever get any from Shelley?" Mike asked.

"Yeah, I get if from Shelley, but penicillin clears it right up."

"Go away, Kevin. Go talk to Terry. Make sure she's . . . go talk to her."

Still grinning, Kevin walked over to Terry.

MacDonnell strayed to the edge of the pool and flopped down on his belly. This movement caused a splash of malt to escape from the bottle, but he decided against licking the drops off the pool tiles when he noticed Annie Wilson swimming in his direction.

"Aren't you coming in?" Annie asked.

"Do I look like a sea nymph?"

Annie clung to the edge of the pool, treading water. She looked over his shoulder. "Kevin's cute. If I were a few years younger . . ."

She did not need to finish the sentence. MacDonnell knew this was no idle threat on her part. To his knowledge (based on innumerable personal phone calls taken in the office, and the frequent delivery of veritable rose gardens) Annie Wilson currently led a string of three lovers, all of whom competed furiously for her attentions. She was able to maintain strict emotional boundaries with these paramours. They might be obsessed with her, but Annie steadfastly, even harshly, preserved an aloof independence — so far.

MacDonnell glanced back at Kevin Marshall. "I think he's homely."

"Compared to you?"

"My mother loved me. Then she died." Mike produced a cigarette and slid it in his mouth. Before he had the chance to light it, a slender hand splashed chlorinated water in his face and batted the menthol up into the air.

Laughing, Annie Wilson propelled herself away from the side of the pool. "You smoke too much."

"Fuck you, Wilson."

Annie swam back to him, beaming victoriously. She gripped the edge of the pool with one hand, allowing the other to trail in the water.

"Sweet Jesus, you are such an . . . Episcopalian," MacDonnell growled. "You know, no matter what we do or don't do, one day we're all going to get very sick, Annie Wilson."

"So? Why hurry it along with cigarettes?"

"Why not?" Mike MacDonnell's answer, meant to be facile, carried an unexpectedly bitter taste which surprised even him. He fell silent, letting his hand droop into the pool and listlessly stir the water, scattering slivers of light. By chance or unconscious design, his fingers drifted until they met Annie's fingers floating on the shivering surface.

For a moment, MacDonnell was unaware they were touching, then a painful awakening drove the breath out of his body.

He looked up — to read instant confusion in Annie Wilson's eyes.

MacDonnell opened his mouth to speak, but the words died in his teeth when she hastily withdrew her hand from his.

He stood up quickly, squared his shoulders. The whisky bottle rose to his bottom lip. "I'm gonna see what Kevin's up to." The words were a lame and winded horse, drowned in a flash flood of whisky.

Annie swam the entire length of the pool twice before she climbed out and joined the others.

Mike MacDonnell, gripped by a new and terrible longing, tried not to watch her dry off with a towel, tried not to map every curve and line and swell of her body. The effort hurt. The poignancy of her flesh, the eyes, the hair, the breasts, the sound of her voice, the way smooth muscle moved smooth limb, pierced him, not just through the heart, but every-where and all at once. He wanted her. Like he never wanted a woman before. Like he never would again.

An hour later, when she casually wrapped herself in an oversized man's shirt and squeezed clenched thighs into a pair of worn-out blue jeans, he found this act of *covering* to be equally exciting. A sultry agent seemed to radiate through her clothes, searing the inexplicably tender flesh beneath his.

The cork went into the whisky bottle. Best to go slow and easy tonight.

Terry Johnson made an attempt to speak with MacDonnell once or twice, but he was distracted by churning emotion and unable to focus on a word she said. Each time her overtures were ignored, she became more withdrawn.

A strange, uncomfortable evening passed slowly for all of them. They sat on plastic Adirondack chairs, drinking, talking about work and fitfully gossiping about students and other staff. On the surface this was quite ordinary, but an odd mood prevailed which invited the disclosure of sensitive personal experiences from two people (novel among Blythewood employees) not given to such revelations. They learned Annie Wilson's parents divorced before she graduated from high school. Her mother remarried and ran a successful antique business. But her father, a gentle alcoholic, died alone in a little room in Seattle, just two years past. In a low voice, Annie told how her mother wept bitterly for the loss of a lost husband. Annie and her older sister flew out to the West Coast for the funeral. It rained for all three days they were there.

Kevin Marshall, spurred by Annie's confession, admitted that his parents separated for several years when he was a boy. His father had been forced to raise all the children by himself. Kevin's parents had since reconciled, but the situation remained troubled.

To prevent Kevin from divulging further details he might regret in a sober state, and to end a theme ripe with the potential for weepy self-pity, Mike MacDonnell rose amidst the circle of plastic chairs and declared, "I had both my parents killed when I was six. My Grit paper route paid for the hit. Anybody need a beer?"

He trotted happily over to a cooler and twisted a cap.

Mike's turmoil over Annie Wilson was thus temporarily supplanted by a cheerful belligerency, most notably expressed when Kevin happened to wander close to the edge of the pool.

MacDonnell loomed behind his friend, asked softly, "What are you doing?"

Kevin stared at the water as if hypnotized. "Not much."

"Why don't you take a dive?"

"Too cold."

"It wasn't a suggestion."

MacDonnell lowered a shoulder and rammed into Kevin's back.

A shrieking, flailing Kevin Marshall plunged into the water.

Annie burst out laughing. "That was mean. How would you like the three of us to throw you in?"

"Do ya think you could?" MacDonnell asked, folding his arms across his broad chest. He took a step back as Kevin clambered out of the pool.

Marshall, blond curls darkened and plastered to his head, glared at MacDonnell. "You are a **fucking** bitch."

In the middle of trying to think of a clever retort, MacDonnell happened to glance in Terry Johnson's direction. She was standing, naked to the waist, staring straight ahead.

"Terry?" MacDonnell frowned. "What are you doing?" In the past, a few insightful people had noticed he suffered from a preposterous touch of the prude.

Terry did not reply. She remained statue still, clutching her tank top in one hand.

MacDonnell forced a light-hearted tone into his voice. "Skinny-dipping's not allowed here. Didn't you read the sign?"

Terry moved her head imperceptibly in his direction. She made him the focal point of a fixed and empty gaze.

"Terry!" MacDonnell almost shouted this time. Annie's housemates, either by chance or circumstance, had come to a window of the house and were peering out at the pool. Earlier, at sunset, Annie had switched on a string of outdoor lights to illuminate the area. Terry Johnson was clearly visible to the young men inside.

"Terry! Get your shirt on!"

Terry Johnson didn't move a muscle.

MacDonnell waved his middle finger at the two college boys and hurried over to Terry. He grabbed the tank top out of her hand and pulled it down over her head. She submitted without struggle or comment.

"Are you all right," he asked. "Are you drunk, high — sick?"

Still no response.

MacDonnell guided Terry back to a chair and gently compelled her to sit.

"It's okay. You're just bombed."

Terry said nothing.

29

The first day of Mike's next shift could be described as active, but more or less typical — except for the fact Annie called out sick. Mike wondered if she was avoiding him.

7:25 am —

MacDonnell arrived to find a staff wrestling with a student in the dumpster. They were grunting like rutting hogs and rolling about in a noisome mixture of mustard, coffee grounds, starchy strands of old spaghetti and fragments of egg shell.

MacDonnell did not ask what was going on. He simply leaned over the lip of the dumpster and inquired, "Is there a problem?"

The student immediately ceased his struggles.

MacDonnell continued towards his office.

There was a car parked in front of the soups door. Exhaust poured from the tail pipe as the engine roared. MacDonnell approached the vehicle and looked in. Ralph Mason, an overnight worker, was slumped in the front seat on top of his abandoned clothing, foot stuck on the gas pedal. Vomit clotted the dashboard and steering wheel. MacDonnell opened the driver side door and was assailed by the stench of regurgitated rye whiskey. Mason, employed six years at Blythewood, had passed the point of containing his drinking to off-hours. Rumor had it he spent the overnights in an alcohol induced state of bliss. Rumors were sometimes true.

"Ralph!"

Ralph Mason raised a wobbly head, spit up another mouthful and said, "Who's got my keys?"

"They're in the ignition," MacDonnell answered. "Man, you can't stay here. Anybody sees you like this and you're done."

Mason nodded and composed himself behind the wheel — as much as any pickled, naked man could hope to do. He slammed the car in reverse and hit the gas. MacDonnell avoided having his feet run over by quickly dancing out of the way. Mason sideswiped a couple of trees on his way down the driveway.

10:30 am —

MacDonnell was reviewing a lengthy incident report from the previous shift. Wesley Rathbun had beaten two staff senseless with a floor-hockey stick. Rathbun had an intense interest in sports and was a bad loser. After his team's defeat in a gym class game, Rathbun attacked both the physical education instructor (an aggressively unattractive woman who insisted on wearing brightly colored underwear which showed through her white nylon slacks) and Joe Sinapoli, a friend of MacDonnell's, who had recently received the Employee Of The Year award. Rathbun pounded them with his hockey stick till the gym teacher was unconscious and Sinapoli was lying helpless on the floor, cradling a broken arm. Rathbun was busily masturbating in the gym teacher's face when he was brought down from behind by another student, ending the rampage. A note in the supervisor's log, regarding this incident, indicated both staff had since tendered their resignations. MacDonnell made a mental note to give Joe a call when he got home.

10:46 am —

Bill Rumgay, atypically in on a Sunday, drifted into the supervisors office like Banquo's ghost. A frown creased the Program Director's narrow brow and his tone of voice was remote, almost imperial.

"Mike? I'll need you to set up a student drop-off for tomorrow morning. I'm taking a few days off, so I won't be able to handle the details."

Not that you ever do, MacDonnell thought, but said, "Who is it?"

"Anthony Reese."

"Where's he going and for how long?"

Rumgay cleared his throat. "He's being discharged."

"Discharged? I thought he was finally making some progress here?"

Rumgay cleared his throat again. "His funding agency cut him off. We are not a charitable organization."

MacDonnell plugged a well of laughter. "Where are we leaving him?"

The program director shrugged. "The Rockland County DSS office, the nearest homeless shelter — it doesn't matter. We need to move him along."

MacDonnell nodded again. Rumgay left without another word. The supervisor looked up at the sign hanging on the wall.

WE CARE

But not very much. The irony was nauseating. But what should you expect from a place advertising a fifty-five percent cure rate for sex offenders and a seventy-five percent cure rate for fire setters, all well beyond figures forecast by reputable treatment facilities, all without any post-discharge follow up or client tracking? If the Blythewood Lords of Fancy proclaimed something to be so, well . . . so let it be. Who was Michael Francis MacDonnell to argue with his betters?

1:05 pm —

Nicky Trim was brought to the supervisors office by his staff. Trim was clutching his crotch with both hands.

"What happened?" MacDonnell asked.

Nicky Trim, face wrinkled in pain, replied, "I was taking a nap after lunch and Johnny Clarkson ran into my room and bit me on the balls." The student began to sob.

Trim had kicked Clarkson in the groin during a fight two months ago. Johnny had a long memory, a savage vindictiveness and — like the Mounties — always got his man. He was one of Mike's favorite students.

MacDonnell looked at the staff. "Did you call the nurse?"

"Yes. She said she won't leave her office."

"Okay. Take Nicky back to his dorm and I'll see what's up with the nurse."

"What about the fucker who bit me?" Nicky asked.

"I'll take care of it."

MacDonnell climbed the stairs to the third floor of the main building to find Donell Crews, a skinny little wretch from the streets of Baltimore, pounding on the nursing station door with a brick.

"What are you doing, Donell?"

Crews squealed and aimed the brick at MacDonnell.

"Throwing that at me will be the worst and possibly last mistake of your life."

Crews' lower lip drooped as if he had a fishhook in it. He laid the brick carefully on the floor.

"Now get back to your team, Donell. And don't let me ever catch you wandering around here by yourself again."

"They said you wasn't here."

"They were wrong. Get lost."

Crews scurried down the stairs.

MacDonnell knocked on the nursing station door. "Rita, are you all right?" Rita May was an LPN who worked two days a week to fill a hole in the nursing schedule.

There was a moment of silence, then a rustling. The door swung open. Rita May already had her coat on.

"I quit! I freakin' quit!" She stomped on his foot as she flew past.

Three in three days. Nearly a record for staff bail outs.

2:30 pm —

MacDonnell was doing routine security checks on the dorms. He walked into the first floor lounge in Dorm Two.

Missy Amadon had been a staff since July. She was unconditionally lazy and suffered from a persistent cough the more streetwise students identified as a 'crack-hack.' At the moment she was reclining on a couch and allowing a student to massage her bare feet. Ecstasy rendered the boy glassy-eyed and drooling.

"What's going on?" MacDonnell asked.

Missy sat up hastily. The student mewed in disappointment when the plump pink toes were removed from his grasp.

"Nothing," the girl protested. "I've got cramps in my feet, that's all. It's not like I was getting off on it. I had most of my uterus removed a year ago."

MacDonnell blinked once, twice, a third time. "Missy, I'll need to see you in my office later."

3:20 pm —

'Baby' Huey Washington was lying under a pile of staff in the TV lounge; which was understandable considering Washington was close to seven feet tall and weighed in excesses of 400 pounds. MacDonnell asked what had happened. A sweaty, breathless childcare worker, sprawled across the student's neck, gave him the details.

"Get up, Huey," MacDonnell said.

Childcare workers scattered like fleas leaping off a Saint Bernard. MacDonnell planted a hand in Washington's back, propelled him up the stairs to his bedroom.

"Sit down."

Huey Washington's bed sagged under his titanic weight. "You ain't gonna scare me, Mike," the boy blustered in a high, childlike voice.

"No? Well, maybe I won't. Maybe I'll give your mom a call and let her know how you've been behaving this afternoon. Do you think she'll like that? Do you think she'll be proud of you, Huey?"

Big tears began rolling down the boy's plump cheeks.

"You're fifteen now, Huey. It's time to start acting like a young man and not a spoiled brat. Didn't I overhear your mom tell you that on her last visit?"

A choked sob. "You don't like me anymore, do you?"

"Anymore? I *never* liked you." MacDonnell let a smile leak out. "Wipe your nose, and cut the shit for the rest of the day — or I will give your mom a ring."

"Am I on restriction?"

"Yeah."

"Do I gotta stay in my room for twenty-four?"

"You should, but if you can control yourself, I might let you get out at dinner time. It's all up to you."

The boy's eyes brightened. "Did you see the Yankees picked up a new pitcher who drinks a lot of beer?" There were posters of baseball players covering the walls around Washington's bed. "I live right next to the Stadium."

"So I've heard." MacDonnell looked at the boy for a moment. In a short time, after a few more years of being institutionalized and preyed upon, in every way possible, by smarter and more aggressive clients; after an endless procession of incompetent, or indifferent, clinicians, Huey Washington would be a hopeless wreck; a perpetually frustrated, uncontrollable, raving behemoth, destined for backwards and straitjackets and the Thorazine Shuffle.

"We're having tacos tonight, Huey."

The boy giggled. "Can we watch the Cartoon Channel after supper?"

"If you can do it without getting in restraint again."

MacDonnell left the bedroom and passed the sweaty-faced staff who had been in on the restraint.

"Somebody should put the kid on a farm," the childcare worker said, "and let him eat all he wants and take care of animals."

"Not fucking likely," MacDonnell said and kept walking.

4:10 pm —

Team Four was busy cleaning up after an arts and crafts period. One of the staff present, Audrey Ringer, was once again bragging about her appearance, several years previously, on a popular television game show. Audrey resembled a blond medicine ball. She was capable of talking about herself and not much else.

"So, I picked Whoopi for the win," she was saying. "You know she's the star of the show? Anywho, the question is, 'Which president dropped the atom bomb on Japan in 1945?' Well, Whoopi says Harry Truman. Now, I don't know if it's the correct answer or not — who would know something that goofy? — but I do know Whoopi really likes me, so I agree . . . and win the game. You won't believe how much . . . "

The other staff in the room were not paying much attention to Audrey. They'd heard her stories too many times. Only Derrick Post, a large and simple-minded student from New Hampshire, was listening with rapt attention. He had also heard the tale many times, but it never failed to fascinate him. He wanted to be on a game show himself someday. He walked over to Audrey Ringer and interrupted her breathless recital of winnings.

"Audie? Can I be on Nollywood Scares?"

Audrey Ringer rolled her eyes and loosened an exaggerated sigh.

"Of course not, Derrick. You have to be smart to get on TV."

Mike MacDonnell walked into the room in time to witness Derrick Post drill Audrey Ringer in the face with a fist like a slab of New Hampshire granite.

Ringer made an odd sound, something like "*Breep*," as she bounced off the floor. It was the last sound she would make until a paramedic revived her in the back of an ambulance.

MacDonnell held a hysterical Derrick Post in restraint for the better part of two hours.

6:15 pm —

A nervous figure slipped into MacDonnell's office from the outside door.

"Darren?" The supervisor's shock was genuine. "What . . . you shouldn't be here."

Darren Lindsey had been fired a week ago. It was a strict Blythewood policy not to allow terminated employees back on campus. This was an instance (the only one) when administration encouraged the supervisor on duty to summon the police. There had been some tense, and nearly violent, episodes in the past.

"Mike, you gotta help me." Lindsey's words had a breathless quality as if he were unable to draw enough air to inflate them. "I gotta have my job back."

"Darren, I —"

"Jesus, dude, they fired me for nothin'. The weed wasn't mine. I don't smoke anymore, my wife does. She's got MS. You know it. *They* know it. It makes her feel better, relieves some of the symptoms. Jesus, there's an article in the New England Medical Journal to prove it. The cop pulled us over 'caus my headlight was out and then he smelled grass in the car. My wife had just finished a joint. But it wasn't any big deal. Just a ticket — just a ticket for fucks-sake. Nobody's going to jail."

"Darren, I know all about it. There were people who stood up for you with Rumgay and the board, but it didn't make any difference. When the story appeared in the paper, the board —"

"Those bastards said they were firing me because I didn't live up to Blythewood's ' code of conduct.' What the fuck does that mean? I know for a fact half the board of directors have DWI convictions, or should have, and the rest have coke spoons shoved up their noses twenty-four-seven — *including* that squirmy little cock, Rumgay."

"If I could help—" MacDonnell wasn't going to. Bill had made it clear further staff protests in the matter of Lindsey's termination would result in others joining him on the unemployment line.

"Dude, I've got a sick wife and three little kids. I don't want to beg, but what the hell am I supposed to do? I need my job and they need my health insurance. I've worked here for nine years. I've been named employee of the month so many times I can't remember, and employee of the year twice. I've never been written-up or gotten a bad evaluation. What the fuck? What the fuck?" The man's entire body began shaking.

Mike MacDonnell got up from behind his desk and locked both doors into his office. He asked Lindsey to sit down. The former childcare worker slumped dejectedly into a chair. The supervisor returned to his desk, pulled out a sheet of clean white paper from a drawer and began to carefully write.

When he was finished, he looked up and said, "I can't get your job back. Rumgay and the board don't give two-hoots-in-hell for you or your family. They don't care how long or how well you worked for them. I know they spout a lot of nonsense about their concern for the workers. And I know how they like to show up at funerals with flowers and a meat platter whenever somebody's granny dies, but that shit's just self-serving public display. We're no more than furniture to the people who run this place. This —" MacDonnell neatly folded the sheet of paper in three and placed it in an envelope bearing the Blythewood logo. "This is a recommendation I am not allowed to give you. It includes my name and home phone number. There are a lot of residential schools in the area. Just make sure they call me, nobody else. I wish I could do more, but I can't. Good luck to you and your family."

7:20 pm —

It was near the end of shift. MacDonnell could not wait to get out and get a drink. He'd planned to ask Annie to join him tonight, to test his new and powerful feelings. Her call-out made that impossible. Oddly enough, he was glad. Booze would be enough of a companion for him tonight. He sat on the edge of his desk tapping his foot against the metal leg, waiting for one of the night shift supervisors to relieve him.

Bonnie Quirk, one of the clinicians, burst through the office door instead.

"Hi, Mike," she barked like an agitated seal.

MacDonnell cringed. The clinician's last name observed her behavior. She was loud, manic and aggressive in both deed and word. Because no one liked her, and despite the fact she set his teeth on edge, MacDonnell had made a modest effort to be polite to her in the past. It had proved an ill-considered foray into good manners. Quirk began targeting him.

"Bonnie, it's Sunday. What are you —"

"I had a lot of paperwork to catch up on," the woman screeched.

"Oh, well, oh . . ." Mike could not look at her face. She was wearing what he called the Aboriginal Fright-Mask: heavy layers of pancake makeup, rouge, lipstick and multicolored eye shadow designed to hide the passage of forty-seven years. Her eyelashes were encrusted with so much black liner, they resembled the spokes radiating from a child's crayon drawing of the sun.

"I've got something to show you," Quirk yelped excitedly. She held up a plastic bass mounted on a wooden board. "Watch this." She pressed a button. The fish began singing, *Don't Worry, Be Happy*. Its tail wiggled, its mouth opened and closed in time to the music, and finally it bent double and stared at MacDonnell.

"Oh, isn't that . . ."

"It's great. It's a birthday present for *Daddy*."

MacDonnell had an innate wariness of aging adults who referred to their fathers as *daddy*.

"It's kind of weird," he said weakly. Where was the night supervisor?

Bonnie Quirk came too close and put her thigh against his. Her perfume was overwhelming.

"Weird works for me, honey," she said — and winked.

MacDonnell much preferred the singing plastic fish.

30

"Want some, Mac?"

Rick Pasinetti held up a chewing tobacco tin for Mike MacDonnell to see. They were moving at 75 mph, north on Route 22 in New York State. MacDonnell was behind the wheel of Pasinetti's old Impala, heading for the town of Hoosick Falls and an all-night pub crawl. Mike had once lived in the town and was intimately familiar with all her bars and taverns.

"No thanks, Rick. I don't chew."

"This ain't chew."

Pasinetti pried the top off and held the can up for another inspection. MacDonnell darted a glance. Even in the gray half-light of early evening, there was no mistaking the white powder inside the tin.

"Where the fuck did you get it?"

"Friend of a friend." Pasinetti produced a silver coke spoon. He dug a healthy serving out of the tin. As he was raising it to his nostril, the car hit a pothole. Cocaine filled the air like a late autumn flurry. Unperturbed, Pasinetti laden the spoon again and shocked his sinus.

"So, Cousin Mongo?" He paused to hawk loudly. "Are there going to be any women?"

MacDonnell shrugged.

"I need to throw a fuck into a broad, tonight," Pasinetti announced. "Preferably one with big — and I mean big — tits."

"You're hung up on breasts. What about nice legs and a cute ass?"

Rick dropped the tin back in his shirt pocket and nodded sagaciously.

"They're fine. But I don't care if a woman's fat and ugly, so long as she has giant tits."

"Breast fed as a child?"

"No, and I've been searching for them ever since." Pasinetti began to sing in a gruff, off-key baritone:

"Oh, give me a home
Where the big titties roam.
And no broads are frigid or gay.
Where seldom is heard
A skinny nag's word,
And the bars stay open all day . . ."

The singing mercifully dwindled to a cheerful humming as he ran out of lyrics.

They turned off Route 22 and onto Hoosick Road. The Impala chased a broad, muddy river past open fields littered with dairy cattle and horses. A scattering of grain silos and old farmhouses gradually gave way to more numerous residential dwellings, until finally the Chevy clattered over a steel bridge into the small town. MacDonnell pulled into a public parking lot across the street from the first neon beer logo he saw glowing in a window.

"Home Plate," Rick Pasinetti read the flickering sign over the door before they entered. "Looks like a dive."

"It is." MacDonnell said.

"Good, I likes dives. Women with those special qualities I seek hang out in dives."

"If these ladies don't suit you, there is a she–male bar next street over."

"Chicks with dicks are best kissed quick."

"Okay . . ." Mike MacDonnell's voice dropped in volume. He was circumspect upon entering any watering hole until he gained a sense of his surroundings. There was more than a hint of jungle paranoia in this. It had served him well in the past.

Richard Pasinetti, on the other hand, rolled into the joint as if he expected to be hailed and feted. A bar to him was a fresh canvas to an inspired artist.

A few heads turned and quickly turned away when they entered. Together the men gave off a vague suggestion of menace. MacDonnell, with his dark, craggy features, Irish glower and hulking proportions, cast a sinister appearance, enhanced by his tangled mass of black hair and the black leather jacket he wore. He looked unkempt, surly. Pasinetti's natural devil-may-care-if-I-commit-homicide swagger issued an almost pheromonal warning to those around him: approach cautiously or not at all.

The two men sat at the bar. Pasinetti turned to MacDonnell.

"You're an ugly fuck."

MacDonnell accepted this for the compliment it was meant to be.

There was a fair-sized crowd in Home Plate this night; mostly blue-collar men and women of varying ages and degrees of wear. The bar was dimly lit and more than a little shabby, but the atmosphere was friendly and the drinks cheap. Music crackled from an old jukebox. There was a pool table off to the left side of the bar and a dartboard on the wall in the back. It was a working class vision of paradise.

"I like this dump," Pasinetti pronounced sentence. Still gripped by the urge to rhyme, he recited:

"I have clinched and closed with the naked Booze,
I have learned to defy and defend,
Shoulder to shoulder we have fought it out —

Yet the Booze must win in the end."

The bartender, a mousey-haired woman in her late thirties, came over to take their order. By the leering twinkle in his friend's eye, MacDonnell knew Pasinetti found her mammary proportions to be satisfactory. When she returned with their drinks, Pasinetti insisted on an introduction.

"The name is Swain Cocksley." He held out his hand which she limply shook. "And this is my associate, Danvers Giddleston the Third— of the Rhode Island Giddlestons."

The woman stared blankly at Pasinetti.

"And your name, dear?" he asked.

"Uh, Chris."

"I am delighted to make your acquaintance, Chris."

The woman bobbed her head and took a few dollar bills for the drinks. She headed back to the cash register for change.

Rick Pasinetti leaned towards MacDonnell and said, "I think she'll blow me."

"Why would you want her to?"

The men sat talking quietly for half an hour or so. Two girls came up to the bar and stood next to them, waiting to order. Mike MacDonnell glanced sideways at the girl nearest him. She was in her mid-twenties, a little plump, but pretty in an ordinary fashion. He was sure he recognized her, but a name failed to suggest itself.

She caught him eyeing her. A smile broke out on her face.

"Mike!" She threw her arms around his neck and kissed him on the lips. "Holy shit, it's been a long time."

"It sure has, sweetheart."

"What have you been up to?"

"Oh, this and that. You know."

"Who's your friend?" Pasinetti interjected.

Fortunately, the young woman thought Pasinetti was demanding an introduction of her companion, saving MacDonnell an embarrassing moment. "Excuse me. I'm such a duh sometimes. This is Karen."

The other girl, about the same age, smiled shyly at the two men.

"Hey, Karen," MacDonnell said, and then to the plump pretty girl, "It's been good seeing you again, sweetheart." He was not going to find her name. It was best to end the reunion quickly and painlessly.

"You too, Mike. Keep in touch." The girl gave him another quick kiss on the mouth. "Call sometime and we'll go out. My number is still in the book."

"Sounds good."

After the girls left, Pasinetti was moved to admiration. "Jesus Gawd, do you have a broad in every port?"

"I wish."

"Did you fuck that one?"

MacDonnell pursed his lips speculatively.

"The charity of women never fails to astonish me," Rick Pasinetti observed.

"Me too." MacDonnell was uncertain why some women thought him attractive, or at least interesting, while others exhibited nothing but disdain. He'd been told once that he looked like a cute mean lion, and his wife had confessed she found him appealing because he looked like a criminal. Lack of convincing evidence either way prompted him to consign this mystery to the shadowy territory occupied by the Loch Ness Monster and spontaneous human combustion. "I ain't every woman's cup of tea," he admitted, stubbing out a cigarette in a Coca Cola ashtray.

"I've noticed certain lower forms of mammals find you simply irresistible," Pasinetti said.

"It's my sweat glands that attract them."

Rick tapped the tin in his shirt pocket. "I have to use the bathroom." He left.

MacDonnell got up from his barstool and stretched. He stood for a while, slowly sipping his beer and looking into the mirror behind the bar. It reflected the entire room. MacDonnell saw men and women paired off for the night, their faces mobile and eager; he watched the pretty plump girl gossiping with her shy friend Karen, and at the next table, a middle-aged couple holding hands and singing along to a country and western tune on the jukebox. In a shadowy corner by himself, an old man with wooden fingers coughed his life away over a glass of whiskey and a pack of Pall Malls.

This smoky, living watercolor filled MacDonnell with a profound, if momentary, sense of loneliness. He dropped his eyes to the dark surface of the bar, but could not clearly detect his image in its dull shine. A spasm of guilt struck and vanished. He envisioned Michelle waiting patiently at home, plotting his execution.

He raised his head and said out loud, "Fuck her, fuck me, and fuck the world."

In the next moment, as if by a wish granted, a heavy metallic object crushed Mike MacDonnell's ankle against the bar rail.

"Shit!"

"Sawee, sawee. I dust wanna pay poo." The tiny, distorted character piloting the offending device fumbled at a joystick control with palsied hands, finally managing to back the whirring electric wheelchair off MacDonnell's trapped leg.

"Sawee, sawee," the little man repeated in a high-pitched gasp. "I dust wanna pay poo."

Despite the human oddities the Blythewood supervisor had grown accustomed to, this fellow ranked high on the sliding scale of strange looking. He was of indeterminate age, maybe twenty, maybe forty-five. The head was a shiny, mottled melon, the features infantile daubs of clay. Sharp, crooked teeth filled a lipless gash which seemed unable to fully close, and strands of brown fur clung to skull, face and arms. Black watery eyes gave a disturbing, almost inhuman impression.

"Watch where you're going in that rocket ship, young man," Mike cautioned in a friendly tone. It was impossible to feel anger towards someone whom fortune had so vigorously ignored.

The little man's head bobbed up and down on a celery stalk neck.

"I dust wanna pay poo." He wiggled a tortured claw at the pool table.

MacDonnell gave a half salute as the fellow hummed off towards his goal.

Rick Pasinetti returned in time to witness the electric chariot and its occupant fail to negotiate a successful stop and slam full force into the pool table. The little round head bounced off the edge of the table with a meaty *thwack*. Unconcerned (and apparently uninjured) the little man backed up and began orbiting the table in search of a pool stick.

"Who's the hamster in the wheel chair?" Pasinetti asked.

MacDonnell whimpered, "I dust wanna pay poo."

"You know, I've worked with orcs for fifteen years — I don't need to see them out at a bar."

"Gee, aren't you the humanitarian?"

"No, I mean it, Mac. He should be back at the group home playing Candy Land with his worker, not spinning around a bar like a runaway roll of toilet paper. What's he here for? To give the locals something to stare at?" Pasinetti erupted in a short burst of derisive laughter when the poor chap in question sent the entire rack of pool sticks clattering to the floor. "See what I mean? Jesus Gawd, I can't watch him put his eye out." Pasinetti turned his back — and then a second later slapped the bar with his hand and stalked over to the pool table. He replaced all the sticks in the rack, except for the one he handed the little man.

"Careful with this."

A huge grin split a gnome face. "Thhhaaank ooooo."

"Yeah, that's okay,"

Pasinetti headed back to the bar.

"Way to go, Mangler," MacDonnell said. "You showed him a thing or two."

"Up yours."

Chris the bartender came over to Pasinetti and took his hairy hand in hers. "That was awful darn sweet of you. Dennis has trouble with things sometimes."

Pasinetti manufactured a smile meant to be charming. "It was my pleasure, dear. In some ways, it reminds me of the time my comrade Danvers and I were with Chinese Gordon in the Sudan. After Khartoum fell, we were forced to disguise ourselves as Bedouin dancing girls. The humiliations we suffered at the hands of the Dervishes were unspeakable. Not since Lawrence has a man been so cruelly used."

MacDonnell wondered if Rick practiced these flights of fancy in front of a mirror at home.

"Were you two in the Army?" Chris asked innocently.

"Indeed we were, dear. Danvers and I were military advisors to the Inuit during their fabled struggled for independence from the Hanseatic League."

"Lyndon Johnson should have stopped that war," Chris opinioned.

It was Pasinetti's turn to stare blankly at her.

"Right?" She sought support for her bold foray into the arena of political history.

"Of course," Pasinetti agreed slowly. "I concur avidly."

Mike MacDonnell ended the discussion by ordering a beer. When Chris retreated, MacDonnell nudged Rick on the shoulder. "I think Dennis over there could whip your girl in a game of let's count to ten."

"I likes 'um dumb."

"You got it."

They spent the next few hours drinking, laughing and debating every topic which offered itself for consideration, which did not include Mike's fellow supervisor; he studiously avoided mentioning *her* name. This conversational ramble suffered only two brief intermissions: once when Pasinetti begged for and received Chris' telephone number, and again when a stranger dared borrow his Zippo without permission.

This last interruption developed while Pasinetti was reminiscing about selling roses in Albany. A thin weasel of a man slunk up to the bar and sat down. This greasy-haired individual nervously popped a Marlboro in his mouth, felt around in his pocket for a light, and then, without so much as a by-your-leave, picked up Pasinetti's lighter from where it lay on the bar.

Pasinetti glanced at the man, but did not pause in his tale, " So, I has a nice location on Broadway, the weathers warm for February and I'm making good money. Along comes this *dude* dressed up like a biker. He's got the leather Harley vest and the leather Harley bandana around his head, he's got the big chain hanging off his pants and them big black engineer boots, the whole shot. As he walks by I says, 'Roses for your sweetheart?' and holds up a dozen for him to inspect. He turns on his heel, looks me right in the eye, and says, 'I give my wife COCK for Valentine's day.' COCK!" Rick Pasinetti's emphasis of that one word caused several heads to turn in his direction. "The fucking idiot. I looks him right back in the eye and says, 'I got plenty of that for your wife too.' The fuckin' guy turns purple and takes a swing at me. I backs up a step and drop kick him in the nuts. That was the end of him. Later, this other vendor tells me the *dude* don't even own a motorcycle, just liked to dress the part."

"I guess his wife didn't get cock or roses for Valentine's day," Mike said.

The greasy character sitting next to them finished his first cigarette and immediately put another one in his mouth. Once again he used Pasinetti's Zippo.

The man barely returned the lighter to the bar when Rick Pasinetti turned on him, snarling, "You might fucking ask before you use my property. I've had that friggin' lighter for twenty years."

"Hey, sorry man." The weasel's face blanched. "I'll ask next time."

"Don't bother. I won't fucking let you have it." Pasinetti snatched up the Zippo and dropped it in his pocket; his face was nearly black. "And stop eavesdropping. Don't you have somewhere else to be, like pumping a cat in the alley?"

The man slid off the barstool and disappeared.

Pasinetti said to MacDonnell, "The balls on that guy."

"I think they're all shriveled up now."

"I knew bastards like him in the Army. They'd *borrow* everything from your mess kit to your goddamned dirty skivvies." Pasinetti gulped his drink. It calmed him, brought back his good humor. "You know, when I was a boy there were only three things I wanted to be, a professional drunk, a union organizer and a sergeant in the US Army. I'm proud to say I've achieved all my ambitions."

"Lucy. Lucy Hewitt," Mike MacDonnell blurted out.

Pasinetti stared at him as if he'd gone slightly mad.

"The girl who was up here earlier? Her name is Lucy Hewitt."

MacDonnell sought her out in the crowd, but she and her companion had left. He shrugged and turned back to Pasinetti. "You want to hit another joint before we call it a night?"

"Ahhh, I'm about done." Pasinetti rubbed red-rimmed eyes. "I drink much more and I'll do something stupid. I could use something to eat, though. Any all-night diners around here?"

MacDonnell was mildly disappointed. He understood his own tolerance for alcohol was abnormal, but he had hoped the coke would keep Pasinetti on his feet at least till midnight.

MacDonnell glanced at the cheap, digital clock on the wall. It was twenty past eleven. He looked back at his friend. Pasinetti was staring rapturously at Chris' chest bouncing like Jell-O filled medicine balls as she scooted up and down the bar.

Mike MacDonnell conceded defeat. "Let's hit the road."

Rick Pasinetti gained his feet with a monosyllabic expulsion of indeterminate meaning; it suggested the clamor of a boar skewered on a huntsman's lance. Pasinetti lifted his remaining cash off the bar and examined it like a poker hand. He called Chris over.

"This is for you, dear." He handed her a twenty dollar bill. "And what does Dinty Moore drink?"

"Who, Dennis? He likes soft drinks mostly. Coke, Pepsi, that sort of thing."

"Good. I wouldn't want to promote drunk driving." Pasinetti handed her a ten. "Get him what he wants."

"You're a sweet man, Wayne," Chris said. She leaned over the bar, caught Pasinetti's face in her hands and kissed the top of his bald pate. A blush covered his head and neck. His gaze, however, remained lowered, not from embarrassment, but in anticipation of generous cleavage revealed. He was not disappointed. Chris' blouse fell open when she hugged him.

"I'll call you, dear," Pasinetti promised. He was positively luminous as the two men headed for the door.

MacDonnell looked at him sideways. "You're a real Don Juan — *Swain*."

"I likes 'um dumb."

The streets of Hoosick Falls were quiet except for an occasional car rattling by. A fresh breeze cleared some of the cotton out of Mike's brain. They strolled across the street to the parking lot. There were still a few cars in it, including Pasinetti's old Impala. MacDonnell absently noted four young men standing around another vehicle at the far end of the lot, but he paid them little heed. Upon reaching the Chevy, Pasinetti climbed into the passenger side, Mike MacDonnell settled behind the wheel. There was an unspoken agreement MacDonnell should always play chauffeur on these little meanders.

"Mac, I'm drunk as a lord," Pasinetti groaned. "I don't know how you do it."

"Vitamin E and coffee enemas." Mike started the car, but didn't put it in gear. The behavior of the four young men grew more animated. They were pounding on the hood and roof of the other car and shouting obscenities. One boy reached through the passenger side window and tried to grab something — or someone. Hoots, whistles and the mindless, abrasive laughter only teenage boys can produce echoed from the walls of the surrounding buildings.

MacDonnell put the Chevy in drive and, without headlights, rolled slowly forward. Streetlamps provided adequate illumination for him to observe the teenagers. At a few feet closer, he was able to identify two figures seated in the other car, two frightened female figures: Lucy Hewitt and her shy friend, Karen.

"Start the car and drive," Mike said, willing Lucy to act.

Both girls remained frozen in their seats. The boy reaching through the window tore Karen's shirt open. She began to cry while he brutally fondled her breasts.

Mike MacDonnell let his forehead bump the steering wheel in a fatalistic nod to the inevitable.

"What's wrong, Mackerel?" Pasinetti finally noticed events were not progressing normally.

"Fucking A!" MacDonnell snapped, not at his friend, and slammed the car into park. "I'll be right back."

He got out of the Impala and walked towards the other car; his face a mask of irritation mingled with bone-weary reluctance. It had been such a fine and easy night, only to end like this.

MacDonnell's approach went unnoticed by the boys, intent as they were upon their prey. He was in their midst before one overweight, pimply-faced kid — in a School Sucks T-shirt — sounded the alarm by yipping in fear and leaving the parking lot as fast as chubby legs could carry him.

This left three agitated monuments to testosterone-fueled stupidity, not including Mike MacDonnell.

MacDonnell maintained a steady bead on the girls' car. The boys fell silent as he rolled past them. One shaved-head, future carnival ride attendant summoned the courage to demand, "Who the fuck are you?"

"Captain Jenks of the Horse Marines."

The boy fell back two steps, dismayed by the ready contempt of this large man. Teenage bravado, and the enchanting allure of an easy gang rape, vanished from the parking lot.

MacDonnell reached the car. "Hi, girls."

Karen and Lucy stared up at him through the windshield, desperate gratitude leaking from their eyes.

"I had a great time tonight," MacDonnell continued. "I'll see you ladies again tomorrow?"

"You ain't datin' both of them!" one boy squealed. To someone who had never had — nor ever would have — a willing date, the idea of a menage a trois was pure desolation.

MacDonnell turned to the kid and smiled. "Who says I can't? You?"

The teenager's guppy mouth remained hanging open, but silent.

MacDonnell sat down on the hood of the car and lit a cigarette. The juvenile jackals fell back into a defensive half-circle in front of the vehicle. Tactically it gave them the most direct line of attack — and the most rapid avenue of escape. One boy, bigger and a shade bolder than his mates, took a step in MacDonnell's direction. MacDonnell recognized him as the little bastard who ripped open Karen's shirt.

"I'm not afraid of you, assfuck!" the teenager brayed. He was caught somewhere between frustrated rage and blind, pants-shitting panic.

Mike MacDonnell took a slow puff on the menthol.

The boy inched another step closer, fell into an absurd parody of a martial arts routine. He made threatening noises (which reminded Mike of a frantic Pekingese barking through a window at a mailman) and chopped the air with both hands. His companions remained hovering uneasily in their positions.

Mike MacDonnell stared into the boy's twisting, rawboned features and experienced an overwhelming urge to smash that face, to destroy the monstrous adolescent arrogance and stupidity — to leave the boy a weeping, bloody mess on the pavement.

MacDonnell slowly straightened up. He flicked his cigarette away. It described a fiery arc in the air.

Enough was enough.

He took a sharp step forward and rapped, "Get the fuck out of here."

Dumb animals and teenage boys can sense fear in other creatures. These boys failed to detect that sweet scent in Mike. Consequently, they ran like hell. Their daring leader emitted a girlish shriek before he turned and fled.

MacDonnell watched the pathetic retreat with relief. He really hadn't wanted to try his hand against all of them at once. Those odds were a wee bit dicey. He turned back to the girls.

"Ladies, next time please just start the car and drive away. I'll give you a call, Lucy."

Mike saw them safely off and headed back to the car. He came upon Rick leaning against a pickup truck. The human fireplug was chuckling to himself.

"You know what, Mac? One of them assholes was yelling, 'He's too big for me' as he ran by." Pasinetti casually tossed away the jagged half of a broken coke bottle. "Do you think if we stopped at your house, your wife would make us a meal?"

"She'd make a meal *of* us," Mike MacDonnell cautioned.

Michelle was a far more formidable adversary than any mob of teenage thugs.

31

Dinner had been completed at Blythewood and Terry Johnson, in on overtime, was sitting idly in the lobby of the main building with her team.

Annie Wilson watched in narrow-eyed disapproval from the door of the supervisors office. She turned to MacDonnell sitting at the desk.

"Tell Terry to take her group over to the Rec Center. You know Bill doesn't want staff hanging out in the lobby with their teams."

"You tell her," he mumbled with lazy indifference.

"Mike!" Annie's voice snapped around his ears like a whip. Their professional relationship centered on a friendly antagonism; however, Annie's tone was not friendly now, it belled with reproachful command.

Since the night at the pool, Mike found himself increasingly unable to balk her wishes on any matter. The more he tried to curb his appetite for her, the more it flourished. He was certain Annie knew his feelings had undergone a radical shift, but her response was an enigmatic avoidance of the issue which left him brittle and uneasy. A part of him even longed for her to mercilessly confirm no hope of an intimate relationship existed. He could have absorbed the blow, put it behind him. But Annie Wilson failed to deliver that humane strike. At times, just to muddy the water a bit more, MacDonnell swore he detected a hint of jealously when she spoke to him about Terry Johnson.

Uncertainty and desire had driven Mike MacDonnell to the doorstep of a small madness.

He rose slowly from behind the desk; a blocky, overweight, black-haired Venus lifted new from the sea.

"Why do you make me do all the dirty work?"

"Take a look in the mirror," Annie replied blandly.

"I can't. You're always in the way."

Annie Wilson tossed her shiny mane, dropped her chin on a perfect shoulder and transfixed him with a playful brand of seductive arrogance.

"I can't help being beautiful."

In the next heartbeat her blue eyes crinkled as she hid delightful laughter behind a raised hand.

MacDonnell lost the power to resist. He would have cheerfully inserted his head in an airplane propeller had she asked him to do so.

He left the office enthralled to a woman who had graduated from college while he had not, who was physically attractive while he was not, who moved in social circles he could not begin to comprehend — and her eyes followed him because he tramped in places she had never been and could never safely go.

MacDonnell's defenses quickly returned as he approached Terry Johnson. A dark cloud was almost visible in the air over her head.

He sat next to her on the couch. "Hey, Terry. How's it going?"

"Fine." Terry was rapidly tapping her foot. Not a good sign. Mike had the frightening suspicion she was waiting to spring a trap on him. Since the striptease at the pool, she'd been distant if not unfriendly.

"Any problem with the kids?" MacDonnell asked politely.

Terry offered him with a contentious glare. "Do you need something, like a life?"

This irritated the supervisor. "Actually, Terry, I'd like you to take your team over to the Rec Center. Administration doesn't —"

"You take them!"

"Come on, Terry."

"No! You come on." Terry's upper body was swaying now like a prize fighter preparing to launch a right uppercut.

"Take your team over to the Rec Center — please." MacDonnell held the lid on his rising temper.

"No," she snapped back. "Why don't you get off your lazy ass and take them over? I'm beat. I don't sit in an office all day. I work for a living."

"It ain't my job anymore, Terry. I'm a supervisor, not a childcare worker."

"Oh? You're a *supervisor*? So what the fuck do you do? Stare at Annie Wilson's tits and play with yourself?"

"That's enough."

"You've changed, big time. You used to understand about working with these kids, what it's like for us line staff. Now you stick your fat behind in a chair and pretend to be somebody."

"Terry, take your team over to the Rec Center."

"No, I won't!"

"Go!"

Terry Johnson sprang to her feet. "I'll go. I'll go home!" She stomped towards the front door, abandoning her team.

Mike, in sudden trepidation, called after her. If an administrator happened by at this moment, Terry would be terminated immediately for violating a slew of Blythewood regulations.

Terry ignored him and slammed the door behind her.

MacDonnell threw policy and procedure and caution to the wind. He rushed out of the building after her. Both staff were now in jeopardy of losing their jobs for leaving an entire team of students unsupervised.

He caught her halfway to the parking lot and blocked her path. "Stop! Please!"

She folded her arms under her breasts and stared at him.

Desperately he promised, "I'll go with you to the Rec Center."

Time was running out for both of them. At any moment someone was going to discover the untended flock in the lounge.

A satisfied smile curved Terry Johnson's lips like a scimitar. She turned on a heel and walked back into the building.

MacDonnell followed after with a vast sense of relief. He stopped in the office to tell Annie he would be going to the Rec Center with Terry's team. Annie treated this announcement, and the subsequent lack of explanation, with silent disapproval. Busily adrift in a sea of back paperwork, she'd missed the entire confrontation; however, intuition told her something was not quite right about the whole thing.

In the Rec Center, Mike MacDonnell helped Terry settle her team into various activities. After this was done, the man and woman sat down together on an old couch and observed the boys fumble at checkers and monopoly, spill a bucket of broken crayons on the floor, pick a variety of scabs and runny noses and generally amuse themselves in the picturesque fashion native to their sundry impairments.

It was almost like old times.

Old times . . .

What had it been? Two years? A bit more? How could it yield anything like 'old times' between two people? Years, many years, were needed to do that. And yet, there it sat. A sackful of months transmuted into a time passage that felt like a decade. Blythewood alchemy, white and black.

MacDonnell looked at Terry, at the strong curve of her face and the restless shadows in her eyes. God help him, but he would be able to close his eyes at any time in his life and recall her features in every detail. They were that fine and handsome.

She glanced up, feeling his eyes upon her.

"I'm sorry," she said in a soft voice.

"Don't worry about it."

"You know I'd do anything you asked me to."

"Then why didn't you?" MacDonnell asked without rancor.

"Because . . ."

She started to cry a little.

Mike MacDonnell stared at the dirty patch of floor between his boots. He wanted to say he knew what she meant. Wanted to say he loved her too; but the words perished in his throat, strangled by the knowledge time had simply passed them by.

Terry wiped her eyes. "Mike, I joined the Army yesterday."

He laughed.

"I'm not kidding. I report in six weeks. I need to get out of this place."

Mike didn't find any words.

"I put in my two week notice this morning. It'll give me some time off before I go."

"The Army, Terry? Is it really . . ."

"Will you write me?"

"Sure," he answered slowly, sadly. "Sure I will."

The end of shift came before long and it was time for them to leave.

32

Mike arranged a going away party for Terry at a Polynesian restaurant in Wessex on the Wednesday afternoon of her last shift. Terry chose the location. For once Mike didn't put up any protest. It was her going away party, after all.

Terry and he were the first to arrive. They sat next to each other at a table in the middle of the empty restaurant and ordered drinks. Both were silent for a bit. MacDonnell listlessly observed the faux Hawaiian decor: the cartoon-bright murals of tropical sunsets, the wicker torches with light bulbs instead of flame, the faded plastic leis drooping on the walls, the tea candle holders, shaped like little scorched pineapples, flickering on the table before them. No Michelin star for this joint. Slide guitar riffs twanged out of speakers mounted near the ceiling. Faintly, from the juke box over in the bar, Don Ho crooned, *I'll Remember You.*

Mike took a breath. "I can't wait for *Tiny Bubbles.*"

Terry looked at him. "What?"

"Nothing. Want another drink?"

"I'm not finished with this one."

"Something to eat?"

"Are you hungry?"

MacDonnell shook his head and took a swig from the beer bottle in front of him. He was uncomfortable and wanted people to arrive so he could hide in the noise, get a handle on the shitty way he felt about Terry leaving. The last thing he wanted to do was ruin this night for her by retreating into a lonely sadness and leading her there with him. He might not see her again for a long time . . . if ever. Things should end on a high note, with a good drunk and good memories. For a second he wondered if he should come on to her after the party, if it would be the right thing to do, a farewell fuck; but he leveled his eyes on the far wall of the restaurant and let that ship sail off into a garish Polynesian sunset. Too late for all that now.

Terry said, "It's cold in here." She hugged herself and moved closer to him, resting her thigh against his. Overcome by a sudden rush of love, he put his arm around her shoulder and pulled her a little closer.

"Yeah, it is. . ." MacDonnell cleared his throat, prepared to say more, but then the restaurant door swung open and Blythewood staff hemorrhaged into their pregnant isolation. He pulled his arm away and she straightened, turned her head to say hello.

Loud, stupid, shy, tired, thirsty, cross, Blythewood's thin denim line filed in echelon. Tables and chairs were pulled together, booze and food were ordered. Two young waitresses, unprepared for this kind of afternoon crush, scurried like mice back and forth from kitchen to bar to dining room. A few minutes before, MacDonnell couldn't wait for other staff to arrive; now, as the noisy activity swelled like a hot-air balloon, he wished they'd go away.

"Jesus," he said to Terry, "I didn't think this many people would show up. You must be popular."

She glanced at him, smiled and went back to chatting with her friends.

At least she was smiling.

Mike leaned back in the chair and finished his bottle of beer. One of the waitresses appeared at his elbow and asked if he wanted another.

"Yes, please."

She leaned forward to take the empty bottle and showed him a little bra and tit. It was an old waitress trick this girl had learned early. Flash a little flesh and get a bigger tip. Just don't get grabby, old son. MacDonnell watched her walk away. Nice ass, too — but not as nice as Terry's. He sighed and wished her thigh still pressed his.

Wish, wish, wish your life away, asshole.

A duet of "Hey, Mike." Two men in their fifties, Jim Smith and John Murray, sat down across from MacDonnell. Jim and John worked the overnight, had been childcare workers for a couple of decades and a couple for nearly as long. MacDonnell had gotten to know them during shift changes, and better after a few weary nights of overtime. Mike considered these two friends — unlike most of the yahoos banging their guts against the table.

Murray, fairly squirming in his chair, slapped a bony knee, and announced, apropos of nothing, "Still won't let me march in the Saint Patrick's Day parade." John's hair was a tangle of gray and he had wet, nervous eyes. His hands shook worse than MacDonnell's.

"You're too ugly. It would scare the little kids and drunks," said Jim dryly. Sober, he tended to be reserved with those he didn't know and sometimes abrasive, even with those he did. He'd been married once, years ago, and his ex-wife and their daughter had begun working the overnight with him a few months back. Recently, the ex-wife's lesbian lover had also signed up, making it a genuine family affair. This led to the occasional clan row in the wee hours, or so MacDonnell had heard.

"Heather stopping by?" Mike asked Jim. Heather was the daughter.

"No. She was dead-tired this morning. Went home to bed."

Too bad. MacDonnell liked to look at her — when he took a break from adoring Annie and mourning Terry. Heather would have made a comforting distraction.

Jim said, "I put in for the soups position."

"So, I heard," MacDonnell replied. "Good for you."

John Murray spat out, "Thank Gawd that dipshit Tom handed in his notice."

"He was an all right boss. We've had worse," Jim said.

"Yeah, Franny Rando," Murray said, referring to the other supervisor on their shift. "That waste of oxygen couldn't find his ass with both hands. He wanders around babbling about samurai warriors. There ain't a thought in his empty skull."

"No," Jim admitted. "But he does the laundry every night."

"He can do me every night."

"He wouldn't want to."

MacDonnell smiled. "Well, Jim, I hope you don't regret moving up the ladder. Our weekly supervisors' meeting could teach CIA torture masters a thing or two."

Jim was about to reply when a minor commotion at the far end of the tables drew everyone's attention.

Greg O'Brien had wallowed into the restaurant. He'd stopped to pat an acquaintance on the shoulder, but succeeded in knocking the man's drink all over him. The guy was yowling a few choice words at O'Brien in between efforts to soak up the mess with cheap paper napkins from a dispenser on the table. The waitress with the nice ass hurried to the rescue with a towel.

O'Brien, unperturbed and chuckling (a sound like a bear might make if it had a badly diseased lung), ambled away from the disaster.

"Oh, Holy Mother," John Murray stage-whispered. "He's coming in our direction."

O'Brien dumped into an empty chair next to Jim.

"Hi, Greg," Murray cackled. "How are you? Sober?"

"You bet."

Jim Smith offered a curt greeting, but didn't look at the man.

O'Brien spent a long minute observing the flame fluttering inside a pineapple candle holder. It seemed a great wonder to him. Finally, he moved a truck load of phlegm in his throat and said, "That's cute. I gotta get me one of them."

"You do that," said Jim Smith. He stood up and asked MacDonnell if he would like to join him for a shot at the bar.

Mike was game. John Murray leapt to his feet, made bug-eyes at O'Brien and declared, "You ain't leaving me here."

MacDonnell asked Terry if she wanted to come with them.

"No, go ahead," she replied, softly. "I'm still gossiping."

The bar was an island of calm. Dark and empty, restrained in its Polynesian kitsch, it allowed MacDonnell to catch his figurative breath. Even the Don Ho retrospective playing continuously on the jukebox wasn't altogether irritating. At least it wasn't Jimmy Buffet. They bought four shots of Jameson — one for the bartender himself — performed the tumbler salute and ordered another round.

Murray, choking a little on the last bump, gasped, "You know, if Greg O'Brien was queer, and the last one on earth, I'd go straight."

Jim spared a quick, uncomfortable glance for the bartender and replied, "There isn't a woman on earth would have you."

"I'll have you know there were quite a few young ladies who sought my attentions when I was a young man."

"Yes, ladies of the evening."

Murray acknowledged this possibility with a good-natured shrug and waved three fingers at the bartender.

Jim said to MacDonnell, "Heard from your cousin Ned lately?"

Smith, like Mike's family, was originally from the Albany-Troy area. He'd dated Mike's cousin many years ago; a fact MacDonnell learned one bleary Blythewood morning.

"No. I don't think he much cares for me. He took a clout at me when I was fifteen, and I chased him around the kitchen table and out of the house."

Murray said, "The guy's a bum. I never liked him."

"You never met him, " Jim said.

"He's still a bum."

"Ned's mother was a sweetheart," Jim said to MacDonnell. "She'd shoot off to the kitchen to make something to eat as soon as you walked in the door, no matter what time it was. But your Uncle Pat? He didn't like me very much."

"I don't think Packy liked a lot of people very much."

"Well, if you should see Ned, ask what he brought back to me from Port-au-Prince."

"Which was?"

"The crabs." Jim took a sip of whiskey, and asked (*shyly?*), "Where's Annie today? I thought she'd be here for sure."

"Connecticut," MacDonnell answered, trying to keep any tell-tale expression off his face.

Murray winked. "Probably got a sugar daddy, a hot little ticket like her."

"I wouldn't know," MacDonnell responded uncomfortably and changed the subject. "Jim, not to stick my nose in where it doesn't belong, but are you going to do anything about Ralph's drinking when you take over the night shift?"

"I have to. I can't let him bring down the whole shift or get somebody hurt because he's incoherent. Franny doesn't notice and Tom ignores it. I won't."

"It's because Ralph and Tom have something going," said Murray.

Jim sighed, "The whole world isn't gay, John."

"About half of Blythewood seems to be," Murray said. "Dykes to the right, dykes to the left. Jesus, it makes me feel like I'm back with the nuns."

"You still need your knuckles rapped."

"The penguins didn't do you any good, Jim."

"I went to La Salle Military, as you well know."

Murray laughed. "Oh, right, the Christian Brothers. No wonder you're a fairy."

Jim turned on him with genuine ire. "In spite of what most people think, no priest, not one, ever put a finger on me or any of my friends. I got a great education and it prepared me for the Air Force."

"The Air Force, there's the culprit." Murray's evil grin showed a few bad teeth.

MacDonnell had the feeling this skirmish was an old one, often repeated. He decided to break it up. "How do you guys handle working four nights in a row on your long shift? Christ, one knocks me on my ass."

"Four nights is tough," Jim admitted. "But then the next week, the other side has the long haul, and we have four days off. Hard to beat that."

"Nights are bad when you're hungover," Murray added. "You just want to find an empty bed and crawl in."

"Which you do," Jim said, then to Mike. "We're not going to stay on nights forever. But, for right now, it's good. A year or two down the road and we'll see what opens up on days."

"Something will be available. You can count on it," said Mike. He dropped a ten dollar bill in the tip jar. "I'm gonna head back to the table. How about you two?"

He led the way. As they approached, it was apparent Greg O'Brien and Terry were holding a conversation. It didn't look good. Her eyes were wide, the expression one of shock or horror or both.

"What's going on?" Mike asked as the three men reclaimed their seats. He glared at O'Brien. The stupid bastard must be barbecuing his parents again.

Terry put a hand on MacDonnell's arm. This confused and thrilled him.

Greg O'Brien lifted a menu, and said, "Just askin' Terry what she'd like to eat. My treat." His voice was a slow, rumbling, drunken drawl. Irritating. Obnoxious. He pretended to scan the menu in his hand. "But then I looked and realized all they have here is Gook grub — there ain't no fried chicken or *colored* greens, no ribs or ham hocks, nothin' she's gonna wanna eat. And for damn sure there ain't any watermelon for desert." O'Brien choked on his own humor.

MacDonnell started to rise like a Titan booster in his chair. Terry grabbed his arm with both hands, begged him to sit down.

"Please don't. Just let it go. *Please, please?"*

Greg, still enthralled by his own brilliant wit, was blissfully unaware how close he was to an ass-kicking.

Jim Smith swatted O'Brien on the shoulder, not gently. "Greg? I need to speak to you outside about something. We can have a cigarette." Jim's voice was sharp, loud.

"Huh? What's that?"

"Outside! I want a smoke." Jim grabbed O'Brien under the arm and dragged him to his feet. Smith's face turned red with the exertion. O'Brien was a big man.

"Whaddya want?" Greg asked as Smith pushed him towards the door. "Smoke? Like ya, James, but you ain't smokin' me . . ."

The restaurant door banged shut behind them.

Terry pulled again on MacDonnell's arm. "Sit down, Mike. He's gone."

MacDonnell did as he was told, but his eyes were still bright with anger. He could only imagine what other rotten things Greg had been saying to her while he was away. Didn't anyone else at the table notice? Were they that fucking drunk? That fucking stupid?

"Terry," he said. "You don't have to put up with that shit. Not from anybody — and especially not from a dirty Irish pig."

"He's half Italian," Murray scolded, his voice jittery, his hands violently shaking. "His mother went to Saint Agnes grade school with my ma. Listen, I'm going to see if Jim is okay. His heart ain't all that good, anymore."

"I'll go, John," MacDonnell said.

"No! You stay put. Nobody needs to get killed tonight." Murray popped out of his chair and scrambled off like a mildly arthritic ferret.

Terry's fingers moved down MacDonnell's forearm and took his hand in hers. "Greg was just drunk, Mike. It's not a big deal."

"Apparently, he's always fucking drunk. So that's the way he is — who he is."

"Please let it go. I'm okay. It doesn't bother me."

No matter what she said, MacDonnell could tell she was hurt. Ambushed at her going away party. No good memories. No good drunk.

Murray and Smith returned a few minutes later.

Jim said in a flat tone, "Greg had to leave. He sends his apologies."

"But not before Jim yanked his tiny balls off," Murray quipped. "I'm gonna put 'um on a ribbon and hang them from the Christmas tree this year."

MacDonnell allowed himself a smile.

After the party was over, and everyone left, Terry and Mike sat in his GTO. They drank beer from his emergency case in the backseat. Afterward, he couldn't remember much of what they talked about that night. Mostly little things, he supposed. They got drunk. Mike asked to see her breasts. She unsnapped her bra and pulled up her shirt. It made him hard, but he didn't touch her. Later, she told him she was scared about joining the Army.

"You'll be fine," he said, not knowing a thing about it.

Terry looked out the car window, blew a cloud of cigarette smoke into the night.

"I don't know. . . I don't think so. . ."

GTO howling at the night. A Michigan banshee. Speedometer pegged. 140 and then some. One hand on the wheel, the other on a fifth of Jim Beam. Running for daylight. Waiting for the scream of glass, metal, the sickening tumble that never comes. Highway actors flashing by: telephone poles, guard rails, trees, fields, farm houses gripped in slumber, hills tossing their shoulders against the road. Past his house.

Running for daylight.

A long, slow breath, almost but not quite a death rattle.

Speedometer receding. 100 . . . 80 . . . 60 . . .

Drop the breaks, crank the wheel. Let the good old bitch kick her ass around, fry the tires. Come about.

No run for daylight.

Not tonight.

33

Mike MacDonnell woke with a grunt. His heart butted against his chest. A slimy film of sweat dampened his brow. He sat up, hawking air, struggling against the grip of a nightmare already forgotten. His eyes darted around the room. The faint glow of a distant streetlight, sifting through the window blinds, cast a few strands of illumination against the shadows crouching at the foot of the bed. Michelle slept on undisturbed; her soft breathing a murmurous sigh.

A bad dream — nothing more.

Mike got up from the bed and went downstairs. For a while, perhaps an hour, he wandered the dark and familiar rooms. He paused in the kitchen, the heart of the house, the place where everyone gathered through the years to talk and tell stories, read newspapers and down vast amounts of coffee and tea and booze; remembered the time his mother had thrown a beer bottle through one of the windows over the sink because her eldest, Jimmy, had heaved a bottle of Bud through the other. "*I* break the windows in this house, hotshot," she had declared to her inebriated son.

In the living room, Mike's fingers ran the length of the mantle over the fieldstone fire place. This was where Christmas began when he was small. Every December 1st, long before the tree was wrestled through the front door, he would carefully lay out little decorations on the mantle: wax figures of snowmen and Santa Claus, little bits of tinsel and garland. It really hadn't looked like much when he was done — MacDonnell had never been burdened with any obvious sense of artistic presentation — but to a little boy, the results seemed nothing short of a miracle. Then over to the bay windows the grown man went. Here is where the tree had gone up, year after year, still did since Mike had moved back after his mother's death. Here is where he would stand for hours, on those long ago winter nights, bewitched by the strings of lights: the big, old-fashioned teardrop bulbs in red, blue, green and yellow, the round glass snowballs whose sharp, spiked edges could cut you if you weren't careful, and the translucent icicles, his favorite, percolating the teaspoon of water inside when they warmed up. Sometimes he would balance toy soldiers in little machine-gun nests of pine needles on the branches, no Christmas cease-fire here, stopping every now and then to close his eyes and breathe in the living scent of the tree. And sometimes he would lay under it with a blanket, staring up along the trunk, always a little crooked, up through the dense weave of limbs and ornaments, waiting, daydreaming, till he fell asleep.

Mike sighed for no particular reason and drifted over to the french doors leading into the dining room. He opened them, but did not enter the room. Instead, he stood in the doorway and watched time fall away, saw all the Thanksgiving and Christmas and Easter dinners, riotous with relatives and in-laws, heard laughter and arguments raised from vanished throats — saw a ghostly flutter of images without the power to disturb a thimbleful of dust.

Mike MacDonnell closed the doors and went back upstairs to his bedroom.

Home.

This was home.

What did that mean?

Mike lived in other houses over the years, had memories of them, not so many to be sure, and not so strong.

Home is where the heart is they say.

All of it and more.

Mike got in bed, stuck his legs under the covers and propped the pillow up the way he liked it. Michelle mumbled something in her sleep and swatted at an invisible fly. The comforter slipped off her shoulder. Gently, so as not to wake her, he pulled it back up again, tucked it in beneath her ear.

Home is where the heart is.

MacDonnell felt lost out on the trail — but with nothing to do about it, he settled back in bed and closed his eyes.

All of it and more . . .

34

Mike MacDonnell stared out the office window, trying not to eavesdrop on Annie's phone conversation, or at least not be obvious about it.

"Look, Carl, we are not going out anymore. Is that clear enough for you? Carl . . . please don't call again." Annie dropped the phone in the cradle. It was a gesture of utter disdain. The conversation with a forlorn admirer had begun on a note of cool distance and ended in an arctic freeze.

Good God, MacDonnell thought, this woman dispatches men like a hunter clubbing baby seals. He hoped never be the recipient of such a frigid execution at her hands. Of course poor Carl's now defunct relationship with Annie had been different from anything MacDonnell shared with her. Carl had been a lover — Mike MacDonnell wanted to be. He'd stopped pretending, to himself at least, he desired anything less.

Things had changed between the two supervisors. They were going out more, staying until the bars closed, and talking about everything under the sun, moon and stars. Afterwards, MacDonnell would trot home, toting another fertilizer sack full of pathetic excuses for Michelle.

"Candy?" Annie raised an eyebrow and held out her hand.

Obediently, he dropped a bag of licorice candies on the desk in front of her. It was Wednesday, which meant not only payday but candy-day as well. MacDonnell would leave campus to cash his check, and, on the way back, stop at the Wessex Mobile Mart to purchase Annie's weekly supply of sweets. There was a slavish devotion inherent in this ritual gift-giving.

"You could say thank you?" MacDonnell reminded her.

"Why?" Annie was cognizant, on some level, that he was hopelessly twined around her little finger.

"Good manners are never excused." He persisted in baiting her though his ultimate goal was his own ultimate submission.

"This from a man who chews other people's gum?" Annie was referring to the incident when MacDonnell, upon the dare of another supervisor (and the promise of ten dollars), plucked an abandoned wad of gum from the lip of a garbage pail and put it in his mouth. Annie Wilson, a reluctant witness to the event, had choked.

"I was hard up for cash — to buy you candy." He lit a cigarette and deftly avoided Annie's resulting lunge across the desk.

"Ha, ha." He was getting good at dodging her Flying Hand of Condemnation.

"Put it out. I'm trying to eat my Good 'N' Plentys."

"No."

"Yes."

MacDonnell blew a cloud of smoke in her face, but his defiance was short lived. He quickly relented and dropped the butt in a half empty styrofoam coffee cup on the desk. There the offending object swam in a greasy tobacco and caffeine stew with several of its pack mates.

Annie Wilson swatted at the haze around her head and forced several racking coughs. "Sometimes you are an asshole, Mike."

With all the care of a lab technician handling an active anthrax culture, she cautiously lifted the coffee cup and placed it on top of a nearly overflowing garbage basket next to the desk. "Housekeeping needs to empty this once in awhile, before you find something else to put in your mouth," she observed tartly. "What does our new head janitor do all day?"

"Scrapes his dirty toes with a putty knife. I'm an asshole?"

"Yes, sometimes. The rest of the time you're just . . . strange."

"As in dark, brooding, yet somehow intriguing strange? Or drooling, giggling, serial-killer-lurking-in-the-pantry strange?"

A smile rose above Annie's genuine irritation.

MacDonnell assaulted the breach. "Wanna go for a drink after work?" There was a shy note in his voice which was not an affectation. He always felt a touch of anxiety when he asked her to go out.

"I was planning to drive down to Connecticut tonight." Annie had a second, part-time job doing kitchen prep at a country inn over the Connecticut line.

"Oh."

"But, I decided not to go till Thursday afternoon. So yeah, we can go out for a drink if you want to."

Mike MacDonnell was elated.

Just then Todd Robertson walked into the office and handed Annie an incident report. Robertson was a new staff. MacDonnell hadn't made up his mind about him yet. Todd did evidence a fawning enthusiasm which made MacDonnell wary, but so far, the childcare worker had committed no overtly idiotic act to warrant supervisory wrath.

Annie, on the other hand, made no bones about the fact she found Todd Robertson attractive. She stopped just short of open flirtation with him.

"Higgy had a little problem in gym," Todd explained. "But I talked him down. He's fine now." There was a dash of cautious self-aggrandizement in the childcare worker's tone and choice of words which set MacDonnell's teeth on edge. It was apparent Todd was in the early stages of Super–Childcare–Worker Syndrome; a debilitating mental disorder which deceived sufferers into believing they were: A) Doing God's Work, B) Possessed of greater insight than any of the mere mortals who had come before them, and C) Capable of healing all the psychic-lepers at Blythewood simply by showing up for work on a more or less regular basis.

"Thanks." Annie's smile was a shade too bright.

"You are welcome." Todd's eyes made a brief, but thorough examination of her chest.

"Todd, you better get back to your team," MacDonnell suggested abruptly.

"Oh. Sure, Mike." The childcare worker shrugged and left the office.

Annie said, with dreamy conviction, "He's such a nice young man."

"Uh-huh." MacDonnell picked up the incident report and frowned at it. Robertson's handwriting had a neat, contained quality which inspired unreasoning contempt in the supervisor. "He writes like a girl."

"What did you say?"

"Snap out of it, Mrs. Robinson." MacDonnell allowed the report to flutter back to the desk. "Are you going to do the staff supervisions this week?"

"It's your turn."

"It's never my turn." He hated doing supervisions. It was an official formality he found significantly inferior to buying someone a drink for a job well done or — on rare occasions — treating an obdurate fool to a volcanic eruption of foul language. Whenever possible, he pawned the task off on Annie Wilson.

Today, she simply shook her head and continued popping white and purple cylinders of licorice candy into her mouth. MacDonnell took heart. It was not an outright refusal.

Annie burped and did not excuse herself. This caused MacDonnell to experience a curious annoyance with her. Rudely passing gas did not fit his meticulously contrived image of her flawlessness. It made her seem too ordinary, too human — too much like all the other girls he'd known and forgotten.

There was a knock at the outer door. Another new staff (there were always plenty of them) sheepishly poked his head inside the office. Billy Stewart was three inches past five feet and his chubby features had the soft, nebulous appearance of an under-baked gingerbread man. He was slow of foot and wit, but conscientious in the performance of his duties, once he understood them.

MacDonnell motioned for the young man to enter. "What's up, Billy?"

Stewart waddled reluctantly into the office. It took him a moment to gather his fragile thoughts before he blurted out, "There's something ain't right over at the Ad-on." He directed his words at Annie Wilson. Mike MacDonnell scared the piss out of him.

MacDonnell prayed they were not about to be subjected to some rambling account of a felonious raccoon's unauthorized entry into the small, prefabricated unit serving as Team Three's classroom.

"What's not right, Billy?" Annie asked patiently.

"Well, sir — you know Peter the teacher?"

"Yes," MacDonnell answered, impatiently. Peter Holland was the instructor in Team Three.

Billy Stewart flinched at the dark timber in MacDonnell's voice, but summoned the nerve to continue. "Well, the rest of my team's out on the ball field for gym, but he's got Marty Dodge alone in the Ad-on — and the door's locked. I don't guess it's probably right."

The hairs on Mike MacDonnell's neck prickled. "No, it ain't right." He darted a look at Annie Wilson. "I'm going over to check this shit out. Come on, Billy. You lead the way."

The supervisor's sudden and intense suspicion was due to the individuals involved. Marty Dodge was a badly impaired boy of fourteen who wore a boxing helmet as protection against severe drop-seizures. He suffered from Cerebral Palsy and an organic thought disorder which compelled him to verbally fantasize about raping his mother and then running her over with a lawn mower. Marty was highly sexualized in his demeanor towards others and, consequently, highly vulnerable to abuse.

The teacher, Peter Holland, managed to dwarf Marty Dodge in every category which might be deemed aberrant or peculiar. From his congenitally disheveled appearance, to his penchant for wandering around campus with his fly unzipped, talking to himself, Peter had established a frightful reputation in five short months of employment.

As he hurried towards the school building with Billy Stewart, Mike MacDonnell was once again forced to marvel at the arcane processes which granted someone like Peter Holland a position at Blythewood. It seemed having a pulse and a nominal claim to human ancestry were the only prerequisites.

The Ad-on, as the name implied, was a modest, self-contained addition to the school building. It had only one point of entry, a gray aluminum door which could be locked from the inside. In management meeting, MacDonnell frequently protested against this feature. It was inherently dangerous, on many levels. Everyone agreed with him and nothing was ever done. Fortunately he had a key to the door on his supervisor's master-ring.

It was a hot day for September. MacDonnell was panting by the time he reached the Ad-on. He fumbled with his keys, finally found the right one, and quietly unlocked the door. He took a deep breath and entered ahead of Billy Stewart.

It was cave-dark inside. MacDonnell blindly sought the light switch on the wall next to the door and flipped it on — to reveal Peter the teacher and Marty the student locked together on an old battered couch in a corner of the classroom.

Marty, wearing nothing but his black boxing helmet, was laying face down, hands duct-taped behind his back, convulsing in what appeared to be a grand mal seizure. White foam leaked from blackened lips.

Peter Holland, pants tangled around his ankles, froze in mid-thrust at the student's quaking rear. The teacher's penis and cartoon-red pubic hair were caked in shit.

Holland's eyes went white with terror and he screeched something Mike MacDonnell would never tire of retelling whenever the incident was recalled. It became one of his favorite Blythewood quotations:

"My girlfriend won't give me any!"

It was a monstrously inane and ridiculous thing for Peter Holland to shout. And yet, there was something miserably sincere about it, something which made the situation even more appalling.

Mike MacDonnell's throat swelled. "GET OFF HIM!"

Gasping for air, Holland stumbled back a few step, fumbling with his pants and underwear. He lost his balance and toppled to the floor.

MacDonnell, now in a calm and measured voice, told Billy Stewart to call the nurse and take care of Marty until she got there — then he moved on the teacher.

Holland barely had time to buckle his belt before he was grabbed by the nape of the neck and dragged out of the classroom. The teacher was not a small man, but he offered no resistance. All the way to the office, MacDonnell tried to think of something suitably vicious and threatening to say, but nothing occurred to him. It was like attempting to decide what kind of cheap, pungent wine serves best with a catshit soufflé.

MacDonnell towed Holland into the office and shoved him in a chair.

Annie Wilson's wide-eyed curiosity was unpleasantly satisfied as her partner described, in blunt detail, the events at the Ad-on. When rapt horror receded, she notified administration — and then the police. This was too serious a matter for even Rumgay to consider covering up.

MacDonnell stood at Holland's side like a plumber hovering over a clogged toilet: the odor offended, but he was prepared to tear the thing apart if necessary.

The teacher retreated into an incoherent state. He mumbled spittle wet nonsense to himself while his shaggy red eyebrows squirmed like mice tossed in a campfire. By any definition, Peter Holland was an unlovely man. Fat-bellied and pug-nosed, his pale blue eyes seemed engaged in an unceasing migration to the middle of his knotted forehead. There was something odd in the motion of his flabby limbs, as if an alien intelligence had imprecisely designed them to approximate the function of human extremities. Most of the students (and some of the staff) called him Porky Pig — often to his face.

MacDonnell grew tired of Holland's twitching. When Annie turned her head away for a moment, he slapped the teacher hard on the back of the head. Holland hardly noticed. He'd become fixated on the wastebasket next to the desk, gazing at it with single-minded devotion. Without warning, he grabbed the styrofoam cup on top of the trash heap, the one MacDonnell had used all morning as an ashtray, and drained its murky contents in one big gulp.

Annie Wilson's eyes grew large and round as dinner plates. Mike could feel her stomach somersault.

"Thirsty?" he asked the teacher politely.

Primordial, filter-chewing grunts were Holland's only response.

Faith Minor appeared at the office door a moment later. There were bags under her sour eyes, bags big enough to frighten a seasoned bellhop. She motioned for MacDonnell to follow her back into the next room. The supervisor balked and gestured wordlessly at Holland.

Minor shook her head and jabbed an index finger at her feet. There was no mistaking the silent command. Reluctantly, Mike MacDonnell left the office.

Peter Holland became absolutely still for a moment, then he lunged to his feet, head tossing like a red roan pony with a neurological disorder. Annie Wilson jumped up, moved between him and the outside door. The teacher grabbed Annie by the hair and slammed the back of her head into the wall. She cried out in pain and shock.

Annie's vision danced, shivered between light and blackness, caught something big and dark, like a thunderhead, moving through the office doorway.

MacDonnell seized Holland, spun him in the air and brought the man's ugly face crashing down on the edge of the desk. The choreography was instantaneous and brutally perfect.

Holland's subsequent screams of agony were halted by MacDonnell's hands closing around his throat.

"Mike! Stop it! Mike!"

Dimly, through the black typhoon rushing in his ears, MacDonnell heard Annie's voice, felt her hands on his rigid forearms.

He relaxed his grip.

Holland sprawled on the floor, gasping for air. There was blood everywhere from a deep gash over the teacher's left eye. A squirming mouse brow was nearly torn away.

MacDonnell wiped his hands on the teacher's rumpled shirt and stood up. There was a loose, watery feeling in his arms and legs, the physical residue of an authentic desire to kill.

He croaked at Annie, "Are you all right?"

"I'm fine. Are you okay? You're white as a sheet."

MacDonnell nodded. He noticed Faith Minor standing in the door-way and raised his hand to tip her a rude gesture, but thought better of it, and instead dismissed the assistant program director with a brief, contemptuous wave. Minor spun on a spiked heel and stalked away.

He turned to Annie, hand still raised, and almost put it on her shoulder. But gentle, nonverbal expressions were then, as always, difficult and uncomfortable for him. Instead he said, "I'm sorry."

"What are you sorry for?" Annie asked. "I'm all right. It's not your fault this creep attacked me."

"I should have been here to watch him."

"I am a supervisor too, you know."

"That's different."

"How?"

"It doesn't matter if I get attacked." It was something a faithful watchdog might have uttered if granted the power of human speech.

"That has to be the dumbest thing I've ever heard you say — and I've heard you say a lot of dumb things. It must matter to somebody."

The corner of MacDonnell's lip lifted. "My mother loved me —"

"And then she died," Annie interrupted with mock impatience. "Or you had her killed. I know, I know. But what about Michelle?" This was well-meant, but awkward. It crackled in the air between them like a static discharge.

Peter Holland began rooting around on the floor and attempted a return to an upright position.

MacDonnell offered the teacher a casual glance before grinding him back down on the floor with a boot heel.

Annie noticed the bleeding wound on the teacher's head. "Should we get a nurse down here to look at his eye? It's pretty bad."

MacDonnell ignored this. "Do you need a nurse?" he asked with real anxiety.

A curt expulsion of air indicated how asinine she found the question. She picked up a box of candy and began gobbling like a famished hen. The issue of her well-being was closed.

MacDonnell admired her fortitude. Nothing in Annie Wilson's previous existence could have prepared her for the things Blythewood offered like glimpses of squalid pornography at a peep show. That she could maintain a sense of poise was remarkable. But then to him, she was most remarkable in every way.

After the State Police carted a squealing, bleeding, Porky Pig Holland away, MacDonnell began chain-smoking. His rapid puffing was matched by Annie's nonstop inhalation of candy. This nervous consumption served as a safety valve for both of them, since the use of more potent mediums of relaxation were, for the moment, out of the question.

"I need a couple blasts," MacDonnell admitted.

"Mike?"

"Yeah?"

"Thanks."

"You're welcome, ma'am."

"Do you believe any of this happened?"

MacDonnell chuckled humorlessly, "Life here in Purgatory Junction can be a nasty proposition."

"I think I am going to Connecticut tonight. I need to get away from all this for a while."

MacDonnell nodded and tossed a cigarette through the outside door. It flickered on the ground and died.

She needed to get away from it all and he needed to be with her.

Jesus, would anything ever work out like it should?

35

Annie Wilson strolled into the office a half hour late on Sunday morning.

"Good of you to join us," MacDonnell said. He resisted looking up from the stack of incident reports he was reviewing.

A video cassette case dropped from Wilson's hand and clattered on the desk.

"What's this?" MacDonnell picked it up curiously. *The Man Who Would Be King.* Where did you get this?"

"I rented it at a video store in Connecticut. I remembered you saying it was your favorite movie. Can you make a copy of it?"

"You bet."

"Please get it back to me by Wednesday?"

"I will." MacDonnell reached for his wallet. "How much do I owe you for the rental?"

"Don't be a jerk." She flicked his ear with her finger.

MacDonnell was not able to express the enormous satisfaction her touch gave him. However brief, however incidental, physical contact with her left him mute, unsteady — and redeemed.

"Why do you like the movie so much?" Annie asked.

"Did you watch it?"

"Yes . . ."

"And you didn't like it."

"Not really. I think Sean Connery is handsome as hell, though."

"They say he's gay."

"He is not."

A black eyebrow arched. "Hey, believe what you want, but he's been cocked more times than a Colt revolver."

"Why are you such an ass?"

MacDonnell shrugged. "It takes a lot of practice. Dare I ask what your favorite movie is, Miss Wilson?"

"There's a film called *The Night Porter,* with Charlotte Rampling and Dirk Bogarde, I find interesting."

"Isn't it about Nazis or something?"

"Something like that."

"I would have guessed you for an aficionado of the French cinema."

"Funny you should mention it. I just saw *Jean de Florette* for the first time. It's —"

"Oh, good God. Why can't I be wrong once in a while?"

Annie's blue eyes transmuted into dark slits of scornful sarcasm.

"Do you do anything to stimulate what I will generously term your intellect? Do you ever read?"

"Uh — no. It's kind of a sensitive subject. You see, Dr. Moreau hasn't completed my transformation yet. But someday . . ." Mike crossed his eyes, shoved an incident report in his mouth and chewed nosily.

"Books. Do you ever read books?"

MacDonnell spit the paper out on the desk. "Yes, Annie Wilson, I read books."

"What kind?"

"The kind with little black words in them — and those wonderful covers featuring hunky male models decked out like cross-dressing buccaneers waiting for a cabin boy to flog."

She tilted her head towards the ceiling. "Why do I bother?"

"Because I'm so fascinating?" His eyes wandered the white curve of her throat.

"Are you able to talk to me like a normal human being?"

"You consider yourself qualified to determine what's normal?"

"I know you're not. Now, what is your favorite book?" There was a stubborn set to her chin, a grim determination to outlast him.

"I like a lot of different things."

"Such as?"

"Oh, the usual. Steinbeck, Joyce, Hemingway . . . Beatrix Potter."

"You don't have one special book?"

"Of course I have a volume of *My Treasured Memories* in which I scribble all my girlish secrets before I go to bed at night. Other than that,

I'd have to say I liked a novel called *A Confederacy of Dunces* a lot. Made me laugh my ass off. I don't know if it's my favorite book, because that's kind of a silly thing to try and determine — especially since Camus' *The Stranger* made me laugh even more, though I don't think it was supposed to." He paused for a moment to let her appreciate his intellectual superiority, then with great and exaggerated reluctance, "Now, I suppose, you'll want me to ask what your —"

"Katherine Anne Porter."

"That's not a book, that's a writer. However, one of her works always comes to mind when I think about this place."

"I like all of her works," Annie continued, ignoring him. "When I was in junior high, I had to do a report on Porter, so on a whim, I wrote to her — and she wrote me back. It was so neat to get a letter from somebody famous. I still have it."

"So, you don't have a favorite book, you have a favorite note?"

"You don't even try to listen —"

"They say she was a lesbian. Preyed on young, budding virgins, mainly through written correspondence, there not being an internet and all."

"Oh, they do not."

"And they say she had a love-child by Bond — James Bond. They made it sleep in a basket of fruit till it was a toddler, which, when you think about it, seems rather apropos —"

"Shut up, will you? I was going to ask if I could borrow the book you mentioned."

"If I had a copy, you could have it, Annie. I stole one from a college library years ago, but lost it somewhere along the way. Jesus, I'm not sure if it's even still in print."

MacDonnell wore a mildly triumphant smile on his face. He loved provoking her, demanding her attention be riveted on him and him alone. It didn't matter if Annie found him funny or infuriating.

They talked some more about books and then breeds of dogs and places they would like to visit someday. The hours drifted kindly by. Finding a way to escape from the reality of their job, to make the shift pass quickly, was instinctive and paramount. Neither one of them spoke about the incident with Peter Holland. So many unhappy things occurred at Blythewood few could achieve — or at least maintain — a fever pitch notoriety. Even something as abhorrent as a staff sodomizing a student would invariably be displaced by some ugly new burlesque. No one was left unharmed by the poison yield of these ephemeral calamities; they simply failed to notice the damage being done. It was, in essence, cognitive irradiation, odorless, colorless, painless — and deadly to the soul.

The only antitoxin was trust in another, and often that trust, that faith, ripened into something even stronger.

36

MacDonnell stopped at a Newbury supermarket to buy a few groceries. He was coming around the head of an isle when an all too familiar voice hailed him.

"Mike!"

Bonnie Quirk's rattling shopping cart increased to ramming speed as it approached. MacDonnell had to step quickly out of the way to avoid a collision.

The clinician wailed, "What are you doing here?" Her makeup looked like the smeary reflection of stoplights on a rainy city street.

MacDonnell lifted a case of beer in mute testimony.

"Let me show you what I just bought," Quirk said gleefully. There were a number of bags in her grocery cart. She ripped one open. "I got these at Hot Rocks." Hot Rocks was an adult novelty store on Tyler Street. Quirk first held up a pair of grape-flavored, edible men's underwear in a thin cellophane wrapper, followed by a square box emblazoned with the colorful legend '*POCKET PUSSY.*' She leaned forward and leered, "More presents for *Daddy*. He'll get a real kick out of them. *Daddy* just loves joke gifts."

Since Bonnie Quirk was in her late forties, MacDonnell estimated her father must be in the neighborhood of seventy. The idea of a wrinkled old man prancing around in edible grape underwear — provided by his daughter — flourishing a 'Pocket Pussy' did something strange to the Blythewood supervisor's stomach.

"I have to pay for this beer," he said faintly.

"Wait a minute, wait a minute. I've got something else to show you." Quirk's hands stabbed into another bag, emerged with several small, multicolored foam balls. "These are Stress Balls for my therapy group," she explained. "When the boys get agitated, they can squeeze these instead of acting out. I picked them up over at New World Games. Aren't they a wonderful idea?"

MacDonnell was forced to agree. Since Bonnie Quirk's group was made up entirely of sex offenders, there was something strikingly appropriate in issuing them Stress Balls.

MacDonnell looked at her. "I have to run now, Bonnie. There was, uh, there was a volcanic eruption at my house tonight."

37

MacDonnell and Annie Wilson were walking back to the office after a routine inspection of Dorm One. September continued its unusually warm weather. The air was stale and humid. MacDonnell hated it. He longed for the autumn chill. Halfway to the main building, Annie stopped.

"Look at my legs," she demanded. She was wearing a pair of khaki shorts from L.L.Bean.

"Why?"

"Do they look all right in shorts? I think I'm starting to get spider veins on my thighs." She rolled up the hemmed cuff to afford him a better view.

"They're fine," MacDonnell pronounced curtly and resumed walking.

Annie caught up to him. "Do you mean it — or are you just being nice?"

MacDonnell, desperate to maintain a dispassionate dignity, looked her square in the eye. "They are fine. Perfect. Okay?"

Annie Wilson beamed.

38

2:30 pm.

On a Wednesday.

Magic time.

A release from the cage.

An invitation to drink —

With Annie Wilson.

Unfortunately, it was only 11:30 am and Annie was gone on a med run to the emergency room (one of the students had lodged the stem of a pen cap in the head of his penis) with Todd Robertson. Mike wasn't happy about it. He'd begun to intensely dislike Robertson. The young man was lazy, undependable, attractive, an ostentatious self-promoter, and, MacDonnell was sure of this, a secret coward. Most of all, he disliked Robertson because he incessantly flirted with Annie Wilson and she enjoyed it. Mike spent most of the time outside the office, frowning, smoking and waiting for the van to return.

The phone finally summoned him back into the building.

Wisps of smoke were still billowing from MacDonnell's flaring nostrils as his huge head barged in the office door — to catch Junior Monroe peeing in a foam cup on the desk.

Junior was a roly-poly teenager whose emotional and intellectual growth had been eternally arrested at the age of two. He had a jolly laugh, a perpetual grin splitting a round-apple face and a wicked delight in escaping from his team and pissing in cups, coffee mugs, glasses and open soda bottles; all in the infantile hope someone would make an awful mistake. In six years at Blythewood, Junior's victims had tasted his success a number of times.

"JR!" MacDonnell shouted. It was unfortunate he startled the boy in process. Urine splashed the entire surface of the desk, soaking telephone, log books and incident reports.

Junior's eyes ballooned and he exploded in gleeful laughter. Dripping instrument still in hand, the teenager dashed out of the office door hollering his abiding and nonsensical battle cry, "Gonna fuck mommy up. Gonna fuck mommy up."

Mike MacDonnell looked at the steaming puddle on his desk for a moment and then closed his eyes in mute despair. The phone continued to ring.

The mess forced the unhappy supervisor to summon one of the facilities more noxious employees: Gordy Burdick. Gordy, Blythewood's new head janitor, was a man who lurked around unexpected corners tidying up the debris of day-to-day existence at the school, and who always appeared to be physically listing to port as he carried out these menial pursuits. MacDonnell often wondered if there were some sort of optical illusion involved in this perception, or if Gordy's ungainly body actually did bend and twist slightly to the left. The janitor's personal appeal was further diminished by the fact he perpetually smelled of sweat and dirty underwear and caustic cleaning solutions. And permanent layers of grime were etched into his skin like dirt tattoos.

Worst of all, Gordy suffered an advanced form of oral dysentery which made MacDonnell dread these moments when he was forced to request the janitor's presence. Only the stench of urine compelled Mike to take such a desperate measure.

Gordy Burdick arrived with a cleaning rag, a bucket of filthy water that smelled worse than the piss, and a moronic grin anchoring the left side of his slack face.

"Hey, Mike. We haven' fun yet? What's new in the zoo?"

Burdick's greeting never varied from day-to-day, week-to-week, month-to-month and year-to-year. If he accosted Mike MacDonnell a dozen times in the course of a single day, those words were repeated verbatim and with an excruciating duplication of tone and inflection. This relentless, mind-boggling inanity made those twelve syllables a pack of yammering hounds which could chase the supervisor from one end of Blythewood to the other.

"Hey, Gordy. People up your way still walking backwards?" Mike deliberately avoided eye contact. "There's a bit of a mess here I need you to clean up."

Any reasonably sensitive person would have interpreted Mike's body language, and the thinly veiled contempt of his greeting, as clear indications he did not wish to engage in friendly banter. But Gordy Burdick was not a reasonably sensitive person. He was from Nottingham, a small city near the Vermont border, viciously rumored to have the highest rate of incest in New England. It was an old joke, in the surrounding towns, that asked, 'If a husband and wife in Nottingham get divorced, are they still brother and sister?' The janitor might well have been the product of some unnatural coupling between siblings, or even variant, antique species. His shambling gait suggested the clumsy struggle towards bipedalism of a hitherto unknown primate or early hominid. And bathing was clearly a foreign concept. His stiff, filthy hair seemed bent on mutating into a kind of greasy antler above his head.

Gordy Burdick plowed into the office, took one look at the desk and hee-hawed like a donkey, "Somebody tinkle-winkled all o'er your stuff."

"Yeah . . . I know."

"You want me to clean it up, right?"

MacDonnell's face had gone expressionless. "That's the general idea."

Burdick noisily tackled the urine spill, and then — much to Mike's misery — lingered to socialize.

"Hey, did I tell you about them loons livin' up on my street?" the janitor asked balefully.

MacDonnell slumped into his chair and stared at his drying desktop. He could not bear to look at the man.

"I said, did I tell you about them loons on my street," the janitor repeated forcefully. He could not — would not — be ignored.

An expression came over MacDonnell's face now, an expression which mingled seething annoyance and dread. "What was that?"

"Yeah, them loons, right?"

"You've got crazy people living on your street?"

"Naw, naw." Once again the braying laughter. "Loons. Them big birds."

"Birds?" MacDonnell forced himself to look at the man's face, at the wayward front teeth and the weathered skin covering the knobby (*empty?*) skull like an old, loose fitting baseball glove.

"Yeah. Got a nestin' pair of 'um up on my street."

MacDonnell longed to feel his hands around the janitor's throat. He could disinfect them later. "You have a nesting pair of loons living on a city street?"

"Yup. You can hear 'um at night, right. They make this weird call — and one time when my sweetie passed out in front a' The Pig's Pink Ear, I saw 'um walkin' down the street while I was tryin' to get her upin her feet."

"You saw loons strolling out of a bar?"

"I didn't say they was in the bar, least I didn't see 'um there. Nawww, you're jokin', right?"

Mike MacDonnell felt as if he'd been given the lead in some awful, country-fried Fellini film.

"Hey, speakin' uh jokes, I got one for ya. Wanna hear it?" Gordy asked.

NO I DON'T, YOU STUPID MOTHERFUCKER!

But a weak voice, "Go ahead, Gordy." Surrender to the inevitable. He'd hopelessly fallen into the clutches of Ming the Merciless Janitor. Why prolong the agony?

"Why is six afraid of seven?"

"Excuse me?"

"Why is six afraid of seven?" The moronic grin deepened.

"Uh, what?"

"Because seven *eight* nine. Get it?" Gordy Burdick's guffaw held the faintest hint of intellectual superiority. "It takes a while to figure it out, right? You have to *think* about it."

"Yeah, yeah you do." Mike wondered where he might find a bottle of Lysol. Maybe somewhere on the janitor's corpse?

"Hey, did I tell you about me and the girlfriend winnin' big at the Cart Mart employee picnic this summer? It's where my honey works, right? Damn, we musta hit every raffle and drawin' they had that day. We won five-hunnered in cash and two tickets to Australia."

"Fart Mart's giving away free trips to Australia?" Mike MacDonnell asked miserably.

"You bet. I talked to my supervisor and got me some time off before Turkey Day, right? That's when we're goin'. In November, right?"

"Have fun."

"Too bad we got to go in the winter, though."

"It'll be spring down under, Gordy."

"Huh?"

"Never mind. Be sure to pack heavy coats and boots."

"How about it, right? Well, I guess I better be headin' over to the school buildin'. The new housekeeper they hired last week, uh, Stanley Bainbridge? He ain't doin' the trick, right? Keeps complainin' he can't get everythin' done in the time I give him. Man, I can do the school buildin', Dorm Two, and help the cook with Sunday brunch in half the time it takes Stanley to clean the principal's office, right?"

An unpleasant image sprouted in MacDonnell's mind: Gordy Burdick dirty-elbow deep in a vat of tuna and mayonnaise merrily mixing away. The supervisor shivered.

"See you, Gordy. Have a nice vacation." So many weeks till Thanksgiving.

"Not if I see you first." Burdick exploded with laughter. He finally turned around and left the office — just in time to snare a hapless staff passing by the door. "Hey, Ted. We havin' fun yet? What's new in the zoo? I got a joke for you, right?"

MacDonnell breathed a sigh of relief.

Later, Annie got back and asked Mike where the incident reports were and why the phone smelled funny.

39

Business was generally slow on Wednesday afternoons at the Four Tables. It didn't start picking up until the Blythewood people began filtering in around three. Mike MacDonnell was first through the door today, and he exhausted the advantage nervously gulping beer and waiting for Annie Wilson.

He sat where he habitually sat now (where *they* habitually sat now), at the far end of the taproom, in a corner by a window. From there he could look down on the road and restlessly scan for the approach of her Subaru station wagon. No matter how many times she assured him that she would be stopping by for a drink, no matter how many times she reminded him there were a couple of quick errands to run before she could get there, relentless anxiety would plague him until she arrived. He had grown afraid of losing a chance to spend an afternoon with her; afraid some unforeseen and malevolent obstacle would leap into her path. For a man not yet thirty, MacDonnell was remarkably free of the illusion endless time and opportunity were his to spend at will. Every instant, with things and people that mattered to him, was counted and savored to the best of his ability and to the best circumstance would allow. He wasted many things in his life, but never those rare moments which come along for everyone, but which most everyone, sometimes, ignores or forgets. He was uncommon in this ability to grasp the significance of a seemingly ordinary excerpt of time. But it brought MacDonnell little contentment. To understand a moment is to understand how fleeting it is, how irretrievable, how soon it marches on to somewhere else — and on to an ending.

But still he craved them.

When he spotted her car, his heart picked up its pace. He kept his eyes tacked to the window, though, watching a white slice of cloud, the only one in the seamless sky, drift over the pretty Wessex houses and distant hills. It wasn't until he heard the groaning protest of heavy door springs and hinges from the Tables' entrance that he turned in his chair.

The first sight of Annie coming around the corner, long legs striding and ponytail swinging, brought an ache of pleasure to his body; pleasure in the way she walked, in the shine of her hair and the sea-color in her eyes. The bright afternoon light had seized her, made her shimmer like a mirage in his dark gaze.

"Took you long enough," he said mildly.

"Took me long enough? We left work half an hour ago."

He had nothing to say. Anticipation had turned thirty minutes into an eternity.

Annie ordered a bottle of dark beer and they sat and talked for a while, mostly about Blythewood and how glad they were another week's shift had come to an end. MacDonnell wasn't glad, but he dutifully seconded her opinion on the matter.

Annie finished her beer, quickly for her, and looked up at the clock behind the bar. "Mike? Why don't we go for a drive?"

"Hmmm?" He had a mouthful of suds.

"I don't know . . . it's a beautiful day and I don't want to sit around with a bunch of Blythewood people. And they're going to be here at any minute."

"Sure, let's go for a drive. We'll stop at a package store and buy some beer."

"Beck's Dark or St. Pauli Girl," she warned.

"Then you're paying half. That shit's expensive. Of course, so is a real St. Pauli Girl."

"Yeah, yeah. Let's go, Jamoke."

"*Jamoke*? Wow, you'd sound really cool if it was nineteen-fifty-six."

Annie got up from the table. "No smoking in my car."

"We can take mine."

"No. I'm driving. I'm not into reaching warp speeds this afternoon."

"You can drive my GTO."

She looked at him in surprise. "You never let anybody touch that car, let alone drive it."

"I was only kidding."

But he hadn't been.

Hours later, they sat in her car at the crest of Shaker Mountain, looking up at a sky on fire.

"God, what a beautiful view," Annie said.

"Yes it is," he agreed, but he wasn't looking at the sunset or the deep blue valley below.

"Mike?"

"What?"

A long pause. "Nothing . . ."

MacDonnell put his bottle of beer between his knees and lit a Newport — only to watch the cigarette take wing on a shower of sparks and fly out the window.

"I said no smoking."

"Thanks," Mike said. "Now I've got a hot ash in my eye, and beer all over my lap. It looks like I pissed myself."

"Would you like me to rush you to the emergency room?"

"Sarcasm doesn't suit you very well," he said, rubbing his eye.

"And being a crybaby doesn't suit you."

MacDonnell sighed. "Well, you've discovered my secret. I'm nothing but a big, fat sissy."

Annie Wilson laughed. Together, they watched the sun fail and night come on.

40

Warren Zevon was singing about drinking up all the salty margaritas in Los Angeles as the GTO turned off the highway and onto Bly Hollow road. Pavement quickly gave way to gravel, and houses to fortress clusters of trees brushed by sunlight and the surging colors of autumn. Mike MacDonnell slowed the Pontiac and turned up the stereo. He was angry — angry with Michelle. He'd asked for sex — bluntly but not rudely, not like a pissed-off redneck wife-beater — and (as was usual now) been refused.

"Come on, baby, please. I'm not a priest. I didn't take a vow of celibacy — and neither did you. I need to get laid. It's been fucking months. You know, the Catholic Church condones sex for married couples?"

"Stop that talk!" she had cried, as if he were somehow threatening the foundations of Mother Church — or at least the foundations of her untidy sanity.

A fatal attempt at humor followed next, though looking back on it, Mike wasn't sure if he'd intended to be funny at all.

"I bet if I had a pussy, you'd give me some more."

Michelle slapped him so hard, he'd actually seen black spots dancing in front of his eyes. He'd been punched by grown men to less effect. MacDonnell was forced to smile as he turned off the road and onto a grassy lane cutting through the wall of maple and pine and tangled underbrush. At least he had gotten some kind of physical contact from her.

The lane was broad enough and smooth enough for a car to safely pass, and it brought Mike to a bowl-shaped clearing, an oasis of little stones and scrub grass, wide as a fair-sized parking lot. This was his favorite refuge when he wanted to be by himself, to think — or drink. He found it long ago during a back road ramble. At first, MacDonnell thought the place must be a building site, but when no structure ever appeared, he realized there had to be another answer. It came one spring day as he was idly exploring the edges of the clearing and happened upon bits of disintegrating paper targets nailed to tree trunks, coffee cans blossoming with rusty holes, clay pigeons, whole and shattered, spent cartridges and beer cans. A private shooting range was not an unknown use of open land in a place like Cornwall. Everyone owned a gun of some kind and hunting held the social imperative and appeal golf enjoyed in more upscale communities. So far, MacDonnell had never interrupted anyone's target practice, and no one had ever disturbed his solitary ruminations. The land wasn't posted, and he felt comfortable coming here whenever he chose to.

Mike opened both car doors so he could hear the stereo and sat on the hood, drinking beer, two six-packs worth. The latest emotional badminton match with Michelle hadn't started out about sex at all, now that he thought about it. She had interned herself on the living room couch for the day, complaining of a mild cold. Along about noon, a demand for a cup of tea was issued forth.

"Where's my sandwich?" she had asked when he brought the tea.

"You didn't ask for a sandwich," he had replied.

"If you really loved me, you would have known I wanted a sandwich, too."

Thus, forced into the untenable position of defending his mind reading skills, Mike MacDonnell had simply chosen the only escape route open to him: complain about their sex life. There hadn't been any real glandular interest in getting squirmy with his snot-nosed gal and her thinking disorder. It was a handy excuse to start a fight and get away.

MacDonnell tossed a beer bottle into the woods. It joined several years worth of glass and aluminum colleagues.

Ah, well, what was a poor boy to do?

"Not much," Mike said aloud to the birds sweeping in and out of the tree tops.

He cracked another beer. Slowly his mood changed. Anxiety and resentment gave way to contentment. It had something to do with the alcohol, and the music rumbling from the big car speakers, and something to do with being alone, isolated from the world. Mike took notice of a lovely, indescribable quality which seemed to filled the air. It might be no more than an illusion, a kind of self-defense mechanism, but it was comforting. Nothing was really that bad; nothing was hopeless or lost. The answers were all here, somewhere close. He would find them in due time.

MacDonnell took a deep breath. His eyes found another world, just beneath the visible one, where the present mingled seamlessly with the past and waking dreams were not eviscerated by reality.

The apparition of Annie Wilson waited there.

For a while that afternoon, Mike MacDonnell felt all right.

41

MacDonnell had finished his fifth cup of coffee and his fifteenth cigarette of the day when the phone jangled on the office desk. The ring did not end with the distinctive, electronic burp of an in-house call. This was a communication from the real world, out where the sun shone.

MacDonnell picked it up, spoke briefly and then held out the phone to Annie. "It's for you. Somebody named Doug?"

Annie Wilson grabbed the handset. "Doug! How are you?" A coy enthusiasm lifted her voice like helium.

MacDonnell didn't try fighting a frown.

A new lover.

How many did that make?

He settled back into his chair like a hippo drifting down into the silt of a dirty riverbed.

Just before dinner time, MacDonnell found Annie Wilson sitting in the lounge with a student in her lap. Zack White, profoundly retarded and smiling like the vacant-eyed, golden-haired cherub he so closely resembled, had his arm around her shoulder. Annie had a soft spot for the boy and essentially treated him like an infant, in spite of the fact he had a long, undeniably prehensile tongue which could — and did — insert a full inch into either nostril. And when this serpentine appendage was not tickling his sinus, a stubby finger, buried to the second knuckle, did. MacDonnell disapproved of her willingness to have casual contact with the little booger-hound — almost as much as he disapproved of her brand-new, less than casual contact with *Doug*.

MacDonnell stood glaring as Zack White began coughing out a tuneless, staccato rendition of the *Flintstones* theme song. The boy yelped badly garbled lyrics, periodically licked his hands like a cat with fish oil on its paws, violently jerked his head back and forth, and — of course — alternated tongue and finger in his nasal cavities. Annie Wilson smiled indulgently.

Mike MacDonnell shook his head in disgust, said, "Don't ever talk to me about chewing somebody else's gum."

42

"We need another bottle," Rick Pasinetti rumbled. He screwed the cap on the empty pint in his hand and tossed it into the backseat of the car.

"We'll stop at a package store," MacDonnell said, eyes on the road ahead. Flakes of snow fled before the Impala's headlights. Cold had come with October.

"There ain't a package store in Newbury open at this hour."

"We'll find something. It isn't that late."

MacDonnell turned the Chevy onto Hungerford Street.

"Didn't you tell me Greg O'Brien lives around here?"

Pasinetti nodded. "Yeah, right up there on the left. See the camper?"

The car slowed to a crawl and pulled into the driveway of a modest ranch. The vehicle stopped a few feet from an old tow-along, dry-docked on the front lawn. Weeds and long grass had swallowed the camper's tires and were crawling up its aluminum sides.

"No, dogballs," Pasinetti protested. "I don't wanna go in there. Look at the cars. His nest of blood suckers are here."

"Didn't you say he always has a shitload of booze? Let's see if he'll give us a bottle."

"I'm not goin' in."

"I'll take care of it." MacDonnell got out of the car and went up a crude set of concrete steps to the camper door. He entered without knocking.

O'Brien and four middle-aged men, all stewed, jammed the tiny interior.

"Mike!" O'Brien, stuffed into the little dining area booth, greeted him with boozy cheer. "What are you doin' here, man? Wanna drink?" He held up a bottle of good vodka. "If this don't suit you, take your pick." He used the vodka to point at an open storage cabinet built into the wall. There were at least a dozen bottles of liquor on its shelves, all different brands, all expensive.

Side stepping, MacDonnell worked his way through the little knot of bodies and took a quart of Old Grand-Dad down from the shelf. He opened it, took a swig and then stood there, expressionless, staring at the other men. O'Brien and friends went back to their previous diversions and paid him no attention.

Rick had not been wrong. They were a sorry lot, yapping and farting at each other like old, befuddled dogs.

The bottle of Old Grand-Dad rose and fell half a dozen times, before:

"Have any of you ladies ever kissed a girl?" MacDonnell's voice was loud, raw, demanding.

The other men stopped talking and looked at him.

"I said, have any of you ladies ever kissed a girl? It's a simple question."

No response. Dead silence.

"I didn't think so." MacDonnell casually took another swig. "You four. . ." He waved the bottle at O'Brien's friends. "Get the fuck out."

This brought a smattering of drunken, bewildered protest.

"I'm not going to repeat myself. Get out — ***right-the-fuck now!***"

MacDonnell took a sudden step forward as if he were preparing to charge.

O'Brien's cronies fell over each other getting out of the camper.

"What the hell was that?" Greg asked, but he was laughing in his thick, rasping way. He squeezed himself out of the booth, intending to close the camper door. He didn't hear the bottle of Old Grand-Dad hit the floor with a thud, didn't see MacDonnell moving. "Shit, it's okay. After awhile, those guys get on my — "

MacDonnell's open hand cracked across his face with tremendous force. Dull shock ballooned O'Brien's fat face.

Another slap, harder. And another. And another. O'Brien's legs started to buckle. A fifth strike, loud as a rifle shot. O'Brien went down on his knees, blood leaking from his nose, his eyes glassy.

MacDonnell's red and swollen hand lifted again, but O'Brien groaned and slumped over on his side.

That was enough.

A wallet was sitting on the little dining table. MacDonnell emptied it of cash, then stepped over O'Brien and went to the liquor cabinet. He grabbed as many bottles as he could carry and went out to the car.

Pasinetti was standing next to the Impala, smoking a cigarette.

"What the fuck is this?" he asked when he saw the load in MacDonnell's arms. "Greg havin' a fire sale?"

"The sow's gone on the wagon. Open the door, will you? I've got my hands full."

As they pulled out of the driveway, Pasinetti asked, "What happened in there? Why did the children of the night leave so fast?"

Mike MacDonnell shrugged and hit the gas. "Where to now, Mr. Peabody?"

Rick Pasinetti grinned. "My chateau, Sherman."

43

Mike sat in the office, staring at a memo on his desk. He yawned. The memo said something about a mandatory in-service to be held at the Wessex Library on the first Thursday in November. He crumpled the paper and tossed it in the garbage pail next to his desk. He would not be attending any administrative mind-control sessions on his day off.

MacDonnell yawned again and glanced at the clock. It was half past one. Three and a half hours left on shift. A nap would be nice right about now. Too bad administration frowned at such harmless little siestas; not that Rumgay's disapproval would unduly influence Mike MacDonnell.

He yawned a third time. This time is eyes teared up and his vision blurred. When it cleared again, Kevin Marshall had materialized in front of the desk. Mike hadn't heard him enter the office.

"Are we keeping you up?" Kevin Marshall asked.

"Do we always refer to ourselves in the imperial plural?" Mike stretched lazily in his chair.

"Yes. When it's me and my King Johnson." Kevin pulled a chair up to the desk. "Mike, you're a bitch."

"I'm bored."

"By a different nancy-boy every night."

"You seem to spend an inordinate amount of time worrying about homosexual congress."

"Don't bore me with politics, Mike. Where's Annie?"

MacDonnell shrugged, didn't say anything.

"You two having a spat?"

"Yeah, Kevin, we're having a spat," Mike admitted sarcastically. "God, you're insightful."

"She hasn't been going out much lately."

"New boyfriend."

Kevin was quiet for a moment. "That's too bad."

"None of my business."

"So, are we going out this afternoon or what?"

"Is it Wednesday? Is it the last day of my shift?"

"I heard you were doing some OT."

"Only till five. The crew has my permission to assemble at the Four Tables."

"Aye, aye, Ahab." Kevin snapped off a salute. "And may I lick your boots and wipe your poopy behind?"

"You are a sick boy."

Anyone listening to their relentlessly idiosyncratic conversations would most likely have extended the observation to include both men.

The telephone bleated on the desk. The odd, syncopated rhythm indicated it was a campus call.

MacDonnell slapped the receiver against his ear. "Supervisor . . ."

He listened to a frantic voice on the other end for a moment and then said, "I'll be right there." He hung up the phone and said to Kevin, "There's a problem at the school building. Team Six."

Kevin hooked his thumbs in his belt loops and expanded his chest. "I suppose you'll want me to handle it?"

"Maybe when you're older, half-pint."

"You're a bitch, Mike."

"Finish your break. I'll call if I need you."

When MacDonnell arrived at the school building, everything seemed quite normal. He walked down the long polished corridor, past cluttered classrooms filled with bored students staring numbly at the tops of graffiti embroidered desks; past a few teachers attempting the herculean task of educating the unwilling, past the rest of the stalwart faculty who, out of frustration or natural indolence, made no effort at all and allowed wall-mounted television sets to occupy their charges. By all appearances, it was an average school day at Blythewood.

Mike came to the Team 6 door. There was no catastrophic symphony issuing from inside, no rivers of gore flowing over the threshold.

He opened the door and entered the classroom.

Fifteen students and two staff were lined up against a wall, like condemned prisoners waiting to be shot. A dirty finger of fear smeared every face.

The source of all this consternation was sitting on the floor behind a picket of rearranged desks.

Carlos Rivera was sixteen, skinny as a hare and unequivocally as mad as the March variety of the species. This madness usually took a benign, even amusing form; such as the showery April afternoon he slithered around campus in a blond Raggedy Ann wig trying to sell mud pies to staff and students alike. From time to time, however, he would scatter all his marbles on the floor.

This appeared to be such an occasion.

Carlos was holding a long carving knife, undoubtedly stolen from the kitchen, and ranting on about the devil and human sacrifice.

MacDonnell considered the performance a bit theatrical, but gave him full marks for originality. Carlos Rivera had inaugurated Satan worship at Blythewood.

MacDonnell didn't hesitate. He issued no commands, made no attempt at counseling, tendered no flatulent promise of reward should Carlos just put down that darn pointy thing.

Desks flew in every direction as the supervisor violently breached Carlos Rivera's improvised fortress.

MacDonnell's adrenalin was kicking a little, the kid had a knife, but mostly this was done for show. Any excitement he exhibited was generally calculated for effect alone; a kind of psychological suppressing fire meant to intimidate.

Carlos leapt to his feet, holding the knife out in front of him, eyes white at the approach of the juggernaut. He made a wild lunge, but in the process lost his grip on the knife. It fell harmlessly to the floor.

The next thing to fall harmlessly to the floor was Carlos Rivera, face first, carrying Mike MacDonnell on his back.

There was no further struggle. It was simply impossible.

The entire incident took a few seconds. The ensuing ritual to cast out Carlos' demons, only a few seconds more.

"Do you still worship the devil, Carlos — and think he's just the bestest?" Mike inquired with polite interest.

"No, no! I can't breathe!" came the carpet-muffled reply.

"Will you ever worship the devil again?" MacDonnell continued in the same polite, almost diffident tone.

"Nooooo," Carlos wailed, faintly.

"Then you are absolved, my son. Go and sin no more."

Kevin Marshall claimed Mike MacDonnell's style borrowed freely from both Father Flanagan and Genghis Khan. The supervisor rather fancied the image and did his best to live up to the rigorous standards it mandated.

MacDonnell kept Rivera in full restraint for ten minutes. When he was convinced the student was beyond further violent behavior, he began to gradually relinquish his hold. Eventually, Carlos was allowed to self-restrain on the floor. MacDonnell warned him not to twitch a single scrawny muscle. Carlos stayed limp.

MacDonnell got up from the floor, picked up the knife and strolled over to an open window. He lit a cigarette and causally puffed at it, but his eyes never left Carlos Rivera's prone form. The teacher thanked him profusely for his assistance. Mike asked her to open page Kevin Marshall and have him come to the schoolhouse.

Annie Wilson arrived with Kevin. MacDonnell told them about the impromptu exorcism.

Annie asked, unexpectedly, "Did you hurt him?"

The question, the cold accusatory tone in her voice, took MacDonnell back for a moment.

"Not as much as I wanted to," he said with more uncertainty than sarcasm. He handed her the knife. "Please take this back to the kitchen and have a little chat with them? Kevin? If you will, take Carlos to the dorm and stick him in his room for twenty-four."

"No problem, Mikey," Marshall answered with a half smile and eyebrows raised in an expression of what-is-going-on-with-you-two.

MacDonnell looked at Annie, asked, "Can I have a word with you?"

"No," she said bluntly and handed him back the kitchen knife. "If you're not going to escort Carlos to his room with Kevin, then I will."

Left with nothing to say, MacDonnell lit another Newport, dropped an elbow on the window sill and watched them go. He glanced over at the teacher. She wasn't bad looking. Tall, nice legs. A little older than he preferred, but hell, she liked him at the moment. That was something.

MacDonnell squibbed the cigarette out the window, waved to the students (one kid returned a middle finger under the desk), and headed out. As he was passing down the hall, a wild figure flew out of the staff bathroom to block his path.

"Is he gone? Is he gone?" Brenda Cormier's grating voice teetered one step away from hysteria. She was the staff who fled the classroom and notified MacDonnell of Rivera's little escapade. Apparently she'd been in hiding ever since.

Cormier was short, dumpy and cockeyed. Her tangled nest of dyed, witch-black hair, and the odd assortment of gypsy dancing girl garments she wore, had not seen a good wash in a good long while. MacDonnell recalled something about her having an infatuation for Rick, once upon a time. He made a grievous error by asking her if she was all right. It was nothing more than the polite inquiry good supervisory form demanded— to Brenda Cormier, however, it was a plea to manifest the arid desolation of her mind.

"I'm okay, okay," she twittered, jerking her limbs like an articulated wooden puppet. "Well … actually, I'm not okay. I'm not okay at all."

MacDonnell could readily second that opinion.

She hissed and said "I don't know if I can work with Satanists."

"Huh? The kid's just torqued in the head, Brenda."

"What if he's in a cult?" Tears came into Cormier's eyes. "Satanists killed my poor Crybaby when I was living in Bennington." Her voice dropped to a conspiratorial whisper. "They cut off her tail and hung her from my mail box and painted a devil sign."

MacDonnell made the cautious assumption Crybaby was a pet of some variety and not some monstrous, nearly human offspring Cormier produced during her breeding period.

"You know what, Brenda? Give the FBI a call. You know the x-files really exist? I'm sure they'd love to hear from you."

Cormier nodded slowly, seriously. "I've contacted them before. It was right after my first husband, Dion, was abducted by aliens. They took him for three days. When he got back, he had marks all over his back and chest and these awful bruises on his neck where they took skin samples. Even his penis was all swollen and raw from some machine they put on it, and …"

Cormier began to weave a lengthy tale of extraterrestrial date-rape. It tightened MacDonnell's grip on the knife in his hand. Luckily, an open page requested his presence in the soups office.

"Sorry, Brenda. Duty calls."

44

"Now what are you trying to poison me with, Donatello?" Rick Pasinetti asked.

"Bourbon. The distributor gave me a deal on it. It's somethin' new, though the label says it's one of the oldest brands in Kentucky."

Pasinetti emptied the shot glass in front of him and made an awful face. "What is it made from? Gorilla shit?" He rubbed a hairy wrist across his wet mouth. "Give me another."

The bartender filled the shot glass again and watched Pasinetti toss it back.

"Well?"

"Tell your distributor more snake heads and gunpowder, less kerosene."

The bartender poured a shot and drank it himself. "That's ... that's nasty."

"It's fucking foul, is what it is. I fell headfirst into a septic tank once and it didn't taste this bad."

"Want another? It's on the house."

"Why not," Pasinetti said. "Hey, I met a relative of yours, an uncle, the other day."

The bartender had a fair idea of what was coming.

"Yeah," Rick continued. " His name was Lorenzo DeEnema. We got to talking and he claimed you would blow a rat for a dollar. Said you'd been that way since you was a boy."

The bartender began shaking his head.

"Don't worry. I defended your honor. I called him a liar and told him I know for a fact you don't charge a dime."

Donatello picked his head up when Mike MacDonnell sat down at Rick's side.

"Beer and a shot?" the bartender asked.

"You know me better than my wife," MacDonnell replied.

"About time you showed up, Mackerel. Donatello was starting to tell me his life story and it ain't a pretty tale." Pasinetti poked a Camel in his mouth. "And don't let the dirty bastard give you the bourbon. It could burn through the armor plating on a Tiger tank." He lit the cigarette. "I hear Terry joined the Army?"

"Yeah."

"Good luck to her."

"She wants me to write her."

"That won't happen."

"Probably not."

Rick Pasinetti nodded patiently. "Don't worry about it, Cousin Mongo. I've never trusted a man who writes letters. Hey, Donatello? Do you mind if I smoke a blunt in here later on?"

"What do you think?" the bartender growled.

"Anyone ever notice you smell like a used condom?"

Donatello splashed tonic into a glass of ice and vodka, brought it to Pasinetti. "No, they ain't," the bartender said. "Anybody ever notice you look like one?"

"Which reminds me," Mike said to Pasinetti. "I talked to an old girlfriend of yours the other day."

"I've never had a girlfriend, dogboy — just encounters of the third kind."

"This encounter is named Brenda."

"That fucking lunatic?"

"She's looking pretty good. Lost a lot of weight," MacDonnell lied.

"I don't care if she weighs a hundred pounds and ninety of it tit. She's got a face like a pin worm crawling out a cat's asshole. And she is a sick, sick unit."

"She told me she still loves your hairy ass," MacDonnell lied again.

"Someone should have locked that broad up by now," Pasinetti said. "Jesus Gawd. She made my life miserable for months. Stalked me like a panther in and out of Blythewood. Kept trying to get me in the rack. I finally tells her, 'Honey, you're too much woman for me. You'd kill me in bed.' She looks at me, blinks twice, and then goes absolutely ape-shit berserk. They were paving the driveway at Blythewood then, and she runs over to a backhoe and beats her head against it till she starts to bleed — all the while screaming my name at the top of her lungs."

"I thought you might be getting a little lonely by now."

"I'd rather date a rat with an abscess."

"No plans for a steady relationship . . . with a human female?"

"Ohhh, Mac." A comically tortured expression coiled Pasinetti's features in a fisherman's knot. "I love getting laid, but I have never been any damn good at relationships, if such things exist. Either the women end up hating my guts, or I ends up hating theirs." Rick grinned. "I'm too much the swine."

"Maybe you never found the right girl?"

"Mac, some men never find the right girl because they're not the right man. Some people are meant to be alone. I'm one of them." He belched and pounded his chest like an ape. "So, how's everything going at the Wood? How are you getting along with your partner there, Annie Oakley?"

"Good, good. No problem."

"Really? A top-shelf woman like her? I figured she'd wanna poison you by now."

"Maybe she does." Mike rubbed his eyes with the palm of his hand. "This afternoon Annie told me she's taking a month off work to go to Hawaii with her boyfriend."

"Hawaii? Good Gawd. That'll cost a pretty penny. Her boyfriend must have the Bank of America between his legs. Rich people." Rick snorted. "You know where I'd go? Fort Ticonderoga up on Lake George. The old man used to take us there every year when I was a kid. Beautiful country. And the history? The French and Indian War? Gawd, it's always fascinated me. You know, during the Revolution the Continentals planned the assault on Fort Ti right here in Newbury. At a tavern, of course. There's still a patch of old cobblestone, over by the library, where the tavern stood."

MacDonnell nodded, not really listening. All he could think about was Annie spending four weeks in paradise with her boyfriend.

Pasinetti continued, "Well, anyway, there's a break for you. You get to fly solo for a month, and not have to put up with any crap from Miss Manners."

"Lucky me."

"Yeah. Too bad about Terry, though. She was salt of the earth, Mac. Salt of the earth." Pasinetti raised his glass, drained it. "I'm goin' out back and smoke a joint. Wanna come?"

45

Mike MacDonnell was miserable for the entire month Annie was gone. He worried about her flying around in airplanes, worried about her getting into trouble with strange people in strange places — worried about all the time she was spending alone with Doug.

Mike's discontent manifested itself in frequent bouts of bad temper, especially at home. One evening he was attempting to extract ice cubes from a cheap plastic tray. Michelle had asked him for a glass of Coca Cola. His anger began to rise as each time he loosened a few and turned the tray over in his hand, more cubes would fall in the sink or on the floor than in his waiting palm.

Frustration finally detonated a powder keg.

"You stupid-fucking-motherfucking-dirty-bastards!"

The plastic tray was smashed into pieces and the remaining ice cubes scattered like tiny comets across the kitchen — just as Michelle entered, looking for her soft drink.

"What's going on?"

"Not a fucking thing!" her husband yelled.

"I'm not going to clean up this mess!"

"I didn't ask you to." Mike grabbed a broom and dust pan from beside the refrigerator. Still swearing under his breath, he swept up the plastic fragments and chunks of ice and contemptuously dumped them in the wastebasket. "There you dirty fucks."

"Now get one of the spare ice cube trays down from the cupboard, fill it up and put it in the freezer," his wife ordered with equal contempt.

Mike snapped the dust pan onto the handle of the broom and whipped it in the direction of the refrigerator. The flying implements didn't come close to Michelle, but she gasped loudly and took an exaggerated step backwards. MacDonnell ignored her and stalked over to the other side of the kitchen. He ripped open a cabinet — and struck himself in the temple with the edge of the cabinet door.

Screaming, inarticulate rage accompanied the door being torn from its hinges. Michelle watched in horror as he smashed the wooden panel over his knee. She opened her mouth to shout something at him, saw the fury on his face, and wisely decided to retreat from the room. She would wait until the volcano cooled before delivering holy retribution.

In those now quiet moments before his crucifixion, Mike basked in an immense sense of satisfaction. He knew it wasn't entirely rational to believe he'd succeeded in thwarting the nefarious designs of a warped ice cube tray and a flimsy cabinet door. But at such times, when his anger roamed free and unfettered, he found it impossible not to assign malicious intent to inanimate objects which refused to do his bidding.

To make matters worse that month, Arlene O'Connor insisted he attend the in-service training he was so determined to avoid.

"Arlene, I don't want to go."

"Honey?" she asked. "Is that the best you can do?"

"Arlene, it's the best I've got. Wild horses couldn't drag me to that shit shoveling festival."

"You're bad, Mac." Arlene O'Connor smiled. "You're going anyway. Give me a cigarette, honey." She was, as always, in the midst of trying to quit smoking. They were sitting in her office on the second floor of the main building, but she flouted the no-smoking policy whenever it suited her. It was one of the reasons Mike liked her so much.

"Bill wants everyone, who isn't working, to go. He's on his high horse again," Arlene said.

Rumgay had recently been taken by the notion of 'The Blythewood Family': a mythic fraternity of happy-go-lucky staff presided over by the wise and benevolent administrators. Mike thought this feudal utopia had a cultish flavor to it, and often wondered if the program director might not feel right at home barricaded in an electrified compound, handing out the unsweetened Kool-Aid to a grinning, vacant-eyed flock of devotees in those last moments before the FBI assault teams breached the outer perimeter.

Mike MacDonnell believed a job was a job. It should never be the defining aspect of someone's life; at least not by official employment policy.

"By the way, honey," Arlene said. "You're going to be conducting job interviews for your shift till Annie gets back."

"Oh, joy."

It had become a horribly protracted process to fill openings. The interview was actually the simple part, to be followed by endless reference checks, haggling over salary, in-service training to prepare the victim; and finally, a two week on-campus observation period. The end product was a badly confused, underpaid lump of cannon fodder who might last six months if he/she (and sometimes *it*) proved hardy enough to bear the strain.

Arlene O'Connor dropped a cigarette butt in a cup of water.

"There's one coming up next Wednesday. His name is Timmons Wainwright."

"Can't you do the interviews, Arlene?"

"No time, honey. I've got payroll and everything else."

"Is that the best *you* can do?" MacDonnell asked.

"Pretend I have confidence in your ability to smell shit before you step in it."

"Stop. You're making me blush."

Arlene handed him an application folder.

MacDonnell glanced at it briefly. "Our man Timmons is fifty-six."

"So? I'm forty-nine."

"You're not expected to do restraints."

"No one is while you're around, honey."

"I'm not always around."

"Do the interview. If he stinks, dump him . . . nicely."

"I am a paragon of tact and sensitivity."

"Sure you are, honey."

MacDonnell tucked the folder under his arm and stood up.

"I must have something to do."

"See ya at the in-service, honey," Arlene said pointedly.

Thursday, on the way to the in-service, MacDonnell got a speeding ticket.

He'd put the GTO in the garage for the winter and was driving his wife's Toyota. Going too fast in the old Corolla was a feat he did not consider possible, until the cherry-poppers blossomed in his rearview mirror.

"Where you going in such a hurry?" the Highway Patrol deputy asked in his best officious, little-prick voice.

"I'm late for a very important date."

"Well, you're gonna be even a little bit later than that." For no good reason, the deputy called for two backup cruisers.

Mike MacDonnell held his mouth and forced himself to be civil, even when one of the newly arrived deputies asked if he had any drugs or weapons to declare. MacDonnell stared at the man for a moment, then answered, "Not today, officer."

The first deputy made a great and detailed search of the car while his fellow Stetson Hats looked on admiringly. Their only apparent regret, in the end, was not finding some excuse for having the Toyota towed away.

MacDonnell fumed over this incident for the rest of the drive into Wessex. In his mind he kept picturing the cop's chipper sneer as he slipped the yellow ticket through the window. It enraged MacDonnell when certain individuals, bereft of the common sense necessary to unzip before urination, concluded a gun and a badge elevated them above the general run of humanity. He also hated being forced, in essence, to grovel before men whose intrinsic function was to manufacture revenue for the state and keep the poor away from the rich.

MacDonnell's sour mood would not be lightened upon arriving at the Wessex Library. There were no available parking spaces within a five block radius.

This was a goddamned day off to remember.

MacDonnell was wiping hangover sweat from his face when he stomped into the library. A black scowl remained undisturbed, in fact deepened, as he followed hand printed signs to a second floor conference room.

Inside, assembled from throughout the Northeast, were the lees and dregs of the human service field, including a full bowl of Blythewood drippings. The in-service was conducted by Alan Towle-Twing, Ed.D., L.C.S.W., and his wife, Harmony Towle-Twing, Ed.D., M.S.W. They were professional lecturers, steeped in the inane arcana of the human service field, who held seminars wherever a certified bank check was waved under their noses. A facility or institution, in this case Blythewood, would sponsor a date and location, and interested parties from all over would then register to attend — at a hefty fee. The happy couple made a nice living without the burden of producing measurable results.

This particular in-service, as the sandwich board outside the entrance to the conference room proclaimed, bore the ghastly title *The Tao of Child Care: A guide to understanding the client through a journey of self-exploration.* Mike was vaguely disappointed cyanide capsules were not provided at the door. He found a seat by himself in the back and kept his head down. He didn't want to see or be seen by anybody, least of all by the presenters or trainers or facilitators or whatever the fuck they called themselves.

When these two latter-day vaudevillians commenced their act, MacDonnell commenced covering the backs of mimeographed handouts with sexually explicit doodles of Harmony Towle-Twing encountering a horny rhino on the savanna. He wasn't much of an artist, but it kept his mind off everything being said.

The day dragged on and Alan joined his wife in a three-way, which very much satisfied the rhino. Egrets swooped overhead, shitting on everyone.

At the lunch break, and much to his surprise, MacDonnell discovered Kevin Marshall was also in attendance.

"I didn't know you were here?" MacDonnell said.

"I wish I wasn't. This is beyond dull."

"Wanna go for a drink afterwards?"

"I wish I had a dozen now," Kevin said.

MacDonnell stuck a cigarette in his mouth and lit it. He was standing under a *No Smoking* sign.

"Got a speeding ticket on the way in this morning — in the Toyota. I'm starting to dislike authority figures in all their many guises."

"I don't think they care much for you either. How many times does this make now?"

"That I've been molested by the Boys in Blue?" MacDonnell asked. "Oh, about a baker's dozen over the last six or seven years. Once they nabbed me for unloading groceries in my driveway. I guess they thought I was engaged in a felony forced delivery of a foodstuff."

The afternoon session got underway with Alan and Harmony paying lengthy tribute to their own superior insight and experience. Everyone in the room, excepting two Blythewood staff, offered enthusiastic homage to the couple. From childcare workers to clinicians, nurses to administrators, many in the human service army were attracted to bright and shiny objects, celebrations of the superficial and absurdly paradoxical.

All skepticism abandon, ye who enter in.

And more than a few filled their own interior vacancies with a subtle arrogance verging on self-righteous malevolence.

Itinerant peddlers, like the Towle-Twings, were elevated to the rank of spiritual advisers, high priests and priestesses, slowly stripping away layers of common sense and leaving behind the insectile buzz of New Age dogma — dogma that changed with each fresh issue of *Social Worker Today* and *Healing Crystals Quarterly*.

At one point, Alan Towle-Twing raised his hands in benediction, drew a long dramatic breath and said, "The Tao of child care. For those of you unfamiliar with the concept of Tao, let me explain. Tao is the unknowable source, and guiding principle, behind all of existence. If you don't understand the value of the vase is in its emptiness . . ." He paused to allow the significance of his words to saturate the audience. "I promise you will, by the time I'm done."

A collective, orgasmic sigh leaked into the air.

Mr. and Mrs. Skywalker followed with examples of badly represented oriental philosophy, spouted against a background of synthesized bamboo flutes, zithers and microprocessed sitars twanging from a portable CD player. Somewhere along the way, this anti-Confucian confusion made an ungainly segue into Jung's theory on introversion, extroversion, and the eight personality orientations. This last part of the in-service suggested to MacDonnell a kind of bland psychological astrology, generalized and imprecise by design, relying on the willful participation and belief of the subject to achieve satisfactory results. There was a multiple-choice test to take (MacDonnell checked every box on the sheet) and a discussion of what it all meant.

Not much.

By the end of the seminar, Mike MacDonnell was left wondering how anyone in the room could summon the discipline of language and thought necessary to order a cup of coffee at a doughnut shop.

He met Kevin Marshall on the sidewalk outside the library, and shaking his head, said, "Arlene O'Connor made me come to this damn thing."

"The value of the childcare worker's head is in its emptiness," Kevin remarked.

"I need to find a public bathroom. I'll be right back."

Kevin waited for some time, and when MacDonnell did not return, he went looking for him.

The Wessex police station, a small, two story brick building, was right around the corner from the library, and it was here he found Mike, standing by the open driver door of a parked police cruiser.

"What are you doing, bitch?"

MacDonnell turned only his head, smiled serenely and continued pissing in the front seat of the empty vehicle.

"Mike! Get the fuck out of there before a cop comes out!"

"I needed a public bathroom, and I found one." MacDonnell zipped his fly and strolled casually back to Kevin. "Let's get those dozen drinks."

46

MacDonnell was waiting in his office for Timmons Wainwright to appear for the interview. Unfortunately, Gordy Burdick stuck his head through the open door first. The janitor offered his routine salutation, which sent shivers of ecstatic fury rippling over the surface of Mike's skin. Burdick's rasping voice reminded the supervisor of a cat trying to spit up a half-digested lovebird.

The janitor's eyes narrowed as he spied a smudge on the window of the outer door.

"Wet Willies," Burdick proclaimed in angry triumph. A spray bottle was flourished like a TEC-9 and he stumbled into action. Cleaning solution hissed from the nozzle and a dirty rag squealed frantically against glass. "You see a perfectly good thumb print on a window, and suddenly it takes a big, smeary left turn, right? You know it ain't no accident. It's them Wet Willies, right? Boy, I'd like ta know who's makin' 'um. He'd be cleanin' windows for the rest of his life, right?"

Burdick gurgled low in his throat. It was a peculiar kind of laughter, at once limp and sour and infinitely aggravating to MacDonnell.

"You won't be seein' me for ten days," the janitor declared in the true half-wit's belief everyone was consumed by interest in every plodding detail of the half-wit's existence. "I'm offin to Austria at four tomorrow mornin'. Just me and my honey, right?"

"Oh, yeah, I almost forgot about that. But I thought you won a trip to Australia?"

"I did." Gordy Burdick looked puzzled. "Takin' a flight outta Bradley tomorrow mornin'"

MacDonnell tendered a silent prayer of thanks to God. "Ever been out of the country before?"

"Oh, yeah, you bet. I was in the Army, right? Stationed in Germany and then up on them moors in England."

The supervisor wondered briefly how Burdick could ever have managed to shamble through a close order drill.

"Up on the moors? Where were you posted? Fort Baskerville?"

"Huh? Never heard a' the place. I was stayin' with an English woman up there in England. Let me tell you, she was a reeeel hummer."

"Uh-huh." Mike MacDonnell did not wish to explore this carnal reminiscence. He had the nagging suspicion it might cause some sort of hysterical impotence.

"Did you know England's only fifty miles wide at the widest part? You can walk across it in a day or two, right? I did. Two, three times."

"Fifty miles?" Mike stopped himself from contesting this statement. There was no point in arguing. "Have a safe trip, Gordy."

"Hey, thanks. You too, right?"

Burdick stumbled backwards out of the office and heedlessly collided with Timmons Wainwright on his way in. The janitor ricocheted out of sight and crashed into something loud.

Wainwright teeter-tottered into the office, collapsed in the chair across the desk from MacDonnell, and breathlessly introduced himself to the supervisor.

MacDonnell returned the introduction, not the least bit impressed by what he saw.

Timmons Wainwright was abnormally thin and his white hair had a yellowish cast which reminded MacDonnell of a rumpled, nicotine-stained bedroom curtain. The man looked much older than the age stated on his application and he also appeared to be wearing a woman's overcoat; the garment flared out at the hips and wrists, and the row of buttons was on the *left* side.

Wainwright started to thrash in the chair as if he were having a heart attack.

"Are you, uh, all right?" Mike MacDonnell asked a loaded question.

"Fine, fine," the older man gasped.

MacDonnell was not reassured. If Wainwright could not tolerate a little bump-and-run from a janitor, how in hell would he ever survive a restraint?

"May we proceed with the interview?" MacDonnell asked politely.

"Please. Go ahead. It's what I'm here for."

"I see you were in the Army for quite a while," MacDonnell said, leafing through Wainwright's application. The supervisor wondered if there were a battalion of unwashed misfits — the secret shame of the US military — now being funneled into Blythewood by a crafty government agency determined to expunge all traces of the unit's unseemly existence.

Wainwright, fully recovered now, assembled his forefinger and thumb into a pistol and pulled the imaginary trigger. "You got it, Mr. McDonald."

"And what were your primary, uh, duties in the Army?"

"Have you ever had an assault rifle shoved in your face in a Cyprian airport, Mr. McDonald?"

"No," Mike MacDonnell answered slowly. "I can't say I have."

"Well sir, I have — chasing AWOL GIs across every part of Europe and half of Asia Minor. I'd find them, counsel them, get them the help they needed, if I could, and get them back to their outfits."

"I see."

Wainwright leaned forward. He had bad breath. "With all due respect, Mr. McDonald, I don't think you do. Not unless you were there in Cyprus, face-to-face with a very confused young man holding a weapon on you."

MacDonnell stared at Timmons Wainwright. "So, why did you leave the Army?"

"National security."

"You were a threat to national security?"

"No! I can't talk about it *because* of national security. I took an oath to uphold and defend the Constitution of the United States of America. I'm sure you understand, Mr. McDonald."

Mike was beginning to understand quite a bit. "Mr. Wainwright, what, uh, what skills do you think you could bring to the position of childcare worker which might benefit our clients?" MacDonnell hated speaking this kind of gobbledygook to anyone, but Wainwright's odd responses forced him to fall back on trite, formalized nonsense.

"I think that's obvious. My years of counseling troubled young soldiers. Like I just said." Wainwright was clutching the edge of Mike's desk with both hands. The supervisor noticed the man's fingernails had not been cleaned or trimmed in a long time.

"Do you play the guitar, Mr. Wainwright?"

"What? Is there a position open in the music department? I just happened to have taught music appreciation in the public school system, many years ago."

"No, never mind. Do you have any other interests, qualifications, or abilities you feel might be of advantage to our program?"

Wainwright tossed himself back in the chair. "I understand a great many of these boys have been abused — *sexually* abused."

Oh, Christ, not another Peter Holland.

"That is correct, though I can't go into details with you. Our rules of client confidentiality are pretty strict."

"That's okay, Mr. McDonald," Wainwright began, lifting his lips in an angry grimace. A psychological fetter — one of his last — had come loose. "I understand. But let me just say I know about that sort of thing on a personal level. When I was a kid growing up on South Pearl Street in Albany, my father *fucked* me, my uncles *fucked* me, and an Italian grocer *fucked* me while I was cleaning out his storeroom for a sawbuck — which was good money in those days." Wainwright balled his fists at chest level, extended his thumbs and began snapping invisible suspenders. "I know what your kids here need. Do you understand me, Mr. McDonald? These *fucking* kids need somebody who's *fucking* been down there with them!"

MacDonnell picked up a pen and began tapping it on the desk. The time had come to end the interview — or call for the butterfly net. He opted for the former choice.

"I guess that's about all I need, Mr. Wainwright."

"When do I start?" The old man's eyes were spinning like drill bits.

"We'll notify you of our decision within twenty-four hours. Thanks for coming in. It was nice meeting you." MacDonnell forced himself to shake the man's filthy claw.

"You won't be sorry, *boss,*" Wainwright cackled. He buttoned up his overcoat, on the left, snapped a salute and left the office.

"Jesus, Mary, and Joseph," MacDonnell said. Through the Wet-Willies-free office window, he watched Timmons Wainwright wobble out to the parking lot. In a flutter of pipe cleaner limbs, the man slipped on a patch of ice and sprawled face first on the ground.

MacDonnell exploded in laughter.

Mad as a wet hen, Wainwright lurched to his feet and cast indignant glances in all directions.

"I saw you fall, jackass." Mike snickered with evil glee. He picked up the telephone and dialed Arlene O'Connor's extension.

"Arlene? It's Mike. Timmons Not-Quite-Right is a definite no. I wouldn't hire him to wipe a rabbit's ass with a borrowed handkerchief. I'll fill you in on the gory details later, but you might as well call him today with the bad news. No . . . I'm sure. I don't want this guy showing up here tomorrow morning thinking he's got the job, which he already does."

47

The Sunday Annie returned, MacDonnell was both elated and uncertain. For most of the day he was unable to surmount an awkward shyness around her. Annie was bubbly and effusive, regaling him, and any other staff who would listen, with one Hawaiian saga after another: the pristine beaches, the mountains, the ocean, a rainforest so green it beggared description, and flowers so exotic, so beautiful, no photo could ever capture them . . . on and on. MacDonnell didn't pay much attention to these stories, except when Doug was mentioned. To a man who thought Newfoundland might be a fun place to visit, Hawaii wasn't much of a grabber.

Nerves kept a Newport dangling from Mike's lip throughout the day. Strangely, Annie did not seem to mind this excessive smoking, which he took as a bad sign.

Finally, after dinner, Annie's native intolerance for tobacco awoke. MacDonnell had been lured into a false, and joyless, sense of security by her previous indifference. Without warning, she grabbed the cigarette he was gnawing and pitched it out the office door.

Mike MacDonnell rose from behind the desk, a happy man.

"I'm going to kill you, Wilson."

Annie ducked behind the inside door and slammed it in his face. Her trailing laughter was giddy and excited him.

MacDonnell pushed playfully against the barrier. "You're dead meat, girlie."

Annie had her entire body pressed against the door, holding him off. Her voice was muffled but distinct. "Mike?"

"What?" He continued nudging.

"I have to tell you something."

"Yeah?"

"Doug asked me to marry him."

MacDonnell's heart stopped and started hurting.

"I told him no," she said. "I just wanted you to know that."

His heart resumed pumping blood. He forced the door open and chased her through the building.

48

A funeral procession passed the van as Mike and Annie were returning from a student drop-off. She caught him blessing himself when the hearse rolled by.

"Well, well," Annie said. "I didn't take you for a believer."

MacDonnell, hand back on the steering wheel and eyes on the road, smiled. "Didn't say I was."

The tone of his voice was the only thing casual about Mike today. Annie had kept him in a constant state of excitement. The expensive pair of dark blue pants she was wearing looked like a thin spray coat of liquid silk. She couldn't be wearing panties, not under that second skin. Mike had spent the last several hours in a game of sneak-a-peek: quick glances at her ass, thighs, hips, knees; the back of her legs, the side of her legs, the front of her legs, between her legs. He hoped to Christ she hadn't noticed, couldn't help himself if she did.

"Stop for a drink?" he asked.

"Administration isn't in favor of operating company vans under the influence of alcohol."

"When has that ever stopped us?"

"A drink sounds lovely."

They approached Cranberry Manor, a sprawling Wessex resort and health spa dedicated to the wealthy and famous.

"We could stop here?" Annie Wilson suggested. "Just park the van somewhere out of sight." She was no stranger to Cranberry Manor's opulent confines and pampered delights.

"Do you really think we should?" MacDonnell asked. The idea of walking through the teakwood doors of the Manor's fern bar held all the appeal of being forced, head first, into the anal canal of an encopretic donkey.

Annie gave MacDonnell, and his clothing, a brief once over.

"Maybe not."

MacDonnell, watching her out of the corner of his eye, accepted the appraisal with judicial tolerance. "When you step out with me, Annie Wilson, you're slumming."

He was completely indifferent to appearances; a trait reinforced at Blythewood where a new shirt was guaranteed to become the primary target of some howling maniac's feces-stained claws. Consequently, he wore clothes which were little better than a charwoman's cleaning rags.

And style, to him, was a matter of how you spiked the ball in the end zone.

She, on the other hand, considered a 'rag' to be the silly, seventy-five-dollar periwinkle blouse she'd owned for five years and worn once.

"How about the Four Tables," Annie proposed primly.

"Where else?"

"Drop the van off at Blythewood first."

"Last week I saw this fuck on TV talking about how his wife and four young children had all been swept away in a mudslide, somewhere in California or Oregon. I don't remember exactly and it doesn't matter. Anyway, this jerk-off has these long dirty dreadlocks, the kind that always look stupid on white guys, a ring in his nostril, and this dumb-ass *grin* as he prattles on. They start flashing family photos of his wife and kids — and damn it, I wanted to feel sorry for the poor fuck, for losing his wife and his beautiful little girls. But instead, he keeps talking, and the more he talks the angrier I got, until he finally says, 'Hey man, they were ready, you know? They were ready to go back to Mother Earth and Mother Earth came and took them.' Here this guy has just lost his entire family, and all he can do is reduce this awful tragedy — his tragedy — to imbecilic, New Age cant. I was so pissed-off I spit on the television screen."

Annie said, "It's not so different from when people say it was God's will so-and-so died."

"No, you're right. And I can't stand that bullshit either," Mike growled.

"When you're hurt and grieving, sometimes it's difficult to come up with something clever or thoughtful to say."

MacDonnell picked up his beer mug. "Then maybe it's better to say nothing at all, until you can. Nobody forced the stupid mother-fucker to get on camera and give an interview. Why didn't he show a little dignity and keep his mouth shut? Couldn't do it. Had to go on national television and let everybody know how fucking enlightened he was. He probably got married a month later to some tree-hugging, empty-headed nature bitch who saw him on the boob-tube while she was preparing to bare it all for a PETA Fur Is Murder photo shoot."

Annie, smiling indulgently, put down her glass of dark beer on *their* table in the corner of the Four Tables. "Do you want to get a sandwich? I'm hungry."

"No, thanks. But you go ahead."

"I never see you eat. How do you stay so. . ." Annie's face began to turn red.

"Fat?" MacDonnell finished the sentence for her.

"No. I mean. . . big."

Mike grinned to show she hadn't offended him.

"Well, gallons of booze ain't exactly sliming. But I like to think it's the MacDonnell metabolism. It's how we survived the famine. Doesn't take much to keep us going."

"Do you believe all the nonsense that comes out of your mouth?"

"I can't always tell." *I love you. Is that nonsense?*

"You never talk much about your family, other than Michelle, I mean."

MacDonnell shrugged. "What's to tell? My family moved to Cornwall from Troy when I was an infant. I've got three older brothers, an older sister, a pack of nieces and nephews, cousins. We get together, mostly at holidays, and talk on the phone."

"Mom, dad?"

MacDonnell hesitated at answering this.

There were lots of things he could have told Annie about his parents: how his father, a little boy near death from diphtheria, had his trachea opened — with no anesthetic, on a kitchen table — by an old Jewish doctor who came to the rescue of an immigrant family without access to surgeons and hospitals. Or how a few years later polio shriveled his father's right arm, but didn't stop him from becoming the first in his family to graduate from college; a college where he became the football star who ran for a 73 yard touchdown on a fractured leg. No lie that. Mike had seen an alumni newsletter which proved it: *'Fifty years ago today, Jimmy*

MacDonnell, injured on the previous play, won the final game of the season with an amazing, last second sprint down the sidelines ... "

Or how Jimmy and his brother Hugh, a fearsome street brawler and heavy-weight boxer never knocked down in the ring, had gotten mixed-up with the Irish mob, got out again thanks to World War Two; how after the war Jimmy became the only teacher in a one-room schoolhouse, ages five to eleven, in Slate Run, Pennsylvania, a sawmill and whistle-stop; how at recess, he often joined the kids in throwing rocks at freight trains as they rumbled past in the cut below the school; how Jimmy had led those desperately poor children to loot one of those trains when several cars skipped the rails, and spilled their lavish contents like all the Christmas presents there had ever been; how when Slate Run closed for good, Jimmy met another teacher, Mary Catherine McAndrews, at the new county consolidated middle school, married her, brought her back to New York and started a family. How, as the years ran, Jimmy MacDonnell lost control of his drinking and disappeared on binges, sometimes for days, sometimes for weeks; how Mary Catherine always took him back because she loved him; how she sat at the kitchen table, little diamond tears trembling on her black lashes, refusing to let them fall, feeding her husband Coca Colas and Hershey bars as he fought with everything he had not to touch the bottle. How sometimes it didn't work and a little kid came home from kindergarten to watch his father empty another pint without stopping and then fall out of his chair and lie on the floor as if he were dead; how later the same little kid stood silently at the door of a dark little room, stinking of piss and whiskey, peering in at a soul stripped raw in a bed of delirium and dreams.

How, in the end, James Joseph MacDonnell exiled the urge to scald his throat and became a gentle old man filled with love for his wife and children; how this old man's heart was made whole, even as its beats slowed and became unpredictable and finally ceased altogether while he slept.

Mike could have told Annie all of this, but didn't. Because, at his age, he didn't know how the story should be told, what it might sound like or mean to someone hearing it. And because you didn't talk about your family with strangers, even strangers you loved with all your body and soul.

"My parents both died years ago. My father when I was a kid."

"For real?"

"Yes, but I didn't really murder them. They just got old." Mike emptied the shot glass in front of him. "Same goes for aunts, uncles and grandparents. I was a late in life baby."

"Late in life babies are prone to Down Syndrome."

MacDonnell raised an eyebrow. "Are you trying to make a point, Annie Wilson?"

"No." She sniffed airily. "Just saying."

49

"Jesus Gawd!" Pasinetti screamed, "You drive too fast!"

MacDonnell grinned. He eased off the Impala's throttle and offered Pasinetti a cigarette.

"You only got a couple left," Pasinetti warned. His old Zippo filled the car with brief illumination and the lingering smell of raw lighter fluid.

"Yeah, I know. I'll stop at the Mobile station on the corner and get a few packs," MacDonnell said. "Got any cash left from the bar?"

"Broke as a cripple's back. Spent my last buck on breath mints."

"A wise investment."

They pulled into a Mobile Mart. MacDonnell got out of the car and walked slowly towards the entrance, thumbing through his wallet for dollar bills. When he entered, the woman behind the cash register — a bleach-blond with a round beer gut and a tanning booth glow — said to a male coworker standing at her elbow, "Look at this ape."

Mike overheard the comment. He shambled up to the register, placed both hands on the counter and thrust his face against the glass window separating him from the woman.

"Cheetah want smoke sticks." Then in a normal voice, "Four packs of Newport 100s — please."

The woman's eyes went wide and her leathery skin almost achieved a flush.

MacDonnell rapped the Lexan with his knuckles. "There's a good reason they make this stuff bulletproof."

When he got back to the car, he asked Rick Pasinetti if he looked like an ape.

"No. You're too damn ugly for an ape. Were you comin' on to the blond in there?"

"No."

"I would. Let's see ... we got smokes, beer, and a bottle. Let's take a ride over to New York."

"Hoosick Falls?"

"Naww. Had enough bars for tonight, cockbreath." Pasinetti tapped the windshield. "It's a pretty night. Full moon, little snow on the ground. Let's go till we don't want to anymore."

"It's your gas."

Content in each other's company and the long, echoing feeling only true friends know, they let the conversation lapse and the miles roll.

Eventually a loud belch prompted Pasinetti to ask, "Have a nice Thanksgiving, Mac?"

"Just the best. Michelle refused to put any salt in the mashed potatoes. You?"

"Had dinner with my sister and her family. Got smashed, of course. Then I dressed up like a roundhead and shot a couple of Indians. At least I think they were Indians. They might have been Jehovah's Witnesses. Either way ... " He pulled half a joint out of his coat pocket, lit it and took a long hit. Several seconds later, "You got any hobbies, Cousin Mongo?" The question ended on a strangled cough and a cloud of smoke.

"I like to masturbate and pick quarters up with my toes."

"Who doesn't? No, I mean, like fishing or hunting? Something like that?"

"When I was a kid. Not anymore."

"Gawd, I loved it. Out on a lake in the spring, or in the woods on a crisp fall morning? Nothin' like it in this world. Didn't even matter if I bagged anything."

"I remember the squirrel, but I never would have guessed you stalked beyond city limits," MacDonnell said. There was something incongruous in the thought of Rick slipping through the trees like a portly Hawkeye.

"Why would you? It's better than ten years since I picked up a reel or a shotgun. Isn't that funny? Ten years come and gone like a morning and afternoon. I knew the woods, all these woods, all the way to Lake George. And then one day, for no good reason, it became nothing more than scenery to me." Rick rapped the window with his knuckle. "Nothing more than a moving postcard."

He pinched the roach between his fingers. "What was the name of that chicken-shit childcare worker at Blythewood who started just before I left? You know the one I mean. The one who wanted to be a forest ranger and an astronaut on the weekends?"

"Rodney Jones?"

"That sounds right. Kind of a jittery sort, wasn't he? Nervous as a three-legged toad at a Hessian clog dancing competition." Pasinetti paused to pop the cap off a bottle of beer. "Every week he was about to embark on a new career. He was gonna be a park ranger, then a scuba diver, then a race car driver — it never ended. He was always in the process of becoming, but he never became. As I recalls, he hated me for some reason."

MacDonnell nodded. "One day at work, he admitted to having electric shock treatments when he was a teenager. You told him there wasn't anything wrong with being 'fucking crazy,' and then you started calling him, Roddy Kilowatt . . . to his face. Jones couldn't take it and quit. About a month later he sent you a death threat in the mail, care of Blythewood."

Pasinetti chewed his bottom lip for a moment. "Good thing I never told him where I lives. You ever dream about being rich, dogballs?"

"Who doesn't?"

"I don't. I used to, of course. But I ain't that young anymore. Things are the way they are."

"I suppose that's right."

"Do you ever think about dying?"

MacDonnell made the Impala swerve violently back and forth on the road.

"You better hope not."

"Don't do that again, you fucking idiot," Pasinetti said. "Toss me around like Scotty in an old Star Trek episode. Gawd, that was an awful show."

"No velour shirts in your closet, huh?"

"There ain't room. Too many skeletons." Pasinetti discovered beer foam on his chin and wiped it off on his coat sleeve. "You think there's a heaven?"

Yes. The empyrean between Annie's thighs. "It'd be nice."

"It would. What do ya think it's like?"

"Jesus! Got cancer, Rick?"

"No. I've just been thinking about things lately. I'm older than you."

"Can you still get it up? Then you're not ready to pack it in."

"Never said I was, Cousin Mongo. I just wonder sometimes. I hope heaven is . . ." His voice went soft for a moment, then gathered strength again. "I hope it's a clear morning. One of them sharp days that smell like apples and leaves. There'll be an old hound named Belle at my feet, and a Browning Sweet-Sixteen hanging over my arm — and the woods right up ahead. That don't sound too bad, does it?"

"No, it doesn't."

Pasinetti grinned crookedly. "Naturally, a naked blond with big tits sitting on a beer keg will have to be included."

50

Annie took a job house-sitting for an acquaintance in Foxhill, a wealthy community twenty miles south of Wessex. She invited MacDonnell and

Kevin to join her at the home on the last Wednesday of the month, forgoing the traditional gathering at the Four Tables.

It was one of those raw November days that made MacDonnell think of old sailing ships tossed on storm-wracked North Atlantic seas. Rain sizzled from granite skies and hung icy droplets from withered bracken and dead, sodden leaves. Despite the weather, he felt lighthearted. A house party suggested possibilities a gulping match at the local saloon did not.

Kevin was riding shotgun in Mike's Toyota. Kevin's vehicle, a Jeep Wrangler, remained in the Blythewood parking lot, slowly leaking radiator fluid. Kevin found the problem at shift change and was understandably leery about driving the vehicle to Foxhill, or anywhere else, before he had a chance to fix it.

The Toyota obediently followed Annie Wilson's blue Subaru from Blythewood. MacDonnell laughed and joked the entire way.

"So Kevin? How old is the Jeep? Two years? Is it normal for the radiators to blow out so soon?"

"It's three years old and the radiator's fine. One of the hoses cracked. A little duct tape will get me home tonight," Kevin growled. "Why are you so gay today?"

"I've got a big dick, and we are going to get drunk."

"Annie's taking a risk letting you in her friend's house."

"I haven't trashed a private dwelling since Grant was a cadet."

"Uh-huh."

"O, ye of little faith."

"O, ye of little self-control."

"By the way, Kevin? If you should need to leave before I do tonight, feel free to take my car back to Blythewood. Just leave it there. I'll have Annie give me a ride later on."

"I bet you will. Oh, and how is Mrs. MacDonnell these days?" Kevin asked slyly.

"Why, very well, thank you."

"And where does she think you are this afternoon?"

"Chasing a poor, misguided runaway in the cold, miserable rain."

"That makes what? Thirty, forty runaways this month?"

"I'm not quite that unimaginative."

The rain was falling with redoubled ferocity by the time they arrived at a splendid, three-storied Edwardian residence, ironically termed a *cottage* in these parts. This august home was set on a wide stretch of park-like acreage which gently rose and subsided until it reached a broad stream and a heavy stand of old forest several hundred yards in the distance. Annie pulled into a long circular driveway paved in bleached stone. Her friend, and Annie had assured MacDonnell this gentleman was only a friend, obviously had a great deal of money. His modest little country estate was just that, an estate.

As they got out of the car, Kevin paused to look at the house and then back at MacDonnell. He called out a warning to Annie Wilson.

"Are you sure you want Mike to come in? It might be safer if he stayed in the car."

"Tell him to wipe his feet," she replied, punching a code into the digital alarm system keypad mounted next to the front entrance.

Mike MacDonnell snarled soundlessly and opened the trunk of the Toyota to remove two cases of beer. His upper lip was still curled as he followed Kevin up a broad flight of fieldstone stairs to the front door. When MacDonnell reached the threshold, his foot slipped in a puddle of rain water and he fell full-length through the open doorway, barely avoiding Kevin's rump with the tip of his big nose. One of the beer cases hit the floor and broke open. Bottles rolled across polished hardwood floors, one hissing like a snake and spraying foam from a loosened cap. It sounded like Reptile Night at the local bowling alley.

Kevin Marshall turned and shook his head. "Like I said."

This time MacDonnell made a sound when he snarled.

After the rogue bottles had been collected and interned with the rest of their mates in the biggest, gizmo-laden refrigerator MacDonnell had ever seen, the Blythewood supervisor picked his way through a maze of rooms until he found a large living area. It contained a stereo and a couch and a big picture window. Like Hillary, he'd reached the summit and it was time to plant his flag.

The stereo system turned out to be a disappointment. It was not the high-priced, high-end tribute to esoteric theories of psycho-acoustic design he'd hoped a house of this magnitude might contain. Still, it was much better than what he had, and the Sam and Dave disc he brought from the car sounded pretty good pounding out of the two speakers set in opposite corners of the room. Add a few beers (and maybe a pinch of coke to help the medicine go down) and it would do.

Annie Wilson entered the room. "Those are studio monitors," she said, pointing to the speakers.

"Yep, they are. Tell your friend I would be glad to recommend, Christ, at least a dozen different speakers systems that would sound a whole lot better than these. Studio monitors aren't really meant for the home."

"I suppose yours are soooo much better?"

"No, mine are crap. But, if I ever get any money, I'll buy better ones."

"You know there are more important things in this world than stereo equipment?"

"Are there? Wow. Thanks for expanding my universe, Annie."

She flipped him the middle finger and sat on the couch.

"Where's Kevin?" MacDonnell asked, joining her.

"Bathroom."

"Ah, must have a hair out of place."

"Jealous?"

"You bet.".

"Do you ever comb yours?"

"It's curly."

"It's tangled."

"At least it's my natural color."

"So is mine."

"A natural calico? How unusual. And I forgot to bring your catnip."

Annie lowered her head and brushed the thick mane forward over her face. "See any roots, Jerk?"

"Like a six hundred year old maple tree," he said, but thought, Good God, it's beautiful — she's beautiful.

Annie tossed the hair back over her shoulders and smiled at him. "I hate it when you cut your hair too short."

"Why?"

"You lose all the curls."

"I thought they were tangles?"

She ran a finger through the hair over his forehead. "I don't like it too long or too short." There was a fluent and proprietary intimacy in this gesture that stalled the breath in his lungs.

He wondered if he should kiss her.

"Lice?" Kevin Marshall asked, strolling into the room.

"Speaking of Shelley," MacDonnell recovered instantly, "Where is she tonight?" He was at once disappointed and relieved the moment had ended.

"Digging for *crabs* on the Cape," Kevin replied. He allowed them the couch and dropped into an easy chair off to the side. "Didn't interrupt anything, did I?"

Annie Wilson laughed a little too loudly. "Of course not."

The three of them passed the afternoon and evening with the comfortable ease of the genuine friends they were. There were no hidden animosities and unvoiced personal grievances, no barely concealed competition between the men for Annie Wilson's attention. If Kevin found her desirable, he never allowed it to find expression. He knew MacDonnell was in love, and for Kevin Marshall that fact alone dictated the boundaries of his relationship with Annie Wilson. A formless sense of anticipation began to wear on MacDonnell after a while, making him restless and nervous. He wanted to drink more and rapidly, but resisted this urge, in case he needed to retain some physical proficiency for later on. Just in case he and Annie . . .

The clock was ticking towards eleven when Kevin announced he had to be up early the next morning. "I've got to pick up a hose —" he shot MacDonnell a telling glance, "At the auto-parts store. I'd better be going."

Annie confessed disappointment.

Mike MacDonnell seized the opportunity he'd been waiting for.

"Jesus, Kevin, do you have to go? I'm not even drunk yet."

Kevin read his friend's mind like an open book. "Yes. I've, uh, I've got to get up pretty early, like I said."

An elaborate groan issued from MacDonnell's mouth. "I'm not even finished with this beer. Christ . . . " He wagged his head sorrowfully, then let his face brighten. "Annie? If I let Kevin take my car now, could you give me a ride back to Blythewood later? I can wait till tomorrow morning if you don't want to go out again tonight." To his credit, MacDonnell was able to carry off this bit of carefully planned spontaneity with an air of convincing frankness.

"I guess so . . . "

"Great. See ya, Kev."

MacDonnell ushered Kevin to the door. He clapped the younger man on the back, thanked him and handed him the keys to the Toyota.

Marshall smiled, but issued a warning in the form of an ersatz aphorism. "Don't count on your *tailor* until the zippers fixed."

MacDonnell stared at him for a moment. "Go away, Kevin."

"Mike — you bitch — good luck."

MacDonnell returned to Annie's side with a beer in each hand and wings on his feet.

Annie accepted a bottle without looking up at him and said, "Maybe you should go with Kevin. I have a lot of errands to run in the morning."

"Huh?" MacDonnell was unpleasantly startled. "Kevin's gone."

"Oh . . ."

"Look, Annie, I thought —"

"You thought what?" She turned on him with an edge in her voice. "You thought what?"

"That — that you wanted to have a few more drinks."

"I really don't."

A squirming panic settled in Mike MacDonnell's stomach, forcing him to turn away from her. He wandered over to the stereo and began blindly picking through a pile of CDs, utterly flustered and uncertain of what to do or say next.

Had he so badly misinterpreted her mood — and the entire evening?

He decided he should summon all of his remaining courage and face her.

"Is there a problem, Annie?"

"Problem?" Her eyes became narrow, almost cruel. "I'm not the one who has a problem."

"And I do?" His voice was unsteady. He feared the answer.

"Isn't your wife going to be pissed off you're not home tonight?"

"Probably."

Annie was well aware of the strain in his marriage. He'd never given anyone — not Kevin, not Rick — access to the personal details of his life the way he had to Annie Wilson.

"Probably you belong at home — with her."

"Kevin took my car."

"Too bad you didn't take the car and leave Kevin."

MacDonnell absorbed this blow in stoic silence. There was nothing else he could do.

Annie's inexplicable (at least to Mike MacDonnell) frustration continued to boil over. "What do you want, Mike?" Her voice was a clatter of metal splinters dropped into a hollow iron bin.

MacDonnell was shocked, hurt and taking heavy damage, but he refused to strike his colors just yet.

"Not a goddamned thing," he replied in a lifeless voice. "What do you want?"

"I don't want anything. Can you understand that? I just want you to go." Her expression was as cold as the November rain pelting against the windows.

"Fine. I'll walk." This was his mortally wounded pride speaking. It would have been a march of some twenty miles back to Wessex in foul weather and freezing temperatures.

"Sure you will. Give me a few minutes to sober up, and I'll drive you back to Blythewood."

"I'll call a taxi."

Annie threw her hands up in the air. "Do whatever you want."

MacDonnell took a single step towards a telephone resting on a small, mahogany stand next to the chair Kevin had been sitting in — but then he turned and looked at the woman on the couch, the woman he loved, the woman he worshiped.

"You know what, Annie? You can kiss my Royal Irish Ass!"

Annie Wilson's jaw fell. He had never spoken to her with such outright hostility. It frightened her momentarily. The big, loveable dog she'd picked up at the humane shelter was baring its teeth and growling deep in its huge throat.

MacDonnell sensed her moment of dismay and opened up with all guns.

"What exactly is my crime here?" he asked. "Is it my desire to spend time with you? God knows, there are enough men who do. If it's Kevin, I'm sorry he left and you got stuck with me. Better luck next time!

"I'm just the silly sonofabitch you sit next to in the office every day and go out with every night — the dumb fucking goon who makes sure no kid dares touch you. Sorry I'm not good looking, or rich enough to take you on ridiculous vacations. Sorry I'm a little fucked-up and twisted. Dougie must be so squeaky-fucking-clean he only has to take a shit twice a month, God bless him. But most of all, I'm sorry I fell in love with you. "

"Mike, listen. I'm sorry if you— "

"No. I don't — can't — expect anything from you, and you're not responsible for the shit running around in my head."

She went to him, put an arm around his neck. He pulled away.

"Don't do that," he said. "I don't need anybody's pity."

Annie stepped back and tried to search his downcast eyes. "I didn't want Kevin to stay. You're not the only one who has trouble sorting things out."

"I don't have trouble 'sorting things out.' I know what I want. There's no mystery involved."

She put her hand on his arm. He shook it off. His dignity was unassailable.

Instead. . .

He shifted from foot to foot (doing what his kindergarten teacher had called his 'teddy bear dance') and developed a sudden facial tick which made his eyes blink in a hard, rapid fashion. He coughed, mumbled something unintelligible and finally stared at the floor.

After a moment, "I'll take that ride to Blythewood now, if the offer still stands. I don't have money for a taxi."

When they walked out the front door together, a brief but mortal terror seized him, a childlike fear of being abandoned and forgotten. He almost begged her to let him stay, to let him lie down in a bed next to her and close his eyes — to let him wake in the morning by her side.

Instead, he lit a Newport and got in the car.

51

Cyril Rumgay put in an unexpected appearance at Blythewood an hour after supper had been completed and the students returned to their dorms.

Mike MacDonnell had seen the elder Rumgay on many occasions, but never actually spoken to him. Rick Pasinetti always referred to Cyril as 'Mandrake the Magician' because of his reputed talent for deceit and trickery, and for the manner of his dress, which was decidedly formal and a little quirky. Cyril was rarely seen in public without a black silk vest, a white ruffled shirt, black silk trousers; a black coat, lined in scarlet, usually tossed like a cape over one shoulder, and a silver-handled cane. This unusual sense of sartorial style, combined with the white mane of hair swept back in epic fashion from the high white forehead, would not have made Cyril look out of place in a line-up of suspects for the Whitechapel Murders. And he looked old enough to have been around then.

This evening Cyril arrived in the supervisors office with a flourish of the polished cane. His hair glistened like snow and his eyes were the color of ripe cherries.

"Mister McIntosh, I presume," the old man declared grandly.

MacDonnell did not know how to respond with anything more than a "Hi."

This visitation was entirely unexpected — Cyril hadn't been seen on campus for a year — and thoroughly disconcerting. Cyril Rumgay was three sheets to the wind. The aroma of bourbon swept through the office like mustard gas.

"My son has left for the day?" Rumgay asked. "I found his office unoccupied."

"Uh, I think he's still here . . . somewhere."

Thankfully, Annie Wilson arrived back in the office from a trip to the bathroom.

"Hello, my pretty," Cyril exclaimed.

My pretty? MacDonnell thought. It was obvious Mandrake hadn't scored since Edward Teach was the top Caribbean cruise director.

"Cyril!" Annie was clearly surprised, but unlike Mike, her composure remained intact. "How good to see you again."

"And you, dearie, and you. Lovely as always."

Dearie? Mike MacDonnell nervously shuffled some papers on the desk. He could not easily bear the capricious behaviors and affectations of the rich — not that he had much experience with them.

Annie asked, "Can we help you with something, Cyril?"

"I believe you can." Rumgay swept his cane through the air like a sword. "Which cottage is now reserved for the homosexuals?"

"Excuse me?" Annie's composure took a direct hit.

"Those lads who practice the love which dare not speak its name."

"I don't think I understand — "

"I've decided we should put on a Christmas pageant here at Blythewood. Of course, I'll need the assistance of the homosexuals — but I can't seem to recall where I put them all. They have such a natural affinity for the arts, you know, making costumes, painting sets, singing in those lovely soprano voices so many of them are blessed with. I have yet to meet one who did not possess a Wildean flair for the dramatic."

Mike wondered if old Cyril ever took a look in the mirror.

Perhaps he did.

"When I was at University," Cyril continued, "we would often put on all-male revues. And the faggots simply dominated the proceedings."

"Cyril. . ." Annie began and then faltered.

MacDonnell boldly jumped in. He'd had enough. "The government came and took them all. Shipped them off to San Francisco, I believe. So sorry."

"What?" The maraschinos on either side of Cyril's nose popped. "The Democrats did what?"

"Dad?" Bill Rumgay arrived in the office doorway.

"Willie! There you are." The elder Rumgay half turned, partially lost his bearing and sat heavily on the desk.

Bill put his arm through his father's arm and assisted the old man to his feet. "It's time to go, dad. Mother is holding supper for you."

"Mother? I thought she was dead?"

"No, dad, I mean my mother. Your wife."

Cyril, Willie and Mother — what a heartwarming family unit it must be, Mike MacDonnell thought. A little money, a little booze — a little dementia to liven the stew.

Bill Rumgay led his father to the door. Before he exited, the program director looked back over his shoulder and fixed Mike and Annie with a glare promising immediate termination should any gossip blossom from this impromptu papal visit.

MacDonnell could not resist a slight smile.

"That was . . . interesting," Annie Wilson said when the Rumgays were gone.

Mike nodded and laughed. "Yeah, Cyril's obviously wandering in fairyland. The frock was a nice touch, though."

"He didn't always dress like Dracula or act like that. That's recent. He once was a very stylish, very charming man. It's a sad thing to witness."

"From what I've heard, he was nothing but a lying sleazebag who would have sold his own sister to a cannibal tribe for a clamshell necklace and a goatskin."

"Don't believe everything you hear, Michael."

"Michael? My, Miss Wilson, you sound positively defensive. What? Did you have something going with the old geezer before he got lost in the puzzle factory?"

Annie just looked at him.

"Oh, for the love of God." Mike rose from the desk and headed for the side door. "Don't even joke about it."

"I didn't say a word."

"Jesus-fucking-Christ," MacDonnell muttered as he pushed open the door with his foot. He lit a cigarette with hands that shook a little more than usual. It wasn't that he believed Annie Wilson ever had a romantic connection with Cyril, that was patently absurd; it was just that he couldn't quite dismiss it either. This tiny bit of paranoid uncertainty — insecurity — goaded him, galled him, convinced him, once again, she was so far beyond what he understood, so much more sophisticated in the matters of love and sex, that anything was possible — anything but her ever wanting him.

The cigarette was finished and discarded and the door allowed to close; but he was reluctant to turn and face her, fearing she would in some direct or indirect way confirm his worst fear. Instead, he stood staring through the small window in the door, at nothing.

"Are we going out for a drink tonight?" Annie asked matter-of-factly.

Sunlight filled the room and melted all of Mike MacDonnell's frozen dread.

"If I must."

"Hey, if you don't want to?" she said.

"You don't need to beg."

Annie Wilson chewed her lower lip to prevent a smile.

Kevin Marshall, feeling like a third wheel, sat sipping a Bass and watching Mike and Annie argue and tease each other. He happened to be at the Tables waiting for Shelley when they arrived. Naturally enough, he ended up sitting with his friends. When Shelley called his cell to say she wasn't going to make it, Marshall was stranded in the cheap seats, a spectator.

After a few minutes of listening to Mike and Annie verbally slap, pinch, claw and lick each other, he was forced to wonder — aloud — if the two of them had been secretly married. Both supervisors ignored this comment as absurd and went on with their play.

MacDonnell, to emphasize his contention a certain rock star Annie adored was a talentless hack, brought his fist crashing down on the beer-soaked table. On impact his cheap silver wedding ring split in half and rolled across the wet surface.

It came to rest in front of Annie Wilson.

MacDonnell stared in stunned silence.

Kevin grinned like a mad wolfhound. "If I were a superstitious Irish bitch, I'd have to take that as some kind of sign."

Mike MacDonnell blushed and grabbed the broken ring.

52

A holiday luncheon was held for the students on the second Wednesday in December. An improperly assembled, and consequently lopsided, artificial Christmas tree was erected in the main lobby. The plastic bush leaned into a corner like a drunk hopelessly entangled in the wiring of a flickering, barroom window display. Decorations — made by Team Three from construction paper left over from the Halloween party — were tacked to the walls. This highly original presentation included orange snowflakes, yellow reindeer and a figure that might have been Kriss Kringle, but more closely resembled a black-robed Inquisitor. The tables in the dining room were draped with red and green paper cloths, and piled high with platters of cold cuts, salads, rolls, chips and a wide variety of desserts. MacDonnell had to admit the buffet looked acceptable, though he refrained from eating any of it, opting instead for a quick fade into the background and a tedious wait for two-thirty. As usual, he'd been offered a chance to work a few additional hours, but politely declined. He just wanted the Blythewood Christmas Extravaganza to pass quickly and painlessly.

Bill Rumgay had other ideas.

The program director handed out felt Santa caps, complete with white faux-fur trim and a little bell on the peak, to every department head and supervisor — and insisted they wear them for the rest of the day.

"I want to create a festive atmosphere for the children," Rumgay explained. "And that begins with all of us."

With the alacrity of Wehrmacht officers faced with compliance or the Russian front, Blythewood middle management donned the head gear — even a reluctant and horrified Mike MacDonnell. The felt cap was several sizes too small and perched precariously atop his shaggy black head.

"You look cute," Annie giggled.

Debbie Wittenburg, standing behind Wilson at the time, made a disagreeable face. Watching the two supervisors interact annoyed the nurse to the core of her being. Yet, their dirty love-play (*"The Most unprofessional thing I've ever seen — be a doll and hand me another cruller, will you?"*) did keep Wilson's slutty hands off Bill. The head nurse decided she would have to swallow her disgust and encourage the gruesome couple. Pretending to be Wilson's friend would also provide advance notice should the bitch plan to dump the ugly baboon and make a move on *her* sweet man-meat.

MacDonnell, face redder than his cap, stood grinding his teeth and staring at the floor.

Kevin Marshall walked by with his team and commented, "You look like a gay lawn gnome."

"I'm in hell," MacDonnell grunted.

"Lighten up, Mike. It's only a hat," Annie said.

MacDonnell shot back at her, "Yeah? Go take a gander at yourself in a mirror, Mrs. Claus."

Rumgay eventually returned to the seclusion of his office and Mike immediately handed his Santa cap to Freddy Pickard, a client waiting in the lounge for his turn at the buffet.

"Bill will have your head if he sees you without the hat on," Annie warned.

"He can kiss my fruity, ceramic ass!"

The supervisors walked away and Freddy Pickard began happily munching on the cap's trim. Fortunately the faux-fur turned out to be nontoxic.

MacDonnell managed to avoid Rumgay for the rest of the afternoon and became the only supervisor who didn't wear the hat for the entire day.

At half past two, as MacDonnell and Annie were on their way to the door, a sudden commotion broke out in the dining room behind them. They turned back to witness four supervisors wrestling with a student on the floor. Bright red caps bobbed furiously up and down over a thrashing body, and merry little bells tinkled sweetly in time to a steady toilet-flush of foul language spewing from the student's mouth.

"Are you going to help?" Annie asked. She knew MacDonnell could end the incident in a heartbeat.

"No." He shook his head. "It looks like Santa's Little Helpers have it all wrapped up."

53

Mrs. Kemp arrived to celebrate Christmas with her son Davie. Mrs. Kemp was a middle-aged woman careworn by guilt over her offspring's impairments and the necessity of having him institutionalized. Abandoned by her husband when Davie was a child, she'd struggled alone — and valiantly — to provide everything for a beloved son.

MacDonnell accompanied her to the Team One classroom. Davie had a pattern of becoming violently agitated when she came to visit. This behavior nearly caused a fatal crash on the turnpike during last year's ill-advised attempt at bringing Davie home for a short stay. Davie exploded like a time-bomb in the car and wrenched the steering wheel out of his mother's hands. The vehicle narrowly avoided slamming into the side of an 18-wheeler.

Today, Mrs. Kemp came heavily burdened by cakes and cookies. These sweets were distributed and gobbled up in short order by Davie and his classmates. For the rest of the day, Team One flew on wings of spun sugar.

Davie Kemp sat in his traditional position, cross-legged on the floor, rocking incessantly back and forth, repeating the second of the three words he knew, "Mommy, mommy, mommy, mommy." He was excited, but did not attack his mother.

Several times during the course of the visit, MacDonnell noticed tears welling in Mrs. Kemp's eyes as she tried to engage her son in some form of normal interaction. It was an impossible task and heartbreaking for a woman old before her time. To her everlasting credit, she never ceased making the effort, unlike many of the clients' parents.

She said to Mike MacDonnell, "I think he's speaking much better, don't you"

The supervisor nodded and smiled.

Before she left, Mrs. Kemp handed out small gifts to every student in Team One. Davie's present was reserved for last. She hadn't wrapped it because the process of tearing open packages sometimes sent him into a violent rage. Instead, she placed the round and furry teddy bear in a brightly decorated, easy to open gift bag.

Mrs. Kemp showed the toy to Mike MacDonnell first. "The eyes are photosensitive," she explained. "When you pass your hand in front of them, they flash and the bear giggles and vibrates all over. Do you think Davie will like it?"

"I'm sure of it."

Mrs. Kemp put the bear back in the bag and with brief — but heartfelt — ceremony presented it to her son.

Davie eagerly tore the bag to shreds removing his present. He held the bear up to his face and myopically inspected it. When he moved his head slightly, and allowed light to contact the toy's protruding plastic eyes, the bear began its battery operated high jinks on cue.

This sudden activity from the toy startled Davie. For a moment it looked like he was going to toss the teddy bear away, but then a slow, and uncharacteristic, smile broke out on his homely potato face.

Davie Kemp crammed the teddy bear into the crotch of his purple sweat pants and began chanting, in time to each vigorous pelvic thrust, the last of the three words he could speak, "Bay-be, bay-be, bay-be, bay-be."

The teddy bear cooed, cackled, quaked and frantically twinkled while it was being sodomized.

Mike MacDonnell's eyebrows merged with his hair line. He turned to a horrified Mrs. Kemp and said, "Uh . . . Merry Christmas?"

54

Blythewood supervisors were expected to show up for the staff Christmas party at the Stanton Club — which put Mike MacDonnell in something of a quandary. Since he would never bring Michelle again, it meant she would do her best to prevent his attendance. The previous year, she'd hidden all the car keys.

Michelle didn't resort to trickery this time. Instead, she sniffed and wheedled and begged him not to go without her. A shower of tears fell. In the end, it was to no avail. Mike grunted a string of barely coherent, and not at all logical, excuses and walked out the door. His wife had no way of knowing this ironclad resolution stemmed from the simple fact he was escorting Annie Wilson to the party. Nothing, and no one, would deny him that honor.

MacDonnell even took some care with his appearance that night. He'd gotten a decent haircut (which left his hair not too short and not too long and still noticeably curly) and purchased a pair of black jeans, a blue shirt and a gold chain to wrap around the ankle of the $200 black cowboy boots he only wore on special occasions — receipts were hidden from Michelle. Leather jacket and a splash of passable cologne completed his vision of sartorial splendor. It was — for him — an unprecedented stab at looking presentable.

He met Annie at the Four Tables, had one drink and then drove to the Stanton Club in her Subaru station wagon. Before they got out of the car, she handed him a small package.

"What's this?" he asked. His childlike delight turned into sudden apprehension, "I didn't get you anything. You told me not to."

"It's okay. Open it."

MacDonnell's hands shook as he tore away the wrapping paper to reveal a paperback copy of *A Confederacy of Dunces*.

"It's still in print," she said.

He looked at her. "Thank you."

Mike MacDonnell would never mean those two words more sincerely then he did that night outside the Stanton Club.

Annie had written something on the inside of the book's cover. Because of the uncertain light, he was able to make out only the final two words of the inscription, which, in letters larger and bolder than the rest, read, 'Love, Annie'.

Love, Annie

His heart swelled. There it was, written down in her own hand, forever his — even if he was exaggerating her intent.

Like a miser hoarding an inestimable treasure, he carefully placed the paperback in the Subaru's glove compartment for safe keeping. He wouldn't chance bringing it into the Stanton Club where it might fall prey to misadventure, though he desperately wanted to know what else she'd written. That could wait till later. Mike MacDonnell was truly a happy man.

But some things are not meant to be kept.

Months later, the book would mysteriously vanish, never to be retrieved. He would spend weeks fruitlessly searching for it.

"Let's go inside," said Annie. "I'm cold."

This particular Christmas party would forever remain something of a mystery to MacDonnell. He would be able to recall only sketchy details and vague impressions; chronological order and coherent memory became processes observed entirely in the breach.

It began innocently enough.

MacDonnell, still drifting on clouds because of his gift, sat down at a long table next to Annie. Seated across from them were an elderly couple, an old man in a carefully pressed brown suit and starched white shirt, and an old woman in one of those heavy, brocaded dresses that look as though they have been cut from Victorian drapes. MacDonnell didn't know them, but he nodded politely. They made no response. He said hello politely. They still made no response. He stared at them openly for a full minute or more — but not an aged muscle twitched, not a milky eye blinked. It made the big Blythewood supervisor extremely uncomfortable. Never at ease in social situations, he was tortured by the notion the couple either despised the very face on him — or they were dead.

He touched Annie Wilson's arm. "I'm going to get us some drinks. I'll be right back." He glanced at the couple one more time, still failed to discover any sign of life, and beat a hasty retreat to the bar. With a hearty sigh of relief, he dropped into a chair next to Stan Woitkowski, the head groundskeeper at Blythewood. Woitkowski was a handsome, portly man in his late forties with steel gray hair and calloused hands. He'd been a gunner's mate on a destroyer and a gear-jammer for most of the years after that. A severe case of asphalt fatigue convinced him to tend the lawns and gardens at Blythewood.

MacDonnell nudged him with his elbow. "Why are all Polka-Wops named Stan?"

"Mac!" Woitkowski roared. He was already deep in his cups. "Let me buy you a drink, you dirty bastard. What'll you have?"

"Boilermaker," Mike MacDonnell replied easily.

This would rank as the last untrammeled memory MacDonnell had of the evening. What came thereafter was a chaotic series of fleeting images, blurred faces and distorted noise; all caught, tossed and diced on the whirling blades of a liquor-powered threshing machine.

He remembered capering like a monkey on some kind of raised platform and splashing everyone beneath it with beer from the gushing bottles he held in each hand; he recalled crouching outside the restrooms, swaying on his haunches to loud pulsating music, like a caveman at a tom-tom ceremony, until some wayward and hostile impulse compelled him to hurl passing bodies through doorways marked 'Gents' and 'Ladies', each destination selected to suit the gender of the shrieking victim.

There was a nightmarish flash of slow dancing with Bonnie Quirk, her hand squeezing his ass, and then tenuous recollections of Annie Wilson leading him out of the Stanton Club; of snorting coke with her in the backseat of an old Lincoln Continental, of kissing her on somebody's front porch, maybe hers — of moving on top of her in a rustling bed.

Then blackness.

The next morning he rolled off Annie's disheveled mattress and fell on the floor. She was nowhere to be seen. He crawled slowly over pile carpeting, seeking his abandoned clothes and praying to God he hadn't fatally injured her. After managing to dress, he stumbled down a flight of stairs into a bright living room that smelled of lemon polish. Sunlight, cascading in from too many windows, hurt his eyes.

Annie was hunched over a coffee table, mincing cocaine with a razor.

"Where are your roommates?" MacDonnell croaked.

"They work weekends." Her face was ravaged by the previous night's debauchery, and yet, every sunken hollow and weary shadow captivated him.

He sank next to her on the couch. "I'm really sick."

Without looking up from her task, she pushed a Bloody Mary across the table in his direction. MacDonnell gulped it. There were a pair of new sneakers sitting on the table. He reached over and put them on the floor.

Annie raised her head. "They don't smell. Why did you do that?"

"Bad luck."

He wanted to ask if his distorted memories of lovemaking were even remotely authentic, but her casual indifference to the amount of flesh exposed by an open dressing gown rendered the question unnecessary.

They drank and snorted until an artificial state of well-being had been restored. Then they drove around Wessex in her car, for hours, talking about small things and carefully avoiding any of the larger issues a sexual relationship proposed.

Only once did the conversation verge on acknowledging a transformation had overtaken them. MacDonnell asked Annie to confirm his memory of huffing coke in the backseat of a Lincoln outside the Stanton Club.

"Yes, we did," she replied slowly. "It was Todd Robertson's car. I think he borrowed it from his parents." Her tone of voice, and the expression on her face, indicated something was left unsaid.

"What's wrong? Did I start eating my own boogers, or what?"

MacDonnell was genuinely afraid he had done something horribly stupid.

"No, it wasn't you." She tilted her head away from him. "Forget it. It's nothing."

"Can I be the judge of that?"

"When you got out of the car to take a pee, Todd tried to put his hand down my shirt. That's all."

"I'll fuck him up." MacDonnell's words were not an idle or boastful threat.

"Don't. I took care of it last night."

MacDonnell remained silent, but unconvinced he should let it go. For him there was no longer any question about his right to watch out for her, in or out of Blythewood.

Later in the afternoon, he returned to Cornwall with a bizarre story about an intermittent fuel line problem that temporarily disabled his car, and forced him to spend last night curled up in the pew of a Catholic church, thank God, because he wouldn't have slept in a Protestant one. There were more holes in this fanciful narrative than a leaky boat, but to his surprise and delight, Michelle accepted the implausible excuse without contention. In his great relief, he failed to notice his wife's great despair.

55

MacDonnell felt shaky the next morning.

Michelle left early and was gone for the entire day. He didn't wonder where she was or what she was doing. He was glad she was gone. It gave him time to think things over.

Mike sat at his kitchen table listlessly sipping cups of Earl Grey and wondering if the night with Annie had been anything more than an incidental shot in the dark. Alternately elated and depressed, he desperately wished one thing in his life could be clear-cut and above suspicion. But the drunken tumble with Annie would not — could not — fit into that mold. It was an emotional anthill at best. Mike's reason and concentration were further handicapped by the odd conviction Annie's fragrance lingered on his hands and her taste on his lips.

MacDonnell cleverly deduced he was suffering from a kind of intense sexual aftershock. It both delighted and scared the living shit out of him. There was potential for great pain here.

He wafted aimlessly through the day, and at sunset, with Michelle still away, he rolled out on his porch to drink a glass of single malt from a bottle he'd hidden in the garage. A cold wind plucked at his black hair, tossing curls like little dark waves over ears and brow. Dressed in nothing more than gray sweat pants and a black T-shirt, he refused to notice the brief, inquisitive stares of people passing by in their tightly sealed cars.

Cornwall was surrounded by wooded hills, leafless now and snow blemished. The gathering twilight colored them brown and purple, and wove them through with sparse threads of dark, piney green. MacDonnell allowed unease to slip away and watched those hills — his hills — make a steady turn to tweed. It came to him, in mild revelation, that there was no air so sweet, no light so clear, as that of home. Acquaintances would occasionally ask him why he remained living in tiny, rural Cornwall, so far from his work, so far from everything. His prosaic explanation was always the same: It was where he came from. It was home. To him, no other justification was necessary.

Mike poured another glass of whisky, and at the first mouthful, and just for a moment, felt like a stray-away child. It made him taste the winter cold more sharply and it made him a little sad.

I love Annie Wilson.

"You look like you seen a spook?" Pete the Eskimo commented as he walked past the porch.

Startled, MacDonnell managed to smile and wave at the diminutive man. "You never know, Pete, you never know."

Everybody called Pete the 'Eskimo'(never to his face, of course, because it would have been rude and Pete had a raging temper), but he was actually a Cree who wandered down from Canada decades ago and, for some reason, made his home in Cornwall. He was only a little bigger than a child, less than five-feet tall, and though he was getting on in years, every morning and every afternoon, in all conditions, he would stroll from one end of the village to the other. On Halloween he sculpted the most frighteningly beautiful faces into pumpkins for the Cornwall children; and occasionally, he and Mike MacDonnell would sit together at the Colonial Inn on Main Street and buy each other drinks. Often, when Pete got stiff, he would get angry and berate Canadians, labeling them as "Dirty condescending Scotch bastards."

"Care for a blast, Pete?" MacDonnell raised his glass.

"No, no, no. Gotta finish my walk. We'll sink a few at Christmas, okay?"

"It's a date."

MacDonnell finished his whisky and went back inside. The warmth of his house, after the chill of the night air, quickly made him drowsy. He lay on the couch and dozed until Michelle came home.

56

The following Sunday, on the way to work, MacDonnell stopped at a supermarket to buy some flowers. It was too early for a regular florist shop to be open, if indeed any were open on Sunday, but he was determined to get roses for Annie Wilson. Unfortunately, there wasn't a sweet smelling petal of any variety to be had in the store. He emerged with some kind of weird plant in a pot. When he presented it to Annie in the office, she stared — by turns — at it and him.

"What's this for?"

"I wanted to get you flowers," he said.

"This is a baby palm tree."

"They didn't have any flowers this morning because it's Sunday. They were out of roses."

Annie turned the pot around in her hands. "It's . . . lovely. Are you sure you don't want to give it to your wife?"

MacDonnell shook his head. "It's for you."

57

"You gave her a cactus?" Rick Pasinetti asked in disbelief. He dispersed the cloud of cigarette smoke hovering above his head with a few quick waves of his meaty hand.

"A baby palm," Mike MacDonnell corrected.

"Cyrano you ain't. What ... what ... *what* could a high-class dame like her see in a fat, ugly, sleazy, Mick cockhound like you?"

Mike MacDonnell could only shrug.

"She must have been blitzed and beyond," said Pasinetti, shaking his head until MacDonnell feared he might induce whiplash. "Jesus Gawd, I don't know whether I should be impressed or terrified a giant asteroid is headed for earth."

"The next day, Annie gave me a CD, some girl singer, said it's her favorite new album. Christ, I couldn't get through two songs. I told her I loved it, of course."

"It still beats a cactus," Rick said, "You know, I gave Wifey Dearest a big, red rubber dildo on our second — and last — anniversary. She'd come flouncing down the stairs in this see-thru-negligee while I was trying to watch *True Grit*. I hands here the dong and says, 'Merry Christmas and leave me alone.' She says, 'Come on Rickey, don't you like what you see?' I takes another look. Now I've said she had great tits, but Gawd, her legs were awful. Turned me right the fuck off after a couple years. So I says, 'Dear, you've got legs like a malnourished duck.' That damned dildo raised a welt the size of a Rocky Mountain Spotted Cantaloupe on my head."

"*True Grit*, huh? You a big John Wayne fan?"

"Gawd, no. He was good in that movie, but I never could stand him. Man's man, tough guy — All American hero. Bullshit. He ducked service in World War Two. Did you know that? Got one deferment after another. The only bullet The Duke ever dodged was his own jizz bouncing off a mirror."

MacDonnell laughed, but it faded quickly. "I don't know how to act around Michelle anymore."

"Well, for fuck's sake, don't tell her what you did with Madame Bovary."

"I'm not going to. I just feel bad." MacDonnell wondered why he was divulging all these sordid details. It wasn't because he didn't trust Rick. He did — but spilling his guts was not something MacDonnell had ever been fond of doing.

"Yeah? Well, don't. I never could understand how people bang each other over and over again without getting bored. Seems unnatural." Pasinetti picked at something between his teeth. "Did I ever tell you about the old broad I nailed at the Richmond Terrace Apartments? I had a place there while I was working for the Newbury Highway Department and she was my neighbor. Gawd, she must have been every day of sixty and ugly as a bag of assholes. One night, out of the clear blue, she invites me for a drink on her patio. I'd already had more than a few, so I goes over and has a few more with her. Free booze is free booze. I don't know how it got started, but the next thing I know, we're making out like teenagers." Pasinetti paused as horror momentarily overtook him. "Well, one thing led to another and I wolf-cocked her right there on the patio. I'm sure the other tenants got quite an eyeful. The next morning she's knocking at my door and asking me if I'd like to go out to breakfast. One look at old leatherface in broad daylight kills my appetite, but to be polite, I says, 'Sure, why not?' We goes to the Copper Kettle over on Winston, and doesn't she start acting like we're a married couple? She starts calling me Ricky and patting my hand and talking to me about stupid shit, the way women do when they think they've got a gaff in. Finally she asks me if I'd like to move in with her. I says, 'Are you fucking nuts? We had sex — once. It don't mean we're now husband and Sea Hag.' She gets pissed off and tells me men are no damn good, that all we want is a blow job and a handshake afterwards. So, I says right back at her, 'You've got nothing to complain about. I'm the one who went snorkeling down in the Ever-glades, not you.' We left the Copper Kettle without ordering, and thank Gawd, she never spoke to me again."

"You've led a princely existence, haven't you?"

"I like to think so," Pasinetti said. "Which brings us back to you and Princess Grace."

"How — in the name of Sweet Jesus — does it bring us anywhere in the vicinity of Annie Wilson?"

"Shit can happen to people, and sometimes it seems more important than it actually is."

"Could be," Mike MacDonnell admitted and hoped it wasn't true.

"See the little TV Donatello is watching behind the bar?" Pasinetti asked. The 13 inch black-and-white was beaming like a blue star inside The Alley. "Donatello thinks basketball is important. Every year he brings in the television and watches every game they broadcast. Hey, Donatello? How are the Celtics doing?"

"Good. Up by six."

"You like basketball, huh?"

"No shit."

"You like looking at all them sweaty black men running up and down the court?"

No answer to this.

Rick Pasinetti grinned. "And you say you're not queer?"

Donatello turned his face from the screen for a moment. "Maybe I am — but I ain't gonna be givin' you no sponge baths."

"See what I mean?" said Pasinetti to MacDonnell.

"No," Mike answered honestly.

58

After the holidays, Annie's wealthy friend once again prevailed upon her to watch his home; this time so he could pursue a young lady of France across the continent of Europe. Annie asked MacDonnell if he would mind another trip to Foxhill on Wednesday.

"Sure," he agreed faintheartedly, remembering the last visit there. "I'll let Kevin know."

"Kevin's not invited."

This caveat caused Mike MacDonnell to lose the power of coherent thought for the better part of an hour.

Neither one had spoken about the night of the Christmas party and no further intimacy had taken place. It was as if they both needed time to digest the matter. It seemed that period of reflection had ended.

Wednesday came and they drove to Foxhill in the Subaru. The Toyota remained at Blythewood by Annie Wilson's insistence. Mike, stiff as a board in the passenger seat, stared through the windshield at an incomprehensible blur of onrushing cars, snow banks, buildings and fleeting daylight. He drank a beer from a six-pack at his feet in a vain effort to conquer an odd mixture of numbing terror and overwhelming anticipation. He was painfully aware of Annie's physical presence next to him, but was afraid to look at her.

By the time they arrived, MacDonnell felt disembodied and free-floating. He wafted through the front door and into the kitchen, where he tried to crack a bottle of her favorite German beer, but only succeeded in tearing a ragged furrow in the side of his thumb with the bottle opener. There was little pain, but a great deal of blood. It irritated him that something — anything — should go wrong tonight. He dismissed the injury with a grunt, wiped the offending thumb on his pants and finished opening Annie's beer.

Annie discarded her coat on the kitchen table. She stood very straight and sipped the beer, all the while staring at him, but not speaking a word. There was a strange light in her eyes which was at once impossibly distant and frightening in its proximity.

And she was wearing that *smile*.

MacDonnell had secretly dubbed it the 'Mona Lisa,' a silent, steady, enigmatic seam rising like a shallow moon above her sculpted chin. Annie would use it as a placid disguise to mask her inner feelings; or, when she chanced to let her eyes fall ever so slightly and then ascend again on the swell of a heartbeat, as a weapon of domination and seduction against which Mike MacDonnell had no defense.

Annie Wilson set the bottle of beer on the table next to her coat. She unbuttoned her blouse, shook it back from her shoulders and let it slip to the floor. Mike MacDonnell would always remember the faint shimmer of a white silky bra against ruddy skin.

He took a breath. It rattled in his chest.

She carefully opened the bra and offered him breasts dusted by freckles and scented by the heat of arousal. He took one in each hand and kissed the curve of her throat. Blood smeared the erect nipple he gently squeezed between torn thumb and forefinger.

He found real passion then, something he had only glimpsed before. Years later he would wonder if he had been clumsy or awkward, if he had disappointed her. But that night, no such doubt disturbed him. She was everything — all creation. No other consideration to be made. They moved on to a bedroom and crisp white sheets and passed the hours in each other's arms.

Guilt never reared its corrupt head, then or later. Mike MacDonnell loved Annie Wilson. He loved her in spite of the other men and he loved her without hope of keeping her. The moments she gave him were enough, more than he had a right to expect, all the mercy a raggedy man could look for along a road that already hinted at something dim and endless.

He would never stop missing Annie when she was gone; but only once, long past their parting, did he allow the torment of what might have been to conjure a portrait of her grown old at his side. He would turn away from this sad apparition with a smile that touched only his eyes, and blended equal parts regret and nostalgic longing with wry acceptance that the carrying currents of life moved and resolved in their own fashion and in their own good time.

59

Bonnie Quirk rushed into the supervisors office one afternoon in her usual state of euphoric mania. The makeup, however, had been troweled on with an extra heavy hand. MacDonnell wondered if a precise chisel strike, just above the bridge of her nose, would cause her face to fracture and crumble like old masonry.

"I talked to *Daddy* last night," she squeaked.

"Oh? About presents?"

"He's dying to meet you."

"Come again?"

"I told him all about you. He can't wait to meet you."

To say Mike MacDonnell was flabbergasted would have been an obscene understatement.

"Do you know where Boonville is?" she continued ecstatically.

"Where Daniel Boone lives?"

"No, silly. It's where *Daddy* lives, up near Lake Ontario."

"Oh . . . oh . . ."

"It has the highest annual snowfall on the face of the earth."

"That's . . . that's something."

"There are some long winter nights up there, I can tell you." Bonnie Quirk winked and left a smudge of black eyelash liner on her cheek.

"Don't say? Well . . . " MacDonnell wanted to be anywhere else, but here or Boonville.

"We could go up there this weekend. *Daddy* says it's good I'm finally getting over Sammy."

"Sammy?"

"My ex-fiancé. He's in jail now. He killed a convenience store clerk with a claw hammer."

MacDonnell made a bubbling sound that might have been some form of response.

"In all fairness, Sammy was provoked." A pout trembled on Quirk's candy-red lips. "The clerk refused to let him pay for my Tic Tacs with a hundred dollar bill. Sammy's temper got the better of him. We were high school sweethearts."

"You and the clerk?"

"No! Me and . . . me and Sammy."

The clinician lapsed into a prolonged silence and stared at the floor. MacDonnell thought she might be crying. Finally he cleared his throat and said, "Well, that's too bad."

Quirk wiped her nose on the back of her hand, abruptly turned and fled the office without another word.

Annie Wilson appeared in the doorway and asked, "What did you do to that poor woman?"

"Tried to kiss her."

Annie frowned and Mike sighed.

60

January settled in with a bitter tang. Its first ten days provided cold, cold and more cold. The snowpack turned stiff and coarse like dry white corduroy. If you lost your footing and fell in it, you'd better be wearing gloves or the sharp crystals would cut your bare wrists and hands. To Mike MacDonnell, however, it was as if a sudden spring had found him and lightened his plodding steps. He came to work early, laughed a great deal and let his heart live. The black moods he pretended not to have still came, but they were less dark, less able to drown him in sad, empty thoughts. He was able to build an intellectual and emotional corral for his wife and keep her there.

Monday, the 5th, was the coldest morning of the winter. Mike's hair, sopping wet from a hurried shower, froze in the time it took him to walk from his front door to the Toyota, and froze again as he walked from the Blythewood parking lot to the office door. Inside, he found Annie squirming on the hook of an uncomfortable conversation with Vivie Sandhurst. Sandhurst was a night staff who resembled a fireplug with unwashed hair. She was also living proof heterosexual males hadn't cornered the market on lonely, obnoxious boors. Sandhurst's chief hobby, other than composing dreary folk songs and flogging them on a guitar at local clubs, was hounding straight women with promises of unimaginable carnal delights; the kind only one female could bestow upon another. Her verbal seduction began with an invitation to her home for an 'American Chop Suey Dinner.' This opening salvo never varied. Not once within living memory had Vivie offered her intended victim meatloaf and mashed potatoes, or even a tuna casserole. 'American Chop Suey Dinner' became Blythewood watchwords for the unwelcome advances of either a woman or a man. In this, Vivie Sandhurst achieved a lasting kind of gender parity.

As MacDonnell listened to the conversation, it became apparent Vivie had decided it was time to take another run at convincing Annie Wilson to nibble a little tomato and macaroni. Vivie cycled through the straight girls with the implacable regularity of the celestial procession. Mike caught Annie's eye and smacked his lips together, pretending to kiss someone. Annie grabbed a spiral notebook she'd been doodling in and flung it at him. Vivie didn't blink or pause in her rap as the object flew past her and hit Mike in the face.

A few minutes later the night shift, as they filtered through the office and out to their cars, asked Mike why he was bleeding. The bridge of his nose would bear a tiny, permanent scar where the notebook's partially unraveled wire spine stuck like a dart. Only Vivie failed to notice his bleeding snout. Her eyes were all for Annie Wilson.

For the rest of the day, MacDonnell found himself relegated to a kind of internal exile decreed by the love of his life. Annie was cold, uncommunicative and unrelenting in her distaste for him. This reduced Mike to a pathetic, anxiety ridden mess. The unhappy footman whined a little and tried an assortment of cheap manipulations to win back the favor of his domina, but in the end, head hanging, and a little sickened by his own desperation, he finally gave up and drifted away from the office and the woman enthroned there.

61

"Not smoking anymore, Rick?" Mike MacDonnell asked.

"Naw. I've taken up chew." To illustrate this statement, Pasinetti leaned over the bar and spit a mouthful of tobacco juice into a plastic cup

"Well, good for you, I guess."

"Hey, Donatello? Where the fuck is my drink, you lazy cock-tease."

The bartender muttered something profane and continued mixing.

"So, how's things at the Wood?" Rick asked Mike.

"Same old nonsense. I told you about Cyril, didn't I?"

"About his Christmas visit? Yeah. Mandrake made his mind disappear."

"Annie said he was quite a charmer in his day."

"Did she really? Well that confirms my suspicions about her taste in men."

"What do you mean?"

"Oh, Mandrake was quite the ladies' man in his prime. From what I've heard, he'd fuck anything that would hold still for thirty seconds. Treated his women like gold, they say — except his wife. He used to beat the shit out of her. Probably still does."

"You're kidding?"

"Uh-uh. I use to bang this LPN over at the Medical Center, and she told me the wife would end up in the emergency room every few months with the livin' bejesus knocked out of her — black eyes, broken bones, concussions, the whole shot. Old Mandrake is a certified mother-fucking-wife-beater."

"He never got arrested?"

Rick Pasinetti laughed out loud. "Cousin Mongo, what world do you live in? Rumgay's got money, connections and friends in high places. It's all you need to get away with everything up to murder — and maybe even that. I heard a story about him getting boiled and killing somebody in a car accident back about twenty years ago. Got covered up by the cops and a friendly judge. Don't know if it's true or not. The stories about the wife are."

Mike whistled. "Wow. Annie really can pick 'um."

Rick made an exaggerated show of looking Mike up and down.

"That's what I've said all along, dogballs."

"Fuck you, Rick."

"Hey. I almost forgot. The old man is giving me his new minivan. He doesn't wanna drive anymore. Do you want the Impala? You can have it for free."

"Shit yes." The car was old, but still in reasonable shape, without too many miles on the 350. "I can drive it instead of Michelle's rice burner. She'll be happy." *For about ten minutes.*

"Come over and pick it up tomorrow. Got to warn you, though. The passenger side mirror is missing."

"What happened?"

"Just a little accident. I sideswiped a parked SUV."

"Drunk?"

"Peeled."

62

Vivie Sandhurst's fascination with Annie continued unabated for several days. She put in an unexpected appearance at the Four Tables one Wednesday evening. Fortunately for Mike and Annie, several other staff were present and sheer numbers diluted her woeful impact on the party, at least for a time.

Sandhurst spent most of the night silently, morosely, gulping tequilas. After two hours of this, her eyes grew so dark, she looked like a raccoon on methadone. At about the same time, ill fortune conspired to thin the crowd, offering her a most unhappy opportunity to be heard.

"I had to tell my last lover to leave," she announced in a loud, sloppy drawl. The words, tilted and ponderous, barely caused a ripple in her lumpy and immobile face. The last survivors of the party — excepting two supervisors — took this as their cue and excused themselves. Mike MacDonnell and Annie Wilson were left, face-to-face, with the Queen of American Chop Suey Dinner.

"She wet the bed . . ." Sandhurst's voice dwindled to a faint sob. "Every night, every night, she wet my sled — *bed!*"

"What were you dating?" Mike asked earnestly, "An incontinent border collie?"

"No." Vivie Sandhurst's head rolled down and then up again. She reached across the table and placed a fingered pork chop on Annie Wilson's arm. "Would you like to hear some of my poetry?"

"Oh, Sweat Jesus," MacDonnell mourned.

"I have a weight problem," Sandhurst muttered, licking her lips. "I've had a weight problem since I was thirteen."

"Do tell?" Mike feigned shock. "I thought you were just big-boned."

"I want you to hear a poem I wrote about it . . . my weight problem that is." Sandhurst closed her eyes, tightened her grasp on Annie's wrist, and launched into a faltering recital. She stumbled over words and lines, repeated herself several times, and was openly weeping by the conclusion of the embarrassingly heartfelt and fantastically inept verses.

The piece ended with the line, "When I find the big black hole in my soul, I fill it with ice cream in a bowl."

Mike MacDonnell howled. He laughed so hard his face turned scarlet and he pounded the table.

Vivie Sandhurst stared at him in dumb, drunken horror. She was not used to having her inner child greeted with abject, hee-haw-braying ridicule.

"I've witnessed the resurrection of Dylan Thomas," MacDonnell roared. "Go not gentle into that good night, just stuff your face with Haagen-Dazs, by the spoonful and the pint."

Vivie Sandhurst knocked the table sideways in her stampede out of the Four Tables' big room. Her wails of consummate misery were audible until she drove away in her old Saab.

Back in the bar, Annie sputtered, "That was the most awful thing I've ever seen."

"Yeah, it was pretty bad," MacDonnell chuckled, failing to understand what she meant.

"You are a cruel bastard!"

"Me? Cruel was being forced to listen to her poem."

"She was drunk. What's your excuse for being a heartless prick?"

"Come on, Annie." Mike MacDonnell knew he was in trouble. "I didn't mean to hurt her feelings."

"Bullshit! It's exactly what you meant to do."

Realizing a feather toss of whining, self-serving excuses was not going to do him any good, MacDonnell decided to launch an attack relying on candor as its salient feature.

"Listen, Annie. If someone — anyone — walks into a bar, pours a bottle of tequila down their throat, and then proceeds to spout the worst kind of corny garbage, they should expect to be laughed at. I would. And don't tell me you found her *poetry* inspiring."

"I never said I did. But it doesn't mean I would kick somebody in the teeth when they're that vulnerable."

"Oh, for the love of Christ. She's a professional victim — like just about everybody else in the human service field. They all want to feel bad about something. Vivie wants to feel bad about her weight and about her ex-lover, Lassie Bladder-Leaky. But most of all, she wants you to feel bad for her. That way, maybe she'll get a little mercy fuck from the straight chick. It was all a blatant manipulation."

"That's what this is all about, isn't it? You're afraid she's going to play me the way you do."

MacDonnell's hands met and formed a spire over his nose.

"Annie, if you want to sleep with a troll that's your business. I ain't the jealous type."

It was Annie Wilson's turn to burst out laughing. MacDonnell's face turned beet red.

She stood up and put on her ski jacket. "I'm going home."

"I'm coming with you."

"No, you are not!"

"I'm too drunk to drive."

"The hell you are."

"I want to go home with you."

"NO!"

MacDonnell trailed her meekly out to the parking lot, but then rushed past her to his *new* Impala, jumped in, kicked the motor — and deliberately rammed the vehicle into the three-foot-high, round wooden posts which served as a barrier between the lower parking area and the building.

He unrolled his window and shouted, "Told you I was too drunk to drive."

Annie shook her head, horrified. "I can't believe what I just saw. Are you insane?"

"We better take your car," Mike MacDonnell suggested smugly, a stupid grin lighting his face. He put the Chevy in reverse and rolled it back into the parking space. There was little damage to the car — a crumple in the bumper, a cracked grill. The Impala was a tank.

"What's wrong with you?" she asked when he got in the Subaru.

MacDonnell tilted his head in her direction. "We don't have nearly enough time to go into that."

"Talk about being manipulative."

"I'm far too obvious to be truly manipulative."

"You are a fucking asshole."

"I don't think I've ever heard you swear this much."

"You bring out the worst in people."

"My mother always said that, and then she —"

"*Shut up*, you stupid, idiotic, mindless . . ." Annie ran out of adjectives and slapped him across the face.

That night, they fucked till both of them were sore.

63

Over time, MacDonnell developed simple, less destructive strategies for breaking through Annie's defenses. The success of these tactics depended upon a variety of factors, including alcohol and drug consumption, the flux of minor tragedies and mundane horrors at work, and the natural rise and fall of their own sex drives.

Overall, he found the direct, never-take-no-for-an-answer gambit to be the most consistently effective . . .

"No . . . not tonight. I don't feel like it."

Hesitation spoke volumes to him. He leaned down and kissed her on the mouth, ignoring the people on their way into the Tables, ignoring the cold and the snow swirling around them.

"Please." His lips at her ear now.

"No."

He kissed her again, and softly, "Please."

"No." Weak this time. Resolve was in flight.

A third kiss. "I'll beg if I have to. I don't have any pride."

She put her arms around his neck. "Did anyone ever tell you that you know how to kiss?"

"No."

"You do." She pressed her mouth against his.

64

MacDonnell never knew what to do with himself on those occasions when Annie called out sick. Without the promise of an evening tryst, nothing was interesting or important. It was as if all his psychological taste buds had gone flat.

In spite of the cold weather, he assumed his usual slouching pose in the outer doorway of the office. An endless procession of Newports stained his fingers yellow. The Blythewood supervisor maintained this position with all the diligence and determination of a machine gunner trying to single-handedly slow an enemy advance along some vital route; except in this case, the enemy was apathetic monotony, as much a friendly acquaintance as it was an opponent. MacDonnell usually didn't mind being bored.

During the late afternoon, Stanley Bainbridge slogged past with broom and dust pan, on his way to one of the dorms. Bainbridge was slow, deferential and quiet. MacDonnell always took time to say hello.

"Hey, Stanley, what's up?"

"Nothin' much, Mike," the housekeeper replied in his heavy New England drawl.

"I haven't seen Gordy Burdick in a while. Isn't he back from his trip to Australia yet?"

"Nawww. Ain't likely to ever be, neither."

"No? Don't tell me he went native and became a mop-wielding, croc-hunting Jackaroo?"

Bainbridge frowned. The question confused him. "Nawww. He, uh, he just up and disappeared."

"Disappeared?"

"Aaayuh. Went swimmin' with his girl one day, and just up and vanished." Stanley snapped his fingers. "They think one of them big sharks, them great whites, et him. Left his lady friend alone though, and that's hard to figure. She must weigh a good three hundred pound herself, and all of it cream and butter. Poor old Gordy coulda' hid behind this old broom a' mine. Too bad. They say he were good to her kids."

"Seven, eight, nine," Mike MacDonnell whispered under his breath.

"What's that?"

"Nothing, Stanley."

"I better get these old bones movin'. I'm head janitor now, and there ain't enough hours in the day to get all the work done round here as it is. I do wish Gordy had stayed out a' the salt. Can't figure why he'd wanna go swimmin' in the wintertime, anyhow. Must have been wicked cold."

"It's a mystery, Stanley."

"Aaayuh."

65

A bright Thursday afternoon found a lumpy Mike MacDonnell on the road, fleeing from another domestic detonation triggered by Michelle. At least he chose to give her credit for this particular outburst in the ever lengthening parade of marital strife. He'd made the mistake of taking a brief nap, only to be awakened by his darling bride kneeling on his chest and hitting him in the head with a rock. What compelled Michelle to communicate in this fashion was never revealed. He didn't wait around long enough to discuss the matter. When she was out to maim, it was best to leave her be.

MacDonnell traced the hen's egg on his forehead with the back of his thumb. Smoke curled from the cigarette stuck between his index and middle fingers. The Newport's filter was stained red by a bloody upper lip. He took a final drag on the cigarette, tossed it out the window and grabbed a pint of rye from the passenger seat. He took a long sip and then another. The bottle was half empty by the time he parked the Impala above the Four Tables.

There was a pay phone outside the bar. MacDonnell called Kevin Marshall and asked him to come by if he wasn't doing anything. Marshall said he would be there in an hour. MacDonnell knew he could put the time to good use.

He went inside to the bathroom, cleaned up his face the best he could, then strolled out to the bar. He ordered an Old Bushmills. A girl, two stools down, asked him what Old Bushmills was. She might have been hitting on him, but he wasn't sure. It didn't matter. Annie Wilson was the only woman on the face of the earth.

For the sake of killing time, and to be polite, he started talking to the girl — a decision he instantly regretted. She ended every statement as if it were a question, a verbal crutch, growing more and more common, which he hated.

"I saw a dog in the road? And a car was coming? And the car hit the dog? And I cried? It was so sad?"

Mike wondered how anyone could be so congenitally uncertain of what they were talking about.

Kevin arrived in time to save MacDonnell's sanity. The girl immediately shifted her attentions and launched everything in her sexual arsenal.

She got drunk and horny. Kevin squirmed. Finally, Mike suggested they seek their liquid refreshment elsewhere.

Walking out to their cars, MacDonnell said, "You could have gotten some, Kevie."

"Not my type, *Mikey*."

"No? A little too much, uh, estrogen for your taste?"

"Stop looking at my ass while I walk."

Marshall suggested they try a new bar, The Rail Line, that had opened in Foxhill. He'd heard good things about it. MacDonnell had heard it was nothing more than a meat shop for the Volvo and Saab crowd. Not exactly his kind of haunt, but he agreed. There was nowhere else to go at the moment, and he was drunk enough to imagine it might be fun to invade a yuppie nest.

"Where did you get this old hunk of junk?" Kevin asked when MacDonnell stopped at the Impala.

"Rick Pasinetti. He gave it to me for free."

"He owes you money."

Main Street in Foxhill was elegantly calculated to devour even the most discriminating and wary tourist. Everything was upscale, tasteful, expensive — old weathered brick and ivy. Beyond, there was a pretty little town that fluttered demurely along a shallow river and crept prudently across scenic hills. The two Blythewood staff had to park their vehicles about a block from the Rail Line. It was past five and the bar was already filling up. Its reputation as a local hot spot had been firmly established.

Mike MacDonnell didn't see Annie Wilson and her two female companions when he first entered the bar; they were at the other end of the crowded taproom. In fact, MacDonnell had finished a beer before he caught sight of a familiar pony tail bobbing through the tangle of human bodies.

"Hey, isn't that Annie?" Kevin asked.

MacDonnell nodded almost imperceptibly, gripped by a sudden and peculiar reluctance to acknowledge her, as if to do so would breach some secret contract not to meet on unfamiliar territory, on an unfamiliar day.

"Are those two ladies with her?" Kevin continued. "Holy shit."

"I'm sure Shelley would be pleased with that reaction."

The two women in question, one blond, one brunette, and both flawlessly attractive, stood to either side of Annie at the bar, laughing and talking with her, and occasionally flirting with the small cohort of male admirers they'd gathered. Nor was Annie Wilson excluded from this testosterone-spiked attention. There was a tall young man standing so close behind her that his thigh lightly brushed her ass every time one of them chanced to move, even slightly. And Annie didn't seem to mind the contact.

"I'll go over and see if they want to sit at our table," Kevin Marshall announced brightly.

"Uh, I don't know," MacDonnell mumbled, but it was too late. Marshall was already threading his way through a maze of elbows. He somehow insinuated himself between Annie and the tall young man and tapped her on the shoulder. Annie turned around with an instant smile and began talking to him. MacDonnell couldn't hear what they were saying, but he watched the exchange closely. Kevin said something and pointed back in MacDonnell's direction. Annie's eyes traveled across the bar — and the smile left her face. Mike MacDonnell wanted to hide under the table. Annie didn't want him here.

Somehow, Kevin Marshall convinced the three women to come back to the table with him, much to the disappointment of all the hard-ons surrounding them. It was an intimidating female trio that moved in MacDonnell's direction, making him painfully aware of just how far his gut hung over his belt buckle. Mike didn't get up when they arrived. Instead, he cleared his throat and grunted and looked guilty for being there.

"Hi, Mike," Annie Wilson said. There was a touch of frost in her voice. "Fancy meeting you here."

"Uh, yeah."

"This is Kathy and Jill. Friends of mine from college. They're here for a few days to do a little skiing."

"Uhhh . . . hmmmm." Like a great many natives of the area, Mike had never been on skis; they were for the tourists.

"Kathy and Jill this is Mike MacDonnell. He works for me at Blythewood."

MacDonnell was baffled by this introduction.

Kathy and Jill made brief, polite and perfunctory salutations and sat down at the small table. It was crowded. Annie had to squeeze in next to MacDonnell when Kevin forged an opening between the other two women.

"So, where did you ladies go to college?" Marshall asked. His eyes were dancing in his head.

Jill mentioned one of the Seven Sisters, which didn't surprise Mike at all. These women gleamed with the luster of privilege. It shone not just from the expensive clothes they wore, but from their hair and skin and perfect teeth, in their eyes and speech and manners. Annie Wilson's physical allure was heightened by their proximity as if she'd been drenched in their glistening perfection. MacDonnell found it difficult to look at them or her. They were too bright, too pretty, too cool and worldly-wise. It made him feel like a mudseed — his concocted term for the homely people who struggled to keep old cars on the road and ate boxes of macaroni and cheese, three for a dollar, when they had to; who eagerly spent their blood and jizz, and lost teeth like pennies; the people who never invested in retirement plans and vacation condos, who took comfort where they could find it, and in the end, ate the dirt they pissed on.

"I got my degree from Western New England not too long ago," Kevin Marshall remarked.

"Why are you working at Brightwood?" Jill asked with a seamless mixture of mild interest and contempt. "By the way Annie describes it, it's a perfectly horrid place."

"Well, I've got student loans to — "

Kathy interrupted Kevin. "We could ask Annie the same question."

Annie Wilson sighed and pulled her shoulders back, making breasts rise and nipples press against the light fabric of the shirt she wore.

"Why don't you ask Mike why he's been there for so long?"

This confused and irritated MacDonnell. Was Annie trying to defend herself or insult him?

He decided it was his turn to do a little intimidating.

"I just do it for the dental plan," he said dryly. "Actually, I'm a fully licensed Nuclear Engineer. I took a correspondence course while I was in jail."

"You were never in prison," Annie said with cool disdain. She'd seen this act before.

"How would you know where I've been, *boss*?"

"Okay, I'll play along with this nonsense. What were you in jail for, Mr. MacDonnell?"

"One of my Harvard frat brothers wore my raccoon coat to the big game without my permission. I strangled him on the quad."

Kathy and Jill were perplexed by this exchange. They could tell there was some kind of tension between MacDonnell and Annie Wilson, but they would never, in their wildest dreams, allow themselves to imagine their sorority sister was somehow involved with such an uncouth slob.

It was not an uncanny mystery to Kevin Marshall.

"Do you girls want to shoot some pool?" he hastily suggested to Jill and Kathy. "I saw a table in the next room." He wanted to give Mike and Annie a chance to work their way out of the minefield they'd laid for each other.

"Sure, why not," Kathy replied. "Are you going to come, Annie?"

"No, I, uh, I'm going to finish my drink."

When they were gone, MacDonnell and Annie sat in silence for some time, not looking at each other.

Finally, MacDonnell said, "I'm sorry if I embarrassed you."

"You didn't embarrass me. I just wanted a day out with my friends, without you following me around."

"Following you around? How in hell was I supposed to know you'd be here? I wasn't stalking you. I wanted to get wrecked. And by the way, you seemed to be having a high old time with Mr. Studley at the bar awhile ago. He was riding your ass like — "

"Don't start, Mike. You know better."

MacDonnell's eyes dropped away from hers.

"Kevin and I will leave when he's done shooting pool — though I think he wants to get laid."

"Not a snowball's chance in hell. Kevin would never cheat on his girlfriend."

"How do you know what he'd go for?" This was a shotgun spray of neurotic apprehension that came from deep inside him and had nothing to do with Kevin Marshall. "Anyway, we'll go some place where the girls are a little more within the reach of mere mortals like us."

Annie glanced at him sharply. "Meaning what? That you're looking?" Her turn for a little uncertainty.

Long strands of hair had escaped Annie's ponytail and drifted down across her ear to tease the curve of her white throat. MacDonnell shivered and wanted to touch her more than anything else in the world.

"I ain't looking for anybody," he scoffed. *I belong to you.*

"Then why go?" A quiet and unexpected surrender.

"What about your friends — and Kevin?"

"They can sort things out for themselves. Kevin's cute and they're slutty. What happened to your head?"

"Dr. Frankenstein tried to steal my brain."

"You mean he was trying to put one in?"

He went drunk and without a condom to Annie's bed.

"You'll have to pull out," she said, clutching him fiercely.

"I will."

"Do you love me?"

"You know I do."

"Tell me."

"I love you" over and over again, till it became a chant.

When the moment arrived, he forgot his promise and came inside her. She made no protest and only held him closer.

66

Mike MacDonnell pounded angrily on the front door of Annie Wilson's house. One of Annie's roommates answered the thunderous summons.

"What do you want?" A frightened squeak through a half-open door.

"Is Annie Wilson here?" MacDonnell roared.

"I — I — I think she's in bed," the college boy stammered, mentally trying to prepare himself to hold the door against this ogreish figure risen from the night.

"*Please*—" Mike labored over the word, "tell her Mike MacDonnell would like to speak to her."

A moment later Annie Wilson stomped down the stairs, hair flying in every direction and sleep filling her eyes like potash.

"What!" she demanded irritably.

"Where the hell did you go tonight?"

Annie wrapped her night gown tightly around her waist in an unmistakable gesture. "You were acting like a loudmouthed jerk — again — so I left."

"You left," Mike snorted. "Look, I don't care if you get pissed-off at me, and I don't care if you want to leave, that's your choice — "

"You're damn right it is."

"At least have the common fucking decency to tell me where you're going. I was scared out of my wits. I thought something had happened to you."

"Like what? I was kidnapped by pirates or white slavers? Get a grip on yourself."

MacDonnell spun on his heel. "Fuck you."

"Say, why don't I have a GPS implanted in my head? That way you can — "

"Fuck you!"

"Get back here." Annie started to laugh.

"NO!" MacDonnell jumped in his car and knocked over two trash cans on his way out of the driveway.

67

On her way home from Connecticut late on a Saturday night, Annie Wilson lost control of the Subaru on a patch of ice and slammed into a fire hydrant. She wasn't hurt and managed to limp the car home. The next day at work, MacDonnell offered her the Impala until her vehicle could be made roadworthy. Annie accepted his generosity with some hesitation. The incident at the Four Tables notwithstanding, she knew what a compulsive fanatic he was about his cars. She misjudged him in this instance. An automobile was a trivial matter. Mike MacDonnell would have given her his eyes.

Two weeks later Annie would return the vehicle, leaving it in the driveway of his house. MacDonnell wasn't home at the time. He had taken Michelle grocery shopping. Upon his return, he found the keys over the Chevy's visor and a handwritten note — rolled around a hundred dollar bill — in the ashtray.

> *Mike,*
> *Doug and I dropped off the car. Found your address on the registration.*
> *You weren't home. Thanks for everything,*
> *Annie*

MacDonnell crumpled the note in his fist.

Doug.

Over the past weeks he'd been able to pretend Doug no longer existed. Annie hadn't mentioned him in some time. Now to find out the rich cocksucker had been in *his* car, next to *her* . . .

What had she told Doug? That Mike MacDonnell was an acquaintance from Blythewood — a coworker — who had rented her a car? *("Just a friend, Dougie. Just a friend.")* It was the explanation MacDonnell had shoved down Michelle's throat.

For an instant he toyed with the idea of lighting a Newport with Ben Franklin's visage — but then thought better of it and stuffed the bill in his wallet. A hundred bucks was hard to come by when you were nothing but a stupid, fucking, glorified babysitter without a shot in hell of ever being anything much better.

Mike MacDonnell sat in the front seat of the Impala for some time, staring at nothing and trying to gain distance from his own unhappy and impotent thoughts.

Eventually Michelle stuck her head out the door.

"Aren't you ever coming in?"

That voice. Christ, he hated the sound of it, the way it always scaled a ladder into pleading, whiny insistence. But there was no sense sitting in the car any longer, or defying her grating command.

"I'll be right in."

Michelle disappeared.

MacDonnell opened the car door. The interior lights flickered on and he noticed something on the turn signal arm, something the shadows had concealed from him before: a tiny, tightly wound hair band.

An image invaded his mind of Annie Wilson on her way home from work, taking both hands off the wheel for a moment to free her hair, to let it fall like mercury and gold over the headrest. He knew how that hair smelled and how it felt between his fingers and against his face.

MacDonnell pushed the hair band farther down the stalk, inside the small opening on the steering column — a place no one else would ever find it. There it would remain for as long as he owned the vehicle, a charm and a talisman.

He got out of the car and stood in his driveway, watching his wife's shadow move back and forth across the kitchen window. She must be doing dishes.

His hands began to shake violently.

No more . . . no more . . . no more . . .

Enough was fucking enough. This had to stop — and stop now.

"Goddamn it." He spat in the dirt. "Fuck Dougie."

Mike decided he would wait until morning to tell Michelle he was leaving her. He would drop the news like a bomb, endure the inevitable emotional firestorm, the battering — and then go to work and to Annie.

From the few comments she'd made, he knew Doug would be a formidable adversary. He had more money than MacDonnell, certainly, and a brighter future; but then many people might claim that advantage. MacDonnell convinced himself he could overcome these obstacles, somehow, someway. He knew what love was now and he wasn't going to let it go. Not without a fight and all guns firing. There was simply no other option he could endure.

A bubble of guilt tickled the back of his throat as he lay in bed that night.

"Michelle, I need to talk to you about something in the morning."

MacDonnell could not see his wife's strange smile in the dark.

"That's funny. I've got something to tell you, too."

MacDonnell's brow remained wrinkled until he fell into an uneasy sleep.

Just past dawn on the next day, before the alarm clock had a chance to squawk, Michelle unceremoniously executed all his dreams.

She shook him awake in the dirty light and, before he had time to clear his eyes or swallow the residue of sleep on his tongue, announced she was pregnant.

MacDonnell sat up slowly on the edge of the bed. A hillbilly assassin could have pumped both barrels of a sawed-off 12 gauge into the back of his skull to no effect — although he would have appreciated the effort.

"I took the home test twice. I was going to wait till Wednesday to tell you, so we could celebrate, but I couldn't hold off any longer."

Michelle spun around the bed like a frenzied sprite full of glee.

MacDonnell drove to Blythewood that morning feeling like his flesh had turned to cold clay. He'd been with Michelle once, two months ago, before the Blythewood Christmas party. Her pregnancy was unimaginable and unbearable.

More glad tidings awaited him at work.

Annie Wilson blew into the office, slammed the door and grabbed his arm.

"I think I'm pregnant! I'm over a week late!"

"Pregnant?" MacDonnell mewled. "By me?"

"Of course by you. You're the only one I've had unprotected sex with."

He groaned and then he laughed and then he groaned some more.

"What's wrong with you?" Annie asked crossly.

"Nothing a pair of hedge clippers wouldn't have cured."

"What are we going to do?"

"Don't worry."

"That's not an answer."

"It'll have to do in a pinch."

She warned, "I don't believe in abortion."

"Neither do I," he admitted miserably.

MacDonnell spent the rest of the day with an eerie buzzing in his head, as if every neurotransmission in his brain had been fancifully rerouted by the horror of his predicament. Knocking up Annie was . . . well it was kind of cool, really. Dougie could go skip rope for all the good it would do him now. MacDonnell had claimed Annie in the most primitive and indisputable way a man could. But Michelle's pregnancy was not cool, not pleasant, not joyous, happy or blessed. It suggested the cruel irony of a consummately sadistic Universal Mind.

Michelle had tried every possible means to become pregnant and none had been successful. Now, of all times, for her to discover fertility was simply fiendish.

A terrible choice had to be made and slowly, over the course of the shift, MacDonnell reached his decision. He would find a way to care for Michelle and the child she bore — no son or daughter of Michael Francis MacDonnell would ever want for a father — but he was going to divorce her and marry Annie Wilson, if she would have him. This was by no means a perfect solution, nor even a particularly honorable one, the outcome having been influenced by his own selfish desires; but it was a resolution and granted him a certain anxious serenity for the next several hours.

In the end, all his mental turmoil proved unnecessary.

At ten minutes to seven, Annie danced into the office.

"I just started my period," she said, smiling broadly. "Wanna go to the Tables for a drink? I know I need one."

MacDonnell pretended relief and hid a sadness even from himself. There were no longer any choices to be made, no consequences to be weighed and balanced — no hope. His wife was going to have a baby and Annie Wilson was forever beyond his reach.

The desperate need to hold onto her would prevent him from telling Annie about Michelle's pregnancy. He knew full well Annie would never take him to bed again under those circumstances. An unhappy marriage was one thing, a teary-eyed expectant mother, waiting for the return of a wayward husband, quite another.

68

The March issue of *Gourmet* magazine revealed to Annie Wilson the existence of an Orthodox monastery, about thirty miles north of Cornwall, which produced world-class cheesecakes. Always prey to a sweet tooth, she asked MacDonnell if he knew where it was, and, when he admitted that he had a fair idea, she insisted they take a ride on their off-shift. MacDonnell, of course, could not refuse. He began to mentally leaf through his collection of patented excuses for Michelle.

They made the trip in the Impala. The monastery was situated on top of a steep ridge at the end of a long dirt road. It was slippery going. Patches of ice and dirty snow continuously spun the Chevy's tires.

"I should have brought a toboggan," MacDonnell griped as the tail end of the car skidded one way and then the other.

"My Subaru wouldn't have a problem getting up this," Annie Wilson commented smugly.

"No, it just has problems getting around fire hydrants."

They finally arrived at a wide clearing and a collection of modest buildings insinuated among pine, coarse winter bracken and evergreen brush. Gilt gleamed from a small onion dome set atop a round chapel of dark, rough-cut wood.

"It's a fucking postcard," MacDonnell said dryly.

A brother Nicholas met them as they got out of the car.

"May I help you?" the monk asked. He was bearded and garbed in a simple woolen robe and a nylon parka. His tone was courteous and his accent American.

Mike MacDonnell was mildly surprised. In his sheltered ignorance, he assumed this would be a religious enclave of stammering immigrants. His fondness for stereotypes was once again thwarted.

"Hi, we're here for the cheesecakes?"

"Oh, very good. If you would follow me?" The monk led them to a lovely little store behind the chapel. Inside, twin banks of refrigerated display cases held every variety and flavor of cheesecake imaginable. Annie clapped her hands with delight and rose up on the balls of her feet like a child trying not to miss a passing parade float.

"Calm down," MacDonnell said. "I bet they don't have any in licorice."

"Oh, yes we do," the monk interjected. "Anisette and peach."

MacDonnell drifted off to the side and allowed Annie to wallow in the splendor. She engaged Brother Nicholas in a lively discussion, on how the cakes were prepared, the ingredients used, how they were best served, which lasted for an hour. By the end MacDonnell was yawning and not trying to hide it. Annie finally decided on a plain, covered in black sweet-cherries; a mocha, topped with a thin layer of dark Belgian chocolate; and of course, the anisette and peach. MacDonnell felt slightly nauseous. On his birthday, a few years back, Michelle had made him a blueberry cheese-cake. He consumed most of it that night, come down with a stomach virus by early the next morning, and spent two miserable days throwing up his toenails. He hadn't been able to look at a cheesecake since.

"Let me put these up for you," Brother Nicholas chirped merrily, removing her selections from the display case. While he was tying off the pastry boxes with string, simple good humor and polite interest, compelled him to ask Annie, "Are you two married?"

Annie's eyes went wide. There was a split second of hesitation.

"No. He's married, but I'm not. What I mean to say is that I'm the other woman — I mean *another* woman!" She gestured to MacDonnell with the desperation of a clumsy sailor hanging by his foot from the top rigging. "He's married to the *other* woman. We're just . . . just friends."

A bewildered expression wrinkled the monk's friendly face.

Annie tossed a wad of cash on the counter, buried her face in the pastry boxes and hurried out of the store.

Later in the afternoon, at a roadside restaurant, MacDonnell happily tormented Annie.

"Why didn't you get down on your knees and beg for absolution? Not that he could have given it to you. He wasn't a priest."

"Shut up, Mike."

"Christ, you're not Orthodox. You're not even Roman Catholic. Why the hell did you spaz-out like that?"

Annie tangled her hands in her long hair and stared at the empty lunch plate on the table. "It was just too weird being in a church with you."

"It wasn't a church. It was a bakery."

"I'm never going back there. I don't care how good the cheesecakes taste."

69

Not surprisingly, Mike MacDonnell celebrated his birthday at the Four Tables that year. The party had become something of an annual event. Everyone showed up, friend and foe alike.

Arlene O'Connor appeared wearing a skintight black knit dress. She kissed Mike on the cheek and said, "Honey, you're getting old. I see a few gray hairs on your head."

"Yeah, the bloom is off the rose," MacDonnell agreed. He smiled when she took a seat next to Stan Woitkowski. Rumor insisted Arlene and

Stan were having an affair, and by the way they looked at each other, laughed together, and took note of each other's smallest action and gesture, Mike was convinced this was true. He was glad for them. Stan was divorced and Arlene's husband had passed away years ago. It seemed they were determined to offer each other a little comfort in a world that only grew colder as men and women grew older.

MacDonnell glanced at Annie Wilson and felt a shadow of sadness creep over him amid all the noise and beer and good humor of arriving guests.

Kevin and Shelley came early. Shelley was pleasantly plump, bubbly and not strikingly attractive. MacDonnell was once again reminded of how unimportant appearances were to Kevin Marshall.

MacDonnell winced when Vivie Sandhurst entered, toting a black guitar case covered in purple triangle stickers. He was relieved when she sat at the far end of the table, glumly awaiting an unsuspecting victim to torture with her unique brand of poetry and music. Unfortunately for Sandhurst, everyone knew her routine and carefully avoided the snares she laid; everyone except Keith Rodgers. The blubbery supervisor sat next to her and, after several beers, tried to kiss her.

Even Debbie Wittenburg waddled through the front door bearing her adder tongue and taste for vicious gossip like six-shooters perpetually cocked and loaded. She made a point of gushing over Annie Wilson. Lately the nurse had been trying to curry both supervisors' favor, for reason's know only to Wittenburg. MacDonnell suspected the worst.

After the head nurse lumbered off, Annie leaned her head close to him and said, "God, I can't stand her."

"I thought you two were best buddies?" MacDonnell chuckled.

"She obviously thinks we are," Annie admitted sourly. "Nobody else will speak to her — probably because all she wants to talk about is Bill Rumgay. I think she's got a thing for him."

Mike MacDonnell didn't bother hiding his revulsion.

Jim Smith and John Murray sent their regrets. Jim was recovering from a bad case of the flu that had led to congestive heart failure and a three day stay in the intensive care unit.

Todd Robertson arrived with a blond giggler on his arm, followed closely by the rest of the childcare workers from their shift and a fair number from the other shifts as well.

Only Rick Pasinetti failed to appear. As an ex-employee, and a man of certain tastes, he avoided anything to do with Blythewood. He had, however, left an envelope at the bar that morning addressed to *Brick Jerkhard*. Inside, scrawled in heavy black magic marker on a sympathy card, was the message: *Blow me, Rick*.

There were several other more conventional gifts and cards that night, mostly from Annie Wilson. She confessed to having failed at securing one special surprise.

"What was it?" MacDonnell asked.

"A Strip-O-Gram. I found a service in Springfield, but their girls were all booked up for tonight. I guess there must be a load of bachelor parties going on or something."

"You were going to hire a stripper for me?"

"Yes."

"Good thing you didn't. I would have left."

"Why?"

"Gee, let's see . . ." His tone was arch as he swept the ceiling with his eyes. "It's humiliating, it's degrading — for everybody involved — and it's about as tacky as anything I can think off."

"Aren't you a self-righteous little prude?" Annie snapped.

"Only a true reprobate can allow himself that luxury. You'll find as you grow older, and completely jaded, that bad taste isn't all it's cracked up to be."

The next few hours were filled with laughter and drinking and good humor. There were no arguments or sniping, no insulting remarks, even from Debbie Wittenburg, and consequently, no hurt feelings to be nourished over the off-shift. Mike remained calm and drank slowly. He was funny without being obnoxious and cruel, and held most of his attention in reserve for Annie Wilson when she requested it.

MacDonnell was glad to see everyone and happy when they left. The one thing he wanted for his birthday was to be alone with Annie Wilson.

One by one the guests departed and his wish was granted. He sat with her at an empty table surrounded by empty glasses and empty pitchers and empty plates. There were scraps of wrapping paper sopping up spilled beer and a few brightly colored helium balloons — courtesy of a smirking Kevin Marshall who knew Mike hated such things — dancing on ribbons tied to the back of his chair.

Annie had grown increasingly quiet, almost solemn, during the course of the evening. MacDonnell asked her if anything was wrong.

"No," she replied, and then after a long pause, "Why don't you leave Michelle?"

"I can't."

"Why not?"

"Because, I can't." Mike MacDonnell felt like his throat was full of broken glass.

"Well then," Annie slowly smiled, "why don't you just shoot her?"

MacDonnell laughed. "I've thought about it."

Annie's smile faded. She stared into his dark articulate eyes and said, "I think you will leave Michelle someday, when you're ready. And that's good. But after that, I'm afraid you are going to end up like my father, all alone in a dark little room, with no one near."

A chill crawled along MacDonnell's skin. His native superstition granted her words the weight of unwelcome divination. Annie was right; he would leave his wife one day. He couldn't do it now, because of the pregnancy, but it would happen, eventually. And then? Maybe Annie was partially right about that too. Yes, he might end up alone — forever a guest, forever a traveler — but not dry-docked in some closed little room, rotting and waiting to die. No, there were books to read, lots of them, and places to visit, places he and Annie Wilson had talked about. Perhaps he would go back to school and get a degree in something that interested him, something that opened up his mind again. There were roads and highways in the soul as well as on the living skin of the earth. In the end he might have to travel all of them to find what he needed, but it would be all right. The things he would learn along the way would make it all worthwhile. But allow himself to become entombed within a dark room, within his own flesh? No. Never. She was wrong about that. She had to be.

MacDonnell lit a Newport and popped every balloon floating on the back of his chair with its glowing tip.

"Ah, well. Fuck the future."

Annie's smile returned. She gently put a hand on the back of his wide neck and drew his homely face close to hers.

"Happy birthday," she whispered in his ear and kissed him. Then she stood up, leaving many things unsaid, and put on her jacket.

Mike looked up at this woman, so perfect and pleasing to his eye.

"Thanks for everything, Annie Wilson."

She smiled. "Let's go home, Michael."

There was never any doubt about their spending this night together. An unspoken agreement had been established before the party ever began.

When they arrived at Annie's place, he insisted she go in ahead of him.

"I'll be along presently," he assured her. "I need a little fresh air."

For some time Mike MacDonnell stood alone, outside the circle of light radiating from her house. In a state of absolute stillness, he watched her pull aside the bedroom curtains and bend her face to the glass, searching for him in the black wash of the night. There was a sound, like wind moving through dry cornstalks, and something cold whispered along the curve of his ear.

A shuddering breath racked his body. He let it go and looked beyond her bright window, beyond barren tree branches, softly glimmering like silver filigree in the velvet darkness, and into the empty sky.

No inner voice was necessary to tell him this would be the last time. He felt it in every limb and every hollow of his body.

There would be a final kiss and a final embrace — all on his birthday. He closed his eyes.

It was time to finish the dance and harbor no regrets. What had been was enough.

Michael Francis MacDonnell hurried to the front door of Annie Wilson's house and up the stairs to her bed.

70

Bob Hendricks had been a staff at Blythewood for a few months, but had spent ten years in the field. MacDonnell found him sitting by himself on a bed in one of the student's rooms.

"I thought you were one-on-one with Ernesto?" MacDonnell asked.

Hendricks was big and laconic. He yawned and pointed at a suitcase on the floor. "In there, boss."

The piece of luggage indicated was of the large, soft-shelled variety with a big zippered flap.

Something squirmed inside.

"Ernesto?" Mike MacDonnell asked.

Bob Hendricks yawned again and nodded.

MacDonnell said, "Probably not the best thing to do. You better let him out."

Hendricks' third yawn turned to a sigh. He unzipped the suitcase.

Ernesto Martinez, fourteen, tiny and hyperactive in the extreme, popped up like a rabid prairie dog. He scrambled out of the bag and began racing mindlessly around the bedroom, jumping on and off the beds, literally bouncing off the walls. A sputtering stream of Spanish poured from his mouth.

"See why I zipped him up?" Bob Hendricks asked.

MacDonnell caught Martinez by the shoulders and planted the boy firmly on the bed. "Sit!"

Somehow, though he still fidgeted uncontrollably, Martinez managed to remain in one place — a voluminous testament to the power Mike wielded over even the most impulsive students.

"The suitcase was a good idea," the supervisor said to Hendricks. "I wonder if we could get it incorporated into his treatment plan?"

Bob Hendricks almost smiled. "Ernesto gets to you after a while, boss."

"Hey, Mike! Hey, hey, Mike!" Martinez prattled wildly in English.

"What?"

"Want a blow job?" Martinez flashed an amazing set of pure white, inhumanly sharp teeth.

"Shut up, Ernesto."

The boy turned to Bob Hendricks. "Do you want a blow job, Bob?"

"Uh, gee . . ." Hendricks rubbed his jaw reflectively. "No . . . I guess not."

"Does the Virgin Mary watch me when I pee?" Martinez yelped excitedly. "Can I get back in the bag?"

Mike MacDonnell shook his head and left the room. As he strolled down the hall towards an exit, he heard the chatter of a heavy-duty luggage zipper.

71

Kevin Marshall wandered through the door of the supervisors office.

MacDonnell raised a speculative eyebrow. "What are you doing here? You left hours ago."

Kevin's face was ashen, lacking even the hint of his usual mocking grin.

"Shelley broke up with me tonight."

MacDonnell let three beats pass. "I'm sorry to hear that, Kevin."

"Wanna get drunk?"

"Shifts over in twenty minutes."

At the Four Tables, Mike MacDonnell patiently listened to Kevin verbally spew his guts up, out and all over the bar.

"I don't get it, I just don't get it," Kevin mourned. "It was a stupid argument about nothing. I told her that I applied to Boston College. It offers a B.S. program in physical therapy, and I don't want to be a CCW the rest of my life. I told her that *if* I got accepted, I *might* have to move out there. She flipped. She started crying and asking me why I wanted to leave her."

Kevin covered his mouth with his hand and stared into space for a moment. "It was ugly. I told her I wanted her to come with me, but she kept crying, and asking me how I expected her to leave her family and all her friends. It was awful. And then she said I had to choose between her and college — a college I haven't even been accepted to yet. I tried to reason with her, but she wouldn't budge. Finally I said I was going to school and she said she was going home and not to ever call her again. After all these years, after everything we've been through, it all just gets flushed away . . . "

"She'll change her mind," Mike said.

"No. Shelley's stubborn about some things. We're done unless I give up school."

Marshall drank a lot more over the next couple of hours, talking aimlessly and endlessly about Shelley before finally reaching the tolerable limits of booze and commiseration. Then he climbed wearily into his Jeep Wrangler and left Mike MacDonnell standing outside of the Four Tables by himself.

MacDonnell watched the Jeep's glowing taillights disappear down a deserted street. Kevin would be fine, no matter how things sorted out. He would push until something gave and then keep going. There was no quit in him.

MacDonnell wasn't sure if he could say the same about himself. He stood next to his car feeling . . . lonely. There was no other name he could give to the sensation. It seemed like he was moving down a narrowing tunnel and nothing waited at the end.

A sudden, asphyxiating dread beset him. What if he had no real existence beyond the boundaries of Blythewood? What if that perpetual car-wreck of a place, disdained in so many ways, provided the only cohesion between his body and spirit? Without Blythewood, he might simply cease and vanish in a puddle of molecular chaos. Katie bar the door.

It was an ugly flagellation of the mind, a perverse infatuation — and it would not leave him.

He settled into the Impala for a long ride home.

Half an hour later, at the front door of his house, a moth returned to the cocoon longing to be a caterpillar. Stale air enveloped him, sucked him through an open door.

The moth slept in a bottle of tequila that night — and caught hell from a caterpillar in the morning.

72

On the third Sunday in March, not ten days past his birthday, Annie walked into the office and sat down across the desk from him.

"Mike, I have some . . . good news."

He did not look up from the papers he was reading. The strange timber in her voice sparked a dread conviction in his heart. The end had come more swiftly than he expected.

Her next words fell like heavy stones.

"Doug and I have decided to get married. We'll be moving to California. I think I told you once that he was a software engineer. And, well, a company offered him a really great job. We can't afford to pass it up. I'll have to pick up some kind of work when we get out there. It shouldn't be too hard."

Mike MacDonnell raised his head and smiled at her.

"Good for you, Annie. Somebody needs to get out of here alive."

He felt a strange tingling inside, almost of anticipation, almost of relief. It was as if a hard run race was nearing its inevitable conclusion.

"I'm going to give Bill my notice tomorrow." Annie looked up at the office calendar on the wall behind MacDonnell. "My last day will be Wednesday, April Sixteenth."

"April Sixteenth," Mike MacDonnell parroted the words for no good reason.

Little more than a month.

At ten minutes to midnight, Michelle began to bleed. The baby was gone before the sun rose.

73

Mike had lost a child he never knew by a woman he didn't love. The woman he loved was soon to go to another. Without Annie, work would no longer be a haven from home and Michelle. It would just be there, maybe better than nothing. There was no sanctuary— except for the one found in the bottom of a shot glass.

For days, Mike MacDonnell punished himself. He drank hard and harder — so hard he choked on it and woke the next day feeling he must surely die. These were not hangovers. They were waking premonitions of imminent collapse. The idea he was killing himself, physically destroying his body, would scare him for an hour or so, but then he would regain his feet and by the afternoon be ready to drink again. Michelle, lost to her own mourning, said nothing to him. She became a shadow in a haunted house.

Mike stopped caring with whom he drank after work. Annie only went to the bar on Wednesday afternoons now. There were no more late nights. Staff whom Mike MacDonnell had once avoided like the plague became his dearest companions, so long as they made enough noise and kept the booze running in a steady torrent. Even Todd Robertson enjoyed a fleeting moment as a close confidant during MacDonnell's crash dive. Like a dog, he followed Mike to the bars every night, kept the glasses full and his supervisor's ear filled with stale flattery. Robertson was thrilled to develop an instant relationship with this man who'd shown him little more than badly concealed contempt. Sober, MacDonnell would still cringe at the lowly nature of the company he was keeping, but once it was time to put a drink in his hand, once he needed an excuse not to go home, Robertson glimmered like a newly minted coin.

Todd Robertson's girlfriend at the time was a childcare worker named Holly. She was blond, jiggly and not very bright. She favored tight clothing that squeezed her breasts and behind into protruding beacons of fleshy promise. When Holly opened her mouth sheer nonsense vied with doleful ignorance. She would freely recall, to acquaintance and stranger alike, the graphic details of sexual abuse at the hands of a battalion of former boyfriends and male relatives. Todd Robertson appeared to enjoy these wretched confessions as much as she did.

This suspicion was confirmed one night after the Four Tables closed. MacDonnell went to the couple's apartment to continue drinking. Todd Robertson asked if he would like to watch him have sex with Holly — or better yet, join in the fun.

MacDonnell put his beer down on the floor and stood up. "I've got to go."

"What do you mean?" Robertson protested. "Take your boots off, Mike. Holly loves getting double teamed. It's every girl's fantasy. You know that, right?"

MacDonnell realized in mild horror that Todd Robertson was only attempting to be a good host, offering the use of his girlfriend's pussy like another man might offer a cigar or a drink of expensive whiskey.

"I have to go, Todd." MacDonnell headed for the front door. He needed air.

Robertson, badly confused and disappointed, followed.

"She's clean, Mike. You don't have to worry about that. She douches almost every day, and even her ass sometimes." The childcare worker correctly sensed his fledgling rapport with his supervisor had been mortally wounded, but he wasn't sure why.

Outside, Mike MacDonnell suppressed an overwhelming urge to punch Todd Robertson and jumped into the GTO, freed now by coming spring. He drove off wondering what had possessed him to spend a willing moment with Robertson. Had excessive thirst — and grief — finally separated him from reason? It wasn't that he cared what kind of sex other people liked, he just didn't want to be included in it.

He spent the rest of the night on top of Shaker Mountain, listening to Emmylou Harris and watching the valley below slowly gather light.

Sometime before true dawn, he arrived at a conclusion. Everyone at Blythewood, not excluding himself, was some kind of deviant caught in endless turmoil over whom to sleep with, what gender, how many and what kind of hardware to employ.

Christ, it was numbing.

Blind windows behind blind windows.

All this considered and understood, Mike MacDonnell was forced to admit under the right circumstances — a few more blasts and a little dope — he might have accepted Todd Robertson's offer and taken off his boots.

Well, nobody is perfect.

During the ride back to Cornwall later in the morning, MacDonnell stumbled further into this unusual clarity of thought and, by extension, purpose. A windswept stretch of New York Route 22 became his modest equivalent of the road to Damascus. He realized it was time to end the funereal feast of lies and treachery at home. For all the bizarre and ritualistic madness Michelle chose to misrepresent as love, she deserved, like anybody, the grace of honesty.

MacDonnell was bone-weary from trying to live two lives, and bone-deep exhausted from maintaining the battlements around his wife's fragile Keep of Sanity.

It was time to let it all go for both of their sake.

At the front door of his house, the family house his mother left him, Mike MacDonnell stopped to finally remove his boots. There'd been a brief shower and clumps of damp gray earth had collected in the treads. Michelle would explode if he tracked mud on the floors.

He laughed out loud. What a trained beast he'd let her make of him; a clowning bear in ill fitting human garb, riding a unicycle around the ring, balancing a rubber ball on the end of his nose.

In stocking feet, he entered his home.

Michelle was waiting for him in the kitchen.

"Where have you been?" she cried.

How many times? A thousand?

"With another woman," he answered.

His wife looked frightened. "Don't be funny!"

"I'm not."

Michelle turned away and busied herself washing clean dishes in the sink.

"Michelle?" he called her name softly. He felt old and worn out.

She ignored him.

"Michelle."

"What?" She hung the word on him like a curse.

"I've been with another woman."

"Why are you so mean?" Michelle looked pitifully small and thin. "I just lost our baby."

Her childlike desperation almost shook his resolve. He took a deep breath and accepted he was rotten, rotten to the core — but it didn't change the fact night was upon them.

"I'm leaving," he said. "The house is yours. I just need to get a few of my things."

"I knew this would happen." Michelle cooed the words to herself like a lullaby.

There was a moment of absolute stillness — and then she began hurling dishes at him.

"You fucking son of a bitch!"

MacDonnell stood like a statue, not bothering to duck the missiles flying in his direction. He could not remember how or why he had fallen in love with this woman. It frightened him. To abandon love was one thing; he could accommodate such a conclusion and go on from there. But to remember nothing of it? To find a blank inside himself where, at the least, some sort of emotional bread crumb trail must lead to the heart? That was terrifying. It whispered of a fatal cold and a pathological disconnection.

If the soul existed it swam in the currents of memory. Mike MacDonnell ransacked empty drawers and pried open hollow closets in mind and heart — but there was nothing to find of Michelle. He was unable to substantiate her living presence in his past or present — with her standing right there before him. A grim certainty arose that this disability marked him as the emotional cripple, not her. If he could not detect her trace, it was because he lacked a basic tool, some simple, selfless internal mechanism that would allow him to recall bygone tenderness. It might mean, from the beginning, he was the miserable bastard in all this and she just another child caught in the tangle of years, a little lost, a little confused, trying to find her way in the world, trying to find a way home.

But nothing inside him could — or would — respond to her.

MacDonnell turned away. He felt no pain from the shards of broken crockery and glass lacerating his feet on the way out of the kitchen. A thin trail of bright blood followed him up the stairs to their bedroom. There he stuffed all the clothes and belongings he could find into an old army duffel bag. Just a few worthless things. The inconsequential residue of three decades lived. He headed back down the stairs.

Michelle was staring blankly at the debris on the floor when he returned to the kitchen. She lifted her eyes and said, "Is this because I lost the baby?"

"No." He wanted to cry, but didn't.

"Then I don't understand!" Tears. Tears upon tears.

"Goodbye," he said and walked out the door.

He tossed the duffel bag in the GTO's trunk and forced his bleeding feet into his infantry boots. A brief glance was all he spared the Impala sitting in the garage. He would pick it up later; sometime when Michelle wasn't around.

MacDonnell spared a longer moment to look at his house.

This was where he had been a boy, where he had grown up, and where his parents had lived and died. The palpability of those memories and emotions comforted him a little.

But now it was time to run away from home.

The Pontiac rumbled to life. Before he could get out of the driveway, Michelle flew out of the house and clutched at the side of the car.

She thrust her head through the open driver side window. Her eyes were dry red gullies. "I'm sorry?"

"Me too."

Mike MacDonnell put the GTO in reverse.

74

Mike found a little second floor apartment across town. It wasn't much, but there wasn't much to choose from in Cornwall. He took what he could get.

He did have choices in the matter of his drinking, however, and he succeeded in bringing it under control. MacDonnell wanted to have clear memories of everything he was about to lose.

Mike and Annie spent those last days together at work as if nothing were unusual or would ever change. They still went to the Four Tables on Wednesday, and if they engaged in a bit more reminiscing about old students, old staff and old times, it never descended to the level of trite sentimentality.

They didn't speak about their past relationship. Neither one of them could find the right words nor a comfortable place to start such a discussion. And no matter how much or how little Mike drank on those last afternoons, he neither spoke about leaving his wife, nor asked Annie to spend the night with him. It would have been wrong to do so. The time of their intimacy had passed forever.

Sometimes, after Annie went home, Mike would wander over to Jim's Bar and Grill because he was lonely and didn't know what to do with himself.

Jim's owner, Marie Halprin, was fifty-years-old and a recent escapee from the ranks of Blythewood childcare workers. For over a decade she worked every available hour of overtime, saved every extra penny, until she had enough scratch put aside to buy a bar in Newbury and call it after her husband. On the glorious morning she handed her resignation to Faith Minor, Marie had triumphantly advised the dour APD to stick the letter up her ass. Halprin left Blythewood without any regrets.

Jim's had been open for only a few months and business was still on the slow side. Because of his admiration for Marie, MacDonnell tried to split his time evenly between her establishment and the Four Tables. Tonight he sat in a corner of Jim's, by himself, drinking and silently watching a big screen television. He had no desire for company, female or otherwise, which was convenient; there wasn't anyone else in the bar except for Marie and her husband Jim.

The light from the television screen flickered in MacDonnell's dark eyes and splintered on the bottom of his beer mug when he lifted it to his mouth. Marie had given him the remote control and he flipped leisurely through channels, pausing for a few moments when something caught his interest. He spent most of the time scanning the more obscure late-night cable offerings, looking for programs featuring interviews with artists and writers, religious figures, politicians, pundits, historians, scientists, sports figures — anyone who had something interesting to say. None of them really did. Oh, some had a wealth of clever remarks, and some had wise appraisals of their own lives and professions, but not one said anything remotely useful to a childcare supervisor with a fast car, an infinite thirst and little else. So Mike MacDonnell put his feet up on a chair and watched them, wondering why their lives were so different from his, wondering if it was because he'd never done anything and never been anywhere.

"Mike?" Marie Halprin was standing next to him. She was a tall, stout woman with a strong jaw line and restless eyes.

MacDonnell cleared his throat and put his feet back on the floor.

"Yeah, what's up, Marie?"

"We're gonna close in a few minutes. Last call."

"I'm all set. Thanks."

"I hear Annie is leaving soon."

Mike nodded, but didn't speak.

Something soft and knowing came into Marie's eyes. She'd seen enough of the two supervisors together to make a guess about the nature of their relationship.

The middle-aged woman put a thick hand on the young man's thick shoulder and said, "I was going through some pictures the other day and found something I thought you might like. Hold on a minute." She bustled off to the bar, returning in a few moments with a photograph. "I took this during the student Christmas party a couple of years ago."

It was a picture of Annie Wilson standing with plate in hand at a buffet table. Her face was turned in mild surprise towards the camera and that ambiguous smile was beginning to rise on her lips.

MacDonnell smiled back and put the photograph in the pocket of his leather jacket.

"Thanks, Marie."

"You're welcome, Mike. See you tomorrow night?"

MacDonnell raised his mug. "Till death do us part."

Later, in his tiny rooms, he found the copy of *A Confederacy of Dunces* and tucked the photograph inside it. There it would remain, until both were inexplicably lost.

MacDonnell looked at the book for a while, at the inscription inside the cover, and remembered the night Annie gave it to him. It felt like a hundred years ago. Then he turned off the light and lay alone in the darkness.

75

That April, Blythewood switched payday from Wednesday to Tuesday. It was a minor adjustment for most staff to make, but to MacDonnell it compounded the feeling his whole world was in a state of flux.

On the sixteenth, after work, MacDonnell walked Annie Wilson out to the Blythewood parking lot. He had a dozen red roses and a bottle of champagne on ice waiting in the GTO. They popped the cork on the Pontiac's hood. He could not remember, afterwards, if he made some sort of a toast. He hoped not. In retrospect, such gestures always embarrassed him with their curdling futility.

"Mike, could you do me a favor?" Annie asked him as she sipped the champagne from a plastic cup.

"Sure."

"Doug and I are going to be in town for another week. Could you pick up my last paycheck next Tuesday? I don't want to come back here if I can help it. We could meet at the Tables for drinks that evening? Around eight?"

MacDonnell nodded enthusiastically. This was an unlooked for stay of execution. The condemned man had been granted his final appeal without even asking for it.

76

The twenty-second came and found Mike MacDonnell wanting nothing more than for the shift to end and allow him to rush down to the Four Tables and meet Annie Wilson.

He spent most of the evening standing at the office door, chain-smoking. He would light — or finish — a cigarette, step outside, stare up at the gradually darkening sky, shake his head for no particular reason and then restlessly return to his office. This compulsive orbit was repeated over and over — until his misery was intensified when Bonnie Quirk popped into the office.

"Mike?" For once the clinician didn't screech his name.

MacDonnell groaned out loud. She hadn't bothered him in weeks. Why now? He'd been convinced she'd gone to periscope depth on some other poor slob.

"Mike, I need to be honest with you."

MacDonnell closed his eyes. He didn't want to see what was coming.

"Sammy's up for parole in two years. I've decided to wait for him."

MacDonnell smiled for the first time in days.

"I thought you should know, Mike."

"I appreciate your candor," he said, opening his eyes. "Sorry I never got to meet . . . Daddy."

"Me too." Bonnie Quirk burst into tears and fled.

For some reason the supervisor could not quite put his finger on, he felt bad for her.

Twenty minutes later, MacDonnell was in the car on his way to the Four Tables. Annie's paycheck was on the seat next to him. He kept picking the white envelope up and putting it down again, as if he feared losing it and failing her in this last task. He turned the stereo on to distract himself.

Like a glacier grinding mountains, Ronnie Drew sang:

Oh a hungry feelin' come over me stealin'
And the mice were squeelin'
In my prison cell . . .

Mike uttered an audible sigh of relief when he spotted the blue Subaru in the lower parking tier. Working his first week without her had seemed like the proverbial eternity. Now that terrible longing would be redeemed — one last time.

Inside, Annie was sitting at their usual table — but another man was sitting in Mike MacDonnell's chair.

MacDonnell had never met the storied Dougie, but the omission was about to be remedied.

"Mike!" Annie waved to him across the crowded taproom. Her eyes were bright.

MacDonnell stood still and so did time. The sounds of the bar faded away.

How could she do this to him?

He wished he were blind.

"We're over here!" Annie called again.

Time resumed.

Mike MacDonnell was no glutton for punishment — other than the kind which is self-inflicted — but he could take a lot of it when he had to. This was one of those occasions. He stiffened his back and walked across the barroom floor to *his* table. He handed Annie her paycheck and shook the hand of her fiancé when she introduced him.

"Nice to meet you. Well, I better be going," he said to the wallpaper above the man's head.

"Nonsense," Annie said. "You're not going anywhere. Sit down and have a drink. Doug and I are buying." She patted the chair at the head of the small table.

MacDonnell obeyed mechanically.

"So, Mike, it's nice to finally meet you," Doug began cheerfully.

Please don't say Annie has told you all about me.

"Anne tells me you're something of a legend at Blythewood."

"No, I don't think so."

"He's being modest," Annie said to Doug.

"No one has ever accused me of that particular failing," MacDonnell muttered.

"Well, you know what I mean," Doug concluded with indulgent good humor. "Anne has told me so many things about Blythewood, I almost feel like I've worked there." There was something faintly condescending in this remark.

"Be glad you haven't had the pleasure." MacDonnell was vastly relieved when a waitress arrived to take their order. He asked for a double Bushmills Black and a bottle of Bass Pale Ale. If Annie's offer to buy the drinks was some kind of consolation prize then he was going to make it an expensive one.

The happy couple ordered glasses of Beck's Dark.

After the waitress left, Doug spread his hands wide to include both Annie and Mike in his next question.

"Do you two think you've actually done some good at Blythewood?"

"What do you mean, honey?" Annie asked.

MacDonnell resisted a wildfire yearning to reveal just how many nights he had done *Anne* good. Of course, it would have been a silly boast without any teeth. What could he really claim? A few times over a few months, nothing more.

"Has any student made it after treatment there?" Doug's brow furrowed in what appeared to be sincere interest.

MacDonnell rolled his eyes and answered before Annie could.

"Mostly onto police blotters, Doug. And a few crime-watch segments of local news programs. I'm still waiting for that special child to go national with a multistate killing spree. Or at least a little creative cannibalism."

"That's not funny," Annie said. She had detected a faint whiff of sarcastic provocation in his tone.

MacDonnell glanced at her directly for the first time. She looked so pretty . . .

"No, I suppose it's not," he said and looked away.

"So you don't think anyone is ever helped at places like Blythewood?" Doug persisted.

Before he answered, MacDonnell glanced over his shoulder, hoping the waitress was on her way back with the drinks. "I think some of them are able to help themselves. How much we do for them is debatable. Maybe providing a relatively safe environment and hot meals counts for something. I don't know. And maybe there are better places around I just haven't heard about. I fucking hope so."

"You're not much of a cheerleader," Doug observed. He was trying to be funny.

"No, I haven't been able to do a split in years," MacDonnell admitted blandly. "You see, we don't do much more than warehouse the retarded clients. They're kids no one, including the parents, want. And by the time we get the gang kids and sex offenders, they're too old or too fucked in the head to readily profit from anything we can do for them."

"Why do you stay?" Doug asked. Once again, Mike thought he detected a tangible hint of condescension in his voice.

"It's what I do, Doug."

The waitress arrived on cue. Mike downed the double Bushmills in a swallow and swiped the back of his hand across his mouth. Doug, to his credit, sensed irritation and subdued his curiosity.

The conversation drifted into more generalized small talk that Mike MacDonnell could service with a few offhand remarks. He reserved most of his energies for drinking just as hard and as fast as he could. Unfortunately the booze didn't seem to have the power to dull his senses tonight. He remained uncomfortably aware of Annie Wilson, how she looked, how often she spoke to her fiancé, and how infrequently she spoke directly to him. MacDonnell felt a strange sort of pain born out of this isolation and the whiskey could not touch it.

Oh, the screw was peepin'
As the lag lay sleepin'
Dreamin' about his girl Sal . . .

Doug proved to be, all in all, a basically decent sort. He was smart, not blessed with an impressive sense of humor (he had to lack something), and obviously in love with Annie Wilson. Most unbearable of all, Doug had plans for the future and an idea of how to manage the resources of his existence with at least a trace of ingenuity and self-assurance. Mike and Doug had nothing in common, except Annie Wilson. Doug aimed for a social stratum MacDonnell neither understood nor admired. A glowing description of the life a software engineer might hope to enjoy in California left MacDonnell cold and unimpressed, but also acutely aware, from her words and expressions, that Annie genuinely shared her fiancé's ambitions.

Sadly, sitting by himself at a table with this couple, Mike MacDonnell realized Annie would never have gone away with him. Her rearing and tastes made the selection of a man like Doug inevitable. Only Michelle's ill-fated pregnancy had prevented MacDonnell from making a spectacular fool of himself.

This sparked a moment of irrational resentment towards his wife — that she, however unknowingly, should have prevented anything, good or bad, from happening between Annie and him. But the resentment quickly faded. Thinking about his morbid relationship with Michele was beyond his capacity this evening.

Mike emptied a shot glass (*How many? Not enough*) and wondered what his involvement with Annie Wilson had meant, if anything. Was it all a routine case of coworkers spending too much time together and things getting a little out of hand? Or was it something more complex yet ultimately forlorn and mortally frail? What if Annie Wilson had enjoyed the flattering devotion of the dominant male figure in a dangerous environment for its own sake? What if she'd only given back what was necessary to keep it all to herself, until the time came to move onward and upward to better things? It would explain why she never said she loved him — written it once in a book, but never said it — after all the times he murmured those words to her.

"Self-preservation," Mike said out loud, to no one but himself.

Annie paused in her conversation with Doug for a split-second and flashed Mike an odd look, as if she had guessed what he meant.

And after all, MacDonnell thought as his eyes grew turbulent and dark, maybe his love, his profound desire, was fueled by sexual craving for a girl he knew, deep down, he could never have. Even if there were no Michelle. Even if there were no Doug. Even if Annie Wilson freely and completely gave herself to him, there would never be a future. Mike lived moment to moment, day to day, his eye rarely on the horizon. There was nothing he could offer Annie and there never had been. That was clear now. It would be a cold day in hell when he ever pulled her down into the chill and sluggish sea which must one day claim him.

Sometimes, when you love a woman, the best thing you can do, the only way to show it, is to get out of the goddamned way.

Mike felt a rolling emptiness inside and gulped another round of Doug and Annie's poison. What was the French expression he'd picked up along the line somewhere?

Folie a deux.

Right.

It had all meant nothing — and still he did not want to let her go.

MacDonnell survived the most bitter evening of his life with an edgy dignity breech-birthed in desolation. When it was over, he followed Doug and Annie out to the cars. He waited until Doug was tucked into the Subaru and then called out to Annie, "Come here a minute. I forgot to give you something." The words had a soft, lonely sound to them.

She strolled over to the GTO, smiling that smile.

MacDonnell found it difficult to catch his breath. He opened the Pontiac's door, knelt down and removed a bag of licorice twists and Good 'N' Plentys from under the driver seat. He'd put them there so nobody would steal them while the car was unattended — as if they were worth their weight in gold.

Still kneeling, he looked up at her and asked, "Will you meet me here tomorrow for a drink?"

The request was pathetic and desperate — and in that moment he did not care.

Annie hesitated. "Doug and I still have a lot to do . . ."

"Please." He handed her the bag of candy. "Last time pays for all."

Annie took the bag. She looked down at him and her blue eyes became still.

"I'll see you tomorrow, Mike."

> *Then that auld triangle could go jingle jangle*
> *All along the banks of the Royal Canal . . .*

77

Annie Wilson came alone the next day.

The Four Tables was deserted. Mary, the new waitress, leaned against the bar doing a crossword puzzle. Mike and Annie, two new-made strangers, sat starring at each other across an open graveyard of emotions and memories.

"Anyone else showing up from work?" Annie asked. Her voice was high and fragile.

MacDonnell shook his head and smiled.

"I told everybody we were meeting at the Cantina. It's a new bar over in Newbury."

"You're devious."

"I didn't think you'd want a big crowd from the Wood."

"You were right," Annie said. She cleared her throat and took a sip of beer.

Mike started to say something, but stopped and stared at the wet ring his mug had left on the tabletop.

"Last night?" Annie said shyly. "When you gave me the candy? I really wanted to jump your bones."

The flavor of her words was odd and unsuited to the moment. He was at a loss for a response.

"I — I can't stay very long," she continued hurriedly, sensing her remark had been ill-considered. "We still have some packing to do before we leave tomorrow."

"I'm sure."

"I'll miss you . . . and everybody."

"We'll miss you too. You did a fine job, Annie Wilson. Much better than I ever gave you credit for."

"High praise from the master."

"I'm not a master of anything." MacDonnell forced a chuckle.

The sound scraped at the walls like fingernails.

"You are very good at what you do," Annie insisted in the voice women use to sooth weeping children and wounded men. "I also know you've got the brains and ability to do anything you want with your life."

"Appearances can be deceiving." *I'm no damned good and I never was.*

"Yes they can, and what you appear to be is not what you are. I'm one of the few people at Blythewood who know that. And I'm glad, very glad to have had that opportunity."

MacDonnell looked straight ahead. This was one of those potentially sensitive moments he found so daunting.

In the silence that followed, they drank their glasses of beer and cast small glances at each other.

After all the afternoons and nights spent together in this bar, it seemed ridiculous — to both of them — that this occasion should be so frustrating and unnatural. It was as if the earth had ever so slightly tilted on its axis and the sky subtly shifted its hue; as if, arm in arm, they were staggering off the face of the world. A foreign strangeness had seized familiar surroundings and altered them, utterly, forever.

They finished one more beer and then Annie said, "I guess I better be getting back to the house. I still have a lot of . . . "

Her words were dragged away by their own heavy finality.

In unison they stood and pushed their chairs into that small table in the corner of the taproom. They were still for a moment, reluctant to move. This was where they had come to know each other. For three years it had provided a congenial launch pad for good-humored bickering and lengthy conversations, both equally potent at revealing hearts and knotting them together — till time and circumstance should sort them once more.

Annie Wilson and Mike MacDonnell walked out of the Four Tables, side-by-side, one last time.

Outside the air was cool, but there was growing strength in the clear April light. It poured in like fire at the corners of Mike's eyes. Spring was no more than a warm afternoon and a few green shoots away.

"It's already hot in Southern California," MacDonnell said as they made their way to the upper tier of the parking lot. "I guess it's always hot in Southern California."

Annie nodded, but didn't say anything.

They had almost reached her Subaru when he closed trembling fingers around her hand. The recollection of another afternoon by a pool struck him with terrible force. He would not — could not — let things end this way.

"Annie Wilson," he said, drawing her to a halt. " I think . . . I think you're swell."

He laughed at the farcical ineptitude of his own words even as his heart broke beyond repair. He pulled her tight and rested his head against hers.

Mike MacDonnell knew every hello carries the certain echo of a goodbye. Never again would Annie Wilson swat a cigarette out of his hand, or toss insults and notebooks, borrow his car or demand payday licorice. And never again would she hold him in her arms when loneliness threatened to extinguish all he had ever been or ever could be. Her face and voice had already begun the long retreat into memory. Crowding months and years would alter them, diminish them, leave nothing more than the lingering trace of a few sweet kisses, a few long ago nights — and a white ghost stealing forever through the shadow of his dreams.

"You have a grand life," he said and kissed her ear.

She said softly. "If I happen to get back this way, someday, will you be here waiting for me, Jamoke?"

Mike smiled.

"No. But I won't forget." He took her face in his hands and kissed her.

Something stung Mike MacDonnell's eyes. He turned his head for a moment and let it pass. If he could stand and take this, without flying apart at the rivets, well, that would be something. It's what he had to tell himself.

Mike took a step away from her and said for the last time, "I love you."

She reached out and touched his fine, ugly face, unashamed of her own tears.

"You know I love you? I always have."

These were the sweetest words he ever heard and the last he ever had from her lips. Silently, he watched her walk away.

Nothing now remained unspoken.

78

In the weeks and months after Annie left, Mike came close to losing his job. He was drinking heavily, hungover all the time and increasingly indifferent to his duties.

No one was hired to fill Annie's spot. Rumgay decided to cut costs and have but one supervisor per shift, supported by two lower paid assistant soups. This was the worst time for Mike to be alone in the spotlight. But he didn't give a fuck about any of it, or anything.

Arlene O'Connor saved his hide. She covered for him every chance she could and defended him from the slings and arrows fired by administration. Finally, when it was obvious MacDonnell was not going to pull out of the nose-dive on his own, she confronted him in her office and told him, in no uncertain terms, to get his head out of his ass before he got tossed. This had an effect on him. He started to try again, to pretend at least.

He survived and let the months and miles roll on, to nowhere and back again.

On an afternoon, a few days before Christmas, MacDonnell was summoned to Dorm Two. The new nurse, Maggie Kelly, was having difficulty getting a student to take his meds.

Mike arrived in a surly mood. He walked into the main living area, found the student, pointed a finger at the boy and commanded, "Take the meds now!"

It was as if the supervisor employed a magic wand. The student instantly shed his snakeskin of noncompliance and swallowed enough pharmaceutical jelly beans to alter the chemical composition of Saturn's atmosphere. This paint box of well-being was washed down with a cup of apple juice provide by the vexed nurse.

The boy opened his mouth wide to prove everything had been swallowed and he was ready to return to polite society.

Mike bestowed a curt nod on the student. "No more problems. Understand?"

He waited while the rest of the medications were delivered to the other students. The time was spent watching Maggie Kelly. She was pretty: blond, blue-eyed, a heart shaped face, freckles. A bit of an over-bite gave her a pouting look. He didn't mind that at all. There was a pleasing wiggle in her round little ass when she walked. He didn't mind that either.

She squatted down next to a client sitting in a chair and started talking to him. The loose fitting shirt she wore fell off one shoulder, revealing a black bra strap.

MacDonnell wandered over. "Is there a problem?"

"No. Neil's not feeling well."

"Oh." MacDonnell looked down her shirt. Nice bra. Nice tits.

He left the building, but paused outside the front door to smoke a cigarette. The nurse followed him out a moment later.

"Don't you ever wear a coat?" she asked, putting on her own.

"I left it in my car."

"Thanks for helping with the meds."

She had kind eyes.

"No problem."

Maggie fumbled for something in her voluminous coat pocket, pulled out wads of Kleenex, sticks of gum, a lighter — dropped a paperback at Mike's feet.

Ignatius J. Reilly and the cockatoo rolled their eyes up at him.

"Shit!" Maggie swept up the paperback and stuffed it back in her pocket with everything else.

"Do you like that book?"

"It's a riot." Her blue eyes danced. "I picked it up at the bookstore on a whim. Do you know if he wrote anything else?"

"A novel when he was a kid. He's dead now."

"That's too bad. Well, I better get going. I still have meds to pass in the other dorms. If I have any more problems can I call you?"

"Don't hesitate."

MacDonnell watched her walk all the way to Dorm Three, found himself wondering what she would look like in black thigh-highs and nothing else. This gave him an erection. He hoped it was a good sign.

79

"It's snowing like hell outside."

"Don't tell Donatello. We'll have to listen to live weather updates all afternoon."

"I hope it stops. I've got the Pontiac."

"Where's the Impala?"

"Starter's gone."

MacDonnell addressed the beer and shot Donatello brought him, finished the shot in the first gulp and half of the beer in the next.

"Another," he said, holding out the shot glass. The bartender nodded and fetched the bottle of tequila.

"Mighty thirsty, eh?" Rick commented.

"Hey, why delay the inevitable?" Mike fired back the second shot.

"Why indeed." Rick Pasinetti raised his glass. "Here's to all the boozehounds — and all their ex-wives. Cheers." He tossed off his drink and burped. "Dogboy? I thought by now you and Guinevere of Camels-fuck-alot would have ridden off into the sunset on a snow white Dodge Charger. "

"Gone, Rick. Eight months ago. Moved to California with a software engineer. And I'm a Pontiac man."

"Computer geek, huh? Well, ain't that a kick in the pants. Them dirty bastards. Miss her?

"Sure."

"Can't say I blame you. How many women like that can a stupid Mick bastard like you hope to bamboozle in a lifetime?"

"Not many."

"One's beyond all human reckoning. But I'll tell you what, dogboy. Buy me drinks and I'll be yours for eternity."

"Or until a software engineer comes along."

"That goes without saying. There's just something about a man who sits around all day playing video games," Pasinetti said. Another round of drinks arrived. "We better be careful. I think Donatello's getting jealous."

The bartender wearily wagged his head, took some money from MacDonnell and disappeared into the murk at the far end of the bar.

"So, how's things going at the Wood?"

"Same as always."

Rick slapped Mike on the shoulder and said, "Somebody told me Terry's back in town on leave. Did you hear that?"

"No."

"No? Oh, by the way, I wasn't kidding about buying me drinks. I'm a little short."

"No problem."

"I apologize. I ran into Karl the Red-headed Hobo on my way out and gave him forty bucks."

"Who's he?"

"An old bum. Used to be a hell of a fisherman. He was always in the paper for winning tournaments. As far as I know, he's never had a home since he was a kid. Spends most of the year livin' in the woods. Come October he heads for the shelters, and then, about this time of year, he'll break into a car or a store and get himself tossed into county lockup. The judges make sure they keep him till spring. Anyway, I'm heading out to the van this afternoon, and sees him pushing a shopping cart full of bottles and cans down the street. I stopped to shoot the shit with him for awhile. Gawd, he looked old and skinny — and smelled like a hundred years of farts. I told him I was thinking about doing a little fishing next year, asked where the best place for trout was. He gets cagey and tells me that's for him to know and me to find out. So I says I'll pay him for it, and gives him a pint and a couple twenties."

Pasinetti paused to rub the top of his head with both hands and take a long look at MacDonnell.

"Well, Mac, you managed to escape the clutches of Tiffany Wilson, Queen of the Wasp People and fuck-up your marriage, *all* without contracting a venereal disease. I'm proud of you, boyo."

"It burns when I piss."

"Good. I'm glad it ain't just me that happens to," Rick said. "You ain't heard nothing from her, huh?"

"Annie? No. Not since the day she left."

"Never could figure it out, anyway. What was a classy, well-educated broad like her doing at Blightwood?"

"Looking for something, I guess."

"Did she find it?"

"I don't know. But she was, without doubt, the prettiest girl I ever saw — and the kindest."

"Shut the fuck up before *I* weep in your beer," Pasinetti demanded. He sneezed and wiped his nose on the back of his hand. "She was too good for you, anyway. You aren't the kind of man who could keep a champagne-dame happy."

"No, I'm not." MacDonnell picked up the next shot of tequila.

"Now, I didn't get to know her very well. Like most nice women, she thought I was a dirty pig. Which I am. But what the fuck — I repeat — what the fuck did she ever see in you?"

"I can dance like Fred Astaire."

"The Cousin Mongo Tango? I'll have to admit, you gave all us dirty pigs hope for a while."

"I know we were . . . different. But sometimes I wonder if she still thinks about me, where I am, what I'm doing." The ghost of a smile settled on MacDonnell's face.

"Cousin Mongo, stumblebums like us don't get to be nobody's secret, undying flame. We're that embarrassing roll in the hay they'd sooner slash their wrists than remember. She probably already forgot your fucking name."

The smile dissolved into Mike MacDonnell's eyes. "I remember her."

He raised his beer glass and laughed for no good reason.

Rick finished off his drink. "How 'bout this summer we go up to Ticonderoga?"

Mike nodded. "Why not?"

"Hey, Donatello? You wanna go see a big fort? Maybe you can get lucky with one of them reenactors. I hear they're all queer . . . "

Mike knew when the summer came they wouldn't go. There would be some reason or another to put it off. But maybe in the fall, or the next summer. It didn't matter really. It was something to talk about, plan for, hope for. That was enough.

"I'm done, Rick. I'm taking off."

"Waddya mean? Gawd it's early. You just got here."

"I want to get home before dark."

"You ain't gonna make it."

"Maybe not." MacDonnell stood up and dropped some bills.

"Careful driving, Cousin Mongo."

Mike MacDonnell put his hand on Rick's shoulder.

"See ya, kid."

The snow showers had blown away south. Stars were scattering overhead. The western horizon was a keeling gun deck blazing cold blue fire.

A Michigan banshee ran for daylight.

BARROOMS

Stephen Slattery

Stephen Slattery was born in Wellsboro, Pennsylvania, and raised in Berlin, New York. For many years he worked as a supervisor in New England residential treatment facilities. Today, he lives in Western Massachusetts with his wife and children.

He can be contacted on Facebook, or at the following email address: swslattery@yahoo.com

BARROOMS